Love Me Back to Life

Copyright

Love Me Back to Life
A Gold Coast Romance Series – Book One

Published by Elle G. Mraz
Distributed by CreateSpace

Edited by Anna Campitelli

ellegmraz@gmail.com
https://www.facebook.com/ellegmraz

First Edition: August, 2015
First Printing: August, 2015
Printed in the United States of America

ISBN (eBook) **978-0-9966947-0-4**
ISBN (paperback) **978-0-9966947-1-1**
ISBN (hardback) **978-0-9966947-2-8**

For Elizabeth

Acknowledgements

Writing this book was a lot of fun because of the awesome people who surround me on a regular basis at the hospital. Yes, it is a complete work of fiction. But it wouldn't have come to life if it weren't for the wonderful support of my fellow nurses, patient care techs, secretaries, rehab therapists, doctors, transporters, and friends in registration. I am surrounded by good people. Life-saving people. What an honor it is to work with such an incredible group of professionals.

I want to especially thank my loving family for putting up with the crazy wife/mom version of me as I burned the midnight oil: writing all night, working all day, then dragging on my days off. You have my heart.

And a monster shout out to my dear friend, and hard-working editor, Anna. Never would have finished this without you. Thank you!

Prologue

Kendall Matthews races up I-95, wildly weaving around cars despite the sparse late-morning traffic on this ill-fated Wednesday, September 17. Her heart races along with the speed of her Jeep, begging for him to hold on, imploring all the powers of the universe to keep him going, to make him fight, to make the phone call from his crew captain be the worst practical joke ever imagined. She won't even be angry if that's the case. She will laugh. She'll do anything to make what he said not be true. It's impossible. She and Dan are forever.

They are forever.

Kendall jolts her Jeep into park, jumping out at the entrance of Palm Beach Hospital's emergency department, leaving the keys in the ignition, the engine still running. She sees a sea of firefighters in the halls behind the clear sliding glass doors. Ariel is already there, Gulfstream University where she teaches just a few blocks away.

And Kendall knows. Despite every cell in her body willing it not to be true, she knows.

As the sliding glass doors open to her weakened body, the crew and Ariel turning to the sound, Kendall collapses to her knees, the outside world caving in as the adrenaline runs dry – having surged like a rogue wave through her veins the moment she got the phone call twenty minutes earlier, and now disappearing below the surface, leaving her breathless. Not a single word crying from Ariel's mouth registers with Kendall as she stares vacantly at the blur of people rushing toward her.

There's only a ringing: a singular note of damaged neurons in her brain firing away in vain – the echo of life being stolen before its time.

"I can't breathe. He can't breathe," she whispers, gasping for air as Ariel cradles her on the hospital entryway mat, the automatic doors unapologetic in their attempt to close until they abruptly bounce back open, over and over again.

Chapter 1

Walking up the stairwell to the second floor of the Dolphin Bar and Restaurant, Kendall Matthews dialed up her vixen character. The burnt-umber stain of the well-worn cedar planked walls harbored years of salted cigarette smoke – a warning sign, if she ever needed one, that a clean escape wouldn't be found up those stairs. She dragged her hand forlornly along the humid, smooth planks, leaving behind an oily fingertip trail – perhaps a way back, if she lost her self too much tonight.

Cue game face… and subsequent gagging sounds.

She estimated needing at least a dozen internal eye rolls on standby for her behavior this evening – possibly accompanied by a few shots of shock.

On one level, she found the whole scenario desperately depressing, almost permitting pity to rain upon herself. People in the depths of despair shouldn't have to explain themselves. She was mourning after all. She welcomed her randy side, inviting it to take charge for a change.

Stage four-and-a-half of grief: promiscuity. *Why the hell not?* Maybe it was an express lane to acceptance. Very cutthroat.

Or deep throat?

Either way, she had to learn something different about life sans Dan.

She had convinced herself that a character escape was perfectly practical. Actually, a necessity and completely justifiable. Before she knew it, she'd have prunes for ovaries and sagging tits. Might as well use it all now. She didn't care if it had been a decade since she'd really used her bait 'n' catch tactics on a man. It's not like she'd had a thick layer of dust on her clit before Dan, so she'd be damned if she'd let it happen after marriage.

Best way to learn to ride is getting back on after falling off. Or something like that.

Except, she hadn't fallen, or failed.

The unbidden thoughts of Dan's death fueled the fiery anger that she'd been turning over for the last couple weeks.

What she really needed was a good laugh: one that would happen when she recalled this night years down the road. One of those full on belly guffaws. When all the ache, all the monotonous movement, all the despair making her virtually unrecognizable to herself – when all that *shit* was tossed to the wayside and she could reflect back on this period of her life as a distant memory, then she'd laugh out loud. Perhaps she'd even share her experience with someone else going through the unimaginable, providing that crucial comfort that there is no right way to recover from such devastation. *Do exactly what feels necessary in the moment to see another day – just keep moving forward.* Yes, there would be laughter when she shared the tale of tonight's promiscuous adventure.

Her shoulders sank with the binding wrap of her black widow web. She'd tell herself anything at this point to get one foot in front of the other. A widow on the prowl definitely deserved an eye roll.

As Kendall precariously balanced on the crag of reason, she weighed her final two options. She could continue to wade through the mental anguish of mourning that at least held fast to firm ground... or, she could choose to venture further out into the unknown by freefalling into another man's arms. At least, she thought, the potential emotional upheaval of the latter carried no painful past.

Tonight is just another Friday Fuck Night – an FFN. That's all, nothing more. Totally doable. Fuckable.

Immediately, as if on cue, in came *shame*. She hadn't even done a single thing yet, and already the chastising thoughts came barging through, despite having worked through them for the better part of a month with Ariel Duval, her go-to sounding board and confidant in all things. Not ready to surrender to the ridicule within, Kendall grabbed her phone from her purse to shoot off a text to Ariel.

KM: **Fuck it. I'm going in and I'm having an FFN. AAAAAAHHHHHH!**

She paused for a minute at the top of the staircase, hugging the shadows of the ominous corner she wanted to turn. No, *needed* to turn. The walls of grief had been hitting her in the head for far too long; at some point, her head had to hit back, knowing full well a breakthrough might not be made – just a breakdown.

She waited. Her phone whistled twice and a wave of relief washed over her.

AD: **"One must still have chaos in oneself to be able to give birth to a dancing star." Your chaos is in full force. Now go dance.**

Ahh, yes, Friedrich Nietzsche. Ariel loved using her go-to philosophical quote for all life's dramas.

Kendall ate it up, clinging to the quote as her new mantra. The words were exactly what she needed to jump in with both feet, entering the realm of never going back.

Kendall turned the corner and sank below the surface.

Act I, Scene 1. She had this.

The minute the briny beer-cologne breeze rustled through her highlighted honey-toned hair and the pounding bass drum of the live band echoed in her chest, Kendall owned her character once again – just like slipping into her perfect pair of fuck-me jeans. The familiarity of it gave her the rush she'd been seeking. She did her obligatory scan of the bar with lips slightly parted and a raise of the heel, knowing full well the extra half inch made no difference whatsoever in her vantage point.

While several potential suitors attempted to lock eyes with her, it was no time to look around. She had to stay focused.

Then she saw him: standing at a high top on the outdoor balcony, forearm resting on the table edge, a pint of beer in hand, casually chatting with her colleagues Mark DeGraff and Dr. Rodin. He wore dark blue jeans and a button-down white shirt with various blue stripes creating a geometric pattern. His sleeves were rolled up, the bottom untucked. Ever so simple and casual, yet honestly, he could have been wrapped up in a patient's soiled linens like a toga and would still look delicious, since the packaging had no bearing on tonight's agenda. He was facing away from the entrance, awarding her a clear shot of the ass she'd admired many times before but had never considered as a married woman.

From strictly a physical standpoint, it was an undeniable fact that Dr. Anson Allaway – from his build to his swagger to his dreamboat eyes – was one delicious piece of ass. Hospital staff at Gold Coast General secretly dubbed him *Double A*, not only for his tireless work ethic in the OR but also for his rumored Energizer-Bunny nocturnal exploits. Kendall counted on this nickname to deliver that night – fully charged.

Dr. Allaway had been at GC General some five years, brought on by South Florida's world-renowned neurosurgeon, Dr. Hardit Patel. Dr. Patel nabbed Dr. Allaway (and his flawless reputation as a new board-certified neurosurgeon) shortly after his fellowship in Texas. While Dr. Allaway's playboy antics died down as his savvy surgeon skills soared, he definitely hadn't settled down. The occasional rumor still managed to pop up, feeding the nurses' gossip circles in the ICUs and on the neurology floor.

Kendall remembered all too well the first time she saw him. She was working night shift in the neuro ICU and had already heard all the rumors about the new doctor. She'd had her doubts. His computer photo in the physician directory definitely showed he was good looking, but *fuckable* could only be determined in person.

Then, around 10:30 one night, he came in to check on a patient – and the air charging around him was electrifying. Married only a few months at the time, she clearly remembered straightening out her rings and keeping them visible, just to make it known to him that she was far from market material.

Looking back, she knew the diamond flash was all for her own benefit. Cheating had never really been a thought during her marriage to Dan – but a friendly reminder of her commitment to him (when certain people came around) never hurt.

After that night, Dr. Allaway had settled in as one of her go-to hospital flirts: the men of GC General she'd built a solid rapport with and could throw out the occasional sexualized innuendo without ever worrying if it would cross any creepy borders. Leonard Bautista, or Leo, had previously held the top spot – a fellow nurse who could definitely rival Dr. Allaway in Kendall's fantasy GQ cover shoot with his Filipino tan, flashy smile, and lashes for miles. But he no longer worked bedside in the intensive care units, so they rarely crossed paths anymore. A handful of other doctors – one in neurology, one in infectious disease, and another in hematology – didn't necessarily make her eye-candy cut, but had quick wits that often left her in stitches, providing a repartee of pure entertainment.

But on this night, it was only Dr. Allaway on the menu. She focused on releasing all her inhibitions, knowing full well he'd need to see her from a purely physical standpoint if she had any hope of sampling the late-night dessert. She was not Kendall the nurse, nor Kendall the widow. She was Kendall the one-night stand.

Kendall strutted toward the high top next to him, where several coworkers stood clustered nearby, engrossed by something on Patricia's phone. Courtney Brown was the first to look up and see her.

"Kendall!" Courtney squealed as she stood up tall. But then her shoulders dropped as she cocked her head to one side, causing Kendall to downshift gears from vixen back to widow.

In unison, the hospital crew standing around the balcony-side high-top tables – as well as several located just inside the balcony doors – turned to focus on Kendall. She'd prepared for this initial reaction.

Without breaking stride, she regained her FFN character and flawlessly greeted her supportive fans. She'd already mastered the tiptoe shuffle with regard to Dan's death, but promised herself that it wouldn't become the focus of conversation that night. It couldn't.

After hugging her circle of close coworkers and graciously acknowledging the nods and sympathetic hand squeezes of several others gathered 'round, Mark DeGraff – who had immediately scurried off to the bar as she'd entered her team's embrace – swooped in, presenting a Kalik Gold. He clinked the neck of his bottle to hers.

"Mmm." Kendall nodded in approval after taking a sip. "Thank you, Mark. This is what I've been missing."

"The pleasure is all mine," he hummed back, overindulgent as always. Oddly, in that moment she found it comforting and silently thanked him for not changing. Perhaps his obsequious manner was, in fact, sincere.

An audible pause hovered over the group's exchanges as everyone took in the subtle (and not-so-subtle) physical differences brought about by tragedy – the most obvious being Kendall's five-month unintentional weight loss. If she were a patient, she might qualify for a nutrition consult. Or a psych evaluation.

Then there was the lackluster hue of her once enviable, vibrant hair; the infinitely hollowed space behind her now dull, green eyes; the general absence of joie de vivre. Even her bronzer, masterfully applied to enhance the contour of her cheekbones with a subtle glow, fell just short of actually masking the sunken look of well-nourished depression.

Kendall almost felt Dr. Allaway's loss of interest as her new status – and the baggage it carried – descended from the raincloud looming above. *Hello, Eeyore.*

She scrambled into Act I, Scene 2.

"I'm fully aware of the black widow dancing across my chest, and honestly, I'm not sure I'm ready to let her go." She took a breath, not expecting her over-rehearsed speech to feel so raw. "But I do know I'll never be ready to move on if I don't get a break from her every now and then. So tonight – I'm just here as Kendall."

All those encircling her, a nearly impenetrable wall guarding her from the outside world, absorbed her words and – finally – her widow's veil ceremoniously drifted to the floor.

The amped-up atmosphere of the populated bar, along with the buzz of life down on the corner of Delray Beach's Atlantic Avenue and A1A below, poured over the wall of friends and electrified the late February South Florida air. Across the street from the bar balcony, Kendall could see whitecaps dancing along the black Atlantic as beams of moonlight scattered across her choppy surface.

The stage was set.

As the black widow retreated, the night became thick with anticipation, granting Kendall her first real reprieve since the night of the accident.

Chapter 2

The rowdy energy of the Dolphin Bar – the low clang of the tip jar bell ringing out over the shouts of drink orders; the over-zealous bass guitarist's amp drowning out his strained vocal cords; even the frequent elbow jabs to the ribs from shuffling around the high-top tables – was in a word, heaven. Kendall wanted to be nowhere else.

As expected, Courtney was loud and hilarious, knocking back perhaps one too many vodka martinis. Patricia checked her phone obsessively, taking pictures to document the occasion and uploading them to every social media account she could. Meanwhile, Rachel, DeGraff, and Kendall laughed it up with silly dance moves, inside jokes from years of working together, and the general alcohol-infused meaning-of-life conversations that always followed their nights out.

Just like old times.

But she wasn't there for the past.

Kendall checked her phone. She'd been enjoying herself for a full fifty-seven minutes and still hadn't engaged *Double A* in conversation. But, make no mistake – she'd definitely chummed the waters.

They had locked eyes three separate times. First, when she'd approached the tables during her grand entrance; next, while naturally scanning the bar after a particularly raucous moment in her tight-knit clique; and finally, after brushing past him on the way to the bar. She'd turned her head, just peeking over her shoulder at him with parted lips, and they'd shared a tasteful, closed-mouth grin. The clear seduction mirrored in his eyes had been beyond exhilarating. *Damn!* She'd felt so alive in that moment, the current of the exchange so tantalizing, that briefly, she'd considered walking right out the door and ditching the rest of her plans.

But the chaos within had reached epic levels – and something had to give.

Standing at the bar counter feeling sexy, all her weight on one foot as the other bounced to the music, she rested her elbows on the polished wood, propping up her cleavage to grab the attention of a gorgeous female bartender. Their fleeting, savory exchange whetted her appetite as she ordered another beer.

The bartender affectionately acknowledged Kendall's order. Kendall flashed a genuine smile of appreciation and turned back out to the crowd to people watch. To her surprise, Dr. Allaway was now standing right next to her with a sly smile.

"If I didn't know any better, I'd say you were hitting on that bartender," he shouted over the music and crowd.

Kendall drank him in, relishing in the opportunity to really enjoy the close-up shot – his tasty mouth showcasing his pristine oral hygiene; his scruffy five o'clock shadow begging to be stroked, perhaps even licked; those striking aqua blue eyes, enhanced by his South Florida tan, drawing her deep inside the mindfuck he seemed to stir within all women (and any number of men). Even his light brown hair, sun-streaked from hours in the surf, had grown since she had last seen him, revealing a subtle wave that was model perfect.

So freakin' irritating. No one should look this good naturally. And be a doctor. An effing brain surgeon. It's simply disgusting.

"Why not? A little flirting goes a long way at a bar. See?" Kendall nodded in the direction of the bartender, hustling back toward them with Kendall's order.

"Here you are. Do you want to start a tab?"

"I've got this" –Dr. Allaway leaned in to read the purple plastic nametag pinned just above the bartender's left breast– "Crystal. Thank you." He handed over a twenty, his arrogance outshining his generosity, then turned back toward Kendall.

"Thank *you*," Kendall enunciated, tipping the bottle toward him, and took a long sip of the refreshing ice-cold beer.

Sure, it was thirst quenching – but it did nothing to cool down the scorching heat in her neck and cheeks. Ordinarily, his cocky confidence would have turned her off, actually relaxing her. But not tonight. Not when the body attached to his ego carried her perceived ticket to escape. Fortunately, the dim lighting masked her flushed face, concealing any self-doubt. Her practiced persona flourished in the cover of night.

Crystal returned with change, and Dr. Allaway dropped a five-dollar bill on the countertop as tip. Although the generous gesture definitely pleased the bartender, it was far too much for a beer, eliciting an unexpected eye roll from Kendall.

"Let me know if you need anything else." Crystal smiled appreciatively at Dr. Allaway but lingered a few seconds too long, the corner of Kendall's mouth curling up with judgment.

"What are you smirking about?" Dr. Allaway inquired with his own delectable grin, teasing her with succulent invitation.

"Clearly, I'm in the wrong business. I think it's a crime nurses can't accept tips, especially considering all the shit we have to put up with," Kendall badgered. "Literally and figuratively. Especially from people like you." She chased her retort with another swig of her beer.

Dr. Allaway pulled out another twenty from his wallet and held it up to Kendall. "Hey, I'd gladly tip nurses. Just tell me where to put it."

Dirt bag.

But, then again...

She lapped up every bit of it. His eyebrows were boldly suggestive and his enticing eyes drew Kendall further into his own well-rehearsed act.

"You'll need more than a twenty to cover my costs. I got mad *skillz*." Kendall played right along, placing her lips around the rim of her beer bottle with a wicked gleam in her eye before she took a small sip.

They shared a lingering laugh, exchanging looks never before dreamt of while at work with one another.

The fact that it was all actually happening, just as planned, felt wildly surreal. Kendall's insides churned, powered by a flurry of endorphins, as the goal of sex with said target drifted deliciously closer. The bounding pulse of her carotid artery drummed in her ears, drowning out the kick pedal of the live band. Finally, she broke their gaze, providing a chance to cool off and catch her breath.

She then noticed Courtney gesturing for her to return to the table. Kendall furrowed her brow, acknowledging her request but declining the offer. Courtney spoke to DeGraff with a look of disapproval. DeGraff, whose back had been facing Kendall, turned to assess the situation. He then waved to Kendall, indicating for her to carry-on and to ignore Courtney's pleas. Kendall laughed and looked back at Allaway.

He was watching a highlight reel of last season's college football games on the flat screen above the island bar, unaware of the across-the-room exchange that had just taken place. Sensing that he'd regained his audience, he glanced toward her, then nonchalantly looked back up at the television.

"So how've you been, Matthews?" he asked, mindlessly taking a swig of his beer, then grimacing at a fumbled play.

Then it hit him: the carelessness of his question, fully wrapped in his douche-bag tone – as if she'd been out gallivanting around having a great time the last few months. It brought to mind his foot-in-mouth fuck-up the morning he'd found out about the fate of her husband.

The day before Dan died, Kendall had been at work in the surgical intensive care unit – like any other day. She had left the neuro ICU a year before in favor of day shift in the SICU. But when the nursing supervisor was in a bind, she'd float her over to neuro because of her background knowledge.

That day, Dr. Allaway had checked out the schedule of nurses for the week; whenever he had a major surgery scheduled, he wanted to ensure he had a strong nurse available during the patient's recovery. Since neuro was going to be short the day of surgery and Kendall was scheduled to work, he'd asked that she be floated over to recover his patient.

Even though it depended on the census of SICU, Dr. Allaway went over to ask Kendall personally if she could be available for neuro that day. He remembered her saying she would have the next day off, so a new assignment would be fine to take on when she returned.

On the day of the surgery, he'd rounded in neuro and was irritated that Kendall wasn't there as planned. When a floor nurse told him she was a no-show for work, his blood pressure rose, royally pissed off that he couldn't depend on her. Overhearing their exchange, another nurse quickly cut them both off – explaining that Kendall's husband had been killed in a work-related accident the previous day.

With the drop of that guillotine, Dr. Allaway's heart sank. The aching loss that he'd buried deep down years before came barreling back in an instant.

From that moment on, he'd curiously found himself hoping to see her once again. Like a gawker to a car wreck, he couldn't shake his interest in seeing how she'd fared in the aftermath – if anything, to compare notes.

"Umm... I mean... you've been missed at the hospital. It's been – what? Six months? Are you planning on coming back?" He downshifted further, nearly suffocating the ardent air that had been pulsating between them just moments earlier.

Kendall graciously smiled at him – knowing full well that if he viewed her as a broken woman, she'd be going home alone. Mustering up the last of her confidence, she replied: "Just over five months. But I'll be back next week. And I'm looking forward to it. I need to get back for my own sanity."

She paused for a second, picking at the splintered edge of the bar counter. After another sip of liquid courage, she slowly let out her line.

"I just need one more thing to get back into the swing of things..." Her heart pounded powerfully in anticipation as she lifted her beer to her lips again, without actually taking another sip. Driven by her now searing-hot confidence, she returned her eyes to his, pupils fully dilated and drawing in all surrounding light as she awaited his response.

Her words echoed above them, stretching across the silence, working to resuscitate the sparking connection between them. And in those few seconds, she swooned in that forgotten feeling of butterflies.

What it would feel like to be held by him, to feel the heat of his chest against hers. His full, sweet lips – to have his tongue exploring all over her skin, tasting every succulent morsel of her body. His eyes! Those Caribbean blue eyes – the way they looked at her, into her, into her soul.

He's just so goddamn sexy.

Suddenly, the possibility of rejection entered her mind. She hadn't expected it. She'd thought her plan was foolproof; she simply had to present herself as ready and willing and he would take the bait with no questions asked. Quite frankly, that's how she'd always viewed him: a fantasy fuck with no strings attached. A sure bet if she ever dared to venture down that road. A cocky son-of-a-bitch who would never actually *have* her because she was just too good for him. Yet if *she* felt so inclined, she'd give him a go-around.

But in that moment, standing there, offering herself like a virgin sacrifice to the unparalleled Adonis – the ball clearly in his court – she saw him as an over-skilled player, one who could easily crush her and her fragile psyche.

Just as the impulse to avert her eyes zipped across her brain, racing to save her from further embarrassment, Dr. Allaway took the bait.

"And that *thing* is?" he asked.

She leaned in, losing herself in the cloak of his cologne, and without hesitation whispered, "I need to be fucked."

His eyebrows arched reflexively, delighted by her choice of words but playing it cool, just the hint of a smile escaping from his lips.

He definitely found her attractive. And he'd always suspected she had a wild side – this not being the first time she'd caught him off guard with a one-liner. Several times before, he'd walked away from an interaction at work, fantasizing about her potential bedroom behavior. Yet he'd always dismissed it soon after, since she was not even remotely available.

Now there she was, handing over a clear invitation. Not just for sex, but for high-stakes fucking. He found the challenge intoxicatingly seductive.

Dr. Allaway placed his empty glass on the counter top, then leaned toward her as if going in for a kiss. At the last second, he diverted his head just to the side of her face, forcing Kendall to control her shallow, rapid breathing. Gently squeezing her waist with one hand, he whispered so close that his lips grazed the fine hairs of her ear. "Give me a minute and I'll take you away from here."

He pulled back to read her expression of agreement, then casually snaked through the crowd toward the hospital crew.

Kendall, the resounding beat of her heart booming in her ears with *holy shit this is happening* adrenaline bubbling up through her neck, chugged back half her beer while keeping an eye on Dr. Allaway. He spoke to DeGraff and bumped shoulders with a few others to signal that he was heading out before turning back her way. She carefully avoided Courtney's glowering glare.

Kendall took one last gulp, then set the bottle down on the slick wooden counter and examined it, rolling her lips together in thought. As she realized she wouldn't be finishing her beer, Dan's playful words, *that's alcohol abuse*, worked their way to the forefront of her brain.

Dan. She gritted her teeth.

"No," she whispered.

"Ready?" Dr. Allaway asked, placing his hand on the small of her back, catching her off guard once again.

Her scalp prickled as every hair bristled with excitement. She turned to face him, making his hand slide along her waist to her hip.

"Yes," Kendall answered confidently.

Chapter 3

Dr. Allaway took Kendall's hand with welcomed control and escorted her through the crowd, back around that fateful corner, down the stairs, and outside to his metallic black Porsche *911 Turbo S*. An *Endless Summer* Florida license plate adorned the back of the superbly sleek vehicle, with "AA007" as its vanity tag.

It took everything for her to suppress a laugh, this cherry-on-top show of arrogance begging for her to spout off some sort of derisive jibe. She bit her tongue, but not before the snap judgment settled into her own train of thought. *He's the epitome of a superficial playboy.*

The short drive up the scenic ocean road was surprisingly smooth. Kendall relaxed, her sudden realization that this conquest was in fact no real challenge at all bringing her into a more confident, comfortable state. They resorted to small talk as if at work in the hospital, the flashing neon sign of *Hot, Dirty Sex* seemingly stowed in the trunk.

"I gave DeGraff a ride tonight. Had to make sure he could make his way home," Dr. Allaway explained.

"Oh yeah, no problem. He's always bumming rides from people. His ten speed isn't exactly the best transportation after a night of drinking, I suppose."

Kendall rubbed her fingers along the seam of the black and white leather racing seat, sizing up the ultra-sleek interior of Allaway's Porsche. She'd accept a ride in it over a bike any day.

"Yeah, plus he lives right around the corner. So we're like neighbors."

"That's nice of you. Do you two hang out much outside of work?" She'd always been curious about their friendship, the two having somewhat opposite personalities within the hospital walls.

"Oh, well. On occasion."

Upon arriving at Allaway's sophisticated oceanfront bachelor pad not even five minutes later, it was abundantly clear to Kendall that DeGraff's dingy duplex sat way to the west of the proverbial A1A tracks.

Dr. Allaway pulled the Porsche into his extended curved drive and turned off the engine. Both wasted no time in stepping out of the vehicle, although he did make it to her side of the car to hold the already opened door. Kendall smiled in appreciation but did not lock eyes. She was not looking for chivalry. Or treasured moments.

Just sex.

She glanced around the property, taking in its exterior – the lush Florida landscape, the mix of natural and inorganic materials, the distinct three-storied modern design that stood out from the more commonly seen Spanish, Mediterranean, and Key West-style estates dotting A1A. She had run past the place before, several times as a construction site and maybe once since its completion, but had never known it belonged to him.

Only then was Kendall aware of her own arrogance. She was being welcomed into his private world, a place he'd managed to keep completely separate from his life at the hospital, yet she still assumed so much about him. She ran down the mental list of what she really knew: Dr. Anson Allaway is an oceanfront-living, Porsche-driving, GQ-contending, life-saving brain surgeon. Not bad for a one-night stand. It was time to cut the guy some slack.

The large wooden gate that had opened upon their arrival began to slide out on its track from a coral rock wall, like a pocket door, and then latched shut. Its richly stained amber boards were uniquely arranged in a horizontal fashion, the rustic look somewhat reminiscent of old St. Augustine in North Florida, yet clearly modernized. She found the whole structure far more appealing than the wrought iron gates typically used to keep the common man from polluting the air of these beachfront mansions.

While the design and motion of the gate mesmerized her, the ocean breeze rustled through the trees above, eventually drawing her attention up. The silver swirls of clouds resembled paintbrush strokes along a navy blue canvas, perfectly framed by blackened palm fronds and banyan branches – a night sky like something handpicked from a Van Gogh painting.

Yes, she was sold. The ionized air of the Atlantic sparked a renewed energy within her. As staging went for a hot fling, it exceeded her expectations.

Chaos. Time to dance.

As Kendall turned toward the house, Dr. Allaway was already a few paces ahead watching her, admiring her confident demeanor. For a few breathtaking moments, they just kept still, her body bathed in moonlight, his silhouetted by the front entryway lights of his home.

It was then that he realized she was, and had been, in complete control. All of the thoughts, expressions, and words exchanged between the two of them earlier, down to their subtle nuances – all of it was in her plan. He'd never been hunted so skillfully. And honestly, it was quite the turn on.

But this wasn't just high stakes fucking, he thought. It was the highest form. She needed to feel alive again, and that carried considerable emotional baggage. Did she know they stood on the precipice of destroyed colleague relationships? Was she searching for a relationship to fill the void of her late husband?

"Thank you," Kendall said.

Her kind words jolted his wandering thoughts back to the present – the sincerity in her voice almost too real for Dr. Allaway to accept.

"It's just sex," he dismissed with a shrug, vocalizing his thoughts unintentionally. "Come on in, I'll get you a drink if you'd like." He held out his hand to welcome her to his home.

Kendall walked up the curved drive to the flagstone walkway where he stood and placed her hand in his. His grasp lacked the eager desire from earlier at the bar. If anything, it was stiff – and definitely not the body part that needed to be.

He smiled nonchalantly and walked with her up to the large wooden door, made from the same wood she'd admired on the gate. It was beautifully simple, without carvings or ornate etched glass. She liked everything about it.

"Hey," Kendall said, pulling at Dr. Allaway before letting go of his hand. He turned to face her. "Just to reassure you: I'm not looking for a way into your heart."

Relieved to hear this, and somewhat embarrassed he was so easy to read, Dr. Allaway relaxed and confessed, "Matthews, or Kendall rather, it's... it's not that getting to know you outside of work would be bad. In fact, we'd probably get along great. It's just that... I just don't want you to be expecting that. The last thing I want to do is cause any further hurt for you. You know what I mean?"

"Doctor... uh, Anson? Double A? See?! I don't even know what the hell to call you!" Kendall said, laughing through her embarrassment, lightening the entire mood on the doorstep.

"Anson," he clarified with a smile that reached his eyes. "I've heard about the Double A nickname."

"Anson it is then," she stated matter-of-factly. "The problem is my late husband. I know! He's everywhere I go right now! And yes, I'm grieving. But tonight – if not just for tonight – I've left it all behind. I. Just. Want. To have. Some fucking. Sex." She drew in a breath and apologetically cringed. "And, no offense, but I figured you'd be a safe bet and probably a wiser choice than someone random. At this point, I was willing to see what Bryan could do for me, but turns out he's in a committed relationship." Kendall rolled her eyes in jest, Bryan being a flamboyantly gay respiratory therapist.

Anson's smile broadened again. "No offense taken. And just for the record, I'm not usually this predictable, but I hear what you're saying. And honestly..." He paused, his expression softening. "I'm so sorry for your loss and I apologize for not saying that earlier." A doleful look spread across his face as he reflected on his behavior. "I guess I am more of an ass than I'd like to admit. But with regard to tonight, rest assured, I do get tested regularly. Which begs the question: Are you on the pill?"

"I've got condoms. A nurse always comes prepared," she said with a wink. "And you're not an ass, just a player. No need to apologize."

"I'm not a player," Anson contested.

"You just fuck a lot?"

He laughed, impressed with her wit, raising his eyebrows suggestively as a wolfish grin returned to his face.

Surprised she would just address the elephant in the room like that, Anson respected Kendall's approach. Strangely, he imagined what Dan would look like: a respectable firefighter, surely a good guy who must have played a role in shaping his wife to be so secure and confident in her ways. And now, seeing this whole other side of Kendall, he oddly admired Dan as well. Anson could tell they must have had one of those rare marriages exemplifying love. She was definitely not on a mission to replace him tonight.

No one would compare.

Reeling his thoughts back in once again, Anson snapped his fingers and pointed at Kendall. "Okay, great. Now that we've gotten all that out in the open." He turned back to the door to unlock it.

"So, do you have kids?" he asked. "Nevermind. Ignore that. I don't know why the hell I just asked that. We're clearly spending way too much time talking out here."

"Nope, no kids. And I agree, less talk."

Before he had a chance to fully turn the key in the keyhole, Kendall grabbed his hand, bringing it to her lower back, and pulled his head down toward hers, taking control once again. And Anson was right there with her. He pressed his hips close against hers, rapaciously sucking her waiting lips, the abandoned keys dangling from the lock.

They both inhaled sharply as he repositioned her up against the solid wood door, driving his tongue deep into her mouth, then softly gliding it along the edge of her top lip. With his hands firmly grasping the inside of her back pockets, squeezing and grabbing her, Anson rocked his pelvis into hers, effectively pinning her to the wood.

At first, his drive was purely primal in nature – his goal, like always, to check out mentally and fulfill that selfish gratification often accompanying meaningless sex. But the more deeply he kissed her, inhaling the pheromones radiating from her pores mixing with the sultry air, the more his focus shifted to Kendall.

And Kendall noticed.

The intensity of their exchange was far more exhilarating than she'd anticipated. Considering she'd been kissing only one man for the last decade, she'd expected an awkward vibe to override this new sexually charged contact.

But with Anson? It felt familiar, safe, and right, *so very right* – yet wildly exotic and intoxicating all in the same breath. The alluring dichotomy seduced her, exceeding even the expectations of her active imagination.

Anson tugged gently at her hair before letting his hand glide along her neck and over her covered breast, where he paused to fondle her. Carefully, he lifted the hem of her loosely designed chiffon top, still feeding off her fiery kisses, and slid his hand on to her bare skin, up her back, and to her bra clasp. Her skin submissively hummed under his commanding touch. From her panting mouth, he moved to taste her earlobe and the salty skin of her sleek neckline.

With one snap of his fingers, he undid the clasp, freeing her. His left hand danced lightly along the side of her ribcage to her breast, eliciting an airy giggle from Kendall. He returned to her mouth, relishing in her response, and sealed his grin against hers. His fingertips salaciously outlined the supple bottom curve of her breast, teasing her in hope of that same delightful response, then seductively caressing and squeezing her entire breast.

Powerless against his skilled hand, Kendall moaned into his mouth, arching her back, pressing her breast into his palm, and hardening him with excitement. He massaged her nipple between his thumb and forefinger while sucking at her bottom lip, leaving her breathless. Their tongues met again, the cool saliva coating her swollen lips – lips that burned lasciviously from the rough friction of his stubbly facial hair.

Just as he began to lift her blouse, exposing her breasts to the humid South Florida night, Kendall pushed his chest away, taking Anson aback. He searched her eyes for assurance, respectfully bringing both hands to rest on her hips. A cooling sensation rushed down both of them as he created a gap between his bulging jeans and her pelvis.

"Everything okay?" Concerned, he instinctively stroked her hip bones with his thumbs in a soothing manner.

Noticing the wistful look in his eyes, Kendall smiled reassuringly, enunciating her somewhat erratic breathing with the softest giggle.

"More than okay," she exhaled. "I just thought we might want to pause for a second, so we can remember how to unlock a door and enter a house. Otherwise, I see us unzipping and finding a place amongst your sea grapes."

Anson laughed. "Nah, no need to roll around in the dirt. I'll just hold you up against the door. Then, if you can handle more, I'll take you inside for round two."

"Aren't you the confident one? Last I checked, I had some pretty outstanding skills myself. And I'm guaranteeing you'll be plain worn out when I'm through with you. Don't get too attached. I'll be gone before you know what hit you." With that, Kendall turned, twisted the forgotten key in the lock and pushed down on the handle of the door.

As he held open the door, she looked back at him suggestively and playfully bit her bottom lip. Without warning, Kendall lecherously cupped his confined erection, then skipped over the threshold into his home.

Her playful teasing in this arena was so unexpected, so alluring, *so fucking cute*. Anson was far from the besotted type. Yet here he was, rapt. Kendall was someone he knew for her keen nursing intelligence and professional skills within the hospital walls. And now she was captivating him with a whole new area of expertise, one with which he was far more interested in becoming familiar. He shook his head in amusement and followed her inside.

Chapter 4

The heavy wooden door swung in to an open foyer, and Anson reached along the wall to switch on some lights, illuminating a stunning blue glass fixture dangling above that boasted large water-drop-shaped hand-blown ornamentals. Tiered at various heights, it was as if oversized raindrops were cascading down from the third floor ceiling. The extraordinary chandelier was just the first of many things in his home that would take Kendall's breath away that night.

Without traveling the four steps up from the foyer, she could see directly into the large centrally located kitchen and straight out the wall of windows to what she assumed was the ocean. From her vantage point, she could only discern the reflecting foyer lights and stainless steel appliances set aglow by the moonlight pouring through the windows.

Kendall ascended the slate steps and wandered through the kitchen, dancing her fingertips along the concrete countertop, this time leaving a broken trail. Anson ambled closely behind, breathing in the scent of her light perfume.

She stopped in front of the large glass sliders along the back of the house. The moonlight skipped along a thin strip of ocean just above the privacy fence of sea grape shrubbery, lighting up the entire wooden deck. A staircase blanketed by thick rolling sea grass descended directly to the sandy beach below. Gray silhouetted cirrus clouds streaked the starless sky – and the striking view nourished her tattered soul.

Slowly, she drank it all in, clinging to the hope of renewed life. She smiled fondly as memories of her and Dan strolling along the beach at night flooded her heart. She silently thanked him, choosing not to shut him out in this moment.

Anson approached Kendall and, sensing her reflective state, decided to stand next to her, hands tucked away in his jean pockets. He no longer concerned himself with the emotional scar she bared and allowed the moment to breathe. Looking at her now, he felt something stir deep within the trenches of his heart for the first time in nearly a decade. There was something so pure about her. She looked up at him, her eyes glistening with the threat of tears, and smiled. And then, as if compelled, Anson leaned down to softly kiss her lips, hands still securely stowed away.

Without warning, the newly rediscovered sensation of butterflies consumed Kendall's insides. She instinctively turned her body toward his, drawing him in, connecting deeper. She reached her hands up to his face and hooked her fingers in his hair, heightening the kiss, introducing her tongue into his inviting mouth.

Anson audibly sucked in through his nostrils, letting his breath go slowly through his mouth onto her wet lips. He'd never expected to find this level of passion tonight. He dove in deeper, pulling her close. He tugged at her bottom lip with his teeth and set his hands free to find refuge against her sultry skin. He massaged her back, gently gliding over each bony prominence of her spine before raising the hem of her blouse. Once over her head, he let it loosely fall to their feet. Her bra, still unclasped, slipped off her shoulders as her arms returned to her sides.

Kendall stood in front of Anson, her breasts highlighted in the crisp tranquility of moonlight. Gently stroking the length of her arms, up and down, Anson took in her beauty.

"Oh Kendall," he cooed, his words of worship effortlessly rolling off his tongue. "You're gorgeous. Your skin is incredible. Breathtaking really." He licked his lips and brought his eyes up to hers, a guilty smile teasing the corner of his mouth. "Scrubs hide way too much."

Kendall shied away, hiding behind her humility. Anson's fingertips methodically traced the curves of her figure. He cupped both breasts in the palms of his hands, pushing them upward and squeezing gently, her nipples wedged between his thumbs and forefingers.

Kendall inhaled through a moan, her head rocking back as her eyes shut, blown away by the power of his touch.

He leaned over, needing to taste her. The tip of his hot tongue masterfully flicked and circled her aroused nipple. Every few rotations ended in a tortuous suck, elongating it into his mouth, then sealing it with a hungry kiss, awakening her entire body.

Her skin hummed under his enticing play, making it impossible not to vocalize her pleasure. She embraced his head, pressing his face into her bosom, nuzzling his hair with her nose, swimming in his provocative scent.

Her entire torso was like a live wire, every touch erupting into a shockwave up her spine and down into her groin, stoking the burning fire within. She'd truly thought it would be years before another man could make her body sing like this.

"You. Taste. So. Fucking. Good," Anson announced into her chest as he hastily caught his breath.

His heady words were like a vibrator to her clit, making her question whether she could handle much more foreplay in that upright position. She clenched her jaw, the heated air hissing through her teeth while he worked her over with his tantalizing magic. Her mouth now dry, she licked her lips, time and time again, desperately parched. She let out another moan, grabbing the sides of his head to quench her thirst with his mouth.

Once again, they were tangled in a passionate embrace, tongues intertwined, lips nipped and bit in the heat of the moment, hands freely exploring up and down the other's body. They both reached down to the other's jeans, needing more. Anson bulldozed through her belt, button, and zipper, eager to get inside. But then he pulled back, and locked eyes with Kendall.

"I want to hear it again. What is it that you *need*?" he asked.

"I need to be fucked," she answered breathlessly, her fingertips dipping below the rim of his now unbuttoned jeans, craving his power. She brushed her lips against his, and clarified: "Actually, I need *you* to fuck me, Anson."

It was all he could do not to take her to the floor right then. How had he not sensed this chemistry with her while at work? The pull and control she wielded over his desires – he'd never experienced anything like it.

Anson set fire to her hovering lips, grabbing hold of her belt loops. Dropping to his knees, he slid her jeans straight down around her heeled sandals. He anchored her shoes as she stepped out of one, then the other. He hastily shoved the articles off to the side and then, ever so slowly, he inhaled her inviting fragrance, traveling along the entire length of her silky smooth legs up into the apex of her thighs.

A wave of unbidden goosebumps raced up Kendall's legs, scattering into a visible shiver that cascaded down her entire body. Anson smiled into the soft skin of her inner thigh. He couldn't help but appreciate their juxtaposition: the control she had over him with her words versus the control his touch had over her body.

The front of her panties dampened as he pressed his lips against her, forcefully exhaling through the fine lacy pattern that adorned the front of her black thong, and further frenzying the thousands of nerves in her clitoris. He released his grasp on her calves and seductively slid his hands up the back of her legs, clutching the skin just below her buttocks. He kissed the black lace, divinely torturing her, then released her and stood up.

Rapidly, Anson unfastened his top button and pulled his shirt over his head, throwing it behind him. He took Kendall's hands, leading them to the opening of his jeans. Together, they unzipped and pulled, freeing up most of the pressure on his erection. He sighed with relief.

Through batted eyelashes, Kendall looked at Anson and raised an eyebrow of intrigue, her knuckles grazing the huge bulge in his boxer briefs.

"Please, explore freely," he responded, nodding in approval and then closing his eyes, the leering grin returning to his face in fervent anticipation of her next move.

With virgin-like excitement, Kendall slipped one hand down his boxers, pulling his erection up and out. She now fully appreciated the size of his reputation. She yanked down his boxers and jeans to his ankles in one fell swoop. Without pausing, she knelt down and firmly grabbed his thick shaft in her hand, sliding down to its perfectly circumcised tip. After slowly stroking it a few times, she took the heated head into her mouth and sucked him hard.

"Ahhh," Anson groaned, placing one hand up against the sliding glass door to steady his legs, the other getting entangled in her hair.

His vocalizations fed her appetite and she drew him further into her mouth. Using one hand as a cock ring as the other cupped his scrotum, rhythmically caressing the boys as if they were Chinese meditation balls, she skillfully slid her mouth up and down his shaft, swirling her tongue around, tasting what he had to offer. With every slurp against the tip, she fingered his taint, sending him to the brink.

"Holy fuck! Ooh, yesss. Okay, okay, okay!" Anson carefully pushed her back and pulled her up. "Shit, Kendall. I thought you were the one needing the release," he said, panting, as he leaned more dramatically onto the glass slider.

"I enjoy giving a little to get a little," Kendall said with a sultry smile.

He shook his head. "You're here for one thing. Let me do my job."

Kicking off his shoes and the jeans awkwardly wrapped around his ankles, he grabbed her exposed ass with both hands, wearing that wolfish smirk, and hoisted her up onto his waist. Kendall clung closely to him, impressed with his strength, as he carried her up two flights of stairs to the third floor: his open loft bedroom.

With the moon dramatically lighting the way, Anson laid her down onto a platform bed nestled against a small partition in the room. The entire east wall was a series of floor-to-ceiling picture windows and if the lights had been on, Kendall imagined they would be giving quite the show to any late night beach walkers.

"Time to give you a little," Anson whispered as he positioned himself between her bent knees.

Kendall fell into a fit full of giggles, the subtle movement of the circulating air over her skin wildly arousing her. Instinctively, she captured his head between her thighs, trying to protect her over-stimulated body. But Anson remained diligent in his mission:

kissing her inner thighs as he hooked his fingers inside her panties, rubbing the silky wet surface below.

"Ahh, yeah. You're so wet. So ready to go. I love it," he whispered huskily, massaging the slippery lubricant between his fingers.

Kendall opened her eyes, just in time to see him greedily suck on his fingers. She dropped her head back again and let out an amused groan.

"What?! Are you kidding me?" Anson stared slack-jawed at Kendall, disappointed with her lack of enthusiasm for her own sexual arousal. "You have no idea how fucking hot this is! This is almost enough for me. You taste incredible."

Kendall laughed and tried to redirect her thoughts to less critical ones. Dan was never this wordy. *Anson's definitely different. A good different. A very good different.*

He pulled down her panties, and like a lasso, flung them out behind him, accidentally sending them right over the loft railing.

"Oh shit. You weren't needing those, were you?" he asked, laughing.

"Not at all. Carry on now. There's work to be done here," she said, haughtily directing him back to her open legs.

"With pleasure."

Anson eased his way, once again, up her thighs, nuzzling, tasting, and kissing her creamy sweet skin. With the forefinger and thumb of one hand, he trailed down her closely trimmed hair and gently separated her, nestling his nose into her labial lips and drinking in her aroma. He hummed against her clit as he exhaled, Kendall whimpering and tilting her hips up in ardent acceptance. He salaciously licked and sucked, gradually increasing in speed and voracity.

Kendall pulled and kneaded at his hair, no longer self-conscious about her body's response to his touch. She looked down at him with fervent desire, begging for her release. He caught a glimpse of her euphoric expression. With a wicked smile and bite of his lip, he immediately sank two fingers inside. Flexing his fingers, he rubbed her warm, moist wall with his fingertips, plunging deeper inside after each cadenced withdrawal.

Her leg muscles tightened. She could barely contain it, the release of her chaotic fury building in the trenches of her belly. But Anson – equally aroused by her every jerk and muffled moan, desperate for his own powerful release – jumped up and positioned his body over hers.

Kendall opened her eyes, frustrated by the sudden halt in dedication to her sexual stimulation. But there he was, hovering over her and huskily breathing, his arms locked on either side of her head, pushing into the plush mattress. Seduced by the intensity in his eyes, Kendall couldn't fight the urge to connect with him, reaching up to touch his cheek. Anson closed his eyes, hypnotized as her fingers stroked the rough stubble along his jaw line.

Anson moved, opening his nightstand drawer, and pulled out a condom. Lost in the moment, Kendall had forgotten all about her condoms downstairs.

In one fluid movement, Anson slid inside her, sinking deep down, burying himself completely, all manner of time and sensibility, ceasing to exist as he only experienced the pleasure of her.

"Sweet fuck," Anson exclaimed through clenched teeth.

Kendall gasped and let out a cry, the sensation of his erection so overwhelmingly full and satisfying. She grabbed ahold of him around his triceps, bracing herself for more – and he gave it to her, thrusting himself even deeper.

His pace picked up, pounding into her, again and again, just to the verge of climax. Then he relented, slowly pulsating inside her, grinding himself against her clit. Once more, he brought her body to the brink, Kendall digging her nails into his back and loudly pleading her desire for him to continue.

But he backed off, prolonging their sexual escapade and denying her the very thing she needed.

"Enough of this Tantric bullshit," Kendall mumbled, bucking her hips up and rolling him over, forcing a swap in positions.

Anson grinned, caught red-handed. He'd always wanted to try Tantric sex, but had never felt compelled to make it last this long with any other woman.

Kendall assumed her riding stance, both hands planted firmly on his sculpted pectorals as he locked onto her hips. She slowly raised her bottom, sliding to the tip of his dick – and regained control.

She picked up the pace, Anson matching the rhythm. She then sat up straight and fondled her breasts as they bounced to the beat of their bodies. Anson held onto her tightly, slamming her hips down harder each time. With her head craned back, her pleasure echoing throughout the house – every vigorous thrust more stimulating than the last – Kendall completely let go.

"Yes! Oh god, yes, please, yes!" she cried out, unable to control her volatile response.

Anson quickly followed suit.

"Oh baby! Oh – fuck! Fu-ck!" Anson forcefully ejaculated, his cock throbbing after each orgasmic squeeze of her tight muscles.

Kendall collapsed down onto his chest, their skin sticking to one another as beaded sweat slipped and slid between them. She rotated her hips, triggering intense bursts of muscle spasms throughout her abdomen, reveling in the delicious sensation.

"Goddamn woman," he exclaimed, awestruck as he stilled her hips, far too sensitive to handle any further stimulation in that moment.

They basked in the glow of their orgasms, breathing heavily, and allowed their sizzling bodies to simmer. Anson combed her hair with his fingers, sending Kendall further into her trance of tranquility – and far, far away from her grief.

Un-fucking-believable.

Chapter 5

Kendall had one leg draped across Anson's body, her head resting comfortably in the cradle of his shoulder. She absentmindedly swirled a fingertip around the smooth skin of his nipple. She stared out into the darkness of the room and thought of nothing – yet, felt everything.

"That's exactly what I needed," she purred, planting a kiss on his chest.

"Anytime. That far exceeded my expectations for this evening," Anson agreed, removing the condom and tossing it to the side.

"So... tell me," he continued, settling back down into the pillows, his arm securely around her. "Did you really plan this all out? Like choosing me because you figured I would agree? Or could it have been anyone tonight?"

Kendall smiled, enjoying the simple conduction of sound through his chest as his voice caressed her cheek. She also enjoyed hearing this slightly insecure tone coming from the great Dr. Allaway.

The only thing she had not planned about tonight was how incredible it felt being next to him – their bodies tangled up together, swimming in the sinfully sweet juices of the other, his natural scent filling more than just her senses. She was certain not just anyone could have done this to her tonight.

"Well, like I said earlier: I felt you'd be a safe bet. And I knew I wanted to make it happen before returning to work. So tonight was the night, since I knew I'd see everyone," Kendall answered.

"So, if I wasn't there, who else was on the list?" he asked. "Just out of curiosity."

Sensing the disappointment in his voice, she looked up at him, her chin resting on his chest.

"There was only you. I knew you'd be there tonight."

Anson's smile lit up his face. He kissed her forehead, a gesture he generally would consider too familiar for a one-night stand. But for some reason, Kendall didn't fit into that category for him.

"Well, thank you for that," he said.

Kendall rested her cheek back down on his chest, his contagious grin reaching her face as well. It was then that she began to grow uncomfortable with *how comfortable* she was, fearing the lines were already blurred.

After a minute of lying together quietly, she moved to sit up. A soft chill of air-conditioned breeze whirled over her glistening skin as she scanned the room in the dark.

"The bathroom is just over there," Anson answered, before she had a chance to ask. He reached over and turned on a nightstand lamp.

With the sudden flicker of light, Kendall felt exposed. She looked over at him as he pushed back against the pillows on the headboard, interlocking his fingers behind his head. His perfectly sculpted chest, now misted in the salty dew of fornication, was a beautiful sight to behold. He was so self-assured; his legs stretched out and crossed at the ankles, his erection losing its edge yet the wolfish grin and randy gleam in his eyes remaining. He studied the inviting curves of her body as she sat on the edge of his bed.

"Just let me know when you're ready to go again. You have to admit, we did that first round pretty well. Honestly, I think I'd be up for pulling an all-nighter with you." Anson laid it on thick, leaving no room for interpretation as he chewed softly on his bottom lip.

Kendall blushed, resting her hand on his leg. She really hadn't seen this coming, always thinking her attraction to him was simply wrapped up in physical appearances. Her physical needs were clearly not as disconnected as she thought they were from her emotional ones.

"Don't get me wrong, I really enjoyed it, too. But I'm going to be honest with you," Kendall said firmly. "I'm guessing it's pretty late now, and I can already see the black-and-white, business-like transaction we agreed upon starting to gray. I mean, at least for me. So I should probably get going."

"What?" Anson sat forward, genuinely taken aback. "That graying is what made it exceptional. I mean, we work together, Kendall. There's bound to be some graying. A business transaction? I have plenty of those, and that's not what this is. So, neither of us expected it to be that good – and it was fucking amazing. Don't rush out just because you're happy to be here with me. Stay a while."

Kendall looked out at his loft, contemplating his surprising request.

As if accepting a challenge, Anson suddenly sprung up and grabbed her arm, pulling her down onto him. He rolled Kendall over to her back and pinned her into the bed, bringing her arms above her head and securing them in place. Kendall giggled as she feigned fighting back. Instinctively, he pushed his pelvis up against her, his seemingly insatiable appetite growing. He stared down at her, his expression shifting from one of lust to a much softer look of desire.

Succumbing to their undeniable sexual chemistry and his compelling Caribbean blue eyes, she stretched her neck up to kiss him, meeting him halfway. They shared a slow and sensuous kiss, one that melted away the world and all the heartache they'd buried inside it. He loosened his grip on her wrists and she cradled his head, her fingers massaging his scalp. The kiss intensified.

Anson trailed kisses down her chin to her neck, flexing his hips into her. His hand slid down her torso, exploring, making no mistake about his craving for her once again. He moved to her ear and lightly nibbled her earlobe, chills cascading down her body as the delicious surge of passionate adrenaline returned. Kendall sighed with pleasure.

"Stay," he whispered hotly into her ear, his tantalizing kisses unrelenting as he worked his way back up her jaw line to her opened, waiting lips. "I want you to stay."

Kendall pressed her lips together, savoring his words, storing them and their pure honesty: unmistakable, raw, and unashamed. She opened her eyes, meeting the gaze that intensely pleaded for her to agree.

And then she saw him – not her escape from reality, her means to an end, *just sex, Double A, player-extraordinaire, a superficial piece of ass* – but him, *Anson*. Someone needing to connect and desperately hoping it was with her.

And she wanted to be part of that connection, however fleeting, in that moment. She needed someone to truly see her, see into her once more. It had been so long.

The serene silence of their registered intimacy finally began to fracture, leaving her with a calamity of racing thoughts. She hadn't planned on an encore performance. If anything, she'd counted on callous behavior from him to make it easy. Staying the night was definitely out of the question.

No attachment. No remorse. Just stay the course.

Kendall decided it was her job to make it easy for him to see her go, severing all blossoming connections. She'd keep it light and playful, though. She tilted her hips, gesturing a swap of positions again and he obliged, bringing her on top of him as before. Lacing her fingers between his – her turn to hold him down – she kissed him, tugging at his bottom lip with her teeth.

"So. Effing. Tempting," she seductively growled, before jumping off the bed and bounding off to the bathroom, leaving Anson dumbfounded.

Chapter 6

After using Anson's spotless marble master bathroom, Kendall stared at her mirrored reflection, her neck and chest still blotchy from her potent orgasm. Grabbing her breasts, boosted by all his positive feedback, she admired her feminine figure, feeling powerful. And to top it off, she knew she'd been dynamite in bed. He definitely fulfilled her physical needs – and he'd made it clear his were met as well.

But Anson wanted more. And now there seemed to be more on the line than just physical fulfillment.

She began to battle in her head again. They'd already had sex and did it very well together, so what would be the harm in doing it again? Yet, she knew that tomorrow would be the worst day possible to wake up next to another man. She could not forget that. *No sleepovers.*

They needed to avoid personal conversations. *Stick to the sex.*

She could do that. Not wanting to be overly insensitive, she wouldn't just rush around collecting her garments, high-tailing it out the door to a waiting cab – but in short, that was her plan. *After more sex.*

Anson knocked on the door. She opened it wide, now feeling confident in her bare skin.

"Damn." He paused in admiration, inspiring Kendall to strike a pose. Anson lost all train of thought for a solid five seconds until her laugh broke his trance.

"Way to leave me hanging out there," he scolded, offering her a black cotton bathrobe. "Thought you might like this. Although personally, I prefer what you have on now."

Noticing he'd pulled on some jersey shorts, she accepted his robe. Brushing past him naked, then giving him a full 360, she dramatically swung the robe around her shoulders, loosely draping it over her breasts before tying the belt in front.

He scoffed. "Have you always been such a tease? Or do I just bring it out in you?"

"A tease? Hardly. A woman in control? Definitely." She couldn't resist batting her eyes at him over her shoulder as she walked out into his room.

Again, he found himself enjoying her choice of words – such a role reversal from the hospital, where he barked out orders and she carried them out. Although even in that setting, she had never been a timid nurse.

She finally surveyed the now well-lit loft bedroom, courtesy of the track lighting above. The picture windows were covered with dark blackout shades. She slowly walked along the banister, looking down to the foyer. Up here, she was at eye level with the base of the glass teardrops, recognizing it as an installation piece and not a chandelier.

"This isn't a Chihuly, is it?" Kendall asked.

"Um, I'm not sure about that. I'd have to ask my brother. He picked it out."

"Probably not then. You'd remember the price tag and name otherwise. It's really lovely." She continued to scan the loft, gathering more information about the mysterious Dr. Allaway.

Like the walls throughout the home, the ones in here were smooth, yet pitted, concrete. The bed, along its small partition, divided the third-floor loft into two halves. A charcoal-colored duvet draped the bottom of the California king, their post-coital slate gray sheets wrinkled over the rest of the mattress. Wooden, black cubed nightstands on either side of the bed's black stained platform held two lamps and a digital clock.

On the north wall of the room near the stairs hung an expansive Clyde Butcher photograph of a lone piece of driftwood somewhere along Florida's southwest coast. In front of it, there was a seating arrangement with a light gray sofa; two white, cubed leather chairs; and a small, rectangular black coffee table. A metallic minimalistic desk stood in front of the windowed wall with a large, white flat-screen desktop computer perched on top. On the south end of the room, near the bathroom, was his dressing area: a large built-in closet and a black wooden chest of drawers.

Kendall skated her feet across the soft, luxurious white area rug covering the hardwood floor and picked up a medical journal opened on the desk, casually flipping through it. His room was modern and classy, fitting his personality well.

Anson watched her closely as she navigated the loft, curiously awaiting her next move.

"Where does that go out to?" Kendall asked, pointing to double French doors near the staircase.

"It's an elevator."

"Oh. Wow. How 'bout those?" She turned, pointing at the sliders along the east wall.

"They go out onto a balcony. Did you want to go out there?"

"Maybe some other time," she remarked with a wink, making him smile.

"Would you like anything to drink?" he asked.

"No thank you. Had a glass of water in the bathroom. Love the Clyde Butcher piece. Stunning, really." She looked back at the black-and-white photograph.

"Thanks. I picked that out myself. You know your art. I didn't know the photographer until buying this one. There's another one of his downstairs."

"I'm a Florida girl. Of course I know him. But what this particular piece says about you, I'd like to know even more," she crooned, her eyes becoming slits of intrigue and seducing him all over again.

She sashayed back over to him, untying her robe, allowing it to casually drape open and reveal the inner curves of her breasts. He reached out and separated the opening further, sliding his hands along her skin, pulling her naked body against his. The temperature around them spiked instantly. She draped her arms over his shoulders, her lips loosely parted – wanting, waiting – as her gaze met his.

Slowly, Kendall pressed herself up on the balls of her feet, letting her eyes drop away from Anson's captivating command, and softly kissed his neck once, the pounding of his pulse notably present beneath her teasing lips. As he hungrily squeezed the flesh along her backside and up to her shoulder, she felt his rock hard excitement grow against her lower belly.

Unable to pull away, their mouths ravished one another, reigniting the flickering flame into a blazing bonfire engulfing all rational thought. Anson moved hastily, his lips sampling her jaw, earlobe, then neck, making her body tremble beneath his seductive kisses. He sank his teeth into the slope of her neck, claiming her. Kendall yelped, thrilled by the impassioned bite, her entire being scorched by the surge of oxytocin in her bloodstream.

Tenderly, he slid one hand down her back, pausing to caress the curves of her supple bottom before moving to the front, cupping her, pleased to find her drenched with desire. He eased two fingers inside, teasing and calling her once again.

"Stay the night with me, Kendall. Just one night. I want you more than you know." His whispered confession against her ear sent a sizzling shiver of temptation down her spine as she exhaled through the pleasure of his touch.

But she couldn't respond with her thoughts muddled by moans, her robotic reasoning malfunctioning as her wires got crossed. *How does he do it?* Mere moments before her knees buckled, she managed to pull back and offered up a compromise.

"Believe me," she whispered, trying to catch her breath and bearings, stepping just enough back that his fingers slipped outside of her. She looked up at him. "You're not easy to walk away from. I won't deny it: I do want you again."

Anson's eyes remained fixed on hers, his attentiveness to her words unwavering.

"But I can't stay. So, if you want me, take me now." Kendall's breathing remained ragged. "Any. Way. You'd. Like. Just make it hard and fast," she offered, utterly aroused by his unabashed desire for her company.

Anson did not hesitate to accept. He slipped the robe off her shoulders, letting it fall to the floor, and removed his shorts. He then swept her off her feet once more, cradling her like a new bride, and carried her to his bed. He set her down on the duvet in a sitting position, legs dangling over the foot of the bed, and then, for an eternal beat in time, he hovered just above, poring over every inch of her as he memorized her beauty.

Their eyes met, and the captured depth of meaning was almost too daunting.

"You do realize, if you ever look at me at work the way you're looking at me right now, I might not be able to control myself," Anson divulged, the very thoughts unequivocally mirrored in her eyes.

But Kendall held her breath, burning with fervor and the fear of vocalizing her agreement.

Anson pulled out another condom from the drawer of his nightstand. Standing in front of her, he slowly rolled it onto his erection, watching her study him. She found the tutorial highly erotic, having stopped using condoms years ago. She caught herself staring, mesmerized by his physique. She blinked timidly up at him, his eyes fixed, claiming her.

He raised her up onto her feet. He peered into her eyes with such fiery intensity that she knew: He was really going to fuck her this time. Without warning, he swiftly turned her around, bending her over the bed. She crawled onto the mattress on all fours, keeping her bare ass close to the edge, exposing him to everything.

Anson's expression grew lustfully dark at the view before him, eager to own it. He shifted her hips back and licentiously spit on his hand before rubbing it between her cheeks, down to her anus. Kendall's eyes rolled up, then closed tightly as she groaned with satisfaction, giving him the go-ahead to have his way with her. He reached further, massaging her engorged clitoris and applying pressure to her anus with his thumb. He threw his head back, growing another heated inch, and expanded his lungs to their tidal volume.

"Holy fuck, Kendall – you make me so hard!" With that, he grabbed his cock and slammed into her wet arousal, gripping her hip bones and yanking her back onto him.

Kendall wailed with pleasure, shocked at how easily he slipped inside her, how aroused he made her. It felt so right, *so fucking good*. How could it feel that good when she'd been in so much pain? She wanted more and Anson complied, drawing back and once again, hitting the limit of her pleasure-pain threshold. Over and over he filled her, bringing her to the brink of her senses.

The power of it – the unexpected yearning for each forceful thrust – shattered her mirror of emotional pain. As she found refuge in the arms of another man, all of this heightened emotion stimulated every sexual neuron in Kendall's brain, bringing her to a psychological release she never dreamt of finding that night with Anson.

I can't. He can't. It's too much!

Feeling her potent response building, Anson reached in front and massaged her clit once again. He picked up his pulsating pace and finally, she could bare it no longer. She explosively climaxed, calling out his name, triumphant tears blurring her vision.

Anson immediately echoed her response, coming hard – the sensation overwhelmingly powerful as he anchored himself securely inside her. And then, just as suddenly, he pulled out and brazenly sank into her anus, sky-rocketing their orgasms to another orbit.

"Fuuuuuck!" Anson yelled out over three shallow thrusts. He dropped onto her back, causing Kendall to collapse to the side, the two of them forbiddingly entangled in a state of unsurmountable euphoria.

Her lips tingled as her body shivered, all senses going offline. She heard nothing over the ringing in her ears. Her face felt numb against the duvet and for a moment, she thought she was floating, suspended in midair, like a dream. With her bearings lost, she drifted into an exhausted state of ecstasy.

Anson, curled around her with his arm hanging over her side, worked to catch his breath. He blinked to clear the spots from his vision, then very carefully pulled himself out of her, whispering her name repeatedly. He rolled to his back, slipping into his own state of nirvana, his arm still stretched out beneath Kendall's neck.

They lay silently still in their forgotten bliss for what seemed like an eternity.

***

Kendall, startled by a muscle twitch, stretched out of her fetal position. Looking out to the bright bedroom, she slowly came back down to reality.

She heard a soft snore and turned over to find Anson sleeping on his back, naked, fully exposed, his member now flaccid along his groin, the condom wrinkled in a most unceremoniously and unappealing manner. She sat up on the edge of the bed and felt a warm stream trickling down below. Panicked, she jerked her eyes back to Anson's package.

The condom broke. *Fuck.*

Clenching her muscles, she rushed to the bathroom.

A short while later, after rapidly rinsing off in his shower, Kendall returned to the bedside. Now cloaked in his robe, she was relieved to find Anson still feebly passed out.

That last experience with him was far more intense than anything she could have imagined. Kendall congratulated herself on a job well done, but also tipped her hat to him, knowing full well he was no novice when it came to satisfying a woman.

And hello! Back door surprise! Holy fuck. She'd just had anal sex with Dr. Anson Allaway! *Anal sex and Allaway. Whoa.* That definitely was not the dancing star she'd planned to be tonight.

She couldn't help but chuckle at his skilled, covert move.

Glancing at the clock, she saw it was now after midnight. February 28. A chill ran down her arms and Kendall wrapped the robe around her more tightly.

"Happy Birthday, Dan," she whispered, at a loss for more words.

Fifteen minutes later, after going on a short scavenger hunt for her belongings, a taxi pulled up to the wooden gate. Two short bursts of the cab's horn made her jump as she quickly scribbled onto a scrap of paper.

Thank you for a very full and filling night!
XOX, Kendall
Although it should really be XXX. Wink, wink.

She left the note on the kitchen counter, then rushed out the front door, through the garden gate, and along the coral wall to the waiting taxi. The driver returned her to the Dolphin Bar and Restaurant, where her Jeep Wrangler was still parked. Another twenty minutes later, Kendall was home in Lantana and off to bed, sleeping soundly for the first time since Dan's death.

Chapter 7

Dan and Anson are laughing over beers at the back of the boat, which Kendall is driving full throttle out of the Boynton Beach inlet. The weather is perfect today, and she can't believe how great the three of them are getting along. Dan died and he came back: nothing short of a miracle.

From her captain's chair, Kendall can see right down to the ocean floor. It's all so crystal clear now.

Then, she panics – Dan is sinking to the bottom. But he was just on the boat! She turns for help, realizing she's now alone on board.

She dives into the threatening waters, but Dan is just out of reach. She motions for him to swim to her, but he doesn't respond. She screams and screams - but all is silent under the surf. Now she's drowning, the ocean violent from a storm raging above.

She looks up to the surface and Anson is back on the boat, drinking a beer in the sun. He nonchalantly invites her back onboard. Confused, she turns back to Dan – but he's no longer there.

Her cell phone rings up on deck, and Anson reaches for it. He motions to toss it to her in the water. But that'll destroy it! She resurfaces, gasping for air and frantically searching for her ringing phone.

Kendall sat up in bed with a start. Wide-eyed, she looked all around the room before realizing her cell was ringing on her nightstand.

"Mom?"

"Hey hon. Oh shoot. Sounds like I woke you up. I thought for sure you'd be up by now, considering our last conversation about your sleeping patterns."

"What time is it?" Kendall rubbed her eyes, trying to forget the bizarre nature of her dream. 8:18 a.m. *Impressive*. "Oh wow. After eight. Don't worry. That was really weird. I'm glad you woke me up."

"Did the ring make it into a dream? Vivid dreaming? You're just like me."

Elena Reyes-Graham, Kendall's passionate and protective mother, had been her anchor to life since Dan's death. She also provided Kendall with the hope that she would survive this battle – just as Elena had when Kendall's father had died. But Elena's comparison of herself to Kendall this morning, after the plotted FFN, caused Kendall to shift uncomfortably, only further mocking her as her overworked muscles deliciously tightened against the stretch.

Even more unwelcome in the moment, and in her mind, was a clear image of Anson as she'd left him: worn-out, nude, and sprawled out on the bed – just moments after asking her to stay and boasting that he could go all night. How would she ever manage to prevent that vulnerable image from popping into her head the next time she saw him? Could she still take him seriously as he cockily swaggered into the SICU and began barking orders? Did they really do all *that*? She tried to shake her mind clear.

"Yeah, but you rescued me, Mom. I was drowning," she said, swinging her feet over the side of the bed and surrendering to the fact that she did, indeed, have sex – hot, dirty sex – with Dr. Allaway.

And just like any other day, she needed to keep moving forward.

"Oh, those are the worst dreams," Elena said. "Good thing I called. So, I just wanted to say good morning and that I love you before heading out to get some work done. Do you have plans to see any friends today?"

"Nothing yet," Kendall yawned, walking into the bathroom to assess whether her nighttime activities had brandished her with any physical reminders to match the vivid memories.

Nada.

"Well, I'd hate for you to spend the whole day alone. I'll call again later on if you'd like," Elena suggested.

"Oh Mom, don't worry. Actually, I'll probably give Ariel a call, since its Saturday. We'll do something together, I'm sure. Right now, though, I'm just fine." Kendall appreciated her mom checking in on her, knowing it was Dan's birthday. "Do you have an event today?"

"No – it's Tuesday night. But I don't want to head in tomorrow, so we're setting up today to leave Monday for tying up loose ends. Daniel was none too pleased when I told him to meet me at the gallery by nine this morning. I tell you, he thinks he owns the place. And I think he's under the impression that his weekend nightlife is necessary to the gallery's success – like I should be paying him for clubbing so he can advertise to all the hipsters of South Beach," Elena said, laughing. "Marianna is on vacation this weekend, so he didn't have a choice in the matter. But he's replaceable. Plenty of thirsty new grads looking to break into the world of art."

Kendall rolled her eyes at her mom's empty threat. Daniel, who'd worked for Elena for the last four years, had become her right-hand man and, in many ways, did actually pull in business with his social connections. Elena used to joke to people that she'd liked Kendall's Dan so much that she had to find her own. Only her Dan went by Daniel and was gay.

"Well, college *interns* work for free and are eager for experience. Some assistants couldn't hurt," Kendall suggested.

"Actually, Daniel already brought that up and we're planning a summer internship this year."

"That sounds good. Well, good luck today. Hope you get most of it ready. I still plan on seeing you and Gabe tomorrow. And if you have loose ends left to be tied, I can stop by the gallery to help out Monday."

"We should get most of it done today. But thanks. I look forward to seeing you tomorrow," Elena said. "Gabriel's been asking about you. We kind of got used to seeing you all the time, so three weeks apart seems too long now. Love you."

"Love you too."

Kendall clutched the phone to her chest, smiling. She had a good mom. And brother. She stared back at her reflection in the mirror, shrugging at her unchanged appearance.

Nothing like a phone call from mom to truly awaken you after a night like that.

***

Kendall was well into her run around Lake Worth's scenic Lake Osborne when her phone rang, this time interrupting her music and day-dreaming.

"Hey," Kendall said choppily, clearly labored in her breathing.

"What, are you doing the deed right now?!" Ariel chided.

"I'm running!" she shouted back, almost too defensively.

"Whoa oh-oh! Look who's got some energy still remaining this morning? Guess an all-nighter was not pulled?"

"Ariel, I'm running. Can I call you back when I'm done?"

"When will that be? Are you doing a marathon?" Ariel asked.

"No. I was thinking of ten." Kendall glanced down at her watch and then scanned the path to determine her whereabouts. "I'll make it six instead. I'll call you in an hour."

"You better, *Miss Thang*," Ariel teased, before hanging up.

Kendall turned her music back up, rolling her eyes and picking up her pace.

Less than an hour later, after showering, Kendall plopped down on her couch and called up Ariel.

"So before I start grilling you, did you want to go to the Norton and have lunch at the café?" Ariel asked. "I have some passes from work that are about to expire and want to use them up."

"That sounds nice. What time do you want to go?"

"Well, it's just after ten, so I'd say now, since we can browse around whatever exhibits they have going on and then be ready for lunch. Sound good? I'll pick you up if you'd like."

"Yeah, sure. That sounds good," Kendall agreed.

"Great. I'll be there in fifteen." *Click*. Ariel's conversations never had an end or beginning. They just flowed in and out naturally, all based on her inflection.

A short while later, Ariel pulled her purple Prius up into Kendall's drive, laying on the horn in a most alarming manner to rush Kendall out the door in no time flat.

"Impatient much?" Kendall scolded.

"Uh, yeah! Someone had an FFN last night and needs to spill the beans before we quietly saunter through the galleries of the Norton."

Kendall darted a look Ariel's way, but she knew full well last night was going to be all about kissing and telling with regard to Ariel. In all honesty, Kendall wouldn't have it any other way. She and Ariel had a kindred connection like no other, and in many ways, Kendall needed Ariel to know everything to help her navigate through it all. That's how it'd been with them for nearly thirty years, bouncing every decision off the other, not feeling they'd given it its due process without the other weighing in first.

"I thought we would work our way up to it or something," Kendall said, kidding as Ariel backed out of the driveway.

"Whatever. You're dying to spill and I'm giving you an open door. Let's hear it."

Kendall laughed, relaxing into their high-school girl-talk ways for the first time in a long time. She recalled nearly every moment she'd shared with Anson in explicit detail, only glossing over their ever-so saucy second round, yet emphasizing the unanticipated connection she found with him.

"So it all happened like I planned," Kendall concluded. "But I was surprised by it all at the same time. I mean, I never knew he'd go for it until he did, and then it was like all bets were off. It was hot and intense like I hoped it'd be, but... I don't know..."

Kendall stared blankly out the window as Ariel pulled into the Norton Museum of Art parking lot. When the vehicle coasted quietly to a stop in a parking space, Kendall found her voice once again.

"The way he looked at me, touched me, and then asked me to stay. I mean, it's like there was real intimacy there. I never thought I'd feel that, and I don't think he expected it either."

Ariel powered off the car and angled herself toward Kendall. Ariel's wide-eyed expression jerked Kendall back to the present – Dan's *birthday* kind-of present!

"What?! You wanted to know. Tell me what you're thinking," Kendall demanded, her face heating up with a thousand shades of passion.

"Aside from the fact that I totally creamed myself? Ho-ly fuck, Kendall."

Kendall bowed her head and laughed, almost honored by Ariel's reaction. A most excellent scarlet feather had been added to her cap.

"But seriously," Ariel said. "Okay, so, freaking hot, to say the least, yet... I just don't think you walked away scot-free. I mean, I'm ready to invite him to the wedding. It sounds like that was beyond just a one-night stand."

"Don't be crazy. I'm not going to date him. I'm not ready for anything like that. It was just better than expected. End of story. And you don't know this guy. I mean, he's arrogant and a player and probably a narcissist. Everyone thinks it. Definitely not my cup of tea."

Kendall paused for a moment, picturing the Dr. Allaway she'd become very acquainted with last night. She couldn't help but smile fondly.

"Though, one-on-one," Kendall said reflectively, "I didn't get that impression. Let's just say, I understand why girls swoon over him a whole helluva lot more now than I did before. He's got *skillz*."

"Hey, don't underestimate bedroom talent. You never know – a professional in the bedroom could be a professional in your heart as well," Ariel tossed back. And just like that, the topic of the FFN and Kendall's fiery rebirth dropped out of conversation.

The two enjoyed meandering through the exhibits of the Norton Museum before having lunch at the courtyard café. They split a dessert, raising their decadent chocolate cake bites to Dan, recognizing the depth behind the day in its simplest form. As they walked back to the car several hours later arm-in-arm, Ariel broached the titillating subject once again.

"So, do you think you'll try and contact him?" Ariel asked. "You know, just to be courteous or whatnot?"

"Are we back on Allaway now?" Kendall scolded Ariel with her eyes.

"Were we ever really off him?" Ariel raised an eyebrow. "You've been distracted all day and I'm sorry, but I know you better than to just give you a pass on it being Dan's birthday. So tell me: What's your game plan going into your first day back to work?"

They separated to enter either side of the vehicle, temporarily suspending the conversation. Ariel pulled out of the parking lot before Kendall picked it back up.

"I don't know yet," Kendall answered honestly. "I thought I knew, before the whole thing went down. You know, like just be a little flirty with him, like making more eye contact without making a big deal about it. Our dirty little secret. That sort of thing. Now, I'm not so sure. I think anything beyond ignoring it completely will send a mixed message."

Ariel pondered Kendall's plight for a minute before responding. "Well, do you think he's hoping for something beyond that night?"

"I'm sure he'd be open for an encore performance, like a booty call. But beyond that? I doubt it. I mean, we obviously had some great physical chemistry, but he was clear from the get-go, as was I, so I don't think he's expecting more. What do you think he meant by saying I'm not a business transaction – he's had plenty of those?"

"Maybe it was his attempt to show a higher level of respect for you. You're not lumped into his regular ol' one night stands because, even though he might think he's God's gift to women, he knows you don't think that and guys get off on shit like that – being dominated by a strong woman. On paper he sounds pretty perfect, so I'm sure he's had his share of gold diggers. And it's probably refreshing knowing you weren't after anything like that."

"Yeah," Kendall sighed in defeat. "I'm not after anything like that. I'm not after anything at all."

Ariel looked over at Kendall, offering her a sympathetic smile. The two remained silent for the rest of the ride back to Kendall's house, the radio their only distraction.

"Well, I'm glad you came out with me today, and I'm sure your mind is beyond occupied at the moment," Ariel said lightheartedly.

"Thanks for distracting me. I'll talk to you later. Love you." Kendall smiled back and stepped out of the car.

Once inside, Kendall paced around her house, at a loss for the first time in a while as to what to do. She wouldn't have been planning a big party for Dan, but she definitely would have been catering to his every need that day. If he were at work, she would've stopped by the station to drop off dinner or bring by a cake. If she were at work, she'd have sent off some suggestive texts, priming him for an evening of getting lucky.

But he was dead.

She ended up leaving a voice message for Dan's mom instead.

"Hey Maryanne. I know we're both in the same boat today with our thoughts. Since you were the only one there 35 years ago, just wanted to wish Dan a Happy Birthday. I'll talk to you later. Love you."

The eerie stillness of her home reminded her of the first night she'd spent here alone after Dan died. She looked around, everything tidied up for the most part. No laundry to do. She'd been a force of energy the week before as she plotted her FFN. Now, her zest for life felt zapped once again. Last night was supposed to rejuvenate her, providing a steamy distraction from reality.

And it did. But only for the night. One-night stands were just that. One night.

She'd thought for sure by this time that she'd be back to a regular routine. But every day, she still needed tasks to just keep her moving, until she felt human again. Her return to work would help, providing a much-needed distraction from her disparaging thoughts. But until then...

In a desperate attempt to avoid spiraling back down into the suffocating sadness, she packed up and headed down to Miami to see her family a day early.

Chapter 8

Kendall arrived unannounced at her mom's home, just as Elena and Gabriel were sitting down for dinner.

"Oh my! You're here already! Wonderful," Elena exclaimed, jumping up from the dining table to hug Kendall as she walked through the door. "Why didn't you call? We just picked up some food on our way back from the gallery. Ended up tinkering around there all day. Hon, I would have picked you up something."

Elena stepped back, looking over her daughter's figure. "You've lost more weight, Kendall. Are you eating at all?"

Elena was always concerned about malnourishment, something her Cuban grandmother had instilled in her growing up. *Always err on being overweight rather than underweight because if hard times hit, the underweight ones will go first.*

"Mom, I'm fine," Kendall answered.

"You're too thin, you're not fine. It'd be one thing if I knew you were training for something. But I know you're not. Here, come sit and eat with Gabriel."

Gabriel stood right behind Elena, waiting to give Kendall a hug. The love between them had always been strong, though there'd been a noticeable strain since Dan's death, the two having adored Dan almost equally. For a while afterward, Gabriel had seemed unsure of how to react when Kendall came over and Dan wasn't right behind her.

"Hi Kendall," Gabriel said, greeting her with open arms, his hugs always warming her to the core.

"Hey Gabe. Sorry I haven't been down in a while. That's why I came early. I missed you guys."

"And today's Dan's birthday. You should be with us on Dan's birthday," Gabriel stated matter-of-factly. Kendall looked over at her mom, Elena's expression agreeing with Gabriel's statement. "And, Mom's right. You need to eat more." He pinched her side.

"Yeah, yeah. Don't believe everything Mom says."

Two years younger than Kendall, Gabriel Graham was her pinnacle guide in all matters of the heart. Growing up, everything she did pretty much revolved around her brother and his well-being until Dan had supplanted him as the love of her life.

***

Kendall didn't fully grasp the concept of Down syndrome until she was about seven or eight years old. She'd known Gabriel had it, and that it was a special distinction of his, but she'd had this idea it was something he'd outgrow, like a favorite pair of shoes. Eventually, he'd be too old for Down syndrome, and the family would no longer be concerned about his development in the same manner that they never fawned over hers. She'd figured he simply hadn't reached that point yet because he was younger.

The day Kendall finally realized that Down syndrome was very much a permanent part of Gabriel and would never go away, she retreated. Elena had found her balled up in the corner of Gabriel and Kendall's shared room, crying after discussing the matter with her mom.

"You don't need to be sad for Gabriel. He's perfectly happy," Elena said, moved by her daughter's own process of accepting the diagnosis.

"I'm not sad for Gabe!" Kendall shouted back. "I'm sad for me!"

"I'm not sure I understand, dear."

"It's not fair. Gabe gets all the extra help and he's fine! But now he'll always have Down syndrome. And everyone will always love him more! Who cares if he has it! He's fine!" Kendall blurted out, her face brighter than an overripe tomato.

Elena knew she had gold in her two children, but after that day, she was always a little more mindful of Kendall's feelings, knowing she would be the one to remain strong in face while breaking down inside.

As Gabriel's self-appointed protector, Kendall had always made the genuine effort to put his needs before hers, even if it meant sacrificing her happiness. So when she'd gone off to college up in St. Augustine, she was nervous about whether Gabriel would still be *fine* without her around. Would he remain as social without her constant hovering? Could he defend himself if someone treated him poorly?

When Kendall and Dan met over spring break her junior year – Dan already a friend of Gabriel's – she realized that Gabriel would always be fine. Her anxieties had more to do with her own insecurities, not her brother's. Her role as protective sister no longer seemed necessary.

After getting her degree, she'd moved back south to live with Dan, who had seamlessly stepped into the role of Gabriel's confidant. This gave Kendall the freedom to embark on her new romantic adventure without the worry of how it might affect her relationship with Gabriel. And as fate would have it, her sibling relationship developed a whole new level of respect and understanding. In releasing her need to control the world around Gabriel, she'd allowed herself to become the center of someone else's world – Dan's.

These evolutions had developed simultaneously, completely intertwined as the three of them grew closer by the day. But now, without Dan, a tier of their trinity had been ripped away, and their sibling relationship had to reestablish itself as a dual partnership once again. It was a difficult adjustment for both, no longer having Dan to balance them out.

***

Kendall was grateful for the distraction of catching up with her family at dinner. If she'd stayed home, she would have drowned her sorrows in the two bottles of cab-sauv purchased before her FFN – her back-up plan if the night hadn't gone as planned.

Throughout the evening, however, Kendall could sense her grief returning to a previous stage, leaving anger and reckless abandonment behind to revisit one of unbearable sadness. She felt it building as she listened to her mom and brother converse casually after dinner. She actively suppressed it when she agreed to a glass of wine with her mom out on the front steps of the condo, the thick humidity and sultry cigar smoke of the neighbors next door threatening to choke it out of her. She wondered if this was simply guilt bubbling up over the previous night's activities – delayed feelings that she'd betrayed the memory of her late husband, and nothing more.

It came to a head as she readied herself for bed, the threat of being alone in her thoughts too much to bear. Kendall struggled trying to unfold the queen-sized sleeper sofa tucked away in her mom's sleek, white leather sectional.

"You need help with that?" Elena asked, her voice carrying softly down the hall as she turned off the lights in the kitchen and made her way toward her bedroom.

Gabriel had already turned in, exhausted from all the moving and unpacking done at the gallery that day.

"No, I'm fine. I've got it," Kendall answered, glancing over at her mom's silhouetted figure in the hallway, highlighted by the ghostly glow of her white nightgown.

"Fine," Elena sighed, walking over to her. "You're always *fine*." She embraced Kendall tightly from behind, unrelenting in her squeeze until Kendall further reassured her that she would, indeed, be fine.

"Goodnight then." Elena smiled warmly at her daughter and then let her be, the hallway light turning out a few moments later.

Kendall stood in front of the half-folded sleeper and looked around the darkened condo. Beams from the outdoor street lights slipped through the partially-open slotted wood blinds, creating a hard-lined shadow on the ceramic floor. Kendall thought about the moonlight pouring in through Anson's wall of windows. How she had stood there in front of the sliding glass doors, thinking of Dan and then being touched by Anson, magically forgetting the sorrow that filled every pore of her body, every moment of every day, since Dan's death.

For the first time, she stopped to think about what Anson may have thought when he woke up. At what point did he realize that she'd left? Had he thought about her at all, wondering whether she would get in touch with him somehow? *Doubt it. I'm too broken.* Her desperation had to have been obvious.

The tears began to well up and Kendall felt paralyzed with despair, unable to unfold the bed any further to rest her weary body. Unless she was knocking herself out with Xanax and chasing it with alcohol, sleep didn't provide the respite she needed from the negative thoughts that tortured her all hours of the day and night. Even her dreams hadn't been any kind of escape lately.

Kendall crumpled to the floor, her body heaving in the waves of crushing sobs, the bite of the black widow back with a vengeance after granting her the one night off.

Within a minute, the hallway light came on and her mother's protective arms swathed her, shielding her from further negativity. Elena coaxed Kendall up off the floor, and together, they moved down the hall into the shelter of Elena's bedroom.

Elena held Kendall tightly against her in bed, just as she had done the first few weeks after Dan's death. Kendall wailed into her pillow as she desperately clung to her mom, the fear of facing another morning without Dan devastating her. Elena steadfastly cradled her daughter until Kendall's body submitted, exhausting all its resources, the automaticity of sleep eventually taking control.

Elena stroked Kendall's hair and shed her own tears of exhaustion, her heart besieged by the grief her dear children had experienced since losing Dan. But she worried most about Kendall, whose independent spirit and determination to do it all on her own, not wanting to burden anyone with her troubles, made her especially vulnerable to a hurt this deep. Elena curled her body around her daughter, keeping her hand on Kendall's arm so she would know the second that she woke, just like when Kendall was a small girl. Elena drifted off to sleep.

The light of the following morning carried the delicious aroma of tostadas, ham croquetas, and fried eggs. Kendall opened her eyes and inhaled deeply, knowing her mom must have been awake for a while – and with every intention of putting some weight on her before she drove home.

"Good morning, love." Elena paused over the stove, extending her neck out for a kiss from Kendall.

"Hey Mom," Kendall said, kissing Elena's cheek and then grabbing a mug to make her own cup of café con leche. She looked around. "Where's Gabe?"

"He already ate. You know him, early riser. I sent him out to get some orange juice. I forgot to pick some up and I know you like a glass with breakfast. So how'd you sleep?"

"Surprisingly, not bad. I don't even remember dreaming. You didn't have to send him out for just orange juice. I'm fine with coffee."

"Not a problem. He drinks it by the gallon anyway," Elena replied.

Kendall took a seat at the breakfast nook and rifled through the Sunday paper spread out on the table. Elena brought her a plate filled with food, then sat down next to her with just a tostada and her café con leche.

"Is that all you're going to eat?" Kendall asked, looking sardonically over at her mom.

"Never mind you. Only I get to be the mother today."

The two sat quietly, selecting various sections of the paper and occasionally reading some parts aloud to share a story, all the while dunking their tostadas into their coffees and never mentioning the events of last night. Since Dan's passing, Elena had learned to patiently wait on Kendall's cues, knowing that when the time was right, Kendall would let her in on her thoughts, subtly seeking advice to help navigate her through.

Gabriel returned with the orange juice just as Kendall finished her plate of fried happiness.

"So are we going for brunch?" he asked, putting the juice down on the counter to pour a glass.

"Are you kidding? Mom just stuffed me like it was Thanksgiving. Maybe a late lunch, but no brunch for me today."

"We'll swing by the gallery later and have a late lunch then, okay Gabriel?" Elena suggested. "But first I'd like us to all go to the beach and get a little sun on this gorgeous day. We all need some Vitamin D, right?"

Gabriel looked quizzically at Kendall.

"Don't look at me," Kendall said, just as leery of their mom's plan.

Elena hadn't suggested a family trip to the beach since before their father's passing.

"Do we bring buckets and shovels?" Gabriel asked sarcastically, far more comfortable out on the ocean than on the sand.

"Oh stop. It'll be fun," Elena said with giddiness. "We'll lounge around with books and enjoy the water. When's the last time either of you has been to the beach?"

Kendall and Gabriel looked at each other again, simultaneously shrugging their shoulders.

"Well, then it's settled. Let's get dressed and enjoy it all before it gets too hot." Elena cleared the table and fifteen minutes later, they were all walking to the beach.

Chapter 9

The sun was just beginning to rise as Kendall pulled up onto the fifth floor of the Gold Coast General parking garage. She stepped out of her Jeep, brushing off some lint from her loosely-fitted ceil blue hospital scrubs. Oddly enough, the well-worn uniform comforted her, erasing the last six months in a fleeting moment of reprieve.

Fleeting. Each moment of every day, fleeting. Until there are none.

Kendall had been internally debating the bizarre nature of bereavement and how it should be handled for the last few months. She'd always been a firm believer in just *getting over it* as quickly as possible. When the world ceased spinning, fracturing all previously-known reality into an unrecognizable pile of shards; when it became a mosaic of despair, chaos, and unrelenting denial – the only thing to do was *get the fuck over it.*

By this reasoning, all she needed to do was move forward and do her job, making her new fucked-up reality easier to digest, easier to view, just plain easy. Maybe even appealing. The beauty of the shattered universe would reveal itself, if she just took the steps to normalize again.

Yet, sadly, no one really talked about the slivers and slices one received when obediently moving forward and not taking the time to heal. The gaping wounds created scars that no amount of plastic surgery could rectify.

She looked out over the horizon, watching the warm glow of the sun weave its way in and out of the clouds, lighting up the eastern seaboard. It was a spectacular view of the Atlantic. She recalled making the decision to accept the job offer at GC General seven years earlier, largely based on this view. If anything, it beat out the concrete-and-scaffolding vista at her previous hospital down in Broward County. Even if she had to drag herself to work, at least she'd have something to look forward to every day before the shift began. This morning's solar awakening definitely delivered on that naïve notion.

She turned her attention to the hospital and inwardly groaned. The nine-story beige building was like the towering cumulus cloud billowing miles off the coast. Majestic fingers of radiant light reached around its hardened edges, signaling life and hope of a new dawn. But the stark reality remained hidden within its stormy insides: grief, pain, and the inevitable promise of death.

Or, so it seemed to her now.

A Trauma Hawk circled above, getting ready to land on the helicopter pad. It was time to head in.

Walking through the halls, she smiled and nodded at various hospital employees who were work acquaintances. Most had no idea she'd been on leave, casually noting it'd been a while since they'd seen her. The glamour headshots of the hospital's board of directors, both alive and dead, welcomed her back with their pompous smiles and coifed hairdos. She swiped her badge to enter the dimly lit surgical intensive care unit, with Courtney being the first one to see her walk through the door.

"Hey there," Courtney said warmly. She embraced Kendall tightly, genuinely relieved to see her back in her scrubs. "So happy you're back. Missed you terribly. But don't think I'm not pissed at you for just up and ditching us the other night. You never answered my texts. Tsk, tsk, tsk. You got some 'splaining to do, lil' missy." Courtney poked her, hoping Kendall would be an open book later on in the shift.

"Yeah, yeah. Different mindset that night. Besides, it's out of my system now." Kendall accepted the reprimand, idly wondering if it actually *was* out of her system. "So what storm do we have brewing today?"

"Well, yesterday was brutal – so let's hope we don't repeat that," Courtney said, crossing her fingers.

Together, they walked over to the assignment board, other day shift staff filtering through the doors. Everyone seemed to stop and greet Kendall. Many of them had been at the funeral. Harsh fluorescent light suddenly flooded the unit, the staff collectively groaning as they shielded their eyes like scorched vampires. Kendall looked toward the entryway and saw Nancy, the day shift unit secretary, who always flipped on all the main lights upon walking through the unit entrance. She seemed to think this signature move of hers gave her some semblance of power in the very hierarchical world of healthcare.

And just like that, Kendall was back to work.

By late morning, she'd settled into the busy rhythm of the unit once again. Kendall was grateful that the night charge nurse had purposely given her a "cruise control" assignment: two vented/sedated patients. One was a 19-year-old gunshot victim who'd undergone surgery two days prior, with dual chest tubes and no plans to wean from the ventilator. The other was a 57-year-old man from a motorcycle accident who'd sustained some significant head injuries and needed to further stabilize before he could have neurosurgery. Neither patient had procedures planned for the day, leaving Kendall to fully reacquaint herself with her profession. There was no nagging worry of potential transfers or admissions, as her assignment was full. Besides, she had enough worries already boring a hole in the back of her mind.

Kendall couldn't ignore the fact that Dr. Allaway's group was on the motorcycle accident victim's case. She didn't know if he'd be rounding, or if it'd be Dr. Patel. She hoped she would just see Ken, their nurse practitioner, and one of them would round later on after her shift.

One could hope.

But every single time the doors of the SICU swung open – before they swung open, in fact – she braced herself. Each time she heard the nearly inaudible click of the lock being released by a swiped badge, despite all the alarms, bells, buzzes, and beeps of the SICU, she became near-paralyzed with anxiety, needing to know if it was, indeed, *him* walking through the doors.

After four hours of this exhausting behavior, mentally lecturing herself that her telomeres were fraying at the ends of her DNA strands due to all this unnecessary fight-or-flight stress, Kendall acknowledged that she was completely obsessed and acting way too much like something should result from their one-night stand.

She knew she would have to interact with the ever-so *fuckable*, scratch that, *fucked* Dr. Allaway – she'd known it beforehand, she'd known it mid-orgasm, and she'd known it while waltzing into work today. She'd simply have to move past it just like every other woman he'd fucked in that hospital had had to do.

Oof.

She realized that she was now in *that* category of women. How many there were exactly, she had not a clue. She could only think of two off-hand: Michelle, the physician assistant who used to work in his office, and Ruby, the respiratory therapist who proudly had more employee notches on her bedpost than he did. Not nearly as damning as she'd first imagined, but then again, she really didn't know. She'd heard plenty of other rumors involving OR nurses, new grad nurses, and even other physicians. But everyone enjoyed spreading the rumors, whether they held water or not.

While attending to the 19-year-old, turning him to one side with his father's help, Kendall heard Nancy calling out to her.

"I'm in here!" Kendall announced.

Nancy popped her head in the room. "Doctor's on the phone."

"Okay, thanks." Kendall finished up and politely excused herself from her patient's parents. "I'll be back in a bit."

"Line 3," Nancy said, motioning to Kendall from across the station desk.

"SICU. This is Kendall. How can I help you?"

"Hey," he said, stopping short.

Her face rapidly drained of all blood, pooling into her feet, as she experienced an oversaturated adrenaline response. It was Dr. Allaway. Kendall dropped down into a chair at the desk to avoid vasovagaling from the sudden rush.

"Oh... Hello! Hey. Um... Becker! The motorcycle guy? Uh... Do you want an update?" she asked, fumbling over her words, trying to keep her professional persona and failing miserably.

Why was she so flustered? She'd hunted *him*. She'd fucked *him*. She'd left *him*. Why did she care? Kendall inhaled deeply, away from the phone, attempting to calm her nerves.

"Becker? You have him?" he asked. "No, I don't need to know anything. Well, eventually. I mean... I can come by again later today. I came by early this morning. Ken should be there soon. Why, is there anything I should know right now about him?"

He sounded just as thrown, far from the arrogance he typically exuded while on the phone spouting off orders or strutting through the unit checking on patients.

"Not really. I mean, his vitals are decent enough. ICP is good. Titrated the levo way down, but still have it running at 10 mics just 'cause. A bed did open up in neuro but they're short nurses, so we'll keep him here for now. Probably tomorrow he could be transferred." It was all she could do to recollect herself, focusing everything on the patient's status.

"Sounds like you're back in the swing of things like you wanted. Just thought I would check in on you – or something. I mean... You know. We never talked after... after we... well, you left, so... I don't know. I just thought I should check in. And I already said that," he mumbled, followed by an assumed eye roll as he growled through an exasperated sigh. "Fuck."

Wow. Never had she heard him so far off his game – and his vulnerability was nothing short of endearing. Hearing this private side of him again sent shivers up her neck and across her scalp, a subtle smile emerging as her gaze softened.

"I didn't expect to be this tongue-tied when you answered," he continued. "Just like I didn't expect Friday night to go the way it did, as well as it did."

Kendall flushed a deep red, her cheeks saturating with blood. She intentionally cut him off, as if they were on speaker phone, fearing he might venture down a verbal recap of the night. Utter mortification smothered her, despite those around being none the wiser.

"Okay then! So, if anything should change, I'll give you a call," she said forcefully into the phone, her eyes darting around the unit.

"Oh. Uh, okay. I'll just talk to you later then?" he asked, baffled.

"Sure. That sounds great, Ans- Dr. Allaway." She corrected herself and stopped. She took in another breath and tried to show her appreciation for his call, considering it was thoughtful. "Thank you for calling."

"K." *Click*.

Although it was how he typically ended their work phone conversations, she couldn't help but feel a bit of a sting. She wondered if she'd hurt him. Was he hoping for more? Their night together had gone well, but maybe *too* well? It was supposed to be *just sex*.

He had asked her to stay, though.

She got up from the chair and stood for a minute, staring bewildered at the phone until Courtney's voice snapped her back to reality.

"That was him, wasn't it?!" Courtney accused with a conniving grin.

"What are you talking about?" Kendall dismissed, turning away to head back into her patient's room.

"Don't act all secretive with me, bitch," Courtney teased. "You're beet red and I'm fairly certain there aren't any other doctors around who could make you turn that shade unless you were fighting with them. And that didn't look like a fight. I could see your smile from a mile away."

Kendall rolled her eyes, giving in to Courtney's deductive reasoning. Damn her flushing face.

"Okay! Yes, it was him and I don't even know why it affected me like that. He didn't even call to check on his patient. Honestly, I don't know why he called. Maybe to make it less weird when we do see each other? I don't know. He never struck me as the type to make sure all was well, you know?"

Kendall was on a roll, becoming increasingly aggravated with him for reasons she didn't quite understand. Why was there fault in calling to say hello? Why was she suddenly holding this against him, as if common courtesy was not allowed after a one-night stand? If she'd been so determined to *not* have to deal with him again, she should have fucked a stranger – which she began blurting out through a clenched jaw when Courtney abruptly shushed her.

"Whoa! Little bit feisty there for not giving a shit about him," Courtney said.

Sensing the pressure building behind Kendall's eyes, Courtney dragged her into the empty medication room.

"So you two *did* have sex, didn't you?" Courtney asked quietly. "Was he an asshole and left right afterward? I knew that would happen! Fucking prick! I *told* you not to go!"

"Actually… I'm the one who got up and left his house in the middle of the night." Kendall bit her lip, bracing for Courtney's tongue lashing.

"Oh," Courtney said, mouth frozen in an 'O' pucker. "Soo… you haven't spoken since then?"

"No," Kendall said. Distressed by her poor decision-making, she paced the small room. "I don't know what I was thinking. I just thought it'd be best if I was the one to up and leave before, you know, awkward conversations ensued or my voice of reason returned. I just knew I couldn't be there in the morning." She paused. "Saturday would have been Dan's 35th birthday. There's no way I would've felt okay being there knowing that, and then potentially going for round three come morning."

"Round *three*?!" Courtney squeaked, not acknowledging anything else Kendall had just said.

Kendall blushed. "Potentially! Come on now. It'd been a while. I'm allowed to have sex."

"Of course you are. But shit! Really, what did you expect? You work with him."

Courtney was right. What did Kendall expect? *"Fuck me now, Anson"* and then *"Yes, Dr. Allaway"* the next day?

"I know, you're right. It is what it is, though. It served its purpose and I can't say I really regret it. Now I just have to plow through the awkwardness of knowing a whole other side of Allaway when really, I still don't know him at all."

"Well, good luck with that," Courtney said, sarcasm dripping off her tongue. "But really, I'm sure it'll be fine. Eventually. Just have to get past that nasty acne stage." She stuck her tongue out with mild revulsion.

"Yeah," Kendall sighed heavily, caving to the doomed inevitability of embarrassing encounters and untimely flushed faces. "Whatcha gonna do, right?" She shrugged.

"Well, one thing you can do is tell me all about it! When do you think you'll take lunch?" With eager excitement, Courtney drummed her fingers together in front of her mouth, like Mr. Burns from *The Simpsons*.

"I have to finish charting my assessment on bed nine. And I want to get to seven's dressing change before–"

The med room door swung open and Kendall stopped talking as Carlos entered the room.

"What gossip's going down, ladies?" He pinched Kendall's side in his usual, harmlessly flirtatious manner as he stepped up to the medication-dispensing machine.

"Determining lunch time," Kendall replied honestly, the original reason for the med room conversation conveniently closed.

If Carlos had one iota of suspicion that she'd hooked up with Dr. Allaway, she'd never live it down – and would most likely have to endure numerous painfully drawn-out inquisitions addressing why she hadn't chosen *him* for her back-to-life fuck.

"Well, how 'bout 2:30?" Courtney piped up, grabbing the door handle before it closed.

"Sounds good."

Kendall submersed herself back into work, administering medications here, discussing situations with families there, changing dressings, drawing labs, providing intimately personal care with compassion, and of course, charting, charting, charting. She was actually able to bury the anticipated encounter with Anson (or Dr. Allaway, or whatever he was to her now) to the back of her mind, making the next few hours fly by. Around 2:20pm, she noticed the time and found Courtney.

"It's now or never. All is well and I'm caught up, so either we eat now or wait for the shit to hit the fan," Kendall said.

"Okay, I'll be there in two minutes," Courtney replied, holding up two fingers. She needed to finish up some charting first.

Kendall let Patricia know she was going to get a bite to eat, so she would cover for Kendall. "I'll just be in the lounge if you need anything."

In the break room, Kendall scanned through her phone. She read a couple texts from her mom and brother, wishing her well and hoping that things were running smoothly her first day back to work. She smiled, comforted by her family's love and concern.

If only they really knew. *All is well, Mom, except it's trickier than I thought, dipping your pen in the company ink. Got any tips for that?* Kendall shuddered at the thought.

She was already eating a salad when Courtney busted through the door. "He's out there now!" she shrieked, backing up against the door like the heroine in a thriller film.

Not very amused, Kendall finished chewing and swallowed. "Well, good. I'm in here, and it can wait 'til another day. I don't have anything to say right now about his patient, so no need to chat."

Disappointed her dramatic antics hadn't had the anticipated effect, Courtney slinked away from the door and grabbed her lunch from the refrigerator. Sitting down at the table next to Kendall, she threw out one last ditch effort. "You still have to give me some details."

Kendall rolled her eyes. "Honestly, it's all a blur," she lied, as she had recounted every detail of the night over and over again for the past three days. "I mean, I basically threw out the offer, he grabbed it, we went to his place, made out, and then, one thing led to another. Then it was late, so I headed out. And voila, here I am today."

"Whatever," Courtney groaned in disapproval. "I'll have to get you liquored up before you really kiss and tell." She darted her eyes deviously at Kendall. "Just tell me this: was it good? Or was it *gooood*?"

Kendall laughed. "Oh it was *gooood*. Hot."

"I knew it! So, you want more, don't you?"

"What? No! I mean, I'm not looking to get more. I just don't want to talk about it. You know, making it any more awkward than I've already made it."

"Sure, whatever. I get it," Courtney said begrudgingly.

To Kendall's relief, Courtney changed the subject to what was happening with her patient, and before they knew it, they were back to normal topics like their grievances with their director and the idiocracy of hospital politics.

Patricia opened the break room door, casually poking her head in. "Hey Kendall, Dr. Allaway wants you to know he added some orders for Becker and wondered if you needed to update him on anything."

Kendall felt the familiar flush travel up her neck and into her cheeks. Courtney, whose back was to Patricia, went bug-eyed, staring Kendall down. Kendall laughed, trying to dismiss her own reaction as if it were to something else.

"Oh sorry, Pat. What? Dr. Allaway? No, nothing new to report to him." She smiled stiffly, cocking her head to one side like a malfunctioning robot.

Irritated by Kendall's response, Patricia left. Once the door latched shut, Kendall and Courtney burst into laughter.

Kendall shook her head, wiping tears from the corners of her eyes. "Seriously. What. The. Fuck. Was. I. Thinking?"

They laughed even harder at Kendall's predicament for a few more minutes. Once it was out of their systems, they headed back out to the unit to finish the remaining four-and-a-half hours of their shift.

Chapter 10

As the night crew trickled in – always a welcome sight at the end of the day – those who had not yet seen Kendall continued the warm parade of greetings started in the morning, squeezing her shoulder and planting kisses on her cheek as she sat at a computer closing out her charting.

She felt good, accomplished, nearly normal. She could make it. One day at a time. Her shift went by quickly, her patients were still alive, and well, perhaps the greatest triumph of the day, despite the shallow nature of it: she'd avoided any face-to-face contact with Dr. Allaway. *A win-win-win.*

Her celebration was short lived, however, as right in the thick of shift change, Anson returned.

His subtle cologne awoke her senses first. Then he was there, leaning over her, his arm on the back of her chair as he invaded her personal space and filled her mind with scenes from Friday night – passionately riding him; his tongue and its unmentionable talents; her head on his chest, drinking him in as his breathing slowed. *Stay. I want you to stay.* It was all so vivid, so raw, so… so… unbelievably wanton!

What the hell does he think he's doing?! She gasped.

"Just pretend I'm looking at some lab work," he whispered, dangerously close to her ear as he breathed her in. "Can you step out a minute so we can talk?"

Kendall's mouth completely dried up. She'd never anticipated this overtly brazen behavior while at work. The heat radiating from her face meant she was glowing like an ember, and not in a good way. She needed to get out of there, quick.

"Back again, Dr. Allaway?" Patricia asked, passing by on her way out of the unit. "We never see you this much." Her critical tone didn't fully register with Kendall at first.

The break in Anson's fixation gave Kendall a chance to switch gears. Slowly, she backed her chair away from the desk, giving him full access to the computer – as if that was what he needed the whole time. He stood up straight, assuming she'd respond to his question.

Kendall took in his appearance. He wasn't the same man she'd been with that night. He looked unfamiliar in his typical surgical scrubs – like he was someone else altogether. He was still breathtakingly beautiful, and seemingly relaxed, his respirations even and unlabored. He exuded confidence like the Anson she'd met at the bar, but she still couldn't wrap her mind around this man being the same one from Friday.

"You can use the computer. I'm finished now," she said, offering him her seat, standing up from her chair and continuing to ignore his request for her time.

She never liked being thrown from her game.

He cocked his head to the side, baffled by her behavior. He was used to getting his way at work, especially from nurses.

"Oh Kendall! You're back!" Richard, a seasoned nurse from night shift, unknowingly interrupted their staring contest, reaching out to Kendall to give her a hug. "It's great seeing you, kid. I've got your assignment tonight."

Kendall embraced him affectionately, breaking eye contact with Anson. "Thank you, Rich. I'm ready for report."

"Let me just go to my locker and I'm all yours," Rich replied, heading to the lounge and leaving Kendall once again without a shield from Anson.

Kendall hustled into her patient's room to escape his gaze. She mindlessly checked all the lines and drip rates on her gunshot victim, desperately trying to control her thoughts and focus on anything other than Anson's captivating presence.

Her efforts were futile, however, as Dr. Allaway followed her, pretending he needed to check something even though he hadn't been consulted for that patient.

"Hey, I'm not trying to make this more awkward than it has to be, so running away every time I come around isn't helping anything," Anson blurted out. "I want to straighten out a few things about Friday night. And seeing as I can't seem to speak to you on the phone and you left without leaving your number, well, here at work is the only way I know how to get a hold of you."

Kendall's cheeks heated up again. She was annoyed with his tone and that he felt they had something to discuss right there, at the hospital, in front of a patient – albeit a sedated and ventilated one – smack dab in the middle of bloody shift change. Not to mention, he'd probably never saved her number from the numerous texts she'd sent him over the years regarding patient status. *What a jerk.*

"What's there to discuss?" Kendall asked brusquely, keeping her eyes on her patient.

Anson, frustrated by her lack of concern, glanced out to the unit. He hated feeling an awkward vibe in his castle. He dominated at GC General. Now Kendall was calling the shots, knocking him off kilter. He turned back and moved further into the room. She looked directly at him.

And he faltered again. Her flawless complexion and emerald eyes besieged him through wisps of loosened hair, the weight of her ponytail winning its battle against the elastic band after a long twelve-hour shift. He wanted to touch her, just to feel it once more – the rush, the rhythm, the unrelenting beat of his previously stunned heart.

Her sudden *get to the fucking point* expression broke his trance, and he scrambled back to business.

"Well, the condom broke the second time, and I–"

Kendall cut him off. "I can't get pregnant, if that's your concern." Flooded with unforeseen disappointment, unrelated to her lack of fertility, she looked back down at her patient.

"Oh. Well good. Well, I mean... I didn't know that so... I guess there's no need for concern. And like I said, I'm clean, so you don't have to be worried either."

Kendall's cheeks blazed, this time fuming with anger. She couldn't believe that was what he'd been so focused on discussing at work. Not even a week out from Friday and the only thing he was worried sick over was her potentially being pregnant? *Again, what a jerk!*

"Well good," she agreed, sharing the same tone he'd just used with her. She glanced at him with icy indifference. "I need to give report now, so unless you have something work related to discuss, you need to leave."

Kendall immediately regretted how she was treating him, but knew it was the only way she could maintain her emotional distance.

Anson stood frozen in her stare for several seconds, wanting to say something further but knowing it would be unprofessional and ultimately pointless. Her mind seemed made up about him. He drew in a cleansing breath, knowing she was wrestling with a lot more than just their night together. There was no sense in adding to her grief.

His timing perfect, Richard strolled into the patient room ready for report.

"Hey there, Dr. A. We got a neuro patient here?" Richard asked.

Dr. Allaway curtly turned to leave, ignoring the question, still stung by Kendall's response. Richard looked over at Kendall quizzically.

"No, he was asking about our other patient. I don't know what's up, something to do with scheduling his surgery. I'll tell you about that in a bit. First, let's talk about this one," Kendall said.

As she watched Dr. Allaway exit the unit, it took everything for Kendall to not distort her face in silent screams of frustration. Why should she be disappointed at all? What had she expected? Or rather, hoped for? A dinner invitation?

Once done with her handoff to Richard, Kendall washed her hands at the nurse's station and waited for Courtney to finish up. She replayed her encounter with Anson in her head. He was totally justified in bringing up the broken condom. If anything, that was a rational and practical issue needing to be addressed, fitting perfectly with her desire to keep it all business.

She pulled out her phone and searched for his contact number. She'd never intended to destroy their work relationship. She texted him an olive branch of sorts.

KM: **It's Kendall. Here's my number if you need it.**

She hit send, then thought for a minute. She'd exposed everything the other night, so there was no point in hiding now.

KM: **I'm all fucked up inside. Not sure of the proper etiquette in situations like these. Sorry.**

She stared at her words, second-guessing the familiar nature of them and unsure whether he'd even been looking for some sort of explanation. Yet almost as a personal dare, she hit send. She scrolled through her older texts with him. It'd been nearly a year since they'd had any exchange, with her last text simply asking if she could add a diet to a patient's orders.

Courtney interrupted Kendall's overanalyzing with her readiness to leave. They both swiped their badges to clock out and headed to the parking garage. As they recapped their days, Courtney asked about Dr. Allaway. She'd noticed him leave the unit but wondered if they'd had any face-to-face exchanges. Kendall denied seeing him, keeping Courtney in the dark. She knew too much already.

"So, I'll see you tomorrow?" Courtney asked. "Day three for me." She smiled, turning to walk down the first floor of the garage as Kendall reached for the stair railing.

"Yup, see you in the morning. Thanks for your help today as my sounding board," Kendall said with a laugh, wondering how many other people she'd inadvertently told about her tryst by confirming Courtney's suspicions.

Just after 9:00pm, Kendall plopped on the couch with a glass of wine, bowl of grapes, and a bag of popcorn. She mindlessly searched through some shows before deciding upon the latest episode of *Orange is the New Black*. She still avoided *Breaking Bad*, a show she'd only watched with Dan.

She and Dan used to curl up on the couch together, with Kendall inevitably coaxing him to give her a back massage. She smiled, thinking of Dan's large, calloused hands attempting to knead out whichever back muscle she'd kinked while at work that day. Two minutes in, he would say his thumbs hurt, and she would tell him to forget it, criticizing his meager attempt. He'd be quick to suggest something crass like, "You liked my massage technique just fine last night." She'd push him away, and they'd go back to watching Walter White.

She'd give anything now for one of his pathetic massages.

Kendall popped a Xanax, chasing it with a swig of wine, desperate to be numb. Between the steamy shower scenes on television and *Candy Crush* on her phone, she still couldn't find the distraction she sought from her deeply buried grief.

On top of her loneliness, now there was guilt. Guilt for having ever been annoyed with Dan over his massage technique. Guilt for sleeping with another man the day before Dan's birthday. Guilt for treating Dr. Allaway poorly at the hospital. Guilt for wanting Anson again.

She sank into the couch as hot tears surfaced and streaked down her face. Before long, she found her usual tormented sleep.

***

"I'm pregnant!"

"Holy shit! Really?! Oh babe, that's great. Are you sure you want to do this again?"

"What do you mean? It's already done, and of course. This one is the one, I can feel it. This is the beginning of our new life together. This is our family." Kendall lovingly holds her belly as Dan smiles back.

But then he turns around and walks away.

"Where are you going?"

"It's not my baby, Kendall. We never had a family together."

"Of course it is! What are you talking about! Get back here and raise your child with me!"

"I'm sorry, Kendall. I have to go. And if I were you, I would find out who the father is before he walks away, without even knowing."

"Dan! You're scaring me. I'm not starting a family with anyone else. I started one with you, and now it's here, growing in my belly! Don't you dare walk away from us!"

But Dan keeps walking, never looking back and leaving Kendall alone, hot tears burning her face as she feels the life inside her slowly wither away once again.

Kendall snapped awake, her face buried in the couch cushions. She rubbed her eyes, the lids and lashes heavy with tears. She hated waking up crying. She squinted at the television, a message across the screen asking whether she was still watching, mocking her sad state of existence. She turned off the TV and pushed her aching body up from the couch. Tripping over the grape bowl on the floor, she stumbled but recovered, continuing into the kitchen.

Numbly, she filled a tall glass with tap water and drank it back. Then she filled it again, adding a packet of *Emergen-C*. She waited for the fizz to stop and chewed up a vitamin B-12 tablet. Drinking back the solution, she hoped to ward off any fuzzy after effects the wine/benzo combo could cause while at work in a few short hours. Unfortunately, she'd grown quite familiar with this hangover-avoidance process.

Kendall blindly felt her way through the darkness to her lonely master bedroom. Putting her phone down on the nightstand, she crawled into bed, then set the alarm for 5:30am. The defeat of the night passed over her once again, yet surprisingly, she managed to drift back to sleep.

Chapter 11

Kendall woke up more than ten minutes before her calm ocean wave alarm was set to go off. Grabbing her phone and propping herself up against the headboard, she slowly navigated away from her slumber. Last night she'd missed a phone call from her mom, a text message from Ariel, and there it was: a text message from *him*.

She sat straight up in bed, wide awake. And with masochistic control, she first listened to her mom's message: "Hey honey, just checking to see how your day went. Call me when you get a chance. Love you."

Her message from Ariel also asked about the first day back. But she knew Ariel wasn't referring to nursing. Kendall shot back a quick reply, despite the early hour.

KM: **Work was fine. Like I never left. Tried to avoid Dr. Sex. Epic fail. I'll tell you all about it.**

Finally, she braced herself for Anson's reply. She analyzed her own message one more time.

KM: **I'm all fucked up inside. Not sure of the proper etiquette in situations like these. Sorry.**

He'd texted at 11:38pm. She pressed her thighs together, picturing his room at that hour.

AA: **There is none. I'm sorry if I added to your stress. I'm here if you need anything.**

Kendall appreciated the sentiment of the text: sweet, without being uncomfortably personal. There was also something appealing about connecting with someone who'd had no previous connection to her life with Dan.

Without over-thinking it, she responded.

KM: **Thank you. Truly. I'll try not to run the next time I see you.**

***

Once again, the beige hospital building beckoned to her as she stretched her legs out from her Jeep onto the fifth floor of the parking garage. Today, the feeling of no time having passed since her leave was far less comforting than it had been the morning before. She recalled new moms returning from maternity leave always making that same comment after their three months were over. She'd been out nearly twice that, but life still carried on in its poetically cruel yet necessary manner. She must either swim in the current or sink below again.

The overcast morning prevented any spectacular sunrises from boosting her spirits. The universe seemed to be working against her.

Or rather, her mind – still a groggy haze of wine and Xanax – was. She was pretty sure the board of nursing wouldn't just let her play the sad widow card if she haphazardly hung a cardiac medicine at the rate of an antibiotic or pushed in 5 mg of Morphine instead of 0.5 into a 97-year-old woman who still planned on living for another ten years. With lives in the balance, she needed to pull herself together.

Her thoughts wandered back to the ever-so-delectable Dr. Allaway. With the jitters of their first work encounter behind them, and their texting having removed the sting of their hospital exchange, she hoped they could both move forward and get on with life.

In front of the automatic doors of GC General's entrance, the chime of her phone caused an extra beat in her heart. Reading the text, her face immediately relaxed, then broke into a smile.
GG: **Hi barbie doll. It is gabe. Have a fun day.**

He was probably sitting at the breakfast table with a large bowl of cereal, getting ready for his own workday. She laughed at the reminder that she couldn't so much as think of another man without her brother intervening.

After shift report, Kendall quickly settled into her assignment. She knew there would be necessary decisions regarding Becker, the motorcycle accident victim, and his upcoming neurosurgery. She welcomed the opportunity to bulldoze through her experience with Anson and reacquaint herself with Dr. Allaway.

In the early afternoon, Becker's family gathered around his bed as Kendall gave them an update. The patient's wife requested Dr. Allaway be paged. Not wanting to bother him for an ETA, or risk another face-flushing phone call, she encouraged the family to hold off a little longer. She was almost caught up in her charting and if she timed it right, she could simply greet him nonchalantly and then head off to lunch. That wouldn't exactly be running.

She sat down to chart at her computer when a hand gently covered hers over the mouse.

"No running today, right?" Dr. Allaway's mouth was several inches from her ear as his index finger lightly stroked her knuckle. He then dragged his hand up her arm to her shoulder, planting a small squeeze – and sizzling imprint – before continuing into Becker's hospital room.

Ho-ly hot. That was intense.

She awkwardly glanced about and involuntarily performed a few Kegel exercises, her body betraying her professional senses.

Kendall silently gave herself a pep talk: *Inhale. Focus. Redirect thoughts. Exhale. No attachment. No remorse. Just stay the course.*

But her meditation was short-lived, as Dr. Allaway soon exited Becker's room. His expression changed from professional to familiar when he caught her eye, a hint of a flirtatious smile that acknowledged a job well done for remaining seated.

Watching Anson move toward her in the bright lights – taboo images of him flooding her brain – was wildly enticing. She knew too much. The way his back arched over her and how every exquisitely-toned muscle followed in its rhythmic fashion, flexing along his broad shoulders. Or how his mouth simply hung open in desire for her before she met his lips. How his entire jaw clenched down and his eyes squeezed shut when he buried himself deep inside her. His length, his girth: She no longer had to guess. She knew the exact feeling of having his six-foot-three build claim her and press her five-foot-seven frame down into a mattress.

Did anyone else really even know the color of his eyes? Had they seen into them? For a second, Kendall marveled at the breadth of experiential knowledge she had on this man: this god of the hospital, god of the OR, god of the bedroom.

And suddenly she knew: He was thinking the very same thoughts – about her. Her cheeks burned with a crimson hue by the time he casually grabbed the open computer seat next to her and pulled up Becker's electronic chart.

Kendall assumed a rigid pose, attempting to ignore the electric storm raging all along the right side of her body. If this were *Jurassic Park*, T-rex would have walked blindly by the invisible Kendall. But that was a movie, and freezing in its tracks never fared as well for the damn deer in the headlights. She blinked blankly at her computer screen, searching for two coherent words to string together – anything to neutralize the erotic sensations pulsating throughout her body. She peeked to the side. He looked right back at her.

"So, consent for surgery first thing tomorrow at seven. NPO after midnight. I entered the orders. You back tomorrow?" he asked.

"Uhh. Saturday." Kendall barely found her two words, her tongue stuck to the roof of her mouth.

Her eyes returned to her screen. By now, the chrome grille of his diesel-powered truck would have pummeled her pathetic doe-eyed face.

If only she were so lucky.

"You feeling alright? You look a little flushed," he commented, watching her closely.

"What? Oh. No. No, I'm fine. Well, not really. I mean, I should probably get something to eat soon. I'm just tired, that's all. I didn't sleep much." Flustered, she redid her ponytail, attempting to straighten out her look.

"Okay. Please call me should you need anything," he said kindly.

As he stood up, he invaded her personal space once again, her senses abuzz with visions of the previous week. He rested his hand on her right shoulder, experimenting with touch one last time. Then, his hushed, low tone tickled the inside of her left ear as he spoke: "But call Ken if you need anything on Becker."

Kendall stiffened attentively as the meaning behind his words seeped in. She spun around to look at him, wanting to see if she understood him right.

And there was no question – she definitely had. He winked and then there it was: that cunning smirk. He totally wanted her again.

Well, shit.

She gawked as he exited through the back door, her thoughts scattering, running wild in her brain, knocking themselves out as they hit each other head-on, leaving her gobsmacked. She jumped up and asked a nearby coworker to cover for her so she could run to the cafeteria and get some food to bring back, knowing full well she'd brought a lunch. She then dashed out the back exit after him, into the isolated stairwell.

The bolt of the heavy door echoed along the towering walls, grabbing the attention of Anson, who was already up the stairs. He smiled broadly, waiting for her to join him. Kendall peered up at him suspiciously, pausing for the door to latch behind her, then cautiously ascended the steps.

"Didn't think you'd need me this quickly," Anson teased, again confirming Kendall's interpretation.

"What are you doing?" Her stern voice forced a swift change in his face.

"What do you mean?" he asked.

"This!" she said, motioning her hand between them. "This flirty behavior."

"I'm recognizing that there's chemistry here. I know you're going through a lot right now, but I'm letting you know, I'm here if you need me," he said confidently.

"Here how? As a shoulder to cry on? Or if I need sex?" she asked. "I'm in no shape to sift through innuendos and mixed signals. I mean, yesterday you were worried sick over a broken condom, and today you're – what? Willing to risk it again? Happy I can't get pregnant? I'm just a little confused."

Kendall couldn't handle being in murky waters with him. It was too taxing on her already overtaxed brain.

Anson, taken aback by her accusatory tone, took her arm, escorting her up to the landing where they'd be out of sight should someone open the SICU back door. When they got there, he searched for the right thing to say.

"No. That's not it," he began. "I actually understand where you're at right now, and maybe we can talk about that sometime." He paused, running his hand through his sandy brown hair, giving himself a minute to allow his frustration to dissipate further. "I apologize if I offended you yesterday. I had to broach the subject of Friday somehow and well, that seemed like a necessary topic to discuss. I certainly didn't mean to come off callous."

And then, that rarely-seen look of insecurity, however subtle, resurfaced. "Tell me it's not just me. You feel it, too, when I touch you, don't you?"

Kendall dropped her gaze, betraying her secret, unable to hide the Pandora effect their night together had had on her as well. Her heart rate soared in anticipation, knowing he'd test out their reaction again. His look said it all.

Without hesitation, Anson stepped closer, his hand reaching for her face, his knuckles lightly grazing her smooth jaw line. Kendall helplessly leaned into the touch, her cheek filling the palm of his hand, her eyes closing, skin melting, worries fleeting, just as it all had before. Her heart sailed among the beats of butterfly wings as she let him pull her in close, possessing her, coveting her, needing her. The power of his touch defied all laws of physics as she weightlessly floated in his embrace.

She felt the heat of his breath whisper softly against her exposed neckline, his lips tattooing the memory of their night as the adrenaline of deepest desire coursed through her veins.

Anson kissed her supple skin, his sampling growing in intensity, sending a divine shiver down her accepting body. He backed her up against the cool concrete wall, the weight of his chest and the pressure of his hips rendering her powerless.

The faintest moan escaped her mouth as she exhaled past his ear, further arousing Anson and prompting him to meet her lips. However, the moan also awakened Kendall to the echo of the barren stairwell, snapping her back to the present. Alarmed, she shoved him back.

"I can't do this. We can't do this," she said breathlessly, panicking.

Barely meeting his eyes, she rapidly descended the staircase, skipping the last step and disappearing into the exposing fluorescent light of reality.

Anson cursed under his breath, smacking the wall with his fist. He was at a complete loss – not because of her reaction, but because of his own. He continued his ascent to the second floor, fully perturbed by the spell she had him under and the uncharacteristic steps he'd taken to reconnect with her.

Once back at her unit, Kendall made a beeline for the bathroom, grabbing the unintended attention of Courtney.

"Kendall, are you alright?" Courtney asked, her question ignored.

"Kendall? Everything okay?" Courtney checked again a few moments later, inquiring into the seam of the bathroom door.

"Yeah, I'm fine. I'll be out in a bit." Kendall stared into the mirror, cursing the scarlet skin along the side of her neck as she worked to wipe away the lingering presence of his lips. She fashioned her hair around her neck, knowing it would be a few minutes before her sensitive skin lost its flush.

What the hell am I doing? With contempt, she glared at her reflection.

"What was that all about?" Courtney asked, unrelenting in her inquisition. She followed Kendall back to her computer.

"Nothing. It was nothing."

"Was it Allaway?" Courtney pressed.

"What? No. Just leave it," Kendall said dismissively, shirking Courtney's words away with a wave of her hand.

But true to Courtney's nosy nature, she took this as a yes, as well as an invitation to drag a chair next to Kendall.

"It was!" Courtney whispered back excitedly. "Why is your hair down now? Were you in the stairwell?"

"Holy shit! Do you have some sort of spidey sense for these things?"

Courtney smiled. "You can't bullshit a bullshitter. It's written all over your face. So what happened? I won't leave until you tell me."

"Nothing happened. He just... I don't know. He showed an interest in something happening again. I nipped it in the bud. Let it go. I am. So you need to, too."

Courtney acquiesced; satisfied in getting Kendall to admit more than she liked, but slightly annoyed that she was being so defensive about it. "Fine. But just so you know, I've got my eye on you." Courtney winked wickedly, then returned to her work.

Kendall immersed herself back in her own work, not stopping for lunch, since she'd wasted her break on Anson and couldn't justify more time away from her patients. Actually, she lacked any sort of appetite for real food at that point. Instead, she was craving something never meant to be a permanent option on her mourning menu.

Chapter 12

While carrying an assortment of linens to her patient room, Kendall casually peered into the rooms of the other SICU patients, noticing that Bed 4 had a distinct look of death that went beyond the zombie-stricken expression common to the aged and ailing population within the hospital walls. She stepped into the room to investigate, glancing up at the telemetry monitor above the bed. *Normal sinus rhythm. Totally viable.* However, upon closer inspection, and after palpating the patient's carotid when he failed to respond to her greeting, Kendall quickly determined the guy *was* dead, just in pulseless electrical activity.

Throwing down the linens, she yelled out to the nurse's station, "I need help!" and leaned over the head of the patient to press the *Code Blue* button on the back of the wall. Immediately the unit erupted into a furious frenzy of activity as the code was heard announced overhead. Kendall flattened out the bed and began chest compressions while a team of people rushed into the room, steering the crash cart into position.

Together, they rolled the patient to position a backboard behind him, simultaneously securing two large cardiac pads, then returned the patient to his back, prompting Kendall to resume the chest compressions. Bryan, the respiratory therapist in the unit that day, made his way to the head of the bed and removed the head board, tossing it to the corner, prepping for intubation. Rachel grabbed the ambu bag and mask behind the bed and delivered the necessary oxygen, completing the components of CPR.

The rhythm of everyone – the chatter heard as each person indicated what they were doing or instructed another person to do something – was like that of a jazz symphony: seemingly unlinked notes pulled together to create the controlled chaos often witnessed during a code. The overriding adrenaline, the one note holding true, could be heard throughout the conducted concert, steering everyone as the fight between life and death took center stage and all skilled musicians battled on the side of life.

Courtney and Patricia had already set up the beast of a defibrillator housed on the crash cart. Patricia administered an amp of epinephrine through the patient's IV as Kendall facilitated its travel with her continued compressions. Shortly after, they all stood back – except Rachel, who continued bagging, and Courtney, who had a Doppler buried in the patient's groin. The lack of pulse through the Doppler speaker urged them on.

Another round of CPR ensued, coupled with more cardiac meds. Now the patient was in ventricular fibrillation and Patricia yelled, "Okay we're going to shock, everyone clear!" Everyone released the patient. "Clear!" A delivered shock jolted the lifeless body. Right away, Kendall began chest compressions again and Rachel resumed bagging oxygen into his feeble lungs.

The ICU intensivist arrived on scene, calmly asking for an update. "Let's see the rhythm now."

Again, the team paused to check pulse and rhythm. The patient's condition remained unchanged, and a second shock was delivered as ordered. Without hesitation, Rachel picked up again after the shock and Courtney relieved Kendall, sweat now beading along her brow. Patricia injected another amp of epinephrine from the crash cart, revving up the heart.

After another round of chest compressions, they broke to check the patient's status once more and Kendall announced, "I hear a pulse," as the soft yet familiar rhythmic swoosh of the Doppler sang the returned rush of blood through the femoral artery. They all looked at the monitor as a slow, viable rhythm graced the screen. The patient reflexively twitched, and a calming relief soothed the heart rates of the staff.

The intensivist gave Bryan some ventilator settings, then moved in to set up for intubation. She skillfully inserted an endotracheal tube into the patient's airway, and Bryan verified the position with his stethoscope before securing it to the patient's face and attaching it to the ventilator. Rachel jotted down some orders from the physician on a paper towel as several of the nurses further stabilized the patient.

The team filtered out of the room, one by one heading back to their patients, their abandoned charting, and their various suspended activities as the extended pregnant pause of the unit transitioned into the recovery phase of the code.

Life picked up where it left off, as always.

Kendall retrieved a new set of linens and walked into her patient's room. About an hour later, Rachel thanked Kendall for checking on the patient when she did.

"Oh, yeah, no problem," Kendall said, playing down her appreciation. "I'm glad I did too! Honestly, I had all those linens in my arms and I was looking at the guy like, 'Is this dude dead?' and considered moving on and just throwing out there, 'Someone might want to check on Bed 4,' but I figured I'd just poke him to wake him up."

"I swear he was fine not five minutes earlier," Rachel explained, feeling bad that she hadn't noticed her patient's decline. "In fact, when I saw you coming from the linen cart, it reminded me that he had just asked for a warm blanket. I was getting up to grab that when you hit the code button."

"Well there you go. He was feeling the cold hands of the Grim Reaper creeping in. Besides, I needed a CPR refresher." Kendall laughed, with Rachel joining in, their macabre humor keeping them all moving forward.

Providentially, by shift change, Kendall felt like just another nurse working in the unit – not the mourning widow who had been absent half the year. She was relieved it had only taken two shifts to transform back to her previous role. She was ready to just blend in with the crowd. But at the same time, she was so grateful for the ongoing support of her coworkers that she felt it was something everyone should be the recipient of at least once in their lives, even if tragic circumstances brought it all on. Having a front row seat to the fragile nature of life can take a person to a new level of growth and acceptance.

Good people surrounded her. Life-saving people.

Courtney and Kendall left the unit after clocking out. As they exited, three nurses from the neuro ICU also walked out, merging with them down the hall. One of them was frustrated with a doctor, and Courtney's ears naturally perked right up, always up-to-date on the latest gossip.

"Well, on Monday, DeGraff floated over and said to just let it go, you know, because he snapped at Tina for no apparent reason. Said he was stewing over a girl or something."

"Wait, what? Mark snapped?" another nurse asked.

"No, *Allaway* snapped at Tina and *Mark* said to ignore him because he was just upset over a girl."

Immediately, Courtney's head swung over to look at Kendall.

"And then today, he was all chipper this morning when he stopped in, but went full jerk-mode again tonight. I mean, it's getting real irritating. If it is a girl, he needs to learn to keep his personal life out of work."

If only the lines hadn't blurred so beautifully.

Kendall shook it off, taking it all in with a grain of salt. Courtney, on the other hand, practically busted at the seams as the groups separated in the parking garage.

"Holy shit! Did you hear that?!" Courtney squealed with giddy excitement, shaking Kendall's shoulder as Kendall attempted to keep walking.

"Please. You have no idea how much of that was actually based on anything. So, just ignore it."

"Okay fine! But you heard it, I heard it. And Dr. Allaway definitely had some kind of moment with you today, so… I'm just saying. Pretty intriguing little detail added to the end of our day. Hmm?"

"Okay, I hear you. And now we're done. So, I'll see you next week?" Kendall asked.

"Fine." Courtney rolled her eyes at Kendall, begrudgingly dropping the steamy subject. "Well, I'm thankfully off until next Tuesday! Got the Hibiscus Ball this weekend!"

"Nice. So enjoy your weekend. Stay out of trouble."

Kendall raced up the stairs as Courtney skipped along the first floor. Once out of Courtney's sight, Kendall took out her phone, locating DeGraff's number.

It was unlike DeGraff to divulge such personal information about one of his doctor buddies. He typically steered clear of any type of gossip. Kendall figured Dr. Allaway must have snapped at Tina pretty badly to get DeGraff to cough up some info as a comfort measure. What did he know – and more importantly – how would she get it out of him? She typed up a text.

KM: **I need to know what Allaway said to you after Friday night.**

She climbed into her Jeep and heard the chime of her phone.

MD: **Well hello 2 u 2.**

She stared at the phone, waiting impatiently.

MD: **Because u r u, he said he had a gr8 night. Wanted 2 get 2 know u more.**

Oh. Get to know me?

KM: **So why did you say what you said to Tina???**

MD: **? Not following.**

KM: **I heard you said Allaway was having issues with a girl. Do explain.**

MD: **News to me.**

KM: **Oh come on Mark!**

MD: **U know more than I.**

KM: **Yet I don't. I'm getting mixed messages.**

MD: **You 2 talked?**

KM: **Not really. So… I'm the girl?**

MD: **The only one I know of. He thought he'd hear from u. He asked 4 ur # but I said that should b smthng he gets frm u. He got a bit pissy.**

KM: **Well, I thank you for that. But why would that make him pissy??**

MD: **There was more to the convo but I may have said u were out of his league!**

Kendall glowed. Once again, DeGraff pleasantly surprised her, maintaining his loyalties across the board and not only to those with high-ranking status in the world of healthcare.

KM: **Too funny. See you Saturday, right?**

MD: **W/ bells on! G'nite!**

Kendall let it all marinate for a minute before starting up the Jeep. So, Anson did have a lingering interest. And she'd turned him down. And, like the adults they hopefully were, they would get past it. That information was strangely empowering. But then she shook her head, dismissing any notions of trying anything further with him. The whole business would run its course. It had to.

Kendall's refusal to acknowledge the very real chemical reaction between her and Anson was like ignoring the power of epinephrine on a viable heart. If those infusing it are fueled with determination and selfless drive, hope flourishes. Where there is hope, there is life. And Anson was not ready to let go.

Chapter 13

As was typical after a shift, Kendall's autopilot body mechanics shifted her Jeep into drive as she pulled forward out of her space. She grabbed her phone and robotically stated, "Call Dan." Suddenly, she slammed on her break, stopping in the middle of the parking garage. She idled for a moment, astounded.

Why was she going to call him? To share the news about Anson? To say she was coming home? To let him know she was no longer going to be emotionally broken by his death? If her brain's reflexive neural pathways hadn't even learned to live without him yet, there was no way her emotional ones had.

Slowly, she released the break, allowing the Jeep to roll forward, and called Ariel, needing to hear her voice of reason.

"Hey there," Ariel answered, putting Kendall's entire body at ease.

"I'm just leaving work and I tried calling Dan. When will things like this stop?"

"Aw hon. That sucks. I'm sorry. Is his phone still in service?"

"No. I disconnected it, but I hung up before it even rang. Hey, I never even thought of it – do you want his phone? It's only six months old. Well, a year now, but was only used for six. But when will my brain realize that? Arrgh!"

"Remember when William and I were just starting to get serious? And I called him Greg during an argument even though Greg and I had broken up like two years earlier? It's the same thing. I wasn't thinking of Greg or anything. But Will and I had never really fought before, so the first thing my brain did was go to its familiar place of what to do when arguing with a guy. And well, the last known frequent guy fighter it could recall easily? Greg. So bam, that name jumped out.

"Your brain is going to think of whomever was last and most frequently associated with whatever it is you're doing to help predict what you need to do next. My guess is you felt normal. Back in your normal routine of work and you're heading home and what did you always do when driving home? You called Dan. And I'm sure things like that will happen again. But it'll lessen.

"Be careful, though. Because whenever you fall in love again, you're going to have a real hard time not yelling Dan's name out in the bedroom. Mm hmm." Ariel laughed, then sighed. "Just give it time. And honestly, what you're going to have to do is give your brain new memories. And those usually take lots of time, too, because they're only going to happen when you're ready to move forward." She paused. "And I do need another phone. This one's about to shit the bed."

Best. Decision. Of. The. Day.

"Thanks, Ariel. I knew there was a reason my brain knew to call you right after that blunder." Kendall smiled, feeling great relief in Ariel's practical explanation. "And excuse me, but I did have sex already and managed to *not* call Dan's name out, thank you very much."

"Yeah, but you fucked – your brain knows anyone can be used for a good fuck. Wait until you make looove," Ariel crooned, deepening her voice and drawing out the last word like it was from a Barry White song. The girlfriends giggled, stabilizing Kendall's labile mood for the moment.

"Well, it'll be a while before that," Kendall said. "I don't miss him any less."

"And you shouldn't feel you need to."

"But I thought on some level, I'd be used to the idea of him being gone by now. I mean, I still can't believe it. I still can't believe I'm about to get home and he won't be there waiting." Kendall's voice cracked. "How can any guy ever compare? There's nothing for me without Dan. And the minute I think I might like someone, the guilt is overwhelming. I just miss him so damn much!" She finally let go, her tears free-falling, blurring her vision as she drove to her empty home.

Ariel allowed the moment to draw out, Kendall's sobs punctuating the silence. As Kendall's breathing gradually softened, Ariel offered her support.

"Aw babe. No one expects you to just forget and move on. It hasn't been that long. I hope Will and I are lucky enough to have half the success you and Dan had in your marriage. But never feel you need to showcase that love for the rest of the world. Never feel you need to let someone understand how much Dan meant to you and how awesome he was by remaining sad. Because believe me, they'll know.

"I knew you well before Dan, and you were not the same person of love and strength I know now. Dan helped build that within you. And people will know you had someone unbelievable love you and care for you and respect you like you should be, because everything about you radiates that beautiful fairytale love. You can't keep beauty like that contained! It needs to be shared and you will share it because that's the kind of person you are. The kind of person Dan helped you become.

"Don't think you need to protect his legacy by shielding the love he gave you. Give it out. Give it out generously. Never think that allowing yourself to feel again is wasted or wrong. All men would benefit from a little bit of Dan in their lives, and who better to bring it to them than you?"

Ariel paused, debating in her head whether she went overboard. She waited, assessing Kendall's emotional state. Kendall sniffed, mulling over Ariel's words, letting Ariel know she was still there, still listening.

"And with that said, who might we be thinking we like?" Ariel asked. "Hmmm?"

Kendall snorted, clearing the air, and let out a disgruntled groan. "I don't know. My whole FFN is turning out to be an effing *N*, as in *nightmare*. Well, not really. I mean, in any other situation, it's a fucking fairytale as well. It's obviously just my current state that's making it impossible to be excited."

"Do tell! What happened?" Ariel asked, quickly switching from counselor to eager cheerleader.

"Well, yesterday he called the unit to check on me. Not his patient but *me*. And it was weird. Very not his persona, you know? That was the first time we spoke since Friday. Then he came by the unit and tried to talk to me, but I avoided him. And when he basically cornered me, it was to address the broken condom."

"Broken condom?! What the hell, Kendall? You totally failed to mention that!"

"I'm sorry! I just wasn't overly concerned. I mean, he mentioned getting tested regularly, and well, you know my damned reproductive system. Besides, I still have the IUD. I just didn't let it worry me."

"Yeah, but I'm guessing he didn't know that. I mean, it's definitely something worthy of mentioning!" Ariel scolded.

"I know, I know. Well, so he did. But I snapped at him a bit, and then we seemed to smooth it over via text. So when I saw him today, I didn't expect such a... a reaction."

"What do you mean? *A reaction*?"

"I mean, an actual reaction, like chemical, electrical. He touched my hand and my stomach must have flipped like ten times. And then he basically said he wanted more to happen between us."

"What do you mean, *basically*? I need it verbatim. Like his tone and look along with the exact words."

"He fucking kissed me, Ariel. I mean, seduced me with his touch and kissed my neck making me want to fucking come until I realized where the fuck I was – in the fucking stairwell of my fucking job!"

"Whoa! Okay! Okay. Wow. Shit. Let me think a minute." Ariel definitely hadn't been prepared to hear that.

Kendall drove along angrily, tears drying along her cheeks as she sniffled, her sinuses clogging up, further frustrating her. This was exactly what she'd hoped to avoid when chasing after Anson earlier in the day.

Finally, Ariel gathered up her sage advice.

"Okay, so, you liked it. That doesn't mean anything. You've described him as a dreamboat model and you liked it last week. Why the hell would it be any different now? He's attractive. I mean, yeah, getting it on in the stairwell isn't exactly your professional style, but that aside, no big deal. It doesn't mean you're looking to replace Dan. No guilt. You're a human being with hormones and he's clearly willing to cater to that, so don't over think this one."

Kendall digested Ariel's words, finally nodding in agreement.

"No, you're right. I mean, he's the only guy I've done anything with since Dan. And he is gorgeous. I mean, it's like a *first,* if you will, and it went well, so the butterfly feeling doesn't really mean anything emotionally."

"Exactly. If you want to have more sex, then do it, but do it on your terms. If you can't handle it all emotionally, just say goodbye to Dr. Sex and be done with it. *You* are in control, here, Kendall. The only reason a guy would reach out to you afterward, knowing full well it wasn't anything but a one night thing – I mean, you said so yourself, he clarified that from the get-go – the *only* reason would be because the sex was too damn hot and you are too damn good to give up. That's what I think."

"Har, har, har. Well, if he does think that, he needs to prepare to be disappointed. I can't go the fuck buddy route."

"There you have it, then. Just let him know that and move on. Anywho. I've gotta get going – I still have a bunch of papers to grade. I love you, Kendall."

Kendall's heart swelled.

"I'm just pulling into my driveway. Thank you, Ariel. Love you too."

Fifteen minutes later, like clockwork, Kendall curled up on the couch with a glass of red wine, a microwaveable dinner, and the TV remote. But that night, she stepped back on the rotating planet and continued moving forward. It was a night for *Breaking Bad.*

***

"Hey Mom. Sorry I haven't called," Kendall said through a yawn, pausing her show to answer the phone. "I was just starting to doze. I'm still adjusting to the 12-hour work schedule, without the random naps I was used to."

"I'm sorry, dear. Well, I'll let you go. Just wanted to check in and see how work was going."

"Oh no, it's fine. I'm fine. I'm on the couch, so I'd rather wake up now than at two in the morning. But work is good. Like I never left, which is good and bad. It's an adjustment, like anything."

"Of course. But you're feeling good about going back? Like that was the right move?" Elena asked.

"Definitely. I mean, any longer and I'd be completely out of touch with my nursing skills. It's good to see everyone again and just sort of blend in with the crowd, you know?"

"Well, good. So now you're off until when?"

"Saturday I work. So tomorrow and Friday I'm off. Got anything going on down south?" Kendall asked.

"No, same ol', same ol'. You're more than welcome to come down and spend the night if you're up to driving, unless you have other things to do. Gabe is off tomorrow and works again Friday."

"I might take you up on that. I'll let you know tomorrow."

"Okay, sounds great. You let me know. Love you, Kendall."

"Love you, too, Mom."

It was just after 10pm and Kendall decided, for the first time since Dan's death, to actually turn in rather than prolonging the inevitable. If she wanted to keep moving forward, she also had to include regular sleep patterns in her schedule again.

The relentless rollercoaster of thoughts that typically bombarded her during the evening hours were most noticeably absent that night. She hoped the moments of stillness would become more frequent as she managed to properly categorize the chaos within. Completing the cataloging was not her goal. But she knew she could evolve – not despite the chaos, but because of it. She would create that dancing star and continue on.

She rested her head on her pillow, the soft sounds of *Let Go* by Frou Frou lulling her to sleep and giving her that constant encouragement she needed to see another day.

So let go, jump in.
Well, whatcha waiting for?
It's all right 'cause there's beauty in the breakdown.

As soon as she woke the next morning, Kendall called her mom and drove to Miami, wanting the good vibe to continue with more of those life-saving people she knew would never stop fighting for her.

Chapter 14

The Gold Coast General Hibiscus Ball had long been the must-attend event for the majority of the hospital's employees. For one thing, tickets were far more affordable than for the other major fundraising event of the year, the Coral Gala. But the real appeal was that stories from the Ball lasted for weeks, whereas the Gala simply boasted a who's who of the locally rich and famous.

Kendall and Dan had attended three Balls together and one Gala in the seven years Kendall had worked at GC General. The only reason they'd gone to the Gala was because she had won tickets – and she likened the experience to a sumptuous wedding reception for people she only knew vaguely. The Gala was held at The Breakers of Palm Beach that year. The food was sensational, the drinks overpriced, and the atmosphere somewhat stiff, albeit opulent. The location of the Gala alternated between high-class Palm Beach County landmarks like The Breakers, Mar-a-Lago, and The Flagler Museum.

The Hibiscus Ball, on the other hand, took place at the same location every year: the Coral Beach Club in Manalapan.

The Coral Gala had its home during the autumn season, whereas the Hibiscus Ball bloomed every spring. Both events occurred during the peak snowbird season, when all the big hospital donors were in town – the residents of the North who called South Florida home for three-to-five months out of the year, making the roads impossible to navigate but keeping the local economy fully in the black.

Fortunately, the sticky heat that comes barreling in right around the end of tax season sends them all back north to their long summer days and gorgeous flowering gardens, leaving the local hospital workers (adapted to the thick humidity by way of their hidden gills, seemingly) to once again arrive at work with plenty of time to spare – only to be sent home early due to low census.

And so goes the ebb and flow of living and working in a tropical paradise.

The Hibiscus Ball was the last thing on Kendall's mind as she drove home to Lantana from Miami. Tickets had gone on sale during her bereavement, and she hadn't even considered going with coworkers. So getting ready for any event, let alone the Ball, seemed next to impossible when she received a text from Courtney.

CB: **Hey there! Any plans tonight? Come to the Ball with me.**

Kendall pulled into her driveway. It was 4:20 on Friday afternoon. *Courtney must be high.*

KM: **I just got home from Miami. Literally. In my driveway. Doesn't it start around 5?**

CB: **Yes. Fashionably late. It'd be fun!**

KM: **I think I'll pass. But thanks.**

Kendall grabbed her bag and purse from the passenger seat and hopped out of her Jeep. There was no way she could make this work. The idea alone sounded exhausting. She unlocked the front door of her house and heard her phone whistle again.

CB: **NOOOOOO. Please come! I have DeGraff's ticket bc the jerk picked up work today.**

KM: **I'm sure others would go. How about Rachel? Pat?**

CB: **Pat? Please. Not her. Rachel is out of town.**

Kendall laughed at Courtney's reaction to suggesting Patricia. Those two could only get along when they were buffered by a crowd.

KM: **I work tomorrow.**

CB: **We won't stay late! It'll be fun!**

Kendall walked straight to the kitchen to get a glass of water. She stared at Courtney's text. If she was being honest with herself, she knew the only thing she would do tonight was brew over tomorrow's potentially awkward Dr. Allaway encounters.

Escaping to Miami had been one way to avoid those thoughts – but she hadn't escaped him completely, considering the texts she had received from him Thursday night. First he had asked to talk but she'd declined, using Miami and family as her excuse. Then, he'd asked point blank whether she was back to running from him. She never replied – something categorically different than running, but having the same effect. A potential run-in with him at the Ball was a further deterrent to attending.

KM: **I need to keep my Allaway encounters to a minimum.**

Kendall chuckled to herself, wondering what Courtney's response would be to that. Then, almost involuntarily, she browsed through her closet to see what she would possibly wear if she were to agree to go. Her phone whistled again.

CB: **Oh puleeeeza. This is a hospital event. Not a hookup bar. He won't even be there if he was out last wknd. He's probly oncall.**

Courtney had a point. Since Dr. Allaway had been at Dolphin Bar last weekend – he wouldn't have been so free to fuck if he'd been on-call – Kendall guessed he'd probably be working tomorrow, so attending an evening event tonight would be difficult for him. And dancing could be the key to relieving her building anxiety.

At last year's ball, Dan and Kendall had danced all night. They also had witnessed all sorts of fun hospital drama, as coworkers left together or made out on the beach. Definitely an entertaining evening. With Dan spinning her around on the dance floor and standing by her side as they sipped cocktails, she'd been unstoppable. And they'd been a dynamite couple that night, using the whole scene for secret laughs and their own personal foreplay before heading home to their perfect, string-free sex. Going to the same event with a fellow single coworker almost seemed hypocritical, living life on the other side of the looking glass.

KM: **It's 4:45 now. What's the point? I have nothing to wear anyway.**

CB: **Wear what u wore to Mari's baby shower! It's perfect.**

Kendall spotted the simple, knee-length coral-colored dress with its twirling skirt line. It was Hibiscus Ball appropriate and very comfortable. She hemmed and hawed over it for a minute. She'd just waste away the evening on the couch. Besides, Courtney sounded desperate.

KM: **OK. But I'm not staying out late. Or becoming your DD half way through the night! See you there in 30 minutes.**

CB: **YES!!! AGREED! You'll be home before u turn into a pumpkin! XOXOXO**

Kendall pulled into the drive of the Coral Beach Club, surrounded by a slew of vehicles and running valet guys. Courtney waved, bouncing around like they were heading to prom, or more appropriately, homecoming. Courtney wore an adorable yellow sundress that accented her curvy body in all the right places. Together, they matched the current colors of the South Florida sky, bright and warm energy radiating through their smiles.

"Thank you so much for coming!" Courtney squealed excitedly, embracing Kendall.

"You're welcome. You look great. Very bright and cheery. Have you been to one of these before?" Kendall didn't recall seeing her at the balls she and Dan had attended.

"No! This is my first one! That's why I *needed* someone to be with me!" Courtney dragged Kendall by the arm through the club lobby and into the main ballroom. She delighted in Courtney's over-the-top and bubbly behavior, hoping the effervescence of it all would soak into her own skin.

The buffet-style event's cocktail hour was in full swing. Kendall read over the program and directed Courtney toward the bar to grab their complimentary drinks, since the emcee would be making her formal announcements momentarily.

With Kendall's two glasses of red wine and Courtney's two vodka tonics in hand, they scanned the room, finally finding some coworkers from various therapy departments at a table with one open chair.

Bryan from respiratory waved them over, patting the one empty seat and subsequently standing up to offer his. Everyone willingly shifted around, making space as Bryan located another empty chair and brought it to the table.

"Thanks so much!" Courtney said, graciously greeting everyone with a smile.

"Hanging with the non-nursing crew tonight!" Alexa, one of the physical therapists, exclaimed. She held up her cocktail to toast the ladies.

The emcee's voice suddenly boomed over the sound system, welcoming the crowd of party-goers. Kendall smiled at the festive atmosphere, happy in her decision to take the leap and attend the ball. Just like Ariel said, she needed to make new memories. With her fresh attitude and free alcohol, the air already felt crisper. Maybe even a little daring.

During the buffet train, Courtney and Kendall mingled with their nursing coworkers as they gathered a surf-and-turf assortment of food. Kendall was selecting grilled asparagus from a station when a squeeze of her sides made her jump.

"That shit is garlic'd up. So not only will you have dragon breath, but your pee will smell too!"

Kendall glowered over her shoulder and hit Carlos on the arm. "You're so gross!"

"Well, I can definitely say that you are not. Looking mighty fine tonight, Matthews!" Carlos shouted over the crowd before leaning in to kiss her on the cheek.

Kendall laughed off his compliment. Then she noticed Leonard Bautista, her fellow ICU nurse who'd became a nurse anesthetist two years prior. The two had been dangerously flirtatious with one another before Kendall got married to Dan, never overtly crossing the line but definitely dancing along it, recognizing a clear attraction. Kendall put a hard stop to it all one night when he had walked her to her car and then held her hand, making some comment about owing it to one another to see if there was something there before she legally committed herself to another guy.

They had remained friends, however, and had been able to carry on without hurt feelings, both understanding it wasn't in the cards – perhaps a different time, a different place, but not then. A year later, Leo had left for school and was gone for three years before accepting a job back at Gold Coast General as a nurse anesthetist. He and Kendall rarely bumped into one another now.

"Leo!" Kendall exclaimed, excusing herself past Carlos, then hugging Leo around his neck with her one free hand as she balanced her plate with the other. Leo embraced her tightly around her waist, his six-foot-plus height easily bringing her up to her toes. "Oh my goodness! It's been forever!"

"Kendall: You look incredible," Leo replied. "I've been by SI a couple times to check in, always hoping to say hello to you. I can't imagine what you've been through. God, it's great to see you here, so beautiful and all smiles. You don't know how good that makes me feel." Leo held his heart, genuinely concerned and relieved to see her alive and well.

"Thank you." Her eyes glistened, taking his kind words to heart. "That means a lot to me."

"So, where are you eating? We have to catch up. There's an open chair where I am," Leo offered, his hand gripping her upper arm affectionately.

"Oh, well, I'm eating over there with some coworkers. How 'bout I come by for dessert?"

"Perfect. Dessert's always been my favorite." He couldn't help but wink, giving away a sly smirk. "I'm in the back corner, Table 13, I think."

"Sounds risky, but I'll take it," Kendall teased, giving him a quick hug again.

"I've always admired a risk-taker." Leo flirtatiously kissed her cheek and then disappeared into the crowd.

Kendall turned back to her table, her plate fairly full and her face fully flushed.

Chapter 15

The food was very satisfying, especially considering that the meal Kendall had planned at home consisted of crackers, cheese, and whatever else was easy to grab from her fridge. The therapy table was boisterous and loud, a desirable, yet surprisingly ineffective distraction to Kendall's randy mind.

Another Friday night and not married – what to do, what to do?

She wasn't sure whether Leo was dating someone, but she almost hoped he was, knowing full well they could easily stir up some bottled chemicals from long ago. Without someone to anchor either one down, there was definitely the potential for fireworks. An FFN flashed through her mind, as if she was daring herself to go down that road again, the dangerous combo of spontaneity, alcohol, and not giving a fuck pumping through her veins.

After finishing her food, Kendall looked about the room. Not wanting to seem too eager to join Leo at his table, she made sure enough of a crowd had gathered before deciding to head toward the dessert stations. Courtney had already grabbed some cake and sat back down, in full conversation with Bryan and the others. It was the right time to ditch her date.

"Hey, Court, I'm going to go say hi to a few people, okay?"

"Oh sure. Definitely. But don't leave me hanging when everyone starts to move outside," Courtney said.

"Of course not," Kendall said with a smile.

She picked up two brownies, then searched for Table 13. Leo spotted her first and stood, pulling out the chair next to him. His smile was contagious and she couldn't help but feel a little bit giddy. Maybe even a tiny bit wet.

Kendall maneuvered around the table to his side and accepted the seat with a nod, looking over at the other guests. Her rosy cheeks instantly drained. Directly across from her was Dr. Allaway, watching her closely with his dreamboat eyes, his chin held causally on his thumb, those skilled fingers concealing his wily smile.

"Everything alright?" Leo asked, leaning into her, the change across her face mildly alarming him.

She swung her head around to face Leo. With her mouth completely parched, as all moisture had drained along with her blood, she eyed Leo's glass of water. "May I?"

"Of course." He handed over the glass, still bewildered by her peculiar demeanor.

She took a revitalizing sip of the ice water and avoided locking eyes with Anson again, regaining her composure.

"That was weird," she said, laughing flippantly and flashing him a goofy grin. "Just a strange sensation, like a head rush. Whatever. Nothing a little dessert can't fix." She playfully raised her eyebrows at Leo, carrying on his suggestive message from earlier as she bit into her brownie.

As hoped, he accepted her explanation without question, and they began to converse with one another as if they were the only ones at the table.

Leo divulged his recent single status after a messy break up the previous month, claiming he would never move in with a woman again if he wasn't head over heels. They discussed his job as a nurse anesthetist and how great it was for him. Then, he turned the conversation to Kendall and whether she had applied yet to a nurse anesthetist program, like she had always wanted.

"Actually, yes, I have," she said, proudly cocking her head to the side and waiting for Leo to ask for more details.

"No way! Where? When do you find out?"

"Well, I already was accepted to two down south, your alma mater included." Kendall sat up confidently, casually glancing over at Dr. Allaway. He was chatting with someone standing behind him, seemingly not focused on her at all.

"Are you freaking kidding me?! Kendall, that's awesome!" Leo hugged her tightly, promptly capturing the attention of Allaway once again. "When do you start?"

"Well, uh, I'm not sure," Kendall answered, shrugging. "They're letting me leave it open until May. Found out a couple months back. I don't know how I could financially swing it all now."

The great school debate had already been catalogued away in her brain as something to revisit at a later date.

"Oh wow. That's true," Leo said. "Kendall, I'm so sorry. I will totally help you out if you'd like, just say the word. It'd be an honor to help you out. You amaze me! I'm really so proud of you." He didn't hesitate to throw in a congratulatory cheek kiss.

Allaway completely disengaged from the conversation he was involved in, now trying to follow what was happening across the table. Kendall remained attentive to Leo, triggering Allaway to pull out his phone.

"Thank you. That means a lot to me," she said warmly. "But, I'll figure something out if I do indeed decide to go."

The alert of an incoming message broke Kendall's focus, and she reached for her clutch on the table.

"You *must* keep me informed, whatever you decide. I'll help you out the whole way. I really admire your strength, Kendall. I know I probably wouldn't be able to handle everything as well as you."

Kendall smiled, slightly embarrassed at Leo's gushing over her, and mindlessly checked her phone. Her mouth popped open in surprise.

AA: **And you think Leo will do the trick for you?**

Kendall darted her eyes across the table, but Dr. Allaway had already gotten up from his chair and was nowhere in sight. Half the ballroom had already begun to filter through the doors to the outside bar and deck. Center tables were being moved by the club staff to prepare the area for the dance floor.

"Want to go outside? I think I owe you a celebratory drink at the very least," Leo suggested, sensing Kendall's loss of interest in their conversation.

"Oh, yeah. Um, sounds great." Kendall slipped her phone back into her purse.

As they meandered around the tables, Kendall realized Courtney had already headed outside, as their table was folded up and rolled to the side. The opened doors had a funneling effect on the crowd as it walked through, prompting Leo to take the lead and grab Kendall's hand to help navigate. The contact lacked the tantalizing rush she'd experienced with Anson at work. But it was sweet and not creepy, so she went with it.

Leo looked back at her, his dark, velvety eyes conveying his thoughts clearly as he gently squeezed her hand. Kendall knew full well she'd end up hurting him, but hoped it was just the ambience of the evening clouding his judgment. Nothing that would result in chronic pain.

A live band playing a mix of Reggae music was already in full force outside as the DJ set up inside. Leo led her to a back corner of the expansive club deck, near the stairs to the beach. The sky remained softly lit from the setting sun's hues of purple, orange, pink, and red, providing a perfect backdrop for romance. With noticeable reservation, Leo released Kendall's hand, smiling affectionately at her as she leaned up against the deck railing.

"I can't believe you're here," Leo whispered, taking in the moment. He cleared his throat. "What do you want to drink?"

Kendall blushed. Leo was gorgeous. His naturally tanned skin and million-watt smile; the ultra-sleek black-on-black ensemble he'd chosen for the night that perfectly complimented his thick, ebony-colored hair; his broad shoulders – he was the epitome of the tall, dark, and handsome admirer. She had been willingly airlifted away and then parachuted down into an exotic getaway.

But this potential rendezvous was very local, and would definitely have more confounding consequences than her last one. There was history between them, even if hadn't amounted to much yet. And she knew she was of no use to any man who actually wanted to engage in a relationship – something Leo would most likely desire.

"Champagne!" Kendall blurted out. "We're toasting, right?"

Sending him away on an errand would allow her to analyze all the potential scenarios, rather than staring at him awkwardly any longer

"Great. Don't move," he warned lightheartedly, before getting swallowed into the crowd around the outdoor tiki bar.

Kendall snatched her phone from her clutch and quickly texted Courtney. Admittedly, it wasn't her best plan, but the only plan that came to mind included the addition of a wingwoman.

KM: **Where are you? I'm in the corner by the stairs on the deck.**

She waited for a bit but didn't get an immediate response. She peered over the railing, seeing that the festive atmosphere had already spilled onto the beach. Courtney could be down there.

Leo returned with a glass of champagne and two beers. He handed over the glass flute as her phone chimed, alleviating her building anxiety over the developing situation. Deep down, she knew she had no real interest in hooking up with Leo. It was simply something to do, other than think. But she needed a buffer zone of friends to keep this in control. Otherwise, at some point, she could just cave, losing herself once again, simply to bury Dan further down.

Or was it Anson now?

She checked her phone to read what she assumed would be a text from Courtney, but just like his nickname, Double A kept going and going.

AA: **Don't you have to work tomorrow?**

Annoyed by the jilted lover tone he had taken in his last few texts, she gulped back the glass of champagne before Leo even had a chance to say a toast. She scoured the crowd for Anson's face and with GPS precision, located him leaning along another railing.

"Well, okay! Good thing I brought the other beer at the same time," Leo said, laughing and replacing Kendall's empty champagne flute with a bottle of Sam Adams. "To you and all that lies ahead." He angled his bottle of beer toward hers, then kissed her on the cheek again.

"I'll drink to that!" Kendall agreed heartily, chugging back nearly half the beer before laughing out loud at herself.

She could see the shock in Leo's face, her exuberant behavior a little uncharacteristic. She covered her mouth, some of the beer dribbling out, and recomposed herself.

"Sorry. Really. Thank you. Truly. I haven't had much fun lately." She hugged him around the neck, turning it into a lingering embrace, all while holding onto the watchful eye of Anson.

A follow-up text from Anson popped up on her phone screen, held near her face as she childishly engaged both men.

AA: **Will you be driving yourself home tonight?**

Out of nowhere, the seething anger that had been setting up shop in her heart the last month released its pressure. As Kendall wrapped her arms tighter around Leo's neck, she simultaneously flipped off the object of her scorn. She pecked Leo's cheek sweetly and struck up a conversation, never looking over to Anson again. Anson recognized Kendall's pathetically desperate play and texted her one more time as he left the deck.

Kendall, mind now made up, never bothered to check her phone again, stowing it back into her clutch and recklessly easing into the evening with Leo and all he could contribute to her uncategorized world of chaos.

Chapter 16

It wasn't long before Courtney joined Kendall and Leo, along with a crew of other hospital companions. Although the sun was now swimming deep below the Gulf of Mexico, the outdoor atmosphere of the Hibiscus Ball sizzled, the ambiance of the night transforming into one of spicy celebration. The indoor bass speakers pumped beats out onto the deck. Kendall began to spin in the alcohol infused air, all her thoughts blending, carefree and meaningless.

Within an hour, Kendall had racked up quite a beverage tally: that first glass of champagne, two beers, and a courtesy-of-Carlos shot of Patron. She occasionally sipped on Courtney's Red Bull and vodka, completely disregarding the nagging thoughts of how she'd feel tomorrow at work and further amping up her *fuck it* energy level. When someone suggested they head inside, the group of seven stormed the dance floor as the DJ spun a mix of house and club hits.

Not even two full songs later, Kendall and Leo were grinding on each other – first laughing playfully, simply enjoying the whole festive fury that ensued when the beat dropped. Kendall alternated between partners, dancing up on Courtney and twirling around their circle of coworkers, then with Carlos, but ultimately, back to Leo.

But then Leo pulled her in close, wrapping his arm around her back, his hand pressing her against him. She willingly straddled his leg, their pelvises knocking, bumping to the bass, cheeks flushed against one another, her fingernails grazing the back of his neck and into his hair. The dark ballroom, with its colorful disco lights and crowded dance floor, felt falsely protective.

And then it happened: Leo brazenly crossed that line they had drawn so many years back. He lightly bit her earlobe, sending a wave of fine hairs to stand at attention across her neck and back. He kissed her down her neck as they danced, slowing the pace against one another, her head falling back and permitting every touch of his lips. Before she knew it, his lips were on hers and there they were – on the dance floor, completely exposed in front of their coworkers, tasting the liquor on their tongues, holding their bodies tightly against one another, experimenting with the shelf-life of those stored chemicals.

A quick bump from a couple of rowdy dancers jolted them back to their present surroundings and company, separating them slightly. Their eyes met as they shared a sheepish laugh, Kendall burying her face into his shoulder. He smelled divine and the entire exchange felt completely natural, not a bit contrived.

But no butterflies. Not a one.

Leo took advantage of the halted moment to slip away unnoticed with Kendall, grabbing her hand as he weaved through the raucous dancers. Once off the dance floor, he guided them over to the bar area, still holding her hand, and requested two waters.

"Getting hot in there, eh?" Leo's eyebrows lowered, his extra-long eyelashes further shading his deep brown eyes as he looked Kendall up and down. She smiled back, unsure how else to react in the sobering moment.

When the bartender arrived with their waters, Kendall knocked back her glass in one gulp, welcoming its chilling effect. Despite the copious amounts of alcohol she'd consumed, she couldn't believe how far she'd let things escalate – or how careless and crude she'd become. Kendall quickly asked for another glass. She hoped she could dilute both her alcohol and her raging hormones, saving herself from further embarrassment.

As she waited for her water, Kendall pulled out her phone to check the time – but first noticed Anson's text from earlier.

AA: **Nice gesture. Call me when you need a ride.**

Ugh. She shook her head.

"Wow, it's 9:30 already," Kendall said, breaking her silence and looking back up at Leo.

"Yeah, still early," he responded. "Do you want to go back outside?"

"Actually, I should probably head out. I have to fucking work in the morning." Kendall laughed awkwardly.

"Oh, that sucks."

Leo put down his glass and reached out to Kendall, interlocking his fingers behind her waist and pulling her in close, as if they were a couple. Very aware of the potential prying eyes all around them, she resisted his advance. But she smiled, always smiled, not wanting to hurt his feelings or give him the impression he'd done something wrong.

"What's up?" Leo asked.

"I don't want to have to answer too many questions," Kendall replied shyly, her eyes scanning around the room.

"Well, I think it's too late for that," Leo said laughing and gesturing to the huge dance crowd. "Besides, let them ask. There's no harm in it." He smiled deviously at her, adding, "I could get us a room for tonight instead, if you'd prefer a little privacy."

Kendall declined, rolling her eyes.

"Kidding. But I should probably call you a cab," Leo conceded.

"I need my car to get to work tomorrow. I'll hang out for a bit more to sober up. No big deal. I should be fine in no time. Sweated most of it out anyway." She batted her eyes, smiling brightly and concentrating through each word, hoping he'd buy her act.

"You want to go back out on the dance floor, then?"

And before she did sober up completely – thinking of Anson lurking around earlier, judging her every step, insulting her choice of company, and now offering her a ride and being the irritatingly better person than she – Kendall took the wild leap once again, throwing caution to the wind because, *fuck it*, she could.

"Not really. I know a better way to sweat it out." She took a step toward the ballroom exit, into the main hallway, and then glanced back at him. "Well, are you coming?"

Leo quickly fell in line, grabbing her hand as Kendall led them away from the crowds. In the hall were small rooms with booths for phone calls. Kendall stepped right into one, wasting no time in pulling Leo to her lips. Feverishly, they groped one another like students at a high school dance, needing to finish quickly before getting tossed out by the teachers. Leo buried his face into her covered chest as Kendall hoisted herself up onto the small shelf inside the privacy pocket. She raised her dress as his hand glided up her thigh.

There was no mistaking Kendall's sense of urgency, rushing Leo to move quickly. For the first few minutes he followed suit, enjoying her wildly arousing antics, playing right along as they risked being caught. But when she demanded her purse to grab a condom, something clicked inside for him. He stepped back, almost offended, and not by the request.

With her tousled hair, strap hanging off one shoulder, dress pulled up and panties pulled down just above her knees, Kendall looked desperate. A silk lei choked around her throat and dangled behind her back, completing this pitiful look, one he'd never seen in her before – certainly never as Kendall Graham, and even more shocking as Kendall Matthews, the widow.

"Kendall, this isn't how I want you. Maybe this is what Allaway wanted, but it's not what I want. I can't do this to you like this."

She was horrified. Hearing Leo's confession made her want to die instantly, so she would never have to see his face look at her again like that. The shame. The guilt. The ugliness of a widowed whore. Immediately she slid off the shelf, pulled up her underwear, and bolted past him into the hallway.

"Kendall, wait up. It's nothing against you. You know that. If anything, it's out of respect for you," Leo pleaded behind her, to no avail. "Kendall. Just wait a minute!"

She spun around to face him, staggering, as the room didn't seem to stop its spin at the same rate as her body.

"Don't follow me. Please, Leo. Just let me walk away."

He saw the tears well up in her eyes. She was broken and not looking to connect with him, or with anyone. She only needed to forget.

"Kendall, I–" Leo reached for her arm, wanting to comfort her.

"Please, just don't." Her voice was no longer strong, and the tears fell freely, one by one.

Leaving Leo heartbroken and abandoned in the hallway, Kendall navigated her way back to the circular drive up front, deciding her reality check was sufficient in clearing away her alcohol haze. She handed over her valet ticket and bowed her head with disgrace.

As her Jeep's tires squealed on the damp cobblestone drive, Dr. Anson Allaway stepped forward, accepting the open door to the driver seat.

"Oh god. You've got to be kidding me! Allaway, come on. I need to get home," Kendall begged exhaustively. "I'm at my wit's end and I can't play any more games."

"I know. I see that. Let me take you home." He gestured to the passenger side as another valet held open the door for her.

With a healthy dose of hostility, Kendall marched back to the passenger side and slumped down into the seat. She avoided making eye contact with the attendants, knowing they must witness an insane amount of drunken drama at these events. What had she become?

Chapter 17

In an attempt to drown out her anger, Anson powered on Kendall's sound system and was immediately bombarded by the lyrics of Sia's *Chandelier*. Kendall jumped, turning the music way down and sinking further into her seat of humiliation. She cursed under her breath as she shifted around, still not fully accepting the bizarre outcome for the evening.

"The inspirational soundtrack for tonight?" Anson asked, looking over at her as he stopped the Jeep, waiting to turn onto A1A from the Coral Beach Club property.

"The inspiration for my last *two* Friday nights is more like it," she mumbled. "Spare me your judgment."

"I'm not judging you, just trying to make conversation. I'm sorry. Are you going to tell me where I'm going, or should I just take you back to my place?"

"No!" Kendall snarled far too harshly.

"No, you won't tell me where I'm going? So, back to my place? Remember, brain surgeon, not a mind reader."

His flippant disregard for her situation further fueled her anger.

"No, *not* to your place! Head west on Lantana Road. I'm just past 95."

"I'm not the enemy here, Kendall. Just trying to get you home safely."

"Oh, *I'm* the enemy in this scenario?" Kendall fell silent, halted by her inability to reply rapidly without slurring. "Fuck. Why did I get drunk tonight? Tomorrow's going to be a bitch."

"Yeah, you're probably right. But at least you'll wake up at home." Anson offered up an appeasing smile. But even that smile, and the light scent of his cologne filling her Jeep, couldn't drag her out of her drunken slump.

"Sometimes I'd like to wake up anywhere but there." Her voice softened as she gazed out his side of the Jeep at the lights dancing along the Intracoastal Waterway. "Or just not wake up at all."

Her comment caught him off guard, shifting his role to that of a friend and a concerned healthcare provider.

"Are you drinking yourself to sleep most nights?" he asked.

"Maybe the last month. I don't know," she answered mindlessly. "It's getting bad, though."

Suddenly she felt duped, looking over at him with betrayal as he turned west onto Lantana Road. "Are you a psychiatrist too now? I'm not asking for help. I have plenty of support from those who really care and know me, so please, save yourself from getting to know me."

"Well, maybe that's the one thing I have going for me," he replied honestly. "I *don't* know you. I didn't know your husband. Yet we have established a connection. A rather intimate one.

"And we might both say it was just sex. But like you said, there was a graying. I'm not judging you, Kendall. But I recognize that hollow look and I'm telling you – from an outside perspective – that what you think will help you forget, will end up making you feel empty inside. Your family and friends might not see it like I do because they're already in there with you, supporting you that way. I'm on the outside. And, well, last Friday, I sort of became vested."

They drove along in silence, the reflective atmosphere evolving into one of comfort. Kendall rested her head up against the wall of her Jeep, fighting hard not to doze. She told Anson her address and finally conceded to the exhaustion, allowing herself to completely relax in his presence before nodding off to sleep. In what felt like only a half-minute later to her, Anson tapped her leg, stirring her awake.

"Kendall. Kendall, we're passing over 95."

Kendall jerked awake and straightened out in the seat. "That was fast. Um... just after the next light, turn left."

"Where? Behind that church?" he asked.

"Yes, there's a small road there. You'll see it as you get closer."

Anson approached the turn slowly until he noticed an alley of sorts. He turned the Jeep onto a narrow dirt road, Sandlefoot Lane. Cautiously advancing, he turned the Jeep's bright lights on, completely unfamiliar with this hidden gem of a neighborhood just two blocks in from the congestion of I-95.

"Is it one way?" he asked.

"No. It's just one of those roads where you pull off to the shoulder to let each other pass. It's a really short road along the lake. Right here, the yellow house on the right," she said, motioning for him to pull into her long driveway.

"Lake Osborne?"

"Yeah. It originally belonged to my husband's grandparents. It's kind of perfect. Small, old Florida home but a huge waterfront property."

"Nice." Anson turned to her, relieved they were interacting civilly. "I'll have to come by during the day some time."

But the moment the engine stopped, Kendall opened the door and bolted, no longer angry with him for helping but unwilling to prolong any moments between them – or even to attempt to decipher the meaning behind that last comment. She walked briskly to her front door as he strolled up behind her. She opened her clutch, just as he jingled the keys.

"Looking for these?"

"Of course, that's right," she said.

She took the keys, careful not to look directly at him, and fumbled with them for a minute before finally unlocking the deadbolt.

"Okay, I'm home safe. So thank you, and maybe I'll see you tomorrow."

Anson laughed, shaking his head. "So you want me to just wait on your front step for my ride?"

"Oh right! Shit. Sorry, yes, of course. Come in!" Kendall said, grimacing as her hand smacked her forehead.

If she could just stop picturing him naked, the whole state of affairs would actually be tolerable.

Kendall opened her door wide, quickly scanning the house to see what kind of condition she'd left it in. Her small overnight bag from her Miami trip was still opened on the dining table, some items pulled out as she'd hurried to get ready for the evening. But everything else was in its place.

Knowing she needed to sober up further, she headed straight into the kitchen. Anson sauntered up to the peninsula counter, pulling out one of the barstools as Kendall created her go-to concoction of Emergen-C packets and B-12 solutabs.

"Does that work?" he inquired, nodding to her drink.

Kendall took a minute to drink back the mix, then refilled the glass with tap water and drank that back as well. Sufficiently hydrated, she finally answered him.

"I think so," she replied, somewhat out of breath. "In my experience at least. It doesn't combat the Xanax fog, but fortunately, I didn't take any tonight." She paused, remembering his comment earlier in the Jeep. "I mean, I'm not drunk every night, despite what you might think. Sometimes it just helps me sleep. Shuts off my brain. I think too much." She took in a deep breath, attempting to squelch her loose-lipped rambling.

"I get it. And you definitely weren't drunk last Friday. That night was different, even if you played *Chandelier* in the back of your mind."

Kendall stopped her fidgeting over various papers on the counter and looked directly at him. "Nothing was the same about that night."

Anson smiled at her. He appeared so comfortable, relaxing on her barstool like they had a history that went far beyond just a week. Then she caught a glimpse of herself in the mirror behind him, interrupting their fixation on one another.

"Oh man. I look like shit!" she exclaimed, quickly rounding the counter past him to the mirror so she could wipe away the dark streaks of tear-soaked mascara.

"Don't worry about it – you're just ready for Friday night football, is all," Anson teased, swiveling in his chair to watch her. Kendall looked back at him repugnantly. "What?" he asked. "Okay, you look like shit."

She finally caved and let down her defenses. He'd already seen her naked, possibly making out with another man, and now drunk, looking like a drowned raccoon. At this point, why even care? She walked back into the kitchen, oddly secure in her defeat.

Anson continued, trying his best to re-establish their common ground. "I remember, or more accurately, don't remember, my benzo/beer stage of grief. Be careful with that one. It's a slippery slope not worth harming yourself over."

Kendall met his eyes, curious about his confession yet unwilling to dive deeper, knowing an actual heart-to-heart was not in her repertoire of drunk tricks. So she tried to take him at face value.

"Yeah. I know," she sighed.

Anson quickly changed the topic. "So do you have a dock out back?"

"Uh, yeah. Yes. And a boat with a lift." Kendall tried to remember if he'd mentioned owning a boat, given the proximity of his home to the ocean.

"Oh yeah? What kind?" Anson asked, genuinely interested.

"Sea Fox 236 Voyager," she answered, pride evident in her voice.

"Sweet. I only surf. No real boating skills as of yet. Maybe one day."

Once again, Kendall was struck by just how bizarre this scenario was, making small talk at her home just a week out from their FFN at his place. She watched him, confidently sitting at her counter, oozing with casual sexiness in his black sports coat and crisp, yellow button-down shirt. She couldn't picture him as a sloppy drunk, reminding her once again of how pathetic she must seem. She needed to put an end to tonight's misery.

"Did you call for a cab yet?" she asked.

"Desperate to get rid of me, I see."

"No, it's just that – this is bad. I mean, it's good you brought me home and I'm sorry about how I acted earlier. But seeing me like this for an extended period of time is just bad. Not to mention, embarrassing. I can't even talk right. Fuck." Kendall braced herself against the counter, opposite Anson, and stared at him with wonder. "I mean, it's you, in *my* kitchen now! I can't *believe* we had anal sex."

That outburst caused Anson to lower his eyes with a hint of discomfiture, but with his knowing smile ultimately emerging. Kendall slapped her hand over her mouth, bowled over by her lack of filter.

Must reengage the frontal lobe.

She slid her arms out onto the counter space in front of Anson, clunking her forehead against the Formica counter, and then covered her head with her arms. She groaned into the unsympathetic laminate material, shaking her head in disbelief.

Anson began to laugh. "That's why we have to be on good terms. I mean, who else can you blurt that out to other than the person involved?"

"Don't laugh," Kendall mumbled. "I'm mortified."

"I'm sorry, I'm sorry," Anson said, attempting to curb his enthusiasm for her enticing Freudian slip. "I'm not laughing at you. It's the whole thing. Last Friday to this Friday – never in a million years would I have pictured these nights with you."

"I'm not sure how I'm supposed to take that," Kendall said, her words still muffled.

She then straightened up, looking at him sternly. "But if you have to picture either night, just stick with the FFN, okay? We should both agree to forget tonight's catastrophe."

Anson tilted his head curiously. "F.F.N? There's a name for it?"

"I just can't seem to keep my mouth shut tonight." Kendall hung her head once more. "I mean last Friday, that's all."

"FFN. Okay. Well, you can rest assured, last Friday is still very vivid and easily trumps tonight." Kendall blushed as Anson winked at her with his blazing confidence.

Outside the house, a beeping horn ended their candid moment, both turning toward the sound.

"Well, that's my cue," Anson said, dropping his hands flat on the counter. "You can breathe easy now – I called for a ride when you fell asleep. So, I'll get the meaning behind FFN another day."

He got up from his chair and bit the edge of his bottom lip as he looked directly into Kendall's eyes. "But, if it means what I think it does, let's do it again, and soon."

BAM!

Without pause, as if he didn't just drastically change everything once again, he walked around the peninsula to her. His swagger was impressive, sending Kendall into a sensory overload: her mouth agape, brain stupefied, the crackling of misfiring neurons only heard within as her mind rushed to clear the dense fog of inebriation.

He most definitely wanted her. That he was still seeking something more with her despite every miserable moment of the night was nothing short of a miracle. And well, the flattery of it couldn't be discounted.

"I like getting to know you outside of work, Matthews, even if it involves driving your mean, drunk ass away from someone else." And with that, he gently grasped the sides of her upper arms and affectionately kissed the top of her forehead. "Get some rest. I'll come find you tomorrow."

Anson walked out, leaving Kendall dazed, her drunken stupor evaporating in an instant as the front door closed behind him. She shuffled to the front window to gawk, then went on a wild rampage, searching for her phone to call Ariel.

"Ho-ly shit. Ariel! The doctor just drove me home from a work function because my stupid ass got drunk and hooked up with another coworker. But Dr. Sex is still very much interested in pursuing something beyond last Friday. Aaah!"

Kendall tossed the phone down on the counter after leaving her message. Meticulously, she went over the night once again, trying to recall every word and look exchanged with Anson. Oddly enough, the scandalous exchange with Leo in the privacy booth seemed almost acceptable now. It had to happen. It was all part of her rebirth, one that continued to involve Dr. Anson Allaway.

Reviewing the playbook of the evening reminded her how it all began – *Courtney!* Quickly she sent her a text, letting her know she was home safe after getting a ride. The details of her driver needn't be mentioned. Then she decided to text him.

KM: **Thank you for the taking me home.**

His response was immediate.

AA: **My pleasure.**

She couldn't help but smile. There was no harm in enjoying it, engaging him a little, flirting for fun. She had often flirted with him in some form prior to her leave of absence. Now there was simply a bit more meaning behind it. *Okay! A whole hell of a lot more meaning.*

Kendall washed the night off her face and brushed her alcohol-drenched teeth before surrendering to the comforts of her bed. Her linens and pillow felt particularly cozy now, her entire body slipping deep into a peacefully secure place.

She would make it out okay. Not unscathed, but with life still left to be lived. The smoldering ashes had finally begun to cool, the transformation of Kendall nearly complete.

Chapter 18

"It's time to jump!" the pilot shouts over the blaring propeller engines as the side door of the small plane is flung open, wild winds barreling into the small cabin space.

Kendall startles. What the hell? She's in an airplane? And she's skydiving?

"What?! I don't know how to!" she shouts back, panicked as she sees a man in front of her leap out fearlessly.

"You just jump! You have to! Everyone does!" a voice shouts back – but it doesn't seem to be coming from the pilot this time.

"What do you mean? Don't you need training? Will I be attached to someone at least?" Kendall's heart races as she counts down the jumpers in front of her, knowing her time is coming up.

"No! You jump by yourself. Just pull the cord with your teeth."

This is insane. She tries to peer out the door but knows if she gets too close, they'll assume she's ready and will push her out. Are people really pulling the rip cord with their teeth? Is that how it's done? There's got to be an easier way. A safer way.

She doesn't want to die.

"You're up. JUMP!"

The pilot's standing at the door – she's the only person left to jump. But who's flying the plane? And why does she have to jump? They could just land, learn about skydiving, and then come back up and jump. She considers shouting this idea back, but she knows it's useless. The pilot is right. Everyone has to jump, and death might be a consequence (or perhaps, just a mouthful of broken teeth but a successfully pulled ripcord). Only one way to find out.

Kendall stands up, barely making it to the door as the plane bumps and shakes through the turbulence in the sky. She stands before the door, her heart in her throat, her stomach a knotted frenzy, but her mind blank.

No regrets. Just jump.

She leaps forward and free falls wildly.

And she realizes that her fate is sealed. She jumped without a parachute. She will die. Impact will come any minute, the ground just seconds away. And there's not a single thing she can do about it. Nothing.

Her body relaxes, knowing that in a few seconds all will go blank and she will cease to exist. All her concerns and connections and her entire existence will be gone. Those still alive might mourn her, but she will be done. And this is okay – because she can't change it, only how she thinks of it when it happens. And it's okay. It is okay. It is going to be okay.

Three...

Two...

One...

"Aaahh!" Kendall shrieked, wide-eyed and jerking up frantically from the carpeted floor, having just rolled off the edge of her bed. "Son-of-a!" She rubbed the arm that took the brunt of the fall.

Never before in a dream had she accepted her own death. All previous dreams involving the possibility had always had an escape clause. Or, if she did die in a dream, she knew she still existed and never really panicked. But this one had been completely different. Kendall breathed rapidly, fully grasping the reality of still being alive.

She looked around her room from her position on the floor, noting that the sunlight filtering through the blinds was significantly brighter than it should have been. For a minute, nothing registered as she watched the dust flit about in the beams of light, the room serene and forgiving.

Her mind traced back to the events of the Hibiscus Ball. And like a bolt of lightning, she jumped to attention. It was 7:00am and she should've already been at work!

Kendall quickly called the unit to let them know she was running late, then rushed through a shower. Fifteen minutes later, she sped out of her driveway, her entire collar line wet from her hair and not an ounce of makeup masking the anemic circles beneath her eyes. While driving, she chugged back another

Emergen-C concoction. At a fast food drive-thru, she applied concealer, mascara, and lip gloss and pulled her hair back into a bun. She scarfed down her breakfast sandwich the rest of the way to work.

She hated beginning her day this far behind – not to mention the guilt for letting her coworkers down. Her third day back to work, and she couldn't even be on time.

DeGraff was charge nurse, making her tardiness a whole lot easier to sweep under the rug. Of course, people asked if she went to the Hibiscus Ball and likened that to why she was late. DeGraff had graciously taken report on her patients, so the two sat down to discuss the cases. But before she hit the floor, he delved a little into the topic at hand.

"So, how'd the Ball shape up to be this year?" DeGraff asked.

"Much of the same. Food was good. Dancing and drinking. And of course, all the shenanigans that accompany that combo," Kendall answered, rolling her eyes. "Next time, don't leave Courtney hanging and desperate for a partner in crime. Yours truly is not ready for any more Friday nights."

DeGraff chuckled. "I gather Allaway ended up going then."

"What do you mean, *ended up*?" Intrigued, Kendall pulled her chair closer to DeGraff, lowering her voice. "Did he say something to you?"

"Oh to be young and carefree, my dear Ms. Matthews. All the questions that swim through our wee brains, with answers just out of reach."

"Oh please. Spare me. What did Allaway say to you about last night?"

"Nothing. But I guess something happened worth being said." His evocative tone further irritated her.

"Well, if you're not talking, I'm not talking. I have to get to work."

DeGraff stood up, his eyes toying with Kendall, but she didn't have time to think about it.

Her day picked up rapidly as she worked to make up that lost hour. By 2pm, she was just beginning to chart her morning assessments. Around that time, Alexa, the physical therapist from her table last night, walked into the unit to make her rounds.

"So, it seems like you had fun last night," Alexa said, sitting down at a computer next to Kendall and giving her that knowing look.

Kendall immediately blushed beet red. "Yeah, I need to learn to turn down a free drink."

"What happened?" Patricia piped in, overhearing the two.

"What happens at Hibiscus Ball, stays at Hibiscus Ball," Alexa said, chuckling.

Kendall rolled her eyes and looked over at Patricia, who was clearly annoyed by their inside exchange. "Nothing happened. Eating, drinking, dancing," Kendall said, glancing up at the clock. "Ooh, I didn't bring a lunch today. Is the cafeteria still open?"

"Yeah, they close at three and then reopen at five," Patricia answered begrudgingly, never looking at Kendall.

"Oh good. Would you please watch my patients for a bit so I can grab something and bring it back? I'll bring you some chocolate chip cookies." Patricia couldn't resist both the offer of cookies and Kendall's begging eyes, reluctantly agreeing with a nod.

"Can I work with Bed 6 while you're down there?" Alexa asked.

"Definitely," Kendall said. "We just got him up to the chair, so it's perfect timing. And thanks, Patti-cake! Be back in a flash."

Kendall saved her work and briefly eyeballed her patients before heading out the back exit, walking down to the basement to the cafeteria. Just as she reached for the basement door, it opened from the other side and Anson appeared in the doorframe.

Chapter 19

"Oh!" Kendall said, startled to see someone, then struggling to compose herself when her brain registered that it was him.

Anson smiled at their perfect timing.

"Hey there," Kendall said. "So, this isn't awkward at all. I'm just heading to the cafeteria." She continued to move past him, avoiding any prolonged exchanges.

"So how are you feeling? Heard you were late for work," Anson commented.

"Yeah, never set the alarm last night. Surprisingly, I feel pretty good. Better than I deserve, I suppose. Guess my special remedy still works." Kendall shrugged and moved through the doorframe as he stood there, holding the door open. Then she stopped. "So, what? Did you check in on me again?"

As soon as the question escaped her mouth, she regretted it. It all seemed too familiar now. Too comfortable. Too casual. Some things were better left a mystery, if she ever wanted to get back to simply working alongside him. The more she knew how much or little he cared, the more wrapped up in the idea of him she became.

"I've got my sources," he answered coyly.

Like a Mack truck barreling into her out of nowhere, she remembered Leo's comment about Anson in the privacy booth at the Ball. DeGraff couldn't have been the only one Anson was speaking to about her. She backed up through the door, extending their chance run-in.

"About that," Kendall said. "Have you been talking to people here at work? You know, about us last week?" Kendall directed Anson further into the bottom of the stairwell, pulling him by his wrist and dropping it promptly.

"About last Friday? No. I'm not one to kiss and tell," Anson answered, insulted.

"Well DeGraff obviously knows. And then Leo made this comment to me, clearly indicating he knew something happened between us. I didn't like what he implied at all and I'm real curious as to where he got it from." She crossed her arms, waiting for Anson to fess up. "I mean, you were at the same table, so you two must see each other at work."

"Leo's talking out of his ass," Anson said. "He doesn't like me, so he'll say anything to make me look bad. Besides, I could ask the same thing of you. Your little friend, Courtney, implied I was with you that night earlier this week in front of Glenn in MRI. I mean, this isn't a mega hospital or anything. Word travels quickly around here, especially if it carries anything with grit. So, the question is: Have *you* been talking about us?"

Irritated, both by his rebuttal and Courtney's blabbing, Kendall sharply turned to exit. His comparison was far from fair, as their personal situations – he an unapologetic bachelor, she a widow – weren't even in the same realm.

"Hey." Anson grabbed her arm before she made it to the door, Kendall whipping around with viper-like reflexes. He released his grip, submissively holding his hand up. "I don't want to do this, Kendall – feed the anger you carry around each day. We left off in a good place last night despite everything."

"Anson, it's not happening again, so just drop it already. I'm not looking to be rescued by you."

"I'm not trying to rescue you. I get it. You're numb to it all. But like I said last night, I feel I'm vested now."

"Well unvest yourself! That's the dumbest thing I've ever heard. *I'm vested*. Is that some kind of surgeon term? What the hell? I'm not some patient of yours. There must be a slew of women you can become *vested* in. Go vest with them! Go vest yourself anywhere else but here with me!" Kendall waved her hands wildly as her voice carried up the empty stairwell.

Anson, incongruously entertained by her gestures and liberal use of his term, rightfully shushed her, covering the loose lips that started this quarrel with his hand.

Defeated, she hung her head for a moment, frustrated she couldn't articulate her feelings and annoyed when he just stood there, patiently listening, like the actual human being she never thought she'd see in him.

Traffic in the stairwell was always minimal – even more so on the weekends, considering one needed a hospital badge to enter. Kendall breathed in the musty, industrialized aroma created by the rubber treading covering each step. She found it curiously soothing to her senses, reminding her of Dan's firehouse. She'd never just *hung out* in there before. With the false sense of security relaxing her, she found her voice once again.

Her honest voice.

"It's not because I'm numb," she sighed, her eyes wandering up, examining the underside of the second set of stairs, trying to muster up the courage to say what was next, knowing it was all a bit heavy for yet another stairwell encounter. "I can't let you in because… you make me feel too much already.

"I tried to block you out last night, to see if it's all wrapped up in a crazy ride of hormones, like I'd originally intended that night to be for us. But it wasn't the same. I don't know what it is. I'll admit it. I do feel something when you touch me. And honestly, I haven't stopped thinking about you since that night."

Kendall's heart threatened to burst right out of her chest as she forced herself to look at Anson directly. Before she could run away, she helplessly sank beneath the inviting, smooth surface of his Caribbean blue eyes. The calming presence, unassuming air, and undeniable attraction that she experienced with him washed over her, and she fearlessly swam in the security he willingly offered.

"You asked me to stay," she whispered, stepping in closer. "And, I wanted to. The way you touched me, held me. How we kissed." She raised her fingers up to him, patting the soft pout of his bottom lip. "I can't stop thinking of this."

"Kendall," Anson reverently whispered, surrendering to her as she raised her chin up to his.

And as if needing to answer his call, she embraced him around his neck, kissing her name off his yielding lips, the way she had fantasized doing since deserting him that Friday night.

Anson fully reciprocated, drawing her in desperately close, leaving no room between them. The fiery passion she brought to his mouth filled him down below, his loose hospital scrubs hiding nothing as he turned her around, pushing her back up against the painted cinderblock wall. He couldn't let her walk away this time. His pelvis flexed into her as he grasped the back of her head in his one hand, his other hand bracing himself against the wall, their bodies melting into one another with heated ease.

"God, I want you so badly," Anson confessed breathlessly along her neck as he drank her in, fighting back the urge to fondle her further, fearing he wouldn't be able to hold back.

"Then take me."

Anson fervently filled her mouth with his tongue, devouring her words, and then spun her body around to face the wall. She leaned against his chest as she reached back behind his head, knotting her fingers in his hair. Anson grabbed hold of her free hand and together, they slid down her uniform along her abdomen, slipping beneath the waistband of her scrub pants into her cotton panties. He pulled her in tightly with his other arm, whispering into her ear: "I want to hear you come."

He rubbed his fingers over hers, together massaging her clit, making her wet, ready, and so receptive to his advances. His tongue flicked along her earlobe, making her body tremble. Yet she stifled the desire to cry out, not wanting to make a sound.

Anson plunged further down, sliding his fingers inside her, again breathing into her ear, "Let me hear you. Don't hold back, baby."

Kendall allowed a soft moan to escape, fueling his arousal as he increased the savory technique of his massage against her. She gasped, her body climbing, desperate for the summit. He squeezed her breasts through her scrubs and pushed his erection harder against her bottom, his fingers diving deeper inside.

Their brazen run-in with its forbidden surroundings and unforgiving walls, coupled with the heady adrenaline coursing through their veins, created a state of intoxicating arousal and exhausting alarm as they risked being caught. The dual nature of it all forced Kendall to build rapidly.

She couldn't take the pressure any longer: She let go, her body quietly quivering against Anson. Her back arched as she whimpered breaths in a staccato rhythm, licking her lips through the delicious satisfaction of impulsive waves.

Anson reveled in the moment. He slowed his massage against the twitching of her muscles as he ravished her elongated neckline, drunk on her aroma. Very gradually, he slid his fingers up and out of her pants. He then craned her chin back toward his, immediately sucking on her bottom lip, indebted to her orgasmic response.

The illicit and highly erotic exchange was over in just a few minutes. Never had Kendall been so brash, abandoning all common sense to satisfy such feral instincts. Her brain came back online, firing rational thoughts at blinding speeds.

Holy shit! An orgasm in a dusty stairwell of Gold Coast General. An orgasm in a stairwell. While at work. An orgasm at work. In a hospital. An orgasm in a hospital. An orgasm. An orgasm. An orgasm.

How did one simply return to medicating and caring for patients after something like that? *The food sucks and you want more Dilaudid, even though you can't have it for another two hours? Well, I just had an orgasm some 50 feet away from your bed. Clearly, I no longer give a fuck.*

With reservation, she slowly faced him, looking up through her lashes, feeling exposed, too vulnerable for simply succumbing to a physical reaction. His hot breath rustled over her hair as he panted, despite what seemed to be minimal physical exertion on his part. He kept her locked in against the wall, feeling entirely fulfilled, the pure arousal of giving her an orgasm gratifying his own sexual desire.

"I needed that more than you know. It's a shame I have to wash my hands soon. Kinda wanted to taste that victory all day." Anson flicked out his tongue like a devilish serpent, tasting the tips of his fingers that were just inside of her.

"Gross."

He laughed, bringing her in tighter, and kissed her disapproving scowl.

Without warning, and miraculously not a minute earlier, the stairwell door bolted open as someone entered. Kendall covered her face in Anson's chest, praying she would not be recognized.

"Hel-lo!" said a man's voice, clearly surprised as the shuffling of his feet had halted upon spotting the shadowed couple.

Anson stared at the wall, shielding Kendall, and broke into his domineering surgeon role.

"Get up the stairs!" he barked.

A quick succession of footsteps followed, the man rushing up four flights before exiting the stairwell.

Anson released a suppressed laugh. "Well, if you were worried about people talking before ..."

Kendall did not share in his amusement and moved past him to head back upstairs.

"I have to get back to work," she said.

"Hey Kendall, wait a minute." He caught her arm as she stepped up the first step. "Come here."

He pulled her in close, sealing his lips against her pout. Yet, even then, she could not shake the very unwelcome feeling of post-orgasm regret.

"I dare say I enjoyed myself more than you did."

Kendall smiled weakly. "It's just that... I have to get back to work."

"There's nothing wrong happening here. I wish you could see that."

She kissed him chastely and went back upstairs.

Anson watched her until she disappeared around the corner. He walked back out into the basement, motivated more than ever to have an actual sit-down conversation with her. The only reason he'd been headed up those stairs at all was to say hello to her. And well, he managed a whole helluva lot more than that.

Chapter 20

Kendall walked back out into the unit, moving straight into her patient's room and aiming to blend in like a chameleon. But Alexa had just finished with Kendall's other patient and spotted her.

"Oh hey, so he was able to weight-bear maybe eight seconds before needing a break. We did leg exercises sitting in the chair. His torso control has improved considerably. Whenever he does get moved upstairs, we'll try to increase his sessions to twice a day."

"Great. Thanks!" Kendall answered quickly, not wanting to make eye contact on the off-chance the word *orgasm* was branded across her forehead.

Or *slut*.

She hated that word and shuddered for even thinking it. If anything, isn't that what Allaway was? Did it even matter? She wondered if that was what other female coworkers had done with him – snuck away into the shadows of the stairwell to get it on. The idea did not sit well with her.

She should have just nipped it in the bud. Or better yet, never turned that corner in the Dolphin Bar at all. Was this the chaos she wanted to follow? Being finger fucked in a hospital stairwell, losing all respect and pride for her profession? Just another naughty nurse, surrendering to the cunning ways of a stud doctor?

"Fuck," Kendall muttered under her breath, biting back tears.

"That was a quick lunch," Patricia commented, interrupting Kendall's self-flagellation by walking into the patient's room.

"Oh!" Kendall said, her thoughts evaporating instantly. "Well, yeah. I bumped into someone in the hall and chatted, so it didn't work out." She busied herself with the IV pump before remembering her promise to Patricia. "Oh shit! Cookies! I'll run down right now and get those for you. Sorry about that, Pat."

"It's no big deal. Bumped into someone? Why would that prevent you from getting food? I mean, if you need to go, then go."

"Really, I'll be fine," Kendall insisted, carrying on by grabbing a pair of gloves off the wall.

But Patricia stopped her.

"Hey, what happened?" Patricia asked, touching Kendall's neck where Anson's mouth had been leached on just minutes before. Kendall jumped back defensively.

"Nothing. I was just picking at something." Kendall immediately let her hair down, positioning it in front of her shoulders. "Bad habit, I guess."

"Sure. Whatever." And with that, Patricia left the room.

There'd been a clear disconnect between the two coworkers ever since Kendall's return from bereavement. Patricia had always been slightly cold, never the warm fuzzy friend to gush over baby pictures or become overly concerned with the plight of another. She was supportive enough, for the most part, but never outright helpful. Kendall had dismissed her stiff vibe, believing Patricia was not really comfortable in situations involving empathy, despite being a nurse. But this was now three straight shifts with her that had some level of animosity.

Not even five minutes later, Dr. Allaway entered the unit through the main entrance, carrying a plastic grocery bag. Patricia took note. Without saying anything, he looked up at the bed assignments and walked in the direction of Kendall's patients' rooms. He spotted her hanging an intravenous medication.

"Hey Matthews, I'll leave this at the desk for you," he called into her room, raising the plastic bag up.

Kendall looked back at him, perplexed. She curiously walked toward the hallway, watching as he put the bag down at the nurse's station. He strutted back through the unit doors and out into the hospital hallway.

Patricia, who was sitting at the station, glanced over at the bag and coolly commented, "Looks like you got lunch delivered."

Patricia's words instantly flipped a tension switch between them. Patricia's stare, judging her with a deep level of contempt, bore into Kendall's skull. Before Kendall even understood what Patricia was piecing together, the daggers were thrown.

"So it's true," Patricia said. "You and Allaway. And still at it, apparently. So why the hell did you go after Leo last night? Do you have a third one to swing on Sunday? Never would have guessed it, Kendall, but being a widow seems to suit you well." The words sizzled off her tongue, haughtily proud to have discovered the scarring truth about Kendall.

With the wind knocked out of her, and the sharp words slicing through like razors, Kendall froze, her jaw wide open.

What could she say to refute that? Every bit of it was true. Maybe even Sunday, considering the careless attitude she'd adopted. And now it was out there – out in the unit, free to spread across the hospital like a debilitating disease that needed to be isolated to a negative pressure room. Like a filthy venereal infection, branding her with a scarlet letter. Another hospital whore had made her name. And a widowed one at that.

Just then, DeGraff walked around the corner. Seeing the glassy look in Kendall's eyes, he could tell some sort of showdown had just taken place between her and Patricia.

"Need anything ladies?" DeGraff asked, his easy tone so clearly off key to their booming tension that it barely registered with Kendall.

"Oh I'm just fine," Patricia responded dryly. "I think Kendall, however, might be a little exhausted from all her recent extracurricular activities."

"Shut the hell up, Pat! Mind your own fucking business!" Kendall snapped.

Patricia simply raised her hand up at Kendall in disgust and returned her attention to her computer.

"Whoa, Kendall!" DeGraff said. "We're at work. That was uncalled for."

"Shut up, Mark," Kendall retorted.

"Watch it, Kendall," DeGraff reprimanded, gritting his teeth. "Drop it. You're getting a pass, now let it go and get back to work." She'd never actually pissed him off before.

She'd never done any of this before.

Kendall turned on her heel back to her patient's room, holding back the hot tears threatening just below the surface. Both she and Patricia managed to complete their shifts despite the overriding anger, hovering like a thick fog. As soon as night shift began rolling in, Kendall worked feverishly to finish up her duties, having never stopped to eat the lunch that Anson dropped off for her.

Once outside the hospital, Kendall took in a deep cleansing breath, desperate to rid herself of all the drama she had attracted within its walls. The belittling thoughts came flooding back in – just a week and a half ago, her grief had been real. She had simply been a woman struggling with the loss of her beloved husband.

"Hey Matthews, what was up with earlier?" DeGraff called out behind her.

Kendall waited, knowing her fight was not with DeGraff. It wasn't even with Patricia.

"Mark, I didn't mean to snap at you," she answered with remorse. "I mean, I did but it wasn't you. I'm realizing I'm more fucked up inside now than I was a couple months ago, and I can't seem to get myself on track. Honestly, it's not even what Pat said, although that *was* a total bitch move." She felt the anger boiling up again and inhaled deeply in a conscious effort to suppress it. "Whatever, though. It's me."

"I can see that," DeGraff said. "Shit. There's a hot-button trigger on you these days. If you need to get something off your chest, let me know, okay? I spoke with Pat, and I guess she heard some things about last night at the Ball. And it's none of my business – you are free to do whatever you want in your personal life. I just don't want this to affect your work style and relationships. You're better than that, Kendall. You're one of our best nurses and to see you fly off the handle like that – well, it's just not you."

Kendall nodded in agreement. She didn't want to be that person with the chronic chip on her shoulder, and she'd extended her FMLA to avoid that very thing. Funny enough, if she'd gone back after 12 weeks as planned, she probably would have been the weeping widow, the role people were expecting to see from her now.

"Before you even left, Pat and Leo were dating," DeGraff divulged. "Most people weren't aware, since they kept it under wraps. But when you took leave, they did live with one another for a short time. It's all petty drama and hurt feelings, but she recognizes the need to let it go as well."

"Oh man. I had no clue." Shocked, Kendall reflected on what Leo had said to her about his recent failed relationship.

"Well, you and Pat might need to talk it out at some point to smooth things over, but I'll let you take care of that. Maybe lay low until it all blows over. If you know what I mean." DeGraff shrugged his shoulders.

"Yeah. I know." With her brain wracked, Kendall bowed her head in defeat.

But with DeGraff in front of her, she suddenly wanted more information.

"Hey, so, what's Allaway's deal anyway?" she asked. "I mean, why is he pursuing me like he is? Is it all for a piece of ass? Is that his style? Like a fuck buddy? I mean, why would you say I was out of his league? Because he just likes to use women for sexual favors? Are you trying to protect me from him?"

DeGraff shifted uneasily, uncomfortable with how the conflict-resolution session had side-stepped into a provocative inquisition on Dr. Anson Allaway.

"So clearly you have some questions, and I think the most appropriate person to answer those would be the man himself," DeGraff said. "I'm just someone who happens to know both of you, not a messenger."

"He bought me lunch," Kendall sighed, holding up the plastic bag. "It's weird. Like, if he wants to use me, I'm oddly okay with that. I mean, I'm useless to anyone right now in any other way. I'm a shell of my former self, really."

She grimaced at the possibility of her latest behavior being her new reality.

"But it's a thoughtful gesture like buying me lunch that somehow destroys me further," she continued. "Like it sets me back somehow. I don't know. I'm just not ready for that kind of affection from a man."

DeGraff reached out and hugged her tightly. "Kendall, I hate seeing you like this."

"You and me both," she said. "I don't know, though. This helps. Just letting my thoughts out every now and then."

"Anytime. I'm here for you. And, if you're upfront with Allaway, he'll back down. I know he's not looking to use you. If anything, he's typically the one being used. He's definitely taken an interest in you. You two have more in common than you think, and he's probably just trying to make sure you're okay." DeGraff smiled, offering far more than Kendall ever thought possible.

"Thank you for that. Really. You two are close, aren't you?"

"He's become a good friend over the years," DeGraff said. "But you'll have to get to know him on your own, not through me. Enjoy the rest of your weekend, Kendall, and I'll see you back at the unit. If you ever need to explode again, just let me know. I can be a great sounding board."

"Thanks, DeGraff."

Kendall smiled, a plan for the evening hatching within as the choking darkness of night became ablaze with possibilities. She suddenly needed to be with the one person who unashamedly wanted to be close to her. She would get to know Anson on her own – why not do it now?

Chapter 21

Invigorated by her conversation with DeGraff, Kendall charged her Jeep up to the entrance of Anson's beachfront home unannounced – and ill prepared, as she had completely forgotten about the beautifully crafted wooden gate. For a few moments she sat, idling in the entryway drive, and debated her best move: call him, text him, hop the fence, or drive off?

Or perhaps call Ariel, as it seemed she'd lost her mind completely.

But then the gate rolled back into its pocket. She hunted for security cameras, feeling like a peeping Tom who'd been caught lurking around his property. She inched the Jeep past the coral wall and saw him standing on his front step, as if he'd been expecting her.

After swapping her nursing shoes with flip flops, Kendall approached Anson casually, the gusto with which she'd driven over now squelched. He was barefoot, wearing blue jeans and a simple gray T-shirt that hinted to the sculpted physique hidden underneath.

"Wasn't sure if you'd show. But decided to hold back and let you decide." His beautiful smile made Kendall's insides immediately tingle.

"Wait, what do you mean? You were expecting me?" she aked.

"You didn't get my note? And yet you're still here. Even better." His face lit up further, his look even more endearing. "I gather you never ate lunch."

"Oh yeah, my lunch! Let me get that."

Kendall went back to her Jeep and grabbed the bagged lunch still sitting on her passenger seat. With no time to eat earlier, she'd put the bag – containing a cold-cut sub – straight into the work refrigerator. Now, she rummaged around inside until she found a folded note.

If you feel up to it, come over for dinner tonight as well.

"I didn't see this," Kendall said. "That's thoughtful. An orgasm, bagged lunch, and a home cooked meal all in one day. What more could a girl ask for?"

"I try," he replied. "And here you are, on your own accord. Though, if it wasn't my invite, I am curious about what prompted this visit."

Anson directed Kendall through the open front door, his hand falling to her lower back as he accompanied her inside.

The house was brightly lit, a stark contrast to her previous visit, and filled with the inviting aroma of grilled steak and roasted vegetables. The large flat-screen television on the wall across from the kitchen was showing an old episode of *Star Trek: The Next Generation* – and Kendall couldn't help but feel like she'd just walked into an actual relationship with Anson.

"You're a Trekkie?" she mocked, leaving her sandals at the door before ascending the steps into his home.

"Uh, yeah. All cool people are. I gather you're not."

Moving into the kitchen, Anson grabbed a Heineken and a bottle of red wine, holding them up for Kendall to choose one. She pointed to the beer, then sat on the center barstool in front of the extended concrete counter that she'd playfully skipped her fingers across just last week. She took in the design of his home.

The same antique wood showcased outside had been woven into the interior plan. Horizontally arranged planks jutted out at various depths to break up the towering gray concrete walls, some serving as built-in shelves and others as steps for the eyes to climb. The unique design was unlike anything she'd seen before, and she found herself pleasantly surprised by his taste.

The cool color scheme, with its sterile blues and grays, sang true to a bachelor pad – and was somewhat reminiscent of an operating room. But the contrasting warmth of the wood established a welcoming presence.

His furniture mostly included black leather pieces, along with a few beige chairs and one pale blue chaise. The surrounding décor popped with color in multiple areas: the vibrant, green potted palms in oversized ceramic planters streaked with a rustic red glaze in the living room; the vertically hung vintage, honey wood surfboard above the mantelpiece of the gas fireplace; the small, netted glass fishing floats in varying sapphire blue and emerald green hues arranged on large, wooden pier pilings in one corner. It all revealed a nautical and beautifully artistic side of Dr. Allaway that Kendall had never suspected while at work.

She turned around to look at Anson, who was standing across from her behind the counter. "Wow. I honestly never pictured you as... as..." –her words failed her– "so architecturally expressive." She spread her arms out over the vast space like an orchestral conductor.

"Thank you, I think?"

"I just mean, you have an eye for design. This is really well done in here, and I'm sure it's even more impressive during the day," Kendall gushed.

"I can't take full credit for it, though. My brother's an architect. He designed the whole place. But I did approve his choices. And you know" –he raised an eyebrow at her– "you've been here before."

"Yeah," Kendall said. "But I wasn't exactly focused on the skilled design that night. Kinda got preoccupied with some other skills."

He wet his lips enticingly; her eyes flirted back as she took a sip of her beer.

"Anyway." Kendall pulled away from his undressing stare, pushing them forward. "Your taste in TV brings the whole milieu down a notch."

"Milieu? Where did you learn that big word – in nursing school? And don't knock *Star Trek* if you know what's good for you."

Kendall laughed, fiddling with her bagged sandwich on the counter.

"Here, I'll put that in the fridge for you," Anson said. "You'll have lunch ready for tomorrow."

"Thanks."

Kendall smiled – but then wondered exactly what she *was* doing here. She knew why *she* had headed over. But now, with a dinner date unfolding before her eyes, she couldn't continue on with their simple banter.

"What exactly is going on here?" she asked.

"I'm making dinner," Anson answered, admiring his perfectly cooked rib eye steaks resting on a serving platter. "You make it sound like I have some ulterior motive." He looked over his shoulder at her and winked, leaving so much to be interpreted.

Anson pulled a pan of vegetables from the oven and plated two meals, setting them on the counter in front of her. They made eye contact again, a boyish grin on his face. It was sweet and inviting.

He actually found her cynical attitude adorable. Last week she'd stormed his home, oozing with sex and seduction, taking no prisoners, his heart and hard-on captured simultaneously. Now she sat across from him in her scrubs, hair pulled back in a plain ponytail, her vibrant green eyes wide with wonder and skepticism, questioning his intentions. Yet he still enjoyed every minute of it.

Anson reached for the remote on the counter, breaking their eye contact. "Alas, there was no plan," he said. "I just hoped you'd come over for dinner. But speaking of plans, what exactly did you have in mind when you raced your sex-kitten self over here?"

"Excuse me?" she asked, taken aback by his bold use of a pet name in their rapidly evolving relationship. "Well, I did *not* plan on becoming a meat-eater tonight." She scornfully eyed the steak in front of her.

"What? You're a vegetarian? Shit! DeGraff said you weren't! I'm so sorry about that." Anson swiftly snatched the plate back as Kendall erupted in laughter.

"I'm kidding, I'm kidding!" she said, laughing. "I love steak. Moo! *Udder*-ly delicious." She pulled her plate back from him, his face drained of its prior exuberance. "I'm sorry, I couldn't resist. I guess you did your homework."

He shook his head, scolding her with his sultry eyes as he picked up each plate and brought them over to the impressive, single-slab timber dining table by the back wall of windows. Kendall hopped down from her stool, grabbed her beer, and followed him. She felt considerably more relaxed.

Anson sat at the head of the table, with Kendall next to him at the end. Shrugging her shoulders, she smiled at him affectionately and waited for him to start eating – just to make sure he wasn't harboring any grudges for her prank. He stared back at her, giving nothing away. And then he broke their silence in a most baffling manner.

"I can't," he said.

Anson got up and stormed to the kitchen, pacing like a caged tiger, until gruffly bracing himself over the sink.

She stood up from her chair and studied Anson closely. His broad shoulders rose and dropped dramatically, as if out of breath. And then he looked back at her, his stormy gaze capturing her – and every sexually-fueled hormone she possessed.

He was ready. Beyond ready.

Kendall recognized the headiness in his eyes as he honed in on her, lifting his shirt over his head and dropping it to the floor. His washboard abs, like a model out of a runway show, almost seemed airbrushed under the illumination of the kitchen lights. His body glided straight for her.

She grasped the edge of the table – the view of him, beyond fucking hot. *This* was what she'd come for, what she yearned to have again, what set her heart aflutter with a passionate burn to live beyond her grief. She remained perfectly still, holding her breath, bracing for impact.

Anson possessively grabbed hold of her waist, her body effortlessly lifted into his arms as he ravaged her sweet honey lips with shameless voracity. He sat her down onto the smooth surface of the amber stained slab, his appetite only growing as he sampled every inch along her tempting throat.

Kendall hastily removed her scrub top, pressing her pastel pink bra to his heated chest. She untied the drawstring of her pants and Anson yanked them down, along with the cotton underwear he'd explored earlier in the day. He immediately slipped his long, middle finger deep inside of her, his tongue mirroring its moves within her mouth.

She groaned in ardent acceptance of his kiss, wanting, desperately wanting more than just his fingered touch. She dug her hands into the back of his jeans, finding him bare, and gripped the flexed muscles of his tight ass.

"I want this," she whispered. "I came for this. Anson, fuck me. Please. I need it again."

Kendall's begging set a rapid pace. Anson opened his jeans, his rock-hard erection springing free, and pulled her ass to the edge of the table. Without pause, he lowered himself down onto her, penetrating her, filling her completely. He moaned earnestly, his head bowing down into her chest, lost in her once again. Her intoxicating scent, the heat of her body enveloping him, the unequivocally divine feeling of being deep inside her, flesh to flesh – it overwhelmed him.

"Sweet fuck. Christ, Kendall."

And that was exactly what she wanted from him – his unyielding desire for her, and only her.

Kendall wrapped her legs around his waist as he tilted her back, his one hand firmly planted on the table, the other holding her upright. He pulled back and with the same torturously slow pace, slipped down inside again, gyrating against her and stimulating every nerve of her highly sensitized body. He repeated the technique several times, priming her for climax, knowing the minute he kicked up the tempo, he wouldn't be able to hold back.

They licked and bit, tugged and pulled, panted and moaned, seeking that deeper connection with one another. They both fought the infinitesimal gap between their bodies, unsatisfied, as if the complete carnal consumption of the other would be the only way to feel close enough.

Anson finally picked up the pace, slamming into Kendall forcefully, thrusting harder, faster, deeper, over and over again, unrelenting in his ferocity, bringing them both to the edge of epic release.

"Oh god!" Kendall cried out. "Yes, Anson, yes!"

"Oh fuck, Kendall. I need you to come, baby. I need to hear it. Give it to me!"

Kendall was right there, her orgasm threatening to explode as she wailed with pleasure, her voice carrying high up the concrete walls, filling her with a deep sense of power. She held on seconds longer, reveling in the control she wielded over him, and wanted to hear him plead for mercy.

And he did.

"Fuck, Kendall! I need this! Let go!"

And she did.

Kendall clung to him, biting his neck as intense convulsions cascaded down her body. Anson came long and hard, suddenly pulling out mid-orgasm and icing her belly, leaving both of them breathless. Never had he burned so much for a woman, unable to control his own body's volatile response. His breathing hot and ragged, Anson sank his head onto her shoulder, further heating Kendall's glistening chest.

Together, they returned to baseline.

"Damn!" he exclaimed. "You're such a fucking tease. I love it." He sucked the curve of her collarbone and looked up at her face, meeting her eyes.

"Nope. Not a tease. Just a woman in control."

"Well, you can control me as much as you'd like. Shit." Anson gave her a quick kiss, before resting his forehead on her chest again.

Silence cradled their entwined bodies for a few moments longer, only the occasional suction sound of their sticky skin disturbing the stillness as their chests rose and fell out of harmony.

"So, uh, was I going to get a salad with all this dressing?" Kendall joked, needing a reprieve from the intimacy.

Anson sighed with a smile.

"Let's just say, the pressure's been building for one. Very. Long. Week," he answered.

He stepped back to assess the damage. She smirked coquettishly as his eyes looked to her spread legs, her bare ass sitting on his $15,000 table with a distinct ring of condensation around her. She leaned back on her forearms, her ponytail loose and messy, his cum drying in streaks down her flat abs but globbed around her bellybutton. Her eyes glimmered with wicked delight.

As if taking a photograph with a square-shaped gesture of his fingers, Anson framed her figure, committing her provocative pose to memory for future reference.

"Fucking exquisite. That's what you are." He leaned in and kissed her again.

Anson walked into the kitchen, returning with wet paper towels and his dropped shirt. He handed it all over to Kendall.

"Or I can get you the robe," he said.

"No, this is good. Thanks." She wiped herself down and slipped his shirt over her head, inhaling the enticing, smooth scent of his cologne. "Um, where's the bathroom down here?"

"I keep thinking you've been here more than just once. There's one over there on the right, near the front door. Sorry for the mess." He offered up a guilty smile. "Did you want to shower?"

"No, I'll just be a minute."

After using the bathroom and letting her hair down, Kendall returned to the table, her slender legs stretching for miles while wearing only Anson's T-shirt. He watched her take her seat once again, crossing her legs beneath her.

They sat in silence, all thoughts translated through their eyes. Kendall made the first move, reaching for one of the napkins in front of him.

But he stopped her, holding her hand.

Kendall looked straight into his captivating blue eyes, his affection for her clearly evident as his thumb stroked her knuckles. His invitation to spend the night last week danced around in her thoughts.

He was getting close. Too close.

They both began to speak.

"Sorry, you go ahead," Anson said, deferring to her with a nod.

"I was just going to say, thanks for making dinner."

She smiled nonchalantly, needing to smother the adoring atmosphere Anson had managed to orchestrate. She extended her reach beyond the cradle of his hand and retrieved a napkin, severing their prolonged touch.

Anson sensed it immediately: her resistance. She could handle the sex – unrefined and uncensored – but did not welcome the emotional attachment.

He picked up his utensils and cut into the cold, hardened steak.

Chapter 22

"Wow. That's incredible," Kendall said. "I had no idea you guys were taking on those kinds of spinal cases now. Been out of neuro too long, I suppose. But SICU has been great so, no, I don't think I'll go back. We see a ton: the general surgeries, the complicated ones, and then the overflow from trauma. I'm glad I got the chance to transfer when I did. It's opened up my eyes to a lot more, which will be key for CRNA school – whenever I do decide to go." She washed her last bite of steak down with the remainder of her beer.

"Want another one?" Anson nodded at her empty bottle.

"No, I'm good. Thanks."

Dining together hadn't felt forced for either of them. Small talk about food preferences and upcoming patient procedures naturally flowed, dominating the conversation. They'd even skimmed the surface of Kendall's conflict in the unit, following their less-than-professional stairwell entanglement.

However, all discussion and decisions regarding the borders of their new relationship had remained far offshore, cast to the wayside by Kendall's overriding fear of connecting on a more intimate level.

That was, until Anson stood up to clear the dishes, ignoring the precedent she'd set at the table.

"Kendall?" He paused over the sink, carefully planning his choice of words.

"Yeah?" She walked over to the barstools and stood opposite him, the kitchen counter maintaining a physical barrier.

"I know what I said to you last Friday, before everything happened. About not getting to know one another." He studied her face, which remained receptive, not shutting him out as he approached the forbidden topic once again. "And what I'm going to say goes completely against that. I'd like to continue this, whatever it might be – fully understanding you're not ready to make that dating 'slash' relationship leap. Just something casual. Would you be interested in that?"

She respected his candor. She feared what might evolve from their obvious chemistry if left unchecked, yet was unwilling to just walk away from him as originally planned.

"I don't mean this to be crude, but do you mean like a fuck buddy?" she asked.

"No," Anson choked out a laugh. "Not like that at all. And I don't mean to sound arrogant, but I can get one of those anywhere. I'm not interested in that." He leaned over onto the counter to close the distance between them, lowering his voice as if others might be listening in. "To say I'm attracted to you would be an understatement. To be blunt: I love having sex with you. It blows. My. Fucking. Mind. And yes, I want it as often as you're willing to give it."

An instant, blazing inferno of rushing blood burned into Kendall's cheeks.

Wow. Hot, hot, hot.

She lowered her eyes, unable to handle his scorching gaze, but he immediately took hold of her hands, prompting her to look back up at him.

"I don't want this if you're uncomfortable with it," Anson said. "You can give me clear boundaries, like remaining strictly professional at the hospital. I won't cross that line." He paused. "But when we are together, I don't want there to be this fear of intimacy. Does that make sense?"

Kendall carefully contemplated his words, impressed with his understanding of where she was coming from, but scared by it at the same time. What he was proposing was clear: A budding friendship with hot sex. Something a bit beyond fuck buddy, but shy of a couple. Somewhere in the middle – as long as she was willing to meet him there.

She took in a pensive breath.

"Let me think about it. I mean, I know that sounds ridiculous – you and I both know what I came over here for." She stood up from the counter, her hands conveniently slipping out of his. "But I seem to be a very day-by-day person lately. When I wake up tomorrow morning, I have no clue as to what I'll be feeling about this. You've seen it. It's like I have multiple personalities or something."

"Wake up here," Anson suggested, casting the baitless hook to the wind once again, hoping for anything in return.

"I can't."

"Why not? You're not working tomorrow. I have to head in first thing anyway, so I'd actually have to get some sleep at some point."

"Exactly. I mean, I'd be a distraction. And then what? I have to get up first thing on my day off to drive home? I'm not going to be some intruder hanging out here. We're not dating. It'd be stupid. It doesn't make any sense."

"You wouldn't have to head home when I leave. You'd sleep in. I'd be back probably by noon anyway. I have nothing scheduled tomorrow, just making rounds and then on-call. It's Sunday."

"Anson, listen to yourself. Now you're being ridiculous. No."

"The only ridiculous thing here is how you're reacting. I want to spend more time with you. That's all. Quit putting all this meaning into it. I live on the beach. What could be better on your day off?"

"Anson: You're outlining a full-on relationship when you *just said*, no relationship, no dating. You're out of your mind. Quit pushing me."

"I'm not asking you to move in. Jesus Christ, Kendall! I'm asking you to spend the night with the man you just fucked on his dining room table and have fucked two times before!"

Anson whipped around and jerked open his refrigerator to grab another beer, his aggravation finally boiling over.

Unfortunately, Kendall took his outburst as a cue to head out. In a flash, she was at the front door, rapidly slipping into her sandals.

"What the hell? You're leaving now?" Anson asked incredulously.

Kendall ignored him, storming out the door into the pouring rain, but stopping short of making it to her Jeep. Holding her scrubs tightly against her chest, she backed up beneath the overhang, still only wearing Anson's T-shirt.

"Fuck." She stared out at her Jeep, the distance seemingly doubling in perspective.

Anson arrived behind her at the front door and she bolted past him, marching back into the house.

"I forgot my lunch," she announced petulantly, avoiding his eyes.

"Kendall, come on. Look at yourself. At least take a minute to get dressed."

Snubbing his efforts, Kendall hustled back to the front door. In her mad rush to avoid him, she'd left a wet trail behind her through the house. Inevitably, she tripped over her flip flop, slipping on the threshold of the door and wildly falling backward, her belongings dropping to the ground. But Anson caught her before she hit the stone entryway.

"Holy shit!" Kendall hollered, clinging to his arms as he stabilized her. She quickly surveyed the damage: She herself was unscathed, but the rope thong of her flip flop had ripped from its leather base – and her ego had shattered.

"Dammit." She angrily kicked off her shoe as the downpour outside drowned out their private indoor storm, effectively silencing the tension with white noise.

Without saying a word – knowing she'd regained her footing – Anson released his grasp on her, bending over to retrieve her scattered articles, and pushed the door shut. He calmly took a seat on the entryway steps, not drawing her back into the house entirely, but inviting her to delay her departure.

Kendall slowly acquiesced and sat down next to him, maintaining a small distance but willing to be present.

He examined her broken sandal and then handed it back to her. "Kinos?"

"Yeah. I was due for another pair anyway." Her voice was weak, slightly choked up from running the gamut of emotions in such a short period of time. "I haven't been to Key West in a while. I guess I needed an excuse to go down and buy another pair."

She took the pile of scrubs from his lap, needing something to hold against her bare legs like a security blanket.

Anson put down her lunch bag and inhaled deeply through his nose. He released the air as he leaned forward, his elbows on his thighs. He rested his chin and mouth on his fists, Kendall's keys held within his grasp. She watched as he looked straight ahead at the door, wrestling with the thoughts he wanted to share.

And then he lowered his hands and began to talk.

Chapter 23

"I got engaged in med school to my college sweetheart," Anson said. "One of those long engagements that went right into my residency. I guess I kept waiting for the time to be right to start that part of my life. You know, the family side of things." Anson peeked back at her, her green eyes focused on him.

"I kept putting it off, first saying we'd get married after med school. Then after residency. Probably would have told her to wait until after my fellowship. I was fully committed to her in my mind, it wasn't a matter of cold feet or second guessing. Loved her without any doubt. We lived together.

"But her career was already underway. She taught second grade. She wanted kids and I think that might have been why I put off the wedding, thinking she wouldn't push it too hard until we did get married. I wanted a family, too, just not at that moment. Not while we were still scraping by."

The thunderous roar of rain continued just outside the door, insulating and protecting their conversation, providing a safe place for Anson to finally confide in her – giving their unstable relationship the chance to take that orbital leap to a higher level.

"In my second year of residency, she died."

Anson stared blankly ahead, as if the tragedy was being played in slow motion on an old 8mm film clip projected in front of him – a frozen, haunting memory brought back to life.

"I found her at home drowned in the bathtub."

A small gasp escaped from Kendall, fracturing the stillness surrounding them. Anson's spellbound expression relaxed somewhat as he remembered his company. He looked at her, almost through her, his eyes still visibly lost in the movie reel replay, and continued as if going over the story one more time would give him the clarity he'd been seeking all these years.

"She had epilepsy. As far as I knew, she always took her meds. She was diagnosed when she was a young teenager. She hadn't had a seizure in years, never a single one while I knew her. It wasn't until her autopsy revealed no traces of her meds – along with being nearly ten weeks pregnant – that my world really began to unravel.

"I didn't even know. I mean, she knew. She had to have known. Ten weeks and no meds and she couldn't even tell me – because I was so preoccupied with my career?

"I've never forgiven myself. I saw her that morning when I left and never made an attempt to check in. She was in the tub all day. All fucking day, ten years ago this week."

Kendall gaped at him, horrified. "Oh god. Anson. I'm so terribly sorry."

"I changed that day, the day I got the report. And not for the better. I mean, I excelled in my fellowship and my career became my life. But I shut down emotionally – almost like a self-inflicted wound, hoping out of the suffering I would heal. In one day, I lost the most important person in my life, never even knowing the two most important, life-altering decisions that she had made: stopping her *Keppra* and carrying our future."

He shook his head in disbelief, still not ready to forgive himself.

"I'm telling you this, Kendall, not so we can swap sad stories and commiserate together. But to let you know that what you feel, that out-of-control, grief-stricken panic that surges up anytime you allow yourself to picture what life could be like happy without him, that suffocating emotion – if you let it, it will kill every beautiful part of you until you are left with nothing. And when the opportunity to experience a positive connection with another person comes around, you will be left with nothing to offer. Simply a shell of your former self will remain.

"I know this because I became this. Don't do it to yourself. You're better than that. Far better than me. And maybe you need someone who knows it firsthand to tell you.

"I see you, Kendall. I get it. Don't shut down like I did."

A few tears rolled down Kendall's cheeks as she secured Anson's words to her heart.

A shell of your former self. Was it too late?

"I've never committed to a relationship since her death," Anson continued. "My connection to women has purely been physical. All business. They use me; I use them; we go our separate ways. I set it up that way on purpose.

"Until you. There's something here, Kendall, and I know you feel it, too, as much as you don't want to."

She looked at him, her eyes shining brightly beneath the entryway lights, highlighted by the tears glinting just below the surface. They sat in silence, listening to the rain beat against the door as the echoes of their tragedies reverberated off the walls of their memories.

There would be no escaping her sorrow. There was not an express lane or city detour, involving carefree sex and shielded emotions. There was only time. She would never leave the grieving room with that eureka moment of being finally free from sadness, basking in unfiltered joy. Her lens to the world would always be altered in some way.

Anson knew that, and was willing to sit with her as she found a new way to focus.

There was hope.

Kendall slid closer to him, resting her head on his bare shoulder. He pulled her in, kissing the top of her head, and again, they just listened.

"Thank you for sharing that with me," Kendall whispered.

Anson's hand released her arm and dropped down her back as she repositioned herself, angling in toward him, one leg stretching down the steps and the other bent in, resting on the open floor. She watched him with wonder, feeling herself open up to his guidance.

Kendall had never looked more beautiful to him: vulnerable and free, with the possibility of experiencing true intimacy once again on the table. She was so willing to heed his words, something no one else had been able to convince him to do for an entire decade. And in one sizzling night, she'd unintentionally made him follow. It was exactly what he'd always wanted, yet never thought he'd deserved.

And it terrified him.

He handed over her keys. "You're going to be alright, Matthews. I, on the other hand..." He shook his thoughts clear and stood up, offering his hands to help her off the floor.

Kendall searched his face as they retreated from their safe, private space and back to the unstable world beyond his doorway. Anson tried to distance himself, but her entire being called to him – her dampened hair and lightly streaked cheeks, her small frame swimming in his large T-shirt, her captivating eyes that said she needed him and only him.

He relaxed his stance and cradled her face in his hands, wiping away the path of her tears with his thumbs.

"You're beautiful," he said. "Broken and beautiful. And you will heal."

He released her and walked into the kitchen. He returned with a plastic grocery bag, placing her scrubs and lunch inside. He then took an umbrella from the entryway closet and opened the front door.

"I'll walk you to your car."

Kendall slipped off her one good Kino flip flop, holding the pair against her chest as she descended the steps, a little baffled by his calm nature as he escorted her out. Even though she had been the one to initiate her departure, she thought for sure that their night would continue together, this new summit of intimacy successfully scaled. But instead, they walked out to her Jeep to go their separate ways.

Just before opening her car door, she turned to look at him. Standing beneath his large black golf umbrella, barefoot, shirtless in his jeans, Anson's glacier blue eyes were fiercely cold in the darkness that now surrounded them.

Unsure of what had just transpired, the time from unabashed sweet devotion to platonic partner in mourning quite abrupt, Kendall questioned their status.

"Are we okay?" she asked.

"We're okay. You need to think and so do I. I'll actually be out of town for a couple weeks, starting tomorrow night. Springing that all on you right now wasn't planned." He forced a smile and opened her car door, Kendall climbing inside.

She started the Jeep still puzzled, knowing so much was left unsaid. Now he was the one holding back. She rolled down her window and shouted into the rain: "Can I ask you one more question?"

"You just did." He laughed dryly, triggering an eye roll from her. "Yes, of course." He stepped up to the window, using the umbrella like an awning over her Jeep window.

"What was her name?"

Anson's expression stiffened, then softened. "Grace. Her name was Grace."

"That's really beautiful."

He nodded, that distant look in his eyes returning.

"My husband's name is Dan. Daniel. Well, it *was* Dan. I mean, his name hasn't changed. You know what I mean."

"I do. Dan was a very lucky man. Drive safely, Kendall."

Anson walked back up to his house, went inside, and never looked back. He was counting on the next two weeks to rid him of his untimely exploration of emotion. He needed to get back to the lifestyle with which he was most familiar, convincing himself Kendall would be better off without him. He had already gone too far down the one-way road of self-destruction. She deserved better.

But Kendall drove home filled with hope. She pulled into her driveway just as the rain ceased. She wore his T-shirt for the remainder of the night, introducing the smell of another man to her bed and giving into that connection, that emotional attachment, to someone other than Dan.

Chapter 24

Stepping into the shade of The Old Key Lime House's great Seminole thatched chickee felt very much like coming home. The Lantana waterfront restaurant and bar had been a staple hangout for Station 9 as long as Kendall could remember. Long before Dan, she had been a family member of the firehouse, and she had no intention of severing that connection just yet.

As kids, Kendall and Gabriel had looked forward to the fire department's Friday night at The Old Key Lime House, held once every spring and fall. The tradition had begun following the funeral of a retired firefighter, when old colleagues decided to meet up at Old Key Lime to catch up and reminisce. After that, the station scheduled the event twice a year, whether to celebrate a life or simply to keep the bonds tight among the crew and their families. They affectionately referred to it as Family Fun Night – or FFN – an acronym with which others had taken clear liberties. She'd met Dan here and now, surrounded by those he had loved being with the most, she was saying her final goodbye to him here.

The entire set up for the celebration of Dan's life was exactly how she'd hoped it would be. Despite never really thinking they'd use the plans they'd openly discussed – sometimes at random, other times spurred on by the nature of their jobs – here she was hosting his memorial party, his funeral well behind her.

No one looked at all like they were attending a memorial service, as Dan had been very adamant that his FFN service would simply be Funeral Free Night. The signup sheet for fishing trips with Gabriel on Dan's Sea Fox was already full, with people even adding in extra lines. Upbeat music surrounded them, the soundtrack to a slideshow of family photos and candid firehouse shots that played on the projector screen typically reserved for major sporting events. People were laughing and knocking back their shots and pints – all in honor of Dan.

There was an open mic strictly reserved for upbeat memories, even roasting of Dan if appropriate. And he had specifically told Kendall that if she saw his mom or sister walking over to the microphone with red wine in hand, she'd have to tackle them to the ground, as they would surely sour the whole mood of the event.

But the crème de la crème, Dan's very clear request, probably too macabre for some but very true to his humor and love of adventure, was *The Bucket of BOAs.* A large orange sand bucket one might take to the beach was filled with mini resealable plastic bags containing small amounts of Dan's ashes. The sign in front of it read:

Dan's Bag O' Ashes
Take me with you, not to keep
But on an adventure, releasing me there.
I am gone, but do not weep
As I'm a story we want you to share.

Kendall knew there'd be a handful of people who wouldn't take a BOA, and a handful of others who would want to take a handful. She was happy she'd done it, not concerning herself with what others might have thought – like the grandparents, or the folks who were far more reserved than the two of them had ever been as a couple. It was exactly what he'd wanted. She could almost feel him wrap his arms around her from behind, whispering in her ear, *you did good, babe.*

"Barbie, these are a riot," said Gary, a long-time firefighter who'd worked alongside her dad for 25 years and been a mentor to Dan. "I want to cry and bust a gut laughing all at the same time. How the hell did you come up with this?" He squeezed Kendall's shoulder in a warm side hug.

"Thanks, Gary," Kendall said, delighted to get the exact reaction Dan had envisioned. "It was all Dan, though. He came up with this idea chatting with Gabe one night when explaining the Taj Mahal, of all things. Gabe liked the idea of having a castle built for him after he died. Dan told Gabe that he wanted to be cremated, and Gabe would have to carry him in a bucket everywhere, spreading his ashes so they could still hang out together.

"I was like, *'Where's my bucket of ashes?'* And he said, *'Fine, there can be two buckets of ashes.'* And then all of a sudden, he got real excited saying, *'No, wait! A bucket of BOAs – bags of ashes!'*

"You know how he was with making everything into an acronym," Kendall continued. "He liked the idea so much, he almost wanted to find a funeral to attend to suggest it."

Gary shook his head fondly. "Son of a gun. Well, I can tell you now, Dan's definitely going to do some traveling in his afterlife. Has he ever been to Alaska? Cause he's going next month on a cruise."

Kendall hugged Gary tightly, thrilled he was so gung-ho with the BOA mission.

The celebration went on into the night, story after story being shared with all the guests, people laughing through their tears, hugging Kendall and Gabriel, as well as Maryanne and Anna, Dan's mom and sister.

From GC General, Courtney, DeGraff, and Rachel hung off to the side, learning so much more about their coworker through this small, yet powerfully uplifting, glimpse into the life of her husband. Although they all considered themselves friends, the lines between their personal and professional lives only really crossed at social functions related to the hospital. They didn't really know Kendall, just as she didn't know them. After this celebration, they all wished they'd known Dan better.

Roger, the Station 9 captain, called for everyone's attention over the microphone.

"Hello all. I'm Roger, and I had the privilege of working with Dan for nearly ten years, the last eight as his crew captain. It's been a rough year – one of the roughest we've ever had at Station 9." Roger paused, his hardened expression quivering. "And we're all about honoring the great men and women who have made our crew what it is today. Dan was one of those men. One of the best."

Some of the crew hollered out, cheering for Dan, breaking the sadness that naturally crept up at events like this. Roger raised his beer in agreement, then cleared his throat.

"But our crew would be nothing without the amazing support of the friends and family we call our own. So in keeping with the tradition that we started, following the tragic events of 9/11, I've got five letters here, all written by Dan: one for his mom, his sister, his wife, for Gabe, and then one for all of us." Roger smiled broadly while holding up the last letter, knowing it had to be good. "So, Maryanne, Anna, Kendall, and Gabe, if you want to, come up now and get your letters."

Anna popped up from the table near the microphone and Roger handed her two letters. Gabe dashed up excitedly to grab both his and Kendall's, delivering hers promptly.

"So the way this works is, when you work for Station 9, we make you draft out your *If I Died Today* letter that can be shared with everyone. When your annual performance review comes up, you decide whether to edit what you wrote, keep it the same, or draft a whole new one, depending on what happened that year. The personal letters are optional. Dan revised this letter on his anniversary date back in February of last year. I haven't read it yet, so here it goes."

Roger opened the sealed envelope as people began to joke around, guessing about its contents.

"'Hey all!'"

"There's an exclamation point," Roger said with a smile, trying to hone in on the energy Dan must have had while writing it.

"'If you're reading this, that ain't so good for me. But as I write this, I happen to be in a fine mood as I got...'"

Roger shook his head, grinning, his tan, leathered face actually blushing as he looked back up at the crowd. "Kendall, sometimes we forget people might actually read these, but here I go:

'I happen to be in a fine mood as I got laid this morning by the most amazing woman I know, my wife, Kendall Matthews, and am happy to share it with all y'all.'"

The abrupt hootin' and hollerin,' along with boisterous applause, washed over Kendall as she turned redder than the sun setting in the March South Florida sky. Ariel jabbed Kendall in the side, laughing. Kendall shook her head, mortified, but oddly feeling a great deal of pride.

There was no denying it: they'd had a really strong marriage. She tried to think back to Dan's anniversary date, seeing if she could remember the morning sex he'd been referring to, but couldn't recall anything specific. Roger continued on, interrupting Kendall's wandering mind.

"'And if I'm not quite dead yet, I'm sure to be now after Kendall hears this.'"

Everyone laughed again, a chorus of loud whistles ringing out from a group of firemen.

"Maybe I should just stop there," Roger said, awkwardly wiping the sweat off his round face with the palm of his hand. But he managed to collect himself, and soon the crowd was getting lost in the memory of Dan.

"'I've been at Station 9 for nine years now. As far as I'm concerned, I could be here the rest of my career. I got the best crew, the best location, the best support a guy could ask for. Kendall and I had a rough year last year, and I don't think we would have made it out so much stronger today if it weren't for all of you.'"

***

Immediately, Kendall remembered the morning sex Dan had written about. They had had two miscarriages the previous year, and the emotional recovery from the second one had been far more difficult than the first. With the first one, the biological and scientific explanations of a miscarriage had helped them to rationalize their way through the grief. They knew things like that just happened sometimes. So while deeply saddened, they'd been hopeful for the future, positive they would have no problems a second time.

But their *real* first miscarriage had actually been when they were dating – Kendall had just never told Dan.

So when it happened again, she withdrew, not wanting to have sex at all. Only after some prodding had she finally told Dan about the first miscarriage. He'd tried his best to be understanding and patient with her, but became increasingly frustrated the more she'd ignored him, feeling slighted.

The night before he'd updated the letter, Dan had tried to initiate sex with Kendall again, but she'd resisted and lashed out. They'd both fallen asleep angry, with Dan starting a 48-hour shift the next day. She'd heard him get in the shower that morning and to his surprise, she walked in to join him. She had pressed her naked body tightly against his, crying into his chest. He'd held her close as the shower washed over them – and then, without any spoken words, they'd made love.

It had been overwhelming and beautiful and pure.

She remembered feeling reborn that day, as if he'd given her the strength to move forward. The morning had continued with Dan preparing for work and Kendall simply hanging out, watching him and eating a bowl of cereal on the bathroom counter in one of his T-shirts. They'd exchanged flirtatious looks back and forth, like a couple of newlyweds adjusting to the full access of one another's bodies. He had been just about to leave when he'd noticed she wasn't wearing anything under the T-shirt.

"Are you all commando right now?" he asked, dipping his head down to examine the enticing area between her legs.

Kendall teased him, laughing and waving her oversized T-shirt around, confirming her lack of panties.

Dan lifted her off the counter, Kendall squealing with pleasure. "Ohh no," Dan said. "You can't wave that around at me and not give it up."

With rapid fire, he undid his pants and bent her over the bathroom counter, where they both could watch in the mirror as he took her from behind. She giggled and groaned the whole way through, as he pounded himself into her for a quick, and very arousing, second round.

With both of them fully satisfied, he pulled out and then smacked her ass. "That'll teach ya."

But then he changed his teasing tone, and kissed her tenderly.

"I love you so much, Kendall. You are my life. You're more than anything I could ever want or need. You and I are forever. And whether we have children or not, that won't change."

"Thank you. I know. I love you, too," she said.

"I'll never get enough of you."

Dan smiled and left for work.

***

Kendall concealed her smile as she remembered the scene. Dan was right about the amazing amount of support around them. She knew this was the worst tragedy she'd probably ever have to face, but she was blessed with a loving group of people to help her along the way. She looked up as Roger, smiling through the occasional crack in his voice, finished Dan's kind words of appreciation for his crew.

"*'So that's that. I love you all. I love my wife above all. And here's to another year with you, keeping the adventure going. Dan.'*

"And then there's a *P.S.* further down," Roger added. He shook his head with laughter after reading it. "Leave it to Dan."

"*'Oh and, just for the record, I got laid twice this morning, hence being a bit late. Sorry, Captain. Duty called.'*"

The crowd roared with laughter and applause as Kendall's face plunged back into its crimson wave of embarrassment.

Even after the sun set, the memories and libations continued. Gabriel had already shared two stories, both about fishing trips he had been on with Dan, and decided to head up one more time. He began his story about the BOAs, but stumbled over his words, as the devastation of Dan's death took hold, his train of thought completely derailed.

Gabriel began to cry, immediately prompting Kendall to run up to his side. She put her arm around him and ushered him over to their mom, who'd also been headed toward the microphone as soon as she recognized Gabriel's story getting lost in translation. Everyone hushed, as the heartbreaking sound of his cries shifted the whole atmosphere.

Kendall regained her composure and grabbed the microphone.

"Hello everyone. I didn't plan on speaking tonight. Just figured I'd sit back and watch it all unfold. But, if my brother can get up here three times to address this crowd because he wanted to share the awesomeness that was Dan, then I should be able to do it at least once."

She took in a deep breath, controlling her anxiety.

"Dan loved Gabriel like his own brother. He never referred to him as his brother-in-law. They were the perfect pair. The brother neither of them ever had, and the brother each of them had always wanted.

"If Ariel told you the story of how Dan and I met, she'd say it was lust at first sight. And well, if I'm being honest, she's probably right."

A soft chuckle reverberated through the crowd. The energy slowly began to shift back.

"But the love did come, maybe fifteen minutes later, when I saw how Dan interacted with Gabe. Right then I knew: this guy was a keeper. It was his selfless nature that really captured my heart the first time I met Dan." Her voice cracked slightly. "And, well, who are we kidding? He was gorgeous."

Then, for all to enjoy, Kendall recounted the beautiful way in which she and Dan began their forever.

Chapter 25

Kendall met Dan at Station 9's spring FFN when she was a junior in college, humoring the old man and her mom by tagging along with Gabriel during her spring break. She hadn't even been aware he existed, as her father surely didn't keep her updated on the new young and available firemen.

Dan had recently transferred to the station from Miami. She first saw him while she stood on the dock with Ariel, who she had insisted come along with her to make the night less embarrassing. Most of her dad's colleagues perpetually treated her as if she were still her childhood nickname, Barbie. And Gabriel loved every minute of it, soaking in all the attention and ganging up against Kendall with the fire crew.

Dan rode up to The Old Key Lime House on an orange and black Hayabusa, smoldering in a slate gray suit and black tinted helmet. He had a light pink dress shirt underneath the jacket, with a midnight blue tie matching his Chuck Taylors. Kendall literally stopped Ariel mid-sentence to direct her attention to the parking lot and the fine specimen that had just rolled up.

"Damn! Check out this biker dude. Holy hot, Batman! Suit on a crotch rocket? I'd hit that."

"Yeah, but you'd probably have to do it with the helmet on," Ariel joked. "When he takes it off, I bet you'd want to hurl into it. It's probably more like, Holy aw-hell-nah, Batman. Joker-face. That's all I'm saying." Ariel laughed as Kendall hit her shoulder. "You'll see. Come on now, biker dude, show us whatcha got."

The two giddy college girls waited with bated breath for him to remove his helmet, needing to determine if he was the complete package or only wrapped up in pretty paper. Dan removed his helmet, leaving it on the bike, and turned, revealing only his profile. He lit a cigarette as he turned away. With his back to the docks, he smoked for a few minutes, completely unaware he was in a highly anticipated one-man show for an audience of two.

Still in the dark regarding his two admirers, he finally made his way to the side entrance. Just before heading into the bar, he turned to take one last drag of his cigarette. As he flicked it out into the parking lot, he gave them a real good look at his face.

The girls simultaneously turned to one another with excited surprise.

"Hellooo Batman!"

Dan was tall with a lean build and chiseled jaw line. His angled features were accented by a neatly trimmed chin-strap beard. His brown hair appeared thick but was kept in a close crop. He carried himself confidently, but without putting on airs.

"I told you he wasn't Joker!" Kendall said, feeling vindicated.

"You told me nothing. Should we go and find out who he's meeting here? Probably a bimbo at the bar. Or Catwoman. What do you think?"

"Oh sure, now you're interested."

"Whatever, Barbie. I want tall, dark on dark, and handsome, not tall, dark on fake 'n' bake, and handsome."

"What?! He looked naturally tan. Maybe he's got Brazilian blood. Or ooh! Cherokee! Yeah, Cherokee with a crotch rocket steed. Yum."

"Believe what you want, but his eyes were a raccoon's negative image, like he and the tanner are well acquainted."

"Oh please. You could not see that. Come on. Let's go investigate."

Kendall dragged Ariel by the arm, needing to prove her friend wrong over – what? Time in the tanner? She hoped against hope that everything about this guy would make them both drool.

As they trekked back up the docks to the restaurant deck, they overheard the jeers and shouts of the fire crew upon spotting Dan.

"Ow owww."

"Pretty boy Dan!"

"So you can dress him up and take him out!"

"Where's all that ink now?"

Turned out that the mysterious biker dude was the newest Station 9 sucker, falling for the long tradition of introducing the new guy to the fire crew families at an FFN under false pretenses.

Fortunately for Dan, he was only told he had to dress formally. Others in the past hadn't fared so well.

Dan fought his way through the crowd, laughing it off, feeling somewhat like a tool but also fully accepted by his new crew. He immediately opened up his suit jacket, loosened his necktie, and unbuttoned the top button of his dress shirt. Kendall and Ariel watched from a distance, shocked that he was one of Kendall's dad's guys – the kiss of death for a potential love interest.

"Well, we've got to meet him, don't you think?" Ariel asked. "I mean, at least get a little background information." She bumped Kendall's shoulder, waiting for her to give the go ahead.

"Let's just wait. We'll see how he acts." Kendall – who prided herself on reading people – was always wary of guys who caught her off guard, fearing they might have an edge on her somehow.

The girls headed back to their spot on the dock and enjoyed their drinks, filling each other in on the highlights of various social events at their different colleges. Kendall kept a close eye on Dan, though, not willing to completely write him off despite his unfortunate connection to her overprotective firefighter father.

And then Kendall saw something even more unexpected – Dan high fived Gabriel. The interaction between the two sold Kendall on Dan, before she was even on his radar. Dan seemed so fully engaged in whatever Gabriel had to say, whatever story he had to tell. Kendall knew this guy was the real deal, the full package, the kind of guy you'd be proud to bring home to mom and dad. And there he was, already standing next to her mom and her brother in his suit and tie.

This was no fake 'n' bake fairytale prince; he was Prince Charming in the flesh.

A short while later, Dan escaped to the docks to light another cigarette. Ariel recognized that gone-overboard look in Kendall's eye and knew she was already visualizing a montage of dating Dan, sexing Dan, marrying Dan, making baby Dans, retiring and growing old with Dan. Kendall only shied away from meeting a guy when she really wanted to meet him – and Ariel was ready to step into her much-needed role as Cupid.

"Hey there!" Ariel called out. "So you're the new fireman, eh?"

"Yeah. I'm Dan Matthews. I haven't seen you two at the station before."

He walked over to the girls with an outstretched hand, a distinct tribal tattoo peeking out from his shirt sleeve. His piercing aquamarine eyes, colored with the same palette used to create the breathtaking blues of the Florida Keys, looked directly at them, into them, into Kendall. He had a full set of kissable lips that completed the perfect picture of his face. And then when that sultry mouth smiled, lighting up those eyes, it revealed teeth so straight they could only be the handiwork of adolescent orthodontics.

Esquire, GQ, hell, even Playgirl. Their covers paled in comparison.

"Well, I'm Ariel. And this is Kendall. We don't work at the station."

Both girls shook his hand – but as Ariel hoped, Dan paused to check out Kendall, affectionately holding onto her hand for half a second longer than necessary. His touch electrified Kendall, setting a swirling kaleidoscope of butterflies into flight inside her.

"You're the captain's daughter, right?" Dan asked. "Your brother, Gabe, told me about you."

Kendall blushed, the only thing her body knew to do when her words failed her. She bowed her head, letting go of his hand and prompting Ariel to continue the conversation.

"So you're a fireman who smokes?" Ariel asked. "How ironic. Kendall's going to be a nurse. She's big into health." Ariel scowled at Dan disapprovingly as Kendall's ears heated into a fiery glow.

"Yeah, bad habit. I'm trying to quit. I don't even know why I'm smoking now. Nerves I guess. Being the new guy and all. Apparently I got off easy though, regarding the meaning of FFN. I was told Friday Formal Night."

Dan damped out the cigarette on a piling, removing the end bit of tobacco before sticking it back in the pack and tucking it away into his coat pocket.

"Oh, believe me, you did," Ariel said. "I mean, they keep it kid friendly and all, but be glad they didn't tell you it stood for Fantasy Fest Night! We've seen some pretty crazy outfits over the years, right Kendall?"

Ariel again tried to get her to open up and engage, but Kendall could barely manage a smile, her flushed face betraying her every thought of him.

"Well, I guess I should be relieved then, even if I do look a bit stuffy."

"Nonsense. You look great. What were your exact words again, Kendall? 'Holy hot? Like a Cherokee chief riding in on his gallant stallion?'"

Kendall nearly spurted out her drink, swinging at Ariel as she jumped out of reach. "I did not say that!"

Ariel laughed and skipped past both of them, making her way to the bar. "I think I need a beer now. Need anything Kendall? Dan?"

Kendall glared at the back of Ariel's head, but Ariel never turned to see her reaction. Dan looked down, shuffling in his Chucks, smiling out of embarrassment, and then looked back up at Kendall to see if she'd recovered her normal pigment yet.

Finally, she mustered up the courage to speak.

"I really didn't say that," Kendall insisted. "Ariel just gets a little crazy sometimes. She probably needs to stop drinking before she even starts. Already her mouth is out of control." Kendall smiled weakly, feeling all hope of actually getting to know this guy slip between the dock boards and drown in the water below.

"Hey, whatever. I guess if I got someone like you to notice, this whole suit and tie ended up being worth it."

Dan couldn't deny his own attraction to her and hoped she would open up a bit. Noticing she was done with her drink, he offered her the beer he had just bought.

Kendall looked up at him with an awkward smile.

"Uh, no thanks. My dad wouldn't be too happy. I'm not exactly twenty-one yet."

"Oh. Shit. Sorry," Dan said in a panic, wondering if she was even eighteen. "That was stupid of me."

"I mean, I'll be twenty-one in just over a month, so it's not a big deal. Just that my dad is the captain, and this is kind of a work thing for him."

"Yeah, you're right," Dan agreed. "I wouldn't want to get on your dad's bad side already, anyway, even if you were legal. I've only been here for a month or so. Want me to get you a soda? What were you drinking?"

"Iced tea. But I'm good. Thanks."

The two of them shifted around for a bit more, looking out at the water. Dan turned to look back toward the restaurant, catching Gabriel's eye. Gabriel bounded over to them with Ariel in tow.

"Hey Dan! Did you meet my sister? Her name is Kendall, but lots of firemen call her Barbie."

"Barbie?" Dan asked, raising an eyebrow and looking at Kendall.

She shrugged it off. "It's just a dumb nickname they gave me when I was a kid. For whatever reason, it stuck."

"It's because she looks like a Barbie doll, not a Ken doll!" Gabriel said, laughing.

"Hey, that's pretty clever. Never thought of that. I just moved here from Kendall."

"My namesake," Kendall stated matter-of-factly.

"Really? Were you born down there or did they just like the name?"

"No, that's where she was conceived!" Ariel blurted out laughing, poking Kendall's side.

"What is this? Rip on Kendall's name time?" Annoyed, Kendall crossed her arms as Gabriel and Ariel laughed together.

"Well, I like your name, Kendall Graham," Dan said. "And I'm really glad I got to meet you. I hope I get to see you again sometime soon. Real soon."

Dan smiled, looking only at Kendall. His charismatic eyes melted her swooning heart, which would have slid right through the dock boards to recapture that lost hope if it could.

Dan walked back under the chickee and Gabriel followed, patting Dan on the back once he caught up. Dan looked back at Kendall one last time, smiling, and then immersed himself in conversation.

Ariel turned to Kendall, her open mouth registering her surprise. "He is totally into you! And you, my friend, are totally smitten!"

Kendall stood there, silently watching Dan and Gabriel pal around with the guys, a smile creeping onto her face. Rolling her eyes, she said sarcastically, "Whatever, Ariel. He's so dreamy. I'm going to marry him for sure."

And she did.

Chapter 26

Kendall finished her love/lust-at-first-sight story and the audience erupted in applause, including the patrons dining at The Old Key Lime House that night who weren't even part of Dan's celebration.

Their story was like a fairytale and they had, in fact, experienced the happily ever after. Although they'd only had ten years together, they'd left nothing unsaid, with no unfinished business and no regrets. They'd lived their shared life together as vibrantly and beautifully as one could have hoped, forever memorialized in those ten years.

They were forever – having shared an infinite number of moments in a finite amount of time.

The serene calm she felt in this eureka moment prompted Kendall to step off the stage and take one bag of Dan's ashes from the bucket. She walked out onto the dock. With a string of white lights – that had weathered countless tropical storms and unexpected gusts of gale force winds – lighting the way, Kendall made it to the very spot Dan had held her hand for the first time. She opened the bag, wearing her bravest smile and allowing the tears to fall freely down her face, and released the ashes into the Intracoastal Waterway.

As the night drew to a close, the guests headed home. Kendall and Gabriel said goodbye to their mom, as Gabriel was spending the weekend with Kendall. Gabriel, Kendall, Ariel, and William, Ariel's fiancé, all strolled out to the parking lot together.

"That was great," William said. "Really couldn't have gone any better. Damn that Dan. He even knows how to upstage everyone in the afterlife."

William kissed Kendall's cheek, then encouraged Gabriel to hang out with him, knowing Ariel and Kendall would need to dawdle in their usual fashion of recapping the night's events.

"Thanks, Will," Kendall said, smiling.

"I'll catch up with you in a minute, babe." Ariel released William's hand, replaced it with Kendall's arm, and walked Kendall to her Jeep.

"I know what you're going to ask," Kendall said, giving Ariel permission to broach the subject of a certain doctor as they plodded along, arm in arm.

"Well, it's just that, it'll be two weeks tomorrow since you had dinner at his house. I haven't heard a single thing from you about him since when? The Monday after? And well, it seems like a lot of heavy emotion went down that Saturday, so I just assumed there'd be some sort of follow-up."

"I know. But I told you, after I texted him Monday to gauge where we stood, all he wrote back was that he was pretty busy and would get in touch later. That's it. He's been out of town. That's all I know. Ball's in his court."

"So, there's a court to serve in? I mean, you're open to it?"

"Ariel. I. Don't. Know. Tuesday was a full six months since Dan died. Let's just say, I'm inching forward. Talking to Allaway helped that night, even if nothing comes of it in terms of the two of us. Tonight has definitely helped. I'm looking forward to your wedding in May. I'm thinking about school again. I don't know. I'm just going to keep on keepin' on."

Ariel squeezed Kendall's arm affectionately. "You're amazing. So, did you ever smooth things over with that coworker of yours?"

"Which one?" Kendall asked, laughing lightheartedly before letting out a long sigh. "Yes, for the most part. I mean, we've been avoiding each other. Well, I've only worked with her twice since then. After going out with Leo for coffee last week to smooth things over with him, and hearing some of the shit that went down between him and Pat, I'm not surprised by it all. Only time will really give me the distance I need from the cluster I created.

"Leo's been great, however. Totally understanding and actually very helpful, regarding nurse anesthetist school. I'm feeling like I might do it. I really think I can. Actually, I know I can."

Kendall looked into her purse for her keys, then looked back up at Ariel.

"Making amends with these people, and well, avoiding alcohol for the most part has helped. I don't know, what do you think? Are there twelve steps to grieving or something?" Kendall paused. "I've even met up with Maryanne twice in the last week. Not that we had any issues. She was a great mom-in-law, but it's like, I've hit this milestone of finding closure. Weird, isn't it?"

"Not at all. I think it sounds healthy. Real healthy. You've got a different aura about you now. It's a good one. We were all a bit concerned you weren't going to make it back from wherever you were headed. I mean, I knew you would. I just... I'm really glad today came. I love you so much, Kendall."

They embraced tightly and said goodnight.

Kendall pulled her Jeep up next to Ariel as she approached the Audi where William patiently waited with Gabriel for their girl talk to be done.

"Hey, I'll let you know if he calls or anything," she yelled out through the open passenger door as Gabriel climbed into the Jeep.

"You better!"

Kendall felt lighter as she reflected along the drive home. She'd been measuring her personal growth and healing since Dan's death by the number of everyday activities she reintroduced into her new single life from her old married life. Eating normal meals had been the first one. Sex with another man had been another – a big one. Now, she had worked her way all the way up to a Station 9 FFN. The celebration was exactly what both she and Gabriel had needed in order to start a new chapter.

She quickly ascertained another activity to add to her list of healing.

"Hey Gabe. Maybe we should take the boat out tomorrow."

"Yeah, that sounds good. You think Ariel and Will want to come?"

"Good thinking. We should've thought of this when we were with them, but go ahead and call. My phone's in there."

Gabriel took Kendall's phone out of her purse and dialed.

"Hey, you want to go on the boat with us tomorrow?" Gabriel asked excitedly. There was a pause and he asked again. "Want to go on the boat tomorrow? Kendall said we can go on it."

Confused, Gabriel turned to Kendall, shrugging his shoulders.

"What? Do they not understand you? Put it on speaker."

Gabriel did and held the phone in Kendall's direction.

"Hey there. He's asking if you want to go on the boat tomorrow. I don't know why I didn't think of it when we were just with you, but if you don't have plans already, you should come over."

"Kendall? Who the hell are you with?" the voice questioned harshly.

"William?" She glanced over at the phone and then up to Gabriel. "Who'd you call?"

"I... I think it says Ariel and Will," Gabriel said, uncertain.

"It's Anson, Kendall."

Simply hearing his name made Kendall jump. She quickly snatched the phone out of Gabriel's hand and took it off speaker.

"Anson?! Oh shit. Sorry about that. That was my brother. He must have accidentally called you somehow." Kendall glanced over at Gabriel, who clearly looked apologetic. "Don't worry, Gabe. It was an accident."

"It looks like it says Ariel and Will," Gabriel said, defending his mistake.

"Oh, *Allaway*! I get it. You're right. It kinda looks like Ariel and Will. No worries, bud. Anyway. Sorry about that, Anson. He was confused by the name. I just have your name entered as *Allaway* in my phone." Kendall smiled, winking over at Gabriel, assuring him all was well. "And he's not wearing his glasses."

"What? Is he drunk or just can't read?"

Anson's uncharacteristically cruel tone angered Kendall more than the thoughtless question.

"No, asshole. But *you* sound drunk," she shot back, astounded that this was their first real interaction with one another since that intimate conversation.

"Well, I am," Anson slurred. "Thought about calling you up tonight, but you know, drunk dialing never gets you what you really want. Yet here you are, calling me. And it's a Friday night. Nice. But alas, I'm in Miami. I'll take a rain check on that boat invite or FFN or whatever you want to call it now." Despite his drunken state, he still managed to maintain his cocky composure.

"Well, you were never extended an invitation for anything in the first place, and you certainly are not welcome now!" Kendall felt all the hopeful waiting she'd been storing up for the last two weeks boiling up into a fit full of rage. "Dammit, Anson! To think I've been waiting to hear from you!" Kendall yelled, ending the call and angrily tossing her phone back into her purse.

"Asshole!" she blurted out, making Gabriel jump. "Sorry. You did nothing wrong. That was just an asshole doctor I work with. He's a jerk."

"Sorry I called the wrong number."

"No, don't worry. It's no big deal. Anywho. Okay. Let's refocus. Boating tomorrow. Lake Osborne – or are we hauling it out and going to the Intracoastal?" she asked enthusiastically, trying to harness the good vibe they had been on before the call.

"Not the ocean?"

"No. I'm not ready to take it out there. We're not doing major fishing. Just trolling along."

"Lake is fine," Gabriel settled. "You okay?"

"I'm fine. I'm fine. Lake it is. It'll be just you and me. We'll test it out, our first run, just the two of us. Then down the road, we'll invite others. We have to go over your boating schedule coming up anyway. Looks like a lot of people want to go fishing with you."

Kendall smiled, nearly convincing herself the phone call never happened.

She turned onto Sandlefoot Lane, relieved to be back at home. It wasn't long before both got comfortable, lounging around in front of the television. Gabriel reclined in the La-Z-Boy and flipped through the channels while simultaneously playing games on his phone. Kendall browsed various shoe websites on her phone, stretched out along the entire length of the couch, occasionally glancing over to the TV as a distraction from her hunt. She still needed to find a pair of heels for Ariel's wedding.

Kendall was taking screen shots to send to Ariel when a text message from Anson popped up. Before diving into the drama that quite possibly would follow by engaging him, Kendall looked up at Gabriel.

"I'm going to turn in for the night. What do you say? You should probably get going to bed, too, right?"

"I'll go to my room soon. I'll turn my phone off at 11:00," Gabriel reported, sticking to his own schedule.

"Well, that's in twenty minutes, so goodnight." Kendall pushed herself up from the couch. "Thanks for everything tonight, Gabe. I was really proud of you. Dan would have been, too."

She kissed the top of Gabriel's head and disappeared into her bedroom, closing the door behind her. There was only one way to start the new chapter in her life. She had to turn the page.

Chapter 27

Not wanting any loose ends to distract her once committing to the reading of his text message, Kendall got herself ready for bed. She repeatedly went over her argument before she heard his, as if preparing for court.

He lured you in, then up and left. He never called for two weeks. And when he did, he offended you AND your brother. He's drunk and wants to use you for your body. His baggage goes beyond ten years. He sounded kind of sexy. Wait. What? No, Kendall! No!

"Get it together!" she scolded herself. Looking in the mirror, all the hidden hope she'd been storing careened into view – she couldn't deny the disappointment in seeing his proposition fade away. She hoped he would carry a strong defense, forcing the judge to go easy on him in the end.

Kendall climbed into bed, propping her pillows up behind her, and picked up her phone from the nightstand.

AA: **I fucked up. Forgive me.**

She stared at the text, unsure how to respond – or whether she even should. This wasn't the explanation or defense she'd anticipated. She'd thought for sure there'd be a story about his time off, perhaps about business meetings and nights of reflection. But a five-word apology was all he could muster? If he was simply in Miami, and clearly able to get drunk, why hadn't he tried to reach out before?

Turn the page. Just turn the freakin' page.

KM: **Not sure what you're talking about. Your absence or being a jerk on the phone earlier?**

She waited with bated breath, and to her relief, he didn't keep her waiting long. Their responses to one another popped up in rapid fire succession.

AA: **When can I see you again?**

KM: **Are you still drunk?**

AA: **Maybe.**

KM: **Why are you in Miami?**

AA: **Business.**

KM: **Has this business been going on for two weeks?**
AA: **Yes.**
KM: **How did you fuck up?**
AA: **Another conversation for another day.**
KM: **Then how can I forgive you?**
AA: **Forgive me for being a drunk ass and leaving you hanging.**
KM: **So you're still interested in something between us?**
AA: **Definitely.**
KM: **Did you need that much time to think?**
AA: **You ask a lot of ???**
KM: **I need a lot of answers.**
AA: **Yes and no.**
KM: **Yes and no, what?**
AA: **Time to think. Thought you might need it. Did you?**
KM: **It's been helpful.**
AA: **Did you decide on anything?**
KM: **Not sure. Kind of gave up on you.**
AA: **I kinda gave up on me too. Will you consider it now?**
KM: **What am I considering exactly?**
AA: **Being with me.**
KM: **"Being" with you. What's that entail?**
AA: **All good things.**
KM: **You asking me out Dr. Allaway?**
AA: **Will that make you agree Nurse Matthews?**
KM: **Agree to what?**
AA: **BEING WITH ME!**
KM: **Shouting via text never helps.**
AA: **Are you smiling right now?**
KM: **Maybe.**
AA: **I like you. A lot.**

Kendall stopped typing. Her heart rate picked up, the stunned grin on her face stretching into a full smile.

He liked her. A lot.

Keep moving forward. Keep on keepin' on. So, he never called, never explained himself, was an asshole on the phone, and now he's drunk. Big deal! It's the anniversary of Grace's death. He sounds like you did a few weeks ago. None of it changes the black and white nature of his text message.

He likes me. A lot.

Kendall permitted the giddiness of a budding new relationship to take over.

KM: **That's me right now :)**

Kendall stared at the phone, butterflies all up in a fluttery commotion, and felt this would be a good stopping point for them until he was back in town. And sober. She waited nearly five minutes just in case he responded, then called it a night.

But in the dark of her room, a buzzing blue glow from her nightstand stirred her from her slumber some twenty minutes later.

"Hello?" Kendall answered groggily.

"My confession put you to sleep?" Anson asked, diving right back in as if there was no delay in his response.

Kendall rolled over, rubbing her eyes before responding.

"I thought we were done," she answered, yawning.

"You sound adorable right now. You in your bed?" He seemed even more intoxicated than he had earlier in the evening – though his word selection had improved significantly.

"What are you drinking?" she asked.

"Johnny and I have been talking all night," he slurred. "Well, he's sort of silent. I've been running my mouth."

Kendall giggled – the great Dr. Anson Allaway drunk off his ass. "Hope you don't have anywhere to be in the morning. How much have you had to drink exactly?"

"Don't get all responsible on me right now. Tell me something dirty. Or at least touch yourself and talk me through it. Are you wet?"

"Anson! Seriously, what's gotten into you? I hear nothing for two weeks and now this?"

"I'm a fucking mess. I had to put you out of my mind when I was with clients. But I kept thinking of you, which is why I'm where I am now. Fucking wasted. Calling wouldn't have been appropriate."

Anson struggled to string his words together amongst all his rambling thoughts. And then he began to laugh nervously.

"Oh shit. This is probably worse that I'm calling you now. Fuck. Xavier's calling back. He wants to book something next month. Where do you think we'll be in a month, huh? I'm shit tired of planning this bullshit. Help me out. What do you say?"

"I'm not following. What are you planning?" she asked.

"I don't want to plan. That's the whole fucking point. Let's plan on dating. I only want sex with you anyway. Kendall, I like you. *I like you a lot,*" he said, repeating the last line from his text like the goofy Lloyd Christmas from *Dumb and Dumber.*

"Was that an impression? Anson, this is all very entertaining, but you're not exactly making sense. How 'bout we talk tomorrow when you're thinking more clearly? Then we can talk about dating and whatnot."

The Lloyd Christmas impression was a real buzz kill, souring the entire meaning behind the sweet sentiment in his text. Her swooning butterfly cloud promptly dissolved. The text message version of drunk Anson had been far easier to digest.

"So you're telling me there's a chance!"

"Are you watching the movie right now?" she asked, slighted.

"Okay. Okay. I'm focused. Shit faced, but focused. So tell me before you hang up. Seriously. Would you consider dating me?"

His pathetic attempt to enunciate each word with purpose forced her to just give in, needing to put him out of his misery.

"Okay, I'm game."

"Sweet. G'night, Kendall."

"Night, Anson."

She hung up, her forehead wrinkled. She wasn't looking for a rowdy prepubescent boy. But if alcohol was a truth serum, he definitely liked her. The approach, however, wasn't exactly a turn on. He did keep her on her toes, though. She'd give him that.

With the verdict still out, the resounding chatter of her thoughts dissipated and Kendall fell back asleep. Her typical dream sequence – where she subconsciously worked through the chaos within – was strangely absent that night, the established pathway between her worrying mind and creative force frayed as her subconscious took a reprieve from reality.

Reality would all be there when she awoke – life carrying on, finding its way.

Chapter 28

Midmorning, Gabriel and Kendall pushed off her dock to head north below the Lantana bridge and into the larger body of Lake Osborne. The weather was perfect for cruising around – partly cloudy but no threat of rain, with highs in the low 80s forecasted for the day.

Gabriel had set up some of Dan's fishing gear that had been stored away in the boat shed for far too long. Kendall delighted in Gabriel's knowledge of it all. Gabriel focused intently on his hook knots as Kendall savored the moment.

She needed this. They needed this.

She hadn't heard from Anson yet and expected it'd be a while before she did, assuming his head was hurting something fierce that morning. But the new turn she'd embarked on did have her thinking about something else. Dating someone new, she realized, would most definitely affect Gabriel as well.

"Hey Gabe," Kendall shouted into the wind over the engine. "Gabriel!"

He looked up from the bow and put his pole down, walking over to her in the captain's seat.

"Yeah?"

"I want to talk to you about something."

"Uh oh. What'd I do now?" he asked.

"No. Come on. I want to talk to you about me, you know, now that I'm by myself."

Kendall looked at him and then straight ahead. She hoped he'd be receptive to an adult conversation rather than making light of everything, in his typical joking fashion, as younger brothers often do.

"I don't want to talk about Dan being dead," he objected, right off the bat.

"No. I don't either. I'm talking about me being alive."

Gabriel looked at her quizzically.

"I'm talking about the fact that I was married, very happily, and now I'm not... married. Do you get what I'm saying?" she asked.

"I know you're not married now. Well, you sort of are... Wait. Are you still married?"

"Well, I didn't get divorced or anything. But since Dan's gone, I'm no longer married. Like from a legal point of view, I'm free to marry again if I wanted to."

"Are you going to get married again?"

"Oh, I don't know. Maybe one day, way down the road or something. I don't know... I don't know," her voice trailed off. She'd never really thought about it, even from a pragmatic viewpoint. It simply hadn't crossed her mind.

But dating...

"What I wanted to talk to you about is dating," she said, regaining her train of thought as she slowed the speed of the boat, finding a perfect spot to anchor for a while so Gabriel could cast his line. "What do you think about me dating again?"

"I don't care."

"You're not going to get off that easy. Seriously, Gabriel: If I were to date again, how would you personally feel about that? Like do you think I have to wait a certain amount of time before I can date a guy?"

"Do you want to get a boyfriend?" he asked.

"I guess I do, one day. But I'm talking more like just going out on dates. Nothing serious. Spending time with someone. What do you think about that?"

"I don't know."

"Would you be mad if I dated a guy?" she asked.

"No."

"Okay, so that wouldn't bother you?"

"No."

"Really?"

Her doubt further irritated him. "Really, Ken-dall!"

"Okay." She backed off, the separation of her name's syllables always a tell-tale sign that she was getting on his last nerve. "I just want you to know that I might start dating someone. But don't go and tell mom about it. I'm just thinking about it right now. And I want you to know and to be okay with it."

"Who do you want to date?" he asked, now a bit suspicious.

"Maybe a guy I work with. Maybe," she answered, looking out over Lake Osborne. Several jet skis zipped by and she contemplated jumping on the back of one to escape Gabriel's curious gaze. It turns out that she was the one unprepared for an actual adult conversation.

"The doctor on the phone? Alltheway? The asshole? You like him?"

She darted her eyes back at him, never giving him enough credit for picking up on the subtle cues of socializing.

"What? Are you like Sherlock Holmes or something? It's Allaway," she corrected.

"You said his name at mom's house before when you were on the phone with Ariel," Gabriel said. "It's good if he's a doctor. You're a nurse. It's a good match." Then he laughed, poking Kendall's side before returning to his fishing pole at the bow. "But I don't think you'll date long if he's an asshole!"

Kendall stood there, flabbergasted by Gabriel's bold assessment of her romantic life. Clearly the only person on this boat losing sanity over whether or not she should explore the world beyond mourning was her.

By midafternoon, after catching nothing, eating their lunch, and touring the lake for a while, Kendall steered the boat back to her canal dock. She and Gabriel secured it against the lift and raised it from the water.

"Hey, not bad for the two of us, wouldn't you say?" Kendall asked, bumping Gabriel's shoulder and feeling quite accomplished, as this was always Dan's area of expertise.

"Yeah, not so bad for a girl."

"Whatever."

The two carried their supplies back up to the boat shed and then headed into the house, a renewed sense of their sibling bond firmly taking hold.

Their night unfolded in typical fashion, though the first time in quite a while that it was just the two of them. They dined on Publix deli subs and macaroni salad while playing Scrabble at the table, the TV tuned into the evening news but serving as mere background noise.

Kendall's phone began to ring on the kitchen counter and she sprang up to see who it could be, the thought of Anson calling occupying the forefront of her brain all day — and breaking down the fine fibers of her patience. Had their conversation last night even occurred, if Johnny Walker was the ventriloquist?

But it was Elena, their mom.

"Hey Mom."

Kendall gestured to Gabriel to see if he wanted to talk with her. He shook his head no. For a few minutes, she listened to Elena ramble on before she had to answer a question.

"We're eating and playing Scrabble," Kendall said. "Went out on the boat today. It was good. Got some sun."

Gabriel methodically placed each of his letter tiles down, spelling out the word *FROG*. He added up his points and immediately tapped his watch, growing impatient with Kendall's inattention to the game.

"Okay Mom. I gotta go. Gabe is giving me a look because it's my turn. Here, talk to him for a bit."

Kendall teased Gabriel silently as she handed him the phone, a mimed battle of who had to talk to mom erupting between them. Finally, Gabriel caved.

Kendall found a spot for her word – *HEART* – and walked into the kitchen to grab another glass of iced tea. Gabriel told their mom about his failed fishing attempts, blaming Kendall and her lack of knowledge on where to anchor the boat.

"Wait Mom. I think someone else is calling," Gabriel said, looking at the phone screen. "It's the doctor Kendall is dating."

Kendall's eyes bugged out of her head as she jumped into a frenzy of action. "Give that to me!"

Gabriel just laughed, backing up and away from Kendall, holding the phone hostage on the other side of the table. Kendall could hear her mom asking what was going on, having no clue what Gabriel meant but clearly recognizing the bickering – nothing out of the norm for the two siblings.

"Mom! Tell him to give me *my* phone!" Kendall shouted over the table.

"Bye mom! Gotta go!" Gabriel said, laughing – and managing to accept the incoming call while continuing his game of keep-away. "Kendall's phone," he answered, eager to hear a response from the *asshole* doctor.

"Hello?" Anson responded hesitantly.

"What's up doc?" Gabriel joked. Kendall pummeled him against the wall, forcing the phone from his grip.

"Dammit Gabriel!" she shouted.

Kendall looked down at a near invisible abrasion on her arm from knocking into the dining room chair as she leapt onto him. Gabriel just beamed with pride. Kendall rolled her eyes as she walked away, trying to suppress a smile.

"Hello?" Kendall barked, still caught up in the wave of aggravated energy. "Mom?"

"No. No, I'm pretty sure I'm not your mom," Anson answered, amused yet sufficiently bemused.

"Oh god. I thought maybe he was messing with me. My flippin' brother thinks he's so funny," Kendall said, her voice also directed at Gabriel. He shrugged her off, continuing to fix the tiles on the game board that got shuffled around in the scuffle.

"So, hey there Anson. How's your head this fine Saturday?" Kendall asked, restarting the conversation, her voice overtly cheery.

She realized she was a lot more relaxed knowing Gabriel was there with her. The phone call could actually serve as a litmus test, considering Anson sounded sober. She'd never dated anyone without them first meeting her brother. He'd always been her barometer of sorts. And here she'd been sneaking around with Anson, considering taking it a step further into actual dating, when he still knew nothing about the true man in her life: Gabriel.

"How old is your brother?" Anson asked.

"He'll be thirty, in what is it, just over two weeks? April 15th. Oh man, that's coming up quick. Gabe, what are we doing for your birthday?"

Gabriel shook his head.

"That's just over three weeks away," Anson corrected her.

"Oh good. We've got a little more time. So tell me, how are you feeling today?"

"Wait, I'm not done figuring out the start of my phone call," Anson said playfully. "So, is he older than you?"

Kendall laughed. "Are you trying to figure out my age, or why Gabe and I sound like a couple of teenagers? How old do you think I am?"

"Ooh, dangerous territory," Anson answered.

"Oh please. I'm not old enough to want to hide my age yet. That's for people your age."

"Ouch. How old do you think I am?"

"I asked you first," Kendall countered, a silly smile spreading across her face.

"Fine. So let's see – your brother will be thirty. You two sound close, so I'm guessing close in age. You act a bit bossy, so I–"

"What?!"

Anson laughed. "Do you want my guess or not?"

"Okay, continue with your bogus process."

"So, bossy sister could go both ways," Anson continued. "Either you're older and naturally took on the bossy role, or you're just a little bit younger and never wanted to be bossed around, so you adopted the bossy role."

"Come on already. What's your guess?"

"Well, before I knew your brother's age I was leaning towards 26, 27. But maybe you're actually 28, 29?"

"Really? You thought maybe 26?"

"I can't guess any woman's age younger than me. You all look young. Honestly, my first thought when taking you home that night was not even 25. Then I actually thought about it, because you've been at General for a while now, right? And you were married, so I added a few years. So, how close am I?"

"You were thinking a couple years out of college?" Kendall asked, struggling to get past his very first impression of her.

"I don't know what I thought. I mean, nursing school is two years, right? It made sense."

"I have my bachelor's degree, thank you very much. And you are a terrible guesser. I am older than my brother. Not by much, but I'll be 32 this year."

"Really? When? I definitely didn't think over thirty," he said.

"May first."

"May Day."

"Yeah, no one celebrates that around here, old man," she teased.

"Okay, okay. Then what's your guess for me?" Anson challenged, entertained by their talk.

"I dunno, figured over the hill."

"Whoa! Really? Damn." The zest in his tone immediately depleted, his vanity bruised.

"I'm kidding! I already knew your age. You'll be 37 on 7/11."

"You really do your homework, don't you?"

"I've known that for a while. First of all, you need to know nurses always know more than you. You also mentioned it once a couple years ago, when someone was reading horoscopes at the nurse's station. And, 7/11 is pretty easy to remember. But above all, I'm just awesome like that."

Anson laughed. In the meantime, her brother grew impatient.

"Are you going to play at all anymore?" Gabriel asked with a huff.

"My brother's giving me dirty looks. We're playing Scrabble."

Kendall got up from the couch and walked back to the dining table, putting her arm around Gabriel's shoulder.

"And the only reason he's winning is because he got the word *pizzas* on a double letter, triple word. So, I need to get my act together and come up with a new strategy. Can I call you a little bit later tonight? Are you still in Miami?"

"Yeah, sure." Anson paused. "Is he in from out of town?"

"Gabriel? He's staying the weekend with me. He lives in South Beach with my mom. But every couple of months or so he comes and stays with me. It'd been a while." Kendall smiled at Gabriel affectionately. "Too long really."

"Oh. So you're really close. I see my brothers maybe once a year. I'd say we consider ourselves close, but we're scattered across the country."

"How many do you have?" she asked.

"Two brothers. Three boys in the family. I'm the youngest."

"Now I'm getting the evil eye from him because I'm not wrapping this conversation up."

"Okay. So, yeah. Just call me when you're done." Anson's hesitation was clearly rooted in piecing together the puzzle of Kendall's brother.

"Okay," she said. "Sounds good. Talk to you later then."

Kendall ended the call, but quickly typed up a text to Anson before putting her phone down.

KM: **Gabe has Down syndrome. Just an FYI. :)**

Kendall began putting down the tiles for a new word when her phone rang again.

"Goodness!" Gabriel groaned.

"Oh crap. It's Mom again," Kendall said, quickly answering the call. "I'm sorry! It was all just crazy and I forgot to call you back."

"What were you two going on about?" Elena asked.

"Nothing. It was nothing. Someone else beeped in and Gabe ended the call with you and picked it up with them. No big deal."

"Gabe said something about you dating someone?" The intrigue in Elena's voice immediately caused Kendall to blush, having hoped her mom hadn't caught anything Gabriel had been spouting off.

"No. No. Gabe misspoke. It was no one. I'm not dating anyone." Kendall reached out and punched Gabriel in the shoulder, giving him a snide look.

"Well, okay. I'll let you two go. But Kendall, know this: When you're ready, that's when it's the right time. So any time you're ready to date, whether you were ready last month or whether you're ready next year, that's the time that's right for you. Okay? It doesn't matter what anyone else thinks. It's only when you are ready."

"Thanks, Mom. We'll see you in the morning."

"Okay. Goodnight dear. Love you."

"Love you, too." Kendall put her phone down, looking at it for a second.

It was one thing to have the love of friends and family, cheering her on as a constant stream of support. It was an entirely new feeling to realize that they'd been carrying her that whole time. Now, finally, they were all holding the door open, patiently waiting for her to take her first real step all on her own.

Chapter 29

After losing to Gabriel in their game of Scrabble and then triumphantly winning their rematch, Kendall retired to her room for the evening. She returned Anson's call without hammering through another round of pre-conversation analysis.

"Hey," Anson answered demurely.

"Hi there. Everything alright?" she asked.

"Yeah. Well no, not exactly," Anson said, drawing in a long breath. "Last night you called me an asshole, and I didn't think much of it because, well, I was drunk, and you know how that goes – you're not exactly thinking clearly. You could have – and probably should have – called me a lot worse. I owe you and your brother an apology.

"Frankly, I'm embarrassed by it all," he continued. "I've read over our texts from last night, trying to see what else I may have said. It looks like you forgave me pretty quickly, but I'm very sorry, Kendall, for offending you. Especially if I offended your brother.

"I don't remember any of our conversation later on, though. I see I called you pretty late and we must have talked, unless I left you a long rambling voicemail. But I do think we talked."

Kendall heard a heavy sigh, as Anson wrestled with the memories of his drunken behavior.

"I knew you were drunk. I mean, it doesn't exactly make it okay that you questioned whether Gabe was drunk or just couldn't read, but–"

"Aw fuck," Anson said, full of regret. "Is that what I said? I knew it was something like that. Shit. I'm really sorry."

"You didn't know. Now you do. And perhaps it'll make you think twice before unintentionally insulting anyone, whether you think they can handle it or not."

Anson paused, unsure how to proceed, so Kendall kept the conversation moving forward. "So, if you read over the texts, you at least knew what direction our phone conversation started out in, right?"

He let out a soft chuckle. “Yeah. I’m guessing I was pretty forward. So, what? Did I propose?”

“Yes, but I had to agree to a prenup first. Apparently you’ll get sexual alimony from me if we divorce.”

He laughed again, cathartically, and then let out another long sigh. “Alright, give it to me. Recap the conversation. But be gentle. I’m not sure how much more I can take at this point.”

“Okay, so you gave me your best Lloyd Christmas impression, which kind of took away the sweet sentiment of your text message, knowing the voice behind it. Then you made it clear, once again, that you like sex with me. And you want more of it. And your solution to get more is by dating me. So, you asked me to date you. And that about sums it up.”

“Oh god. Please say you said no to such a raging buffoon,” he groaned.

“Well, I suggested talking today when you were sober, but you were very persistent, worried about something an Xavier had planned for next month or something, and somehow my agreeing would save you some grief. So, I said I was game.”

“Wait – what?”

“I’m game to dating,” Kendall said, smiling and feeling just as surprised by her answer as Anson seemed to be.

“No, about Xavier. What did I say about him?” he asked.

“Oh. I guess he was calling you? You didn’t say anything about him, just that you were sick of planning things with him. You mentioned clients at one point. Does Xavier set up client meetings for you? Do you have to fish around for referrals so people can come up to GC General for surgery?”

“What? No. No. It doesn’t matter,” Anson stuttered, distracted, hoping to get past this portion of their conversation. “Kendall, can you do me a favor? Forget everything from last night. That was way out of my norm. I was in a bad place. Before I knew it, I’d finished nearly two bottles of scotch. I am paying for it today, dearly.

“But I’d like to start over with you. Let’s just make this the first call since we had dinner at my house. I’m sorry I went underground for a bit. Those were two weeks off that were already planned. I tend to escape around the anniversary of her death. I don't share this side of me with anyone, and I'm sorry it all came to a head the way it did."

"Oh. Wow. Of course. I appreciate your honesty. I know a thing or two about needing a pass."

"Thank you," he said with relief. "So, I'll be back in town tomorrow afternoon and at work Monday. Would you like to get together this week?"

"I picked up Monday and then I'll be working Thursday, Friday, Saturday, Sunday."

"Ooh, four in a row taking up the whole weekend. So I could probably see you during the week while at work."

"Okay. But, uh, it's probably better for me that you don't come around the unit just to say hello. Like, no sneaking around any stairwells while I'm in them."

Anson smiled broadly. "You have to admit, though, that was pretty fun, right? Wouldn't mind trying it again."

"Well, sure, if you want this to be like high schoolers behind the bleachers... Is that what you're hoping for?"

"No. I'm just teasing. I get it. I won't corner you or purposely hunt you down when we're both on the clock. My dining table works better than the stairwell anyway," Anson said, laughing, unaware of Kendall's uneasiness with their shift from potential dating to booty call, once again. "But if my schedule permits, on one of your days off during the week, can we plan on meeting up? For dinner, or something."

"Or something," she repeated.

"Not okay?"

"Well, yeah. I mean, we'll figure it out, I guess," Kendall agreed reluctantly.

There was an uncomfortable pause, something they really hadn't experienced with one another before. Kendall wondered whether this was all too forced, the chemistry solely being wrapped up in their physical attraction to one another.

"Well, I'm still nursing this hangover," Anson offered up, hoping to fill the void and end the call.

"Doctoring it," Kendall quipped.

Another pause.

"Oh, right. Doctoring it," he said, catching on a moment too late. "Should have had your nursing concoction." His comment just fed the awkward air that had snuffed every last spark in their conversation.

"Well... okay then. I'll see you Monday perhaps," Kendall said, seconding the motion to bail, feeling it could only get worse.

"K." *Click.*

Kendall shuddered, glaring at her phone screen. She was wholeheartedly turned off by his abysmal goodbye. Some serious resuscitation would be needed between them during the next meet-up – if it even happened this week. And suddenly, she was no longer sure she wanted to devote the energy to all of this. Perhaps this was the conversation they'd both needed to simply move on.

Anson, however, wasn't ready to give up, calling back a short while later.

"Yes?" she answered, her mouthful of toothpaste garbling her speech. She wasn't about to put her bedtime routine on hold for him.

"Brushing your teeth?" he asked.

She spit into her sink before giving him a clearer "yes" and then picked right back up with the brushing. She welcomed his interruption to her mourning, but her oral hygiene? No thank you.

"Okay. I'm done." She made no attempt to hide her over-it tone as she crawled into bed, wondering how the conversation would continue to crash and burn.

"I'll admit, I blew it," he announced. "Clearly, I am horrible over the phone with you. We should do this in person. What are you doing tomorrow?"

"What?"

"What kind of plans do you have for tomorrow?"

"I'll be with my mom and brother."

"All day?"

"Well, for a good part of the day. I'm taking Gabe back down to South Beach in the morning, where we'll meet my mom for brunch. Then, I'll head back home early afternoon, since I have to work Monday."

"Perfect. Maybe I can hitch a ride with you back to Delray Beach?"

"You don't have your car?"

"Nope."

"For two weeks you've been without a car?"

"Driver and a Town Car."

"A driver with a Town Car?"

"That's what I said. Are you angry with me?" he asked, his cocky yet playful tone placating her sardonic one, and she backed down. A bit.

"What?" Kendall asked caught off guard. "No. A little. I mean, I don't know. Gaah. Why am I like this? Really, I'm just feeling a bit uneasy with this evolving arrangement. No matter how you sugar coat it, or whether I think I could handle it, I know I'm not interested in maintaining a friends-with-benefits relationship with you."

Kendall knew turning him away once they were within arm's reach carried a level of willpower she simply did not possess. Nipping the whole arrangement in the bud over the phone was her only hope of expressing her thoughts without creaming her pants first.

"And you suck over the phone, because you don't have your god-bod to back up your mouth," Kendall spouted.

"My what?" Anson asked, laughing. "Okay, so obviously you're second guessing me, and with good reason. I'm not looking for friends with benefits either. I honestly believe there's something here, Kendall, and it's not just the sex – despite my blatant emphasis on the physical. I know that's how it started, but I would really like to spend more time with you."

"Anson, I got that impression the last time I saw you. But everything since then has shown me otherwise. If you're out of town and we can't even talk, then clearly the only thing connecting us is that physical reaction when we're together. And the whole manner of our last call… I don't know, maybe we should just leave it, since it's been two weeks anyway."

"No, hear me out," Anson said, fully committed to turning the conversation around. "Let me make it up to you. Let me prove you wrong. Tomorrow, let's drive back together. If the vibe is as awkward as that last call, then fine, you're right. I'm an asshole who can't see beyond sex. But if there's a spark, let me take you out this week. On a date. In public. I'll pick you up, drop you off, and won't even expect a goodnight kiss."

And there it was, the one little flit of a butterfly wing. Kendall turned off her bedside lamp and snuggled into her pillow, letting his suggestion sink in.

"Well, maybe a kiss," he clarified, their smiles unknowingly shared.

There was a short pause as he waited for her response, his patience wearing thin. "You're killing me here, Kendall. What do you think?"

"I'd like that," she timidly responded.

She liked hearing his voice this way: softly in her ear, while cozy in her bed. Everything felt hushed by the stillness that accompanies the first moments of total darkness – until particles of light filter through, restoring the senses once again.

"You sound irresistible right now," he said, their thoughts now aligned.

"You said that last night on the phone. Well, actually, you said *adorable*."

"At least I was making some sort of sense. Give me a call tomorrow when you're through with brunch. Sound good?"

He was no longer the Dr. Allaway she was accustomed to hearing over the phone. This was bedroom Anson. Stairwell Anson. Sitting on a front step, pouring his heart out, melting her insides, Anson.

"Okay," she agreed. "Sounds good. Thanks for calling back."

"Thanks for answering."

The charming factor skyrocketed dramatically as they both grinned, shying behind the silence that no longer carried that unwelcome vibe.

"Goodnight, Anson."

"Goodnight, Kendall."

Chapter 30

Just after 8am, Kendall practically forced Gabriel into the Jeep so they could head down to South Beach to meet their mom. Sunday brunch at their favorite breakfast spot along Lincoln Road had been a fairly regular routine ever since the death of Elena's husband and her move back to South Beach with Gabriel. Kendall and Dan used to make it down a few times a year, but since Dan's death, Kendall had only missed it a handful of times, keeping up with the tradition in order to bring some semblance of order to her bereavement.

Today's brunch, however, couldn't get started or finished fast enough.

"We never go this early," Gabriel protested, still bitter that Kendall had rushed him through eating his regular pre-brunch bowl of cereal.

"I told you, I have things to do and I can't be spending all day down south when I have to work tomorrow. It's no big deal if we eat brunch around ten instead of eleven. Sometimes you just have to roll with the punches."

Gabriel pulled out his phone, ignoring her reasoning, and settled deep into his world of Minecraft for the duration of the drive.

They arrived at their mom's condo building in the Art Deco District a little over an hour later. After parking and dropping off Gabriel's bag, they walked the two blocks to Lincoln Road with Elena.

"Don't feel obligated to stay for brunch if you need to get back," Elena offered, after listening to Gabriel go on about Kendall being in such a hurry that morning.

"No, Mom, I'm fine. I want to eat. It's just that I don't want to get started too late and turn it into one of our typical lazy Sundays. It's too hard for me to pick up and head back home then."

"I understand. Well, I'm guessing you won't be making it down as often anyway, now that you're back at work. What's your schedule looking like?" she asked.

"The next couple of weekends I'll be working. But I'll be down again after that I'm sure. I know I'm off obviously for Gabriel's party and then Ariel's wedding, since I already got the requests approved. But I'm not sure what my schedule is outside of that. I told them to schedule me where they need me, since I have no other major commitments right now. Plus, I'm picking up shifts here and there."

"That was thoughtful of you. Well, any time you need to head out, don't hesitate, alright?" Elena smiled at Kendall as they crossed the street to their usual spot. The host of the restaurant warmly greeted them from afar, as Gabriel and Elena were well known among the locals.

The weather couldn't have been any more picturesque. South Beach was showcasing the best of her assets as the three dined on their usual breakfast choices out on the restaurant's sidewalk veranda.

While drinking her mimosa, Kendall slowly began to update her mom on the personal growth she'd experienced over the last few weeks.

"This is my first sip of alcohol in quite a while. At least for me," Kendall said, examining the delicate champagne flute like it was some kind of anomaly.

"Oh? Any particular reason?" Elena asked, gently encouraging her to delve a little deeper.

"Well, yeah. I was drinking too much. I mean, not all day or anything, but definitely too much at night. Like a crutch to put me to sleep. It had to stop. So, I just stopped buying wine. And so far, I've found I actually sleep better without it."

"That seems like a keen insight to have. Not too many people would try and change that on their own if they don't feel it's like an addiction. Good for you."

"It wasn't all me. A friend pointed it out, too. I mean, he didn't say I was drinking too much; he just said to watch out for it. And I knew it already. But sometimes you need to hear it from someone else, you know?"

"Sure." Elena took another bite of her omelet, not wanting to pressure her daughter into opening up too much – although she clearly hung on every word Kendall divulged.

"It's been a good couple of weeks, oddly enough. Well, there was this drama at work I had to deal with and everything, but somehow that was okay, too."

"You really looked good on Friday, love. Strong. Like you've found a way to alleviate some of your sadness."

Kendall looked down at her plate, knowing that kind of sincerity from her mom always choked her up if she maintained their eye contact.

"Ariel said I had a good aura," Kendall laughed, validating her mom's conclusion.

"Yes, you did. And you still do. The vibrancy of it seems to be back. No more muted colors. You have a glow.

"Kendall, I've been worried about you. You know me: I worry. But I didn't want to push you, knowing some things just need to run their course. And you're just like your dad when it comes to taking advice, so no matter what I wanted to suggest, I knew it would only make you resist me harder."

"I haven't been resisting you." Kendall looked up at her mom. "Have I?"

"Well, maybe not resisting. But definitely not revealing. I know some things have changed for you recently. I'm not talking months ago; I'm talking the last month. A mother knows. And maybe you don't share it because you're not really sure what's going on yourself. Or maybe you're worried that I would disapprove. I'm not sure. But whatever has changed, it's helped you. I'm really proud of you, Kendall."

Elena reached across the table and took Kendall's hand, squeezing it tight. Gabriel looked up at them and rolled his eyes, Kendall catching his response.

"What? You can't be mom's favorite all the time," she said.

They all laughed, then continued to eat. After a few minutes, Kendall decided to open up more, addressing exactly what Elena's observations had touched upon.

"Well, I haven't been saying much because, you're right, I haven't known what to make of it all," Kendall said. "First, I think I will pursue nurse anesthetist school come fall. I've been thinking about it a lot and I haven't fully committed to the idea yet, but selling Sandlefoot Lane to support me through school is definitely an option I'm considering. When I found out about being accepted, I couldn't even fathom it. But now... well, not only have I wanted this for years, but Dan wanted it for me, too. And the idea of letting him down – even though he's not here – is more upsetting than letting myself down. Does that make sense?"

"Of course. And Dan always wanted you to pursue your dreams," Elena said encouragingly.

"Exactly. And he also wanted me to be happy. And I haven't been. I mean, for obvious reasons, but I've also been purposely avoiding things that might make me happy, as if it wouldn't be fair to him."

Kendall paused to take another sip of her mimosa, sitting back in her chair and digesting more than just brunch. Her mom listened intently.

"So, I'm toying with the idea of dating someone." Kendall quickly stole a glimpse at her mom, gauging her pupillary reaction before she continued. "It's someone that didn't know Dan, and I guess in some ways, I like that. He lost someone, too, a long time ago, and well, there's that common ground – like he knows where I'm coming from and doesn't expect me to be your typical eager date."

"Mm hmm," Elena agreed, nodding.

"I hadn't heard from him for a couple weeks and I felt good about that – like either way, if we do try dating or just go back to being colleagues, I'm fine with it. But he called and he does want to take me out some time. And I admit, I like the idea of dating him. I was worried it might be too soon, like maybe I should just be alone. But now I think I'm ready. I don't know."

Kendall fidgeted with the hemline of the tablecloth, finally heaving her biggest fear off her chest. "I never want to think, 'Oh good. Dan died so I got to meet this guy.' You know? That's about it." Kendall shrugged her shoulders matter-of-factly and finished her mimosa.

"Well. That all sounds like very healthy reasoning to me," Elena said, maintaining as much neutrality as possible – she knew Kendall would hate any overt signs of excitement coming from her. But she couldn't help but to wink, making Kendall roll her eyes.

"Don't be going all gaga over this, Mom," she said. "It's no big deal right now. And I don't want you asking a million questions about him or what's going on between us because when you need to know, I'll let you know. Right now there's nothing to know." Kendall shot her a stern look, then took the last bite of her French toast.

"I didn't say anything," Elena said with a smirk, wiping her mouth with her napkin. "Do I at least get to know his name?"

"Anson," Kendall answered cautiously, knowing full well Elena would roll his name around over and over to try it on for size, giving far too much credence to this nonexistent relationship for Kendall's liking.

Gabriel, who had practically licked his plate of Belgian waffles clean, suddenly chimed in, always following along with conversations as a silent observer until the right moment struck. "He's an asshole doctor. She called him that."

"Oh?" Elena's eyebrows arched, fully intrigued by that tidbit of information.

Kendall groaned, perturbed by Gabriel's big mouth and impeccable timing.

"He is a doctor. And that's all I'm going to say at this point. So consider yourself in the loop now, Mom." She leaned back in her chair and crossed her arms.

"Hmm. Any particular field of medicine? Proctology, perhaps?" Elena asked, casually taking a bite of her omelet in an attempt to suppress her laugh.

"Mom! He's one of the neurosurgeons at the hospital."

"A what?" Gabriel asked, making a face at Kendall.

"A neuro-surgeon," Elena clarified. "That's someone who does surgery on the brain, definitely not the ass."

"Mom, stop! Or… I'll have him do a lobotomy on you," she said petulantly, sticking out her tongue.

Elena erupted in laughter, Kendall relaxing again. But Gabriel looked ready to pounce.

"Well, maybe you should call him a neuro-hole then," he suggested dryly, crossing his arms at Kendall, his knack for one-liners often on par with hers.

Kendall now joined Elena in laughter, Gabriel's cooler-than-ice character melting away into giggles as well. Elena dabbed tears away from the corner of her eyes and then finished her Bloody Mary, motioning to their waiter to bring another round of their breakfast cocktails. With their family bonds fully rejuvenated, all three experiencing a surge in positive energy, they settled into comfortable conversation, basking in the heat of the Miami Beach sun.

***

The family of three leisurely strolled along the Lincoln Mall, watching the other Sunday morning patrons enjoying their meals at the variety of sidewalk cafes. Elena paused from time to time to exchange kisses and hellos with friends, acquaintances, and business contacts, always pointing out her two children in tow – mainly Kendall, since everyone saw Gabriel on a regular basis at the gallery.

The walk almost always transported Kendall back to her childhood as the self-conscious middle schooler, wanting to just blend in instead of stand out the way her mom liked to do. When they had first moved to South Beach from Homestead to be closer to Elena's gallery, being paraded around by her mom was a weekly occurrence.

Gabriel would charm the socks off everyone, her dad would poke fun at his wife's wildly extroverted persona while adoring it all in the same breath, and Kendall would alternate between smiling and rolling her eyes after every introduction. That was family life in South Beach for two years – until Kendall's dad had accepted a position at Station 9 in West Palm Beach. After that, he'd moved the family up to North Broward in a compromise between Elena's zest for spicy city life and his desire to live in suburbia.

The three came up to *Galerie Gabriel* so Elena could pop in to check on things. Always the ever-present and involved owner, she'd basically worked seven days a week for the past 28 years. Though, she generally made her weekends available to Gabriel, who worked three days a week at Gold Coast Reefs, the saltwater aquarium warehouse one block over from the gallery.

When Kendall's parents had gathered enough resources to open the gallery after Gabriel was born, Elena had envisioned Gabriel being the creative force behind it all, hoping he'd find a niche in the art world. But the ocean had captured his attention first, becoming a fish aficionado as a teenage boy. Dan had fostered that interest further after he and Kendall were married, taking Gabriel out on the ocean regularly and getting Gabriel his first job at a pet store in Broward.

When Elena moved back to South Beach after her husband's death, buying a stylish 1200-square-foot two-bedroom condo within walking distance to her gallery, Dan had helped Gabriel get established at Gold Coast Reefs. The small slice of heaven Elena and Gabriel had managed to carve out in the ever-growing congestion of South Beach never ceased to amaze Kendall. The two made city life quaint and charming, Elena's car parked most days out of the week as they walked all over town together.

After hanging out in the gallery for a short time – but before being sucked into any brainstorming sessions regarding upcoming shows – Kendall decided to head back to her mom's home to fire up the Jeep Wrangler and hunt down Anson, wherever he might be down there in Miami.

"Well, it was nice seeing you all," Kendall said, waving to gallery staff members Marianna and Emmanuel, "but I should really get going now, Mom."

"Oh yes. Do you want me to walk back with you?" Elena asked.

"No, that's not necessary. I'll be fine. Hey Gabe!" Kendall shouted at Gabriel, who was perusing the aquatic-themed collage works of a newly featured local artist. "Thanks for spending some time with me this weekend."

"You're welcome. See ya, Barbie. Say hi to the doc."

Kendall rolled her eyes to her mom. "This is why I don't say anything."

Elena smiled in amusement, walking Kendall out of the gallery.

"Thanks for brunch, Mom." They squeezed one another tightly on the sidewalk. "I'm fine, you know."

"I know. I just worry about you. I love you, Kendall."

"Love you, too." Kendall looked back through the gallery windows at Gabriel. "Do you think he'll be alright with me dating someone? He seems a bit hostile about it."

"I'll talk with him. It's an adjustment for him just like it is for you. That's all."

"I did try talking to him about it, but he said he doesn't care if I date."

"I think he does, but only in a protective brother way. He has his emotions to deal with, too, so we'll talk and I'm sure he'll be okay with it. If things do progress in any way, try and involve him a bit. I'm guessing he won't have that instant bond you saw between him and Dan – but I don't want that to concern you, either. Remember: Gabe knew Dan before you did, so he never felt obligated to like him just because of you."

"That's true. I never thought of it that way. And well, there's nothing to get too concerned about yet anyway. It's all trial and error. But you two will know if things move forward. I'll call later."

Kendall smiled and headed back down Lincoln Road to the condo. As she crossed Lincoln, she grabbed her phone to call Anson.

"Hello there. I was just looking for you," he answered, all levels of sexy smooth.

"What? Like a stalker? Where are you?"

"I'm walking north on Collins Avenue. I had my driver drop me off about fifteen minutes ago, figuring brunch hours were fading into just-lunch hours."

"You do remember I was having brunch with my family, right? We're not exactly at the stage of meeting them yet." The sun's radiant heat felt stronger against her face as her insides delighted in his game.

"Well, I thought I'd spot you before you saw me and just wait it out or something. Kinda creepy, hey? So, where are you?"

"Not on Collins. I'm just a few blocks in," she said, picking up her pace. "I'm almost to my car. I'll come pick you up."

"I asked where most people eat out and the driver suggested this road. Where do you go?" he asked.

"Well, there are hundreds of places all around here to eat. But my mom owns an art gallery on Lincoln, so we usually eat near there."

"Damn. He mentioned that area, too, and I chose Collins. Next time."

Kendall could practically hear Anson's sly smile, making its way through the phone and into her heart.

Once at her Jeep, Kendall gave herself the once over in the mirror, grabbing a piece of gum from her purse and applying a light coat of lip gloss after blotting off the beaded-up sweat along her forehead.

She had considered wearing a sundress that morning and was grateful she'd stuck to her more typical brunch attire: a delicate sea-foam-colored tank top and a pair of flat-white shorts. She felt just the right level of sexy cute without trying too hard. Her hair was pulled back with a few loose tendrils framing her face. Elena was right: she did have a glow about her today.

A few minutes later, she spotted Anson standing at a corner, his smile seducing her instantly.

Chapter 31

Wow. Two weeks had been too long. The man was still something to behold, sizzling in his South Beach attire – a pale blue linen shirt and coral shorts, his beautiful blues hidden behind a slick pair of aviator Ray-Bans, the look almost too perfectly plucked from the pages of a *Hunks-R-Us* catalogue. Kendall felt a certain level of possessive pride after seeing a few bikini clad ladies checking him out further. His focus, however, remained fixed on Kendall.

She pulled off to the side, and Anson opened up the passenger door, sliding the seat forward, hoisting a small brown leather duffle onto the back seat. Kendall's heart pounded, his cologne romancing her mind. She reached over and turned down the radio as he got in and closed the door.

"Hey Kendall."

"Hey Anson."

Kendall shook her head, avoiding any prolonged eye contact with him, but did a poor job of hiding her pure pleasure of being his chauffeur for the afternoon. She merged with the traffic of South Beach.

"So your mom owns an art gallery? Which one?" Anson asked.

"Galerie Gabriel on Lincoln."

"I may have been there before." He paused reflectively. "That explains your acute eye."

"My acute eye?" Kendall asked.

"At my place. You noticed all the details. You're into the nitty-gritty. In a good way."

"I'd make a good surgeon," she said with a smile.

"Yeah, quite possibly. Do you think I'd make a good nurse?"

"Not at all."

Anson laughed. "I'd have to agree with that."

Kendall stole a glimpse of him – his face was lit up in a carefree smile, something she never wanted to miss. She drew in a long breath, settling her nerves.

"So how long have you had this Jeep?" Anson asked, continuing to lead their conversation. He ran his hand over the cracked surface of the Wrangler's dashboard. "Looks like it's got some history."

"Maybe five years now. Six? But it's nine years old. I always liked the look of Jeep Wranglers and when we got a boat, I could justify it a bit more. You know? To tow the boat."

"Justify it?" he asked.

"Well, it's not like I need to go over rough terrain or plow through snow to and from work. Here in Florida, what's the point of a big engine unless you're hauling stuff, right?"

Anson pondered her reasoning for a bit.

"It's a gas guzzler," Kendall explained further. "I'll probably end up selling the boat at some point and then trading this in for something with a little better gas mileage. But maybe not." She thought about it for a moment. "It's paid off, so gas is all I pay for. Plus it runs well. Besides, I do like it. Wranglers have this sort of cool look about them. I know – that sounds stupid to say."

Kendall took a breath, realizing her rapid rambling filled in the gaps of silence a little too successfully. She never looked over at him, keeping her eyes fixed on the road despite feeling his eyes on her several times.

"Hmm," Anson expressed, nodding thoughtfully.

"What?" Kendall asked warily.

"Well, I certainly didn't pick my Porsche for any practical reasons. So what? You think it's overkill?"

Kendall glanced at him, before looking straight ahead again.

"If that's your thing, that's cool," she said quickly, backpedaling. "I mean, it's a sports car. A powerful engine comes with the territory, right? It's just that, if I had your kind of money I'd probably buy a Tesla. But that's just me."

"Well, maybe I'll consider a Tesla next. My lease is about up."

"You lease it?" She immediately grimaced, her tone coming off as too judgmental. "Not that there's anything wrong with that."

"I like something new every couple of years. I do own one vehicle, a Mercedes-Benz *G-Class*."

Kendall shrugged, unfamiliar with the name.

"It's like your Jeep. Fits my boards better. Practical." He paused, analyzing her subtle cues. "You think I'm shallow, don't you?"

"What? What do you mean? We're talking about cars," Kendall responded defensively.

"Before that night at the bar, what did you think of me?" Anson asked, getting to the meat of the conversation.

"I don't know. I mean, I didn't."

"Well, at work," he clarified. "If you had to describe my personality to someone – what would you say?"

Kendall laughed, slightly flustered as he probed deeper into the recesses of her mind.

"Fine. Let's see," she said, trying to think back to when she did view him as just Dr. Allaway. "If a patient wanted to know about you, I'd say you were a great doctor with good bedside manner. They'd be in excellent hands. If a new nurse asked about you, I'd probably say the same thing."

"You're smiling. What else would you say?"

"Oh. It's nothing," she said, stifling her giggle. "I mean, every new nurse, whether they're attracted to men or not, comments on your looks at some point. You're a good looking bachelor, Anson. So, it lends itself to... I don't know. Other things." Her smile broadened, but she couldn't bring herself to look at him.

"What *other things*?" he asked, angling himself toward her to lean up against the door frame, all ears in her confession booth.

"Oh, I don't know," she said, stalling. "It'd come up about you being... well, you know... a playboy. Eventually the *Double A* nickname gets dropped, and well, stories follow." Kendall shifted in her seat, guilt-ridden for violating a secret nursing gossip code of honor. "Let's just say, there's an assumption that you're a... just a pretty package of sorts."

"Huh? Like a pretty package of *air*? You guys see me as a dumb jock?" he asked, slightly offended but more amused by this glimpse into the minds of the nurses.

"No. Obviously you're intelligent. You have serious surgical skills and, well, the now confirmed, uh, bedroom skills that I've heard about."

Kendall laughed nervously, briefly leaning her head onto her hand propped up along the window frame, her forehead radiating more heat than the blazing sun.

"I guess the assumption is that, if you were the full package inside and out, well, you'd be off the market by now," Kendall said, failing to make it sound any better.

"Oh. I see. So, I lack depth. Again, you see me as a bit of a shallow person."

Anson could barely contain his pleasure in seeing Kendall squirm, her self-imposed hot seat burning.

"No!" Kendall retorted, now flustered. "Honestly, I didn't really think about it. It didn't matter. You're an excellent surgeon. That's all that mattered to me, when I thought of you. Lots of people remain single – and that's totally fine. And now I know more. It was just a stupid assumption. You asked what I thought. So, now you know. What'd you think of *me* before that night?"

"I thought you were sexy, intelligent, and off the market. So, all thought stopped there."

Kendall swallowed hard. Why hadn't she just answered him like that?

"So what about now?" he continued. "Is the handsome packaging still the foundation of your thoughts when you think of me now?"

Sure, a foundation strongly supported by wet lips and tantalizing orgasms. Feel free to dive in a little bit deeper, Double A.

Kendall delayed her answer as she refocused on the road, navigating the causeway traffic toward I-95, letting her mind retreat from the subject at hand for just a moment longer. But once cruising along, Anson resumed his grilling.

"So, Kendall. What do you think of me now?"

"Well, obviously, I've changed my mind after spending time with you. I know there's more to you than just a playboy surgeon, if that's what you're wondering."

"That's good to know. And if I told you that you're the only person working at GC General whom I've ever kissed, slept with, and pursued – what would you say to that?"

"Did half the female staff leave since I last worked?"

"Ouch!" Anson looked on in disbelief, his playboy reputation having a more rock solid foundation than he'd imagined.

Kendall laughed, instinctively placing her hand on his arm, but then removed it promptly – a disappointment for both of them.

"I'm not worried about who you've been with before me," she said. "Sure, your reputation didn't help my transition back to work, but that was my doing, whether you'd been around the block or not. So, now I'm one of the Allaway conquests. It's fine."

"What? Is that what people think? Are you still getting flak?"

"It's fizzled. Nothing I can't handle."

"Well good," he said, straightening himself up in his seat. "Wow. I had no idea. So, hear me out. You think I've worked my way through the panties of every willing nurse at GC General, and you're flat out wrong. There's some truth to that playboy reputation, but it's misguided at work. This may come as a shock, but I've never had any sexual contact with someone I work with before you. It's all been well outside the hospital walls. But rumors fly and grow roots wherever they land.

"So, aside from your positive view of me as a surgeon – which I am very happy to hear – you have this idea of me being a shallow, self-involved womanizer. I need to change that. There's more to me, despite what you've heard."

"Wait, what about that PA that worked at your office? Not even her?" Kendall asked in disbelief.

"Michelle? No. Damn. What was the basis behind that rumor?"

"Oh, I don't know. That one was considered fact," Kendall said, still wrapping her mind around his revelation. "Ruby the respiratory therapist? There's no way that's not true."

"Kendall, I'm telling you the honest truth. You're the only one. Besides, you were the only one who so blatantly offered it up. Maybe there have been some round-about propositions, but nothing like what you said. That was near impossible to turn down."

Kendall felt her face flush, remembering her blazing confidence that night and unsure how she'd managed to pull it off.

"Okay, so, you don't want me to jump to any conclusions on what dating you would be like," Kendall said, agreeing to move forward. "I get it. And I'll take that into consideration. But that doesn't change all my hesitations."

"Welcome to the conversation. So tell me about your hesitations."

Kendall darted her eyes at Anson – and then melted a little inside. The conversation would've been near impossible if they'd been sitting still, facing one another. They'd never have made it past their greetings.

"Alrighty then," Kendall said, putting her game face on. "So, obviously we have a strong physical attraction to one another; I won't even try to downplay it. You seem to stir things up in me that I feared would lay dormant for years. And clearly, I do the same for you."

Anson smiled, looking down, his unshakeable confidence faltering momentarily. Her blunt approach took some getting used to.

"But you're at a very different place than I am. So maybe you've been the playboy around town and are ready to give it up, wanting to connect with someone on a deeper level. But I haven't been the playgirl – not that I want to become one or anything, but just for comparison's sake. I just don't see my pursuit of this the same way you might see it with me.

"I've never been good with that kind of vulnerability. It took months of dating Dan before I really let my guard down. I sort of feel it being next to impossible at this point – you know: intimacy."

Kendall paused, mulling over her free-floating thoughts, wondering if she should just throw it all out there in the open for consideration.

"Wait," he said. "I thought you were worried *I* only wanted a physical relationship. Are you telling me that's what *you* want now, and I want too much?"

"Ugh. I contradict myself all the time now. Maybe you could do a little exploratory surgery on my brain or something, because I don't know what I want. But since neither of us can escape the confines of this vehicle at the moment, I might as well keep going.

"I worry for my own well-being, going into this," she said. "I've been in sort of a dark place, and that's where I was when I picked you up. But now I'm kind of emerging from it. I don't want to slip into getting attached just because that's what I'm used to."

Anson considered responding, but then she continued, never taking her eyes off the road.

"And how would any of that be fair to you?" she asked. "To have to deal with my misguided emotions? I'd hate to use you that way. It's not worth the risk."

"Neither of us knows what could happen here," he responded. "There's always a risk. And you're right. I am in a different place than you. But don't worry about your attachment to me, in terms of how I'd react. Your guard seems to be fairly strong. And I mean that in a healthy, self-preserving way.

"If you ignore my absence for the last two weeks, I think it's safe to say: I'm the one pursuing this, and you're the one resisting. The risk is all mine."

Kendall finally began to relax. Maybe he would make a good nurse after all, considering the way he put her mind at ease. He certainly knew how to listen.

"My mom said something similar to me today about resisting," Kendall said. "But if I'm the one resisting, how do you explain two weeks ago? After what *I* thought was a breakthrough of sorts – at least for me – you up and left. Or escorted me out. I was ready to give it all a shot right then."

This time Anson looked straight ahead, watching the stream of cars around them on I-95, collecting his thoughts.

"Well, it's safe to say, we both have our baggage. Who doesn't, though, right?" he asked, shrugging.

"I've never opened up to anyone about Grace aside from superficial anecdotes here and there," he began. "With you... well, there's a certain level of comfort, a connection that I haven't had with anyone else. And I know you felt that, too, before I said anything that night. And then you pushed back like you do. So, I opened up, letting you in, but more than I had planned.

"And then I pushed back. I needed you to go," he said quietly.

"But why?" she asked.

Anson let out a long sigh, his fingers tousling his sandy brown hair as the Jeep quarters began to feel tight and smothering.

"Whose brilliant idea was this to drive back together so we could talk?" he asked, forcing a laugh until it evolved into a groan.

"Ah, I don't know, Kendall," he said, working through his newfound claustrophobia. "I suppose if I knew why, I would have jumped back into the world of dating years ago. I just knew you deserved more than someone who had just warned you not to become what he was."

"Oh. So what's changed now?"

"Well, two more weeks of continuing to be that person I warned you not to become was two weeks too many. I couldn't shake wanting to be close to you, hoping you'd give me another shot. My timing was off that Saturday."

"Maybe our timing's still off," Kendall said regretfully.

The circulating air within the Jeep had slowed immensely, the density of their shared thoughts filling the small space like a thick molasses. The blurred highway walls and lamp posts, whizzing by at 80 miles per hour, seemed to disappear. Time stood still – until Anson broke their silence.

"No," Anson shook his head, refuting the idea completely. "It's not timing. At the risk of sounding trite, perhaps I'm like your Jeep – something you like, might even want to show off." He raised an eyebrow, Kendall's expression lightening. "But you consider it excessive and need to justify its existence in your life.

"I'm not practical to you, Kendall. And I get it. But like your Jeep, I'm used and already paid off. Maybe even damaged inside a bit."

Kendall could not fight back her smile, the air increasingly easier to breathe.

"Kendall, I like you. And I'm fairly certain I could, in fact, like you a lot," Anson said poignantly.

With the notorious impression noticeably absent, Kendall's insides floated weightlessly. Somewhere, in the far reaches of her mind, she heard even her super-ego sigh with angelic whimsy, instructing her to just go with it. The more Anson spoke, the more the air cleared, and the more he drifted into her heart.

After a healthy dose of silence, with only the sounds of an overplayed pop hit softly accompanying the rumbling of the road beneath the Jeep tires, Kendall finally spoke.

"So if you're my Jeep, will that old R&B song, *You Remind Me of Something,* be ours?"

"*Because you wanna ride me*?" Anson asked, singing along without missing a beat and then falling into hysterics.

It took a full two minutes to compose themselves, both wiping away the tears of laughter, the weight of the conversation and stress of their pasts evaporating in an instant.

"Whew! Why hadn't I thought of that?" Anson asked, still chuckling. "Great song by R. Kelly. I have it on my phone."

"You do? I wouldn't picture you as the R&B type. The R&B, Trekkie type."

"Oh, Kendall. You have no idea. No idea. This'll be fun."

Kendall eyed him with a wary smile. He stretched his arm out and stroked the base of her neck beneath her ponytail, sending an electrifying chill all the way down to her pink pedicured toes. Her muscles deliciously tightened within. Reluctantly, he pulled his hand back to his lap. He didn't want to start something he couldn't finish.

They rode along for a few minutes, the positive charge of crisp, circulating energy electrifying their skin and causing every fine hair to stand at attention.

"So, aside from running into you at work tomorrow accidentally on purpose" –his voice switched to full swagger mode– "how about getting together on Tuesday evening? You won't be at work. I have two light cases, so I should be out late afternoon. You don't have to work the next day, but I do, so you don't need to worry about my hopes for an all-nighter..." Anson checked her response, sharing her sly smile. "So, what do you say? Hopefully I could pick you up early, maybe five, and we could go from there?"

"In the Porsche?" she asked.

"Well, yeah. Unless... you really don't like the Porsche?"

"I do. I like it a lot actually. Contrary to popular belief, every now and then, I do like to spoil myself with something overtly excessive and unjustifiable," Kendall answered, winking at him.

"Well, that's what I'm here for. Our timing must be perfect."

Chapter 32

Kendall sailed up I-95, surprised at how quickly time had passed. Having Anson along definitely made it much more interesting. But then her phone rang, distracting them both. Anson grabbed it from her purse in the back just as the ringtone stopped.

"It says Ariel. You want to call back?" he asked.

"Oh, I'll call her when I get home," Kendall said, dismissing it.

But then it rang again, prompting Kendall to take the phone from Anson.

"Everything okay?" Kendall asked Ariel.

"What, did you ignore my first call?" Ariel asked, without any true resentment in her voice.

"No, I couldn't reach it fast enough. I'm driving back from Miami right now. What's up?"

"Just got off the phone with your mom. She called."

Kendall tensed, hearing Ariel's tone. She knew Anson had to be the reason for the call.

"She did? That's weird. Hope everything is fine," Kendall said casually.

"Oh yes. Yes, everything's just peachy," Ariel answered back, annoyed. "First she wanted to make sure you're not tricking her into thinking you're doing better. But I agreed with her, that you hit a rough patch, but now you're on the upswing of the rollercoaster ride. So, you know, she seemed happy about that."

"O-kay. But I'm guessing there's more." Kendall stole a glance at Anson, relieved to see him preoccupied with his phone.

"She also wondered whether I knew" –Ariel paused for dramatic effect– "the *guy*. You. Were. Dating."

Kendall took in a deep breath. "Shit. Ariel, it's not what you think. Well, not yet. I don't know what it is. I just haven't had a chance to call you. I can't believe my mom called about that. She's lost it. I'll talk to her. I mean, that's crazy. So, yeah. I'll get back to you after I talk to her."

Anson had now tuned in to Kendall's side of the conversation, stowing his phone away.

"No, no, no. I don't think so, Barbie," Ariel protested. "Your mom can call me any ol' time she'd like. And that's not the only time she's called me before, so don't get your panties in a wad over mom checking in. My panties, however, are in a serious wad. A tight one.

"What the hell? You're dating this guy now? I didn't even know his first name. I now have to get info like that from your *mom*? And by the way, Anson is a hella hot name."

"Okay already," Kendall argued back. "Don't get so possessive over *my* life. I mean, Gabe was over and we were on the boat all day Saturday. Then, in Miami today. I was going to call, I just didn't have time. So we'll talk tonight, when I get home, okay? Geez."

"Uh, I'm on the phone now. Spill the beans. So what? Did he finally call?"

"Well, I'm driving. So I'll just call you when I get home."

"Exactly. So, it's a perfect time to talk. When did he call?" Ariel asked again.

"Um, Friday. On our way home from Old Key Lime. Actually, Gabe called."

Kendall winced, recalling the way it all started, wondering if Anson would even be in her car if Gabe hadn't called him first.

"Gabe called him? What, they already know each other too?!"

"No. Not at all. It was an accident. He was trying to call you. I mean, it was all a mess, but it worked out. Hey, can I just call you later? I have to go."

"Oh. My. Goodness. You're not driving. You're with him!" Ariel's voice increased a full octave.

"I *am* driving," Kendall reiterated through clenched teeth.

"He's in your car?" Ariel squeaked. "Wait a minute! Did he go to brunch with you?!"

"No!"

Kendall looked right at Anson. He definitely knew the subject of their phone call now.

"No," Kendall repeated more calmly. "And, yes, to your first question. So, please. If you wouldn't mind, I'd like to call you back tonight. It won't be late, since I have to work tomorrow."

"Drive safely, talk to you soon!" Ariel hung up.

Kendall tossed her phone into a cup holder with a huff.

"So how's everything with Ariel?" Anson asked, charming as ever.

"Ugh. She's basically my sister. Best friends since age two. So, what happens to me, happens to her, and vice versa. I'd have it no other way, but uh, when *I* don't even know what's going on in my life, it's hard to bring her up to speed."

"So, explaining where I fit in?" Anson asked.

"I liken it to brain surgery," Kendall said, shaking her head.

"Well, I hope it's not that complicated. Down the road we'll have more definition. But there's no need to explain it now. I'm guessing Ariel's view of me is pretty narrow, as well. Right?"

Kendall offered up an apologetic smile.

"Well, at the very least," he continued. "Let her know I enjoy being with you – even with clothes on. Which by the way, you look beautiful."

He had more to say, but his thoughts derailed as he glided his hand over the bare skin of her thigh, squeezing lightly, his pinky stretching up higher to stoke the fire buried within.

The exhilarating burn felt deep in her groin startled her, forcing one hand to drop from the steering wheel on top of his. She took a breath, smiling sweetly, and gently removed his hand, putting it back on his lap.

Anson carried a powerful advantage when in close proximity to Kendall. There would be no fair fights in his presence – not when she couldn't resist his touch.

"Anson? Can I be blunt?" she asked.

"I don't think you're capable of much less."

She tossed him a snide look, then focused back on the road.

"For my own sanity, I need to define everything," she began. "If I can't define what we are to Ariel, that's a problem. It means I don't know what I'm doing or where I'm going. And I need to know these things.

"At the risk of sounding harsh, if there's no definition, I'm not going to jump through any special hoops to make this work. If we can't make our schedules jive, and then days go by where you don't hear from me, I just want you to know, it's not you.

"Family is the most important thing to me. And I'm not sure how you would fit into that. In my family, there's no such thing as casual dating. And I'm definitely not looking for a boyfriend. So, that means: no sleepovers, no meeting the family, no falling in love. Nothing like that."

Kendall stared straight ahead, unsure of where she was going with her rambling.

"I guess, what I'm trying to say is – if I'm being honest – well, without defining us, I do prefer the fantasy idea of flirty fun, great sex, and no baggage."

Anson shook his head and sighed.

"You do have a way with words." He laughed, Kendall looking at him skeptically. "Okay, so aside from your last line, you do realize you just gave me a preemptive breakup speech?"

"No! I didn't mean it like that. I'm sorry," Kendall said ruefully. "I just... I don't know. I suppose, I'm trying to figure it out up front. Then down the road, when lines blur and colors blend, I won't have to think. Or maybe I'm just trying to save face. I don't know. Shit."

She laughed at herself, now wishing Ariel were there to make sense of all her thoughts.

"You've been wonderful, Anson. Very complimentary and flirty. And when I look at myself, from the outside, getting abrasive and dodging your advances – I don't like it. It's not me. It is, but it isn't."

"It's this, isn't it?" Anson touched her again, holding her hand in his. "Affection. Accepting affection from another man. As if the physical affair is understandable, but the emotional one crosses the line."

Kendall's body stiffened, unprepared to hear such blinding truth from him. Anson brought his other hand over on top of hers, sandwiching her hand between both of his.

"I understand everything you're saying, Kendall. I know your heart is healing. I'm not here to make that process harder. I just think we could have a good time together. We don't need to be exclusive, or get serious, or even label it as dating. Whatever you're comfortable with."

He released her hand, Kendall slowly bringing it back to the steering wheel.

"Thank you," she said, her tension dissipating. "I am comfortable with this. With you. Knowing you know I'm gun shy, but still willing to wait it out, as I figure it out. I appreciate that, more than I let on."

Kendall met his eyes and smiled, her racing thoughts, finally, entering a cool down lap. Anson had kept amazing pace; through every faulty start and widened stride, he stayed with her. Until it was time to move them along.

"And for the record," he said. "I completely back the fantasy idea of flirty fun with nonstop sex. So really, the arrangement is quite perfect."

Anson's signature wolfish grin made its first appearance – and now her underwear was wet.

"Uh, I didn't say, *nonstop*," Kendall teased.

"Sure you did. At least, that's how I heard it. So, we should probably get started on that right away, wouldn't you say? We should be at my place in – ten, fifteen minutes?"

"Hey, I thought you weren't even going to give me a goodnight kiss."

"That's for our date. Tuesday. Today's Sunday. I didn't say anything about Sunday."

Without warning, he unlatched his seatbelt and leaned over the console, his hand squeezing her thigh as his fingers dug in below the hem of her shorts, just grazing the moist surface of her panties.

His body ached for her as the distance between them became difficult to maintain. He pulled her earlobe between his teeth, groaning softy.

Kendall sucked in sharply as her eyes sprung wide open, hyper-focused on the road – like a reverse blindfold, unable to get lost in his touch. And he knew it: the steering wheel became handcuffs, anchoring her down, bending her to his will. He provocatively kneaded her inner thigh as he nibbled his way along the slope of her neck, her breathing increasingly erratic.

"I'm driving," she stammered, her mouth parched as it hung open with desire.

"I'm aware," Anson said, smiling against the back of her neck, then deeply inhaling the scent of her hair. "You smell so fucking good. I had to have a taste."

Kendall felt a wild rush through her body as her desire for him built. Then he backed away, readjusting the contents of his shorts. The seatbelt clicked back in and Kendall caught her breath, now fully primed.

"So what kind of food do you like, aside from my steak?" Anson asked, oozing with confidence.

Kendall chortled at his suggestive tone. "I've had better steak."

His smug expression begged to differ.

"Um, anything really," she said. "I could do beef steak one day, raw sushi the next. You take your pick." She bit her lip, playing along with his innuendo.

Anson's smile was almost too wide for his face now.

"Damn, I love the words that come out of that tasty mouth of yours."

Kendall laughed, that powerful four-letter word bouncing around like a pinball in her head. It seemed to slip out of him, so easily.

And then it dawned on her: Love is always justifiable, and never excessive.

Chapter 33

In no time, Kendall exited I-95, heading east on Atlantic Avenue to Anson's A1A home. Their conversation had turned to small talk, discussing South Florida's crazy traffic and unpredictable weather patterns. Anson needed to bring it back to the only topic on his mind: afternoon sex.

"You want to try surfing today?" he asked casually. "Weather's good for some decent starter waves, nothing crazy. It'd be fun to teach someone."

"I don't have a bathing suit with me," Kendall said. "But I'd like to do that someday. I've always wanted to try."

"I operate a nudist surf club. So, you're covered," he said, failing to keep a straight face.

"A bit weak on your delivery. That's all you got?"

"Oh, come on. What would you have said?"

"Uh, maybe something more like, 'Bathing suits are optional, I just want to get you wet,'" Kendall suggested, matter-of-factly.

"I'm pretty sure I already did."

Damn.

In a snap, Anson reached between her legs again, causing Kendall to jump in her seat, pressing her thighs together, screaming as she fought him off.

"Anson! You're going to make me crash!" she screamed, laughing.

She pushed his hand back to his side of the car, the radiant glow of blood rushing to her cheeks further arousing him.

"Is this road trip not driving you fucking insane?! Holy shit, Kendall. I'm about to lose it. You've got some wild sex pheromones."

"I do?" Kendall retorted, reveling in his admitted lack of control around her. "You're the one all sex-crazed, blasting your nympho pheromones out into the atmosphere."

"It's unbelievable how obsessed you've got me. It must be a major culmination of not seeing you for two weeks. And now you're here, just out of reach. What are you doing to me?" He studied her in awe.

"Wow. You really know how to lay it on thick, don't you?"

"Don't say that," Anson said. "I don't want it, if you're not into it. Trust me – turning you on is what turns me on."

"Anson," Kendall said dryly. "I woke up this morning, planning this very moment. And it wasn't just to drop you off."

Kendall parked in his driveway and Anson promptly wrapped his hand around her neck, pulling her in close. Finally, all the energy he'd used to restrain himself during the drive, poured into her through his lips. It all felt so new again, so fresh and enticing. Anson shifted awkwardly over the center console, groping her breast, desperate to feel her heat.

"Anson," Kendall muttered into his mouth, gently pushing him back. "Hey, Anson. Let's go inside."

Her voice was airy and sweet as her hand caressed his cheek, waking him up to the small quarters of the Jeep Wrangler – his claustrophobia now conquered.

They walked together hand in hand. The warm midafternoon sun laced through the banyan leaves above, creating shadows that dragged across their clothes in a hypnotizing fashion. They strolled along, mesmerized by their perfect moment.

This was the new beginning they'd both been seeking – and the feeling was incredible.

They entered his home and Anson wasted no time, pulling Kendall close, pressing his body against hers. His hands clasped the sides of her head as their tongues swirled around one another, desire growing hot and thick. Kendall took control, leading him up the stairs to the third floor.

The sun poured through the three-storied front windows, filling his loft room with natural light. The entire back wall of picture windows was like a phenomenal beachside mural – the majestic Atlantic, vibrant in her shades of greens and blues, with breaking waves of white. The view was breathtaking, and extraordinary, and inspiring... and nowhere near the focus of Kendall's attention. She turned away from it, consumed with the fueling power of Anson's lips.

She sashayed backwards, until the back of her knees hit the edge of his bed, forcing her to sit, her hands dropping to his waist. As she undid his shorts, and he unbuttoned his shirt, they never broke eye contact.

Kendall left his briefs in place, governing its powerful, rock-hard force, just a while longer. Anson kicked off his Reef sandals, and Kendall hoisted herself back to the center of the bed, seducing him with her bedroom eyes. She pulled off her tank top and bra as Anson removed each of her sandals. Now, they were mere moments, from the unbeatable feeling of skin-to-skin contact.

Anson straddled her legs with his arms, slowly crawling onto the bed and up the length of her body. His face fell to her breasts, nuzzling them with his nose, making her giggle. He pulled one of her peaked nipples into his mouth and sucked hungrily. As he savored the taste of her tits, he blindly groped around her inner thighs. Realizing her shorts were still on, he swiftly pulled them down, along with her underwear.

"Kendall," he whispered.

Anson slowly took in the bare terrain of her soft skin, her name a statement all on its own. He bowed between her legs, worshiping her like the goddess she was to him, and kissed the silky flesh of her inner thighs.

Kendall gasped, delighting in her divine treatment.

Then he used his tongue – first teasing and then plunging it into the wet folds surrounding her sex – helping her to embark on an erotic journey of tantalizing pleasure. Anson stimulated her entire body to the core, dipping into the deepest pools of her fantasies and arousing every excitable nerve she had.

Anson's technique was practiced, precise, and unparalleled. And yet, with every calculated lick, he still infused eagerness, only present with true passion.

She cried out as he ravished her – her fingers clawing into the bedding, her body's response building, Anson unrelenting. Every muscle fiber within her flexed, squeezed, and stretched as her legs clenched harder around his head, her toes gripping tighter and tighter into the sheets.

"Oh god, Anson," she called out. Her entire torso convulsed, the crashing wave of her potent orgasm soaking deep into the marrow of her bones, her cries filling his soul with salacious satisfaction.

Anson smiled against her pink velvety skin, lapping up the sweetness of her response. He moved up her belly and curled his body alongside hers. He watched her closely as she cooled down, her mind drifting in the dream of her heavenly orgasm.

"How was that?" he asked, planting petal-soft kisses along her cheek.

"That – Dr. Allaway – was amazing," she murmured. She opened her eyes and slowly focused on his gaze, his cool Caribbean blues welcoming her back to Earth.

"You ready for more?" he asked, dragging his index finger from her parted lips, down the slope of her chin, and circling it around her nipples.

She nodded bashfully.

"You have no idea how lucky I feel, lying next to you like this. It's my nirvana," he said.

Anson's words were so unfiltered – so beautiful to hear. She needed to be closer to him, to fill that void and repair his broken heart.

"Come here," she whispered, pulling him on top of her and passionately kissing him.

But before losing himself in her completely, Anson moved partially off of her, reaching into his bedside drawer for a condom, only to find an empty box.

"Fuck," he mumbled, suddenly pushing off the bed and walking into his bathroom.

"What is it?" Kendall asked.

"Shit. Sorry, babe. I'm out of condoms here. Where's my bag?" He scanned the room, searching for the leather duffle he'd taken to Miami.

"Um, it's probably still in my Jeep. But really, don't worry about it," Kendall said, propping herself up onto her forearms. "I know we were kind of reckless last time... but I assure you, I won't get pregnant. I have an IUD, so we're covered." She slid her foot along the shin of her other leg, attempting to call to him like a sexy siren.

"Oh," he said. "I assumed it was because of infertility reasons."

"Well, that too. Technically, I *can* get pregnant. My body just doesn't seem to know how to *stay* pregnant."

Anson's expression sank, triggering Kendall to stop her seductive pose – the midafternoon sex sent just off stage, waiting for its cue to return.

"But don't worry about that," Kendall said. "This is all a conversation for another day, right? Come back here." She smiled sweetly.

"Right. Definitely. Um, well, let me just run downstairs and grab my bag quick. I bought a box of Trojans," Anson said, heading toward the stairs.

"The IUD is crazy effective, just like condoms," she replied quickly. "So, really, I'm fine without them. It's not like you'll be catching anything from me."

"Of course not. I wasn't worried about that at all. It's more of a precaution for you." Anson stopped short, recognizing the very extinguishing nature of his explanation.

Kendall sat up, bringing her knees to her chest.

"You said you were clean," she said, her voice now small. "That you got tested regularly. You assured me of that."

"I do get tested regularly. Usually, several times a year. You have nothing to worry about, even with our carelessness last time. I was tested four weeks ago."

Anson shifted uncomfortably, crossing his arms over his chest now. He'd had no intention of unloading his typical sexual behavior, and all its dirty laundry, on her now. Not yet, at least.

"Okay," Kendall said. "So you and I were together just over three weeks ago. Then, again, two weeks ago. And all was well. But now, another two weeks later – what?"

"Well, we weren't together," he answered awkwardly.

"Right. You were gone for two weeks," she repeated.

Their uneasy tension grew, and the waiting sex faded further backstage.

"So, we weren't together," he said, again, wishing she'd just leave it at that.

"So?"

"Kendall, what do you want me to say? There were other women," he finally admitted.

"Other women? How many *other women*?"

"I don't know," he said, irritated.

"You don't *know*?!"

"Well, I do know, but – dammit, Kendall," Anson pleaded. "We weren't together. I use protection every time. Every. Single. Time. I'm just trying to protect you. Just in case."

"Protect me? What the hell, Anson? You woo me, like I'm your one and only, and then go fuck around Miami?"

Anson approached her on the bed, but she bolted past him.

"No. We're done for the day," she said angrily, grabbing her underwear and shorts off the floor and rapidly dressing.

"I get the whole, *we weren't dating and you had no loyalties to me*, per se. But for fuck's sake, Anson. I had no idea there'd be a *slew* of women between then and now. I've barely touched myself in the last two weeks. But you? I'm not sure that's someone I can be with. I understand your drunken babble from the other night a whole hell of a lot more now." She fastened her shorts and frantically searched the room for her tank top.

"But I'll give it to you, Anson," she continued. "You're good. A real pro in all of this. The things you say to me, to get me in bed, I mean, you've got a gift. I really believed it. But maybe I'm just desperate. I guess come next weekend, since I'll be working, you'll say those same things to another gullible woman." And then she stopped in her tracks. "Where the fuck is my shirt?!"

Anson had already stood up from the bed, somewhat following her around as she dodged his advances. He located her tank top near the head of the bed and retrieved it, Kendall snatching it from his hands and pulling it on without her bra.

"Kendall," he said softly, coaxing as he reached for her.

But she resisted.

"Kendall, please."

She attempted to step around him, but got caught by his grasp. He pulled her to his bare chest. Fighting back, once held against his skin, was futile.

"Don't," she sulked, Anson hugging her tightly.

"I'm sorry," he whispered, inhaling the vanilla coconut scent of her shampoo, and the very essence of her, deep into his lungs. "I never wanted to hurt you."

Kendall felt an isolated tear run down her cheek, and angrily flicked it away.

"Everything I've said to you is true," Anson continued. "I tried to suppress it all down in Miami, and ended up in rough shape – drunk and bitter. Seeing you today has been exactly what I needed. I'm not looking for other women. Just you. So, please, Kendall. Don't give up on me just yet."

He held her in his embrace, waiting for her to relax into him, to concede. Eventually, she did, and he softened his squeeze, his arms falling down around her waist. She met his eyes, her vulnerability on display.

"I'm sorry," he said again, kissing her forehead. "Are we good?"

She exhaled, then yielded, accepting a soft kiss to her lips.

"But if you want to be with me," she spoke. "There can't be other women. Maybe it sounds crazy, to set exclusive limits right off the bat. But that's my rule. I am not one of many."

"No, you're not. And, I already knew, for me, it wouldn't be anything but exclusive. Kendall, I'm all yours and only yours. Until you decide you've had enough."

She pressed her cheek against his chest. The soothing sounds of his heart, gently thumping in her ear, calmed her further.

She missed hearing that – the very basic, continuous rhythm of life – in someone intimately close to her.

"So… Is there any chance we can pick up where we left off?" Anson asked, hopeful. "Just give me a second. I'll run down to the Jeep."

But Kendall stopped him. "Take me out on Tuesday. Wine and dine me. Seduce me all over again."

She picked up her bra, carefully slipping it back on beneath her top. Grudgingly, Anson grabbed his shirt, as well, and walked her down the stairs.

He retrieved his forgotten bag, with its game-changing condoms, as Kendall started up the Jeep.

"I like this combo you've got on here," Kendall said, smiling, sizing him up in his boxer briefs and open shirt ensemble.

"Tuesday, then," Anson said.

They kissed goodbye.

"Tuesday," she agreed, and then turned around in his driveway.

"If I make it through Monday!" he yelled back.

She laughed and called back to him out her window, "You'll make it!"

But then she had to laugh a bit harder as she exited through the gate. The image of Dr. Allaway, in her rearview mirror, was nothing short of comical: a half dressed neurosurgeon, with – if she'd care to guess – a raging case of blue balls. She didn't take pride in causing them. She simply loved knowing that she was the only woman he wanted relieving them.

Chapter 34

Monday's drop in the SICU census resulted in Kendall floating to the general telemetry floor – never an ICU nurse's idea of a good time. So, when Anson stopped by the unit late afternoon to see her, he was met with disappointment. They managed a few check-in text messages.

Tuesday's official dinner date never happened, despite both Anson and Kendall preparing for it. Anson arrived to work early, successfully rounding on all his patients, and completed both scheduled procedures before 4pm. Unfortunately, just as he was walking out, he was called back to the hospital for a trauma accident with several victims, requiring multiple surgeons. Their text messages, however, carried a far more flirtatious tone.

By the time Wednesday rolled around, Kendall had accepted the idea that their interactions would predominantly involve texts and short phone calls, hopefully interspersed with an actual run-in from time to time. She rather enjoyed the foreplay of it all, as it made for appetizing fantasies. Plus, the freedom from attachment felt possible, with days buffering their bedroom activities. It provided just the right amount of distraction from her grief.

After having lunch with Ariel at Gulfstream University, followed by a five-mile evening run, Kendall prepped for her four-day stretch of work. She'd just finished showering and was walking naked across the living room, carrying a load of laundry, when there was a knock at the front door – freaking her the fuck out.

Rapidly, she threw on her bathrobe and searched for her phone. But then she heard his voice.

"Kendall, you home? It's Anson."

Immediately, she opened the door.

"What are you doing here?" she asked, smiling brightly, shamelessly pleased with his unannounced arrival.

"I've called you half a dozen times," he answered, entering her home. "I brought dinner. Hope you like Thai." He walked past her confidently, wearing his typical office attire: a navy blue suit over a white collared button-down.

The gorgeous factor never got old.

"I was just looking for my phone," she said, spotting it on the couch. "Oh whoa. Five missed calls. Sorry about that. I was in the shower and doing laun-"

Kendall looked up at him and began to laugh. Anson had already put the take-out down on the kitchen counter and removed his blazer. But he didn't stop there.

"Wait. Are you getting naked?" she asked, amused.

"Are you naked beneath that robe?"

Kendall gave him a seductive nod, her entire body heating up in anticipation.

"Good," he said.

The rampant inferno radiating from him made her weak in the knees, her adrenaline spiking. He dropped his pants and ripped open his shirt, Kendall's eyes bugging out as she fought back laughter. He was still in his domineering doctor roll, and right then, she was more than willing to play his obedient nurse.

"Is there something I can help you with? A sponge bath, perhaps?" Kendall asked, demurely.

Anson swiftly closed the gap between them. Before she could say another word, he removed her robe and backed her naked body against a wall, the distance to the bed unfathomably far. He slipped his tongue between her teeth, opening her mouth, making her hungry for him, and pinned her in place with his pelvis. He grabbed her breasts greedily, squeezing and massaging hard, Kendall pushing back into his palm. He then wriggled out of his boxers and immediately rolled on a condom. He hoisted her up, then down onto his rock hard dick.

Kendall gasped, the power of his thrust shaking her to the core. Anson's eyes rolled back, his hot breath draping down her neck, as his body instantly surrendered to her.

"Sweet fuck," he moaned through clenched teeth. He could never deny the insurmountable pleasure he received from being buried deep within the wet layers of her sex.

He thrust upward again, every muscle of his torso and arms, flexing exquisitely as he supported her against the wall. He bit and sucked her neck, pulling her hips down harder, his pelvis rocking up to meet her.

Kendall clung tightly around his neck, marveling at his force, his absorbing strength – all of it confounding – including the abrupt change from an evening alone to being fucked hard against the wall outside her kitchen.

Anson's groans became more guttural, his body working tirelessly against her. She bit her lip in eager anticipation of his orgasm, moaning along – if anything, to get him off. His spontaneous and puckish presentation was undoubtedly exciting. But the bruising nature of it? This was not exactly conducive to her own climactic experience.

He powerfully pounded into her one last time, coming hard, digging his fingers into her sides, then dropped his head to her shoulder. His mouth hung open, wetting the crest of her clavicle. He panted from exhaustion, his hot breath settling down her breasts.

Kendall just smiled lasciviously. A fast fuck: a delightfully wicked necessity at times.

With considerable effort, he held his head up and looked at her.

"Sorry babe," he said. "I've got to put you down." He stood her on her feet, then leaned his head against the wall just over her shoulder, keeping her close with his one arm around her waist.

For a few steamy moments – Anson's beautiful muscles sequined in sweat and Kendall locked in a sultry sauna of arousing aromas – they stilled, listening to the rhythm of their bodies. Kendall stroked his back, trailing her fingers down the curvature of his spine, and waited for him to speak.

"Hey Kendall," Anson whispered, finally greeting her. Cradling her face in his hands, he kissed her softly. "Thank you. I needed that." He rubbed his thumb over her lips, then backed away to give her some room.

"I didn't even do anything. You did all the work," she said, laughing.

"And I've got more in me. I just needed to get that first round out of the way."

Anson pulled his boxers back on and walked into the kitchen to discard the condom.

"So, I've decided: I can't go this many days without you," he called out from the kitchen as Kendall dressed into her robe. "Especially after Sunday. Plus, that text you sent me earlier today."

He returned to her side and pulled her close. Just as she was about to speak, he sucked the air right from her mouth, leaving Kendall breathless – and so very ready for more.

Damn, he was good at kissing.

"I think I'll have to send more texts like that," she said playfully. "I did wonder why I got such a short response, though. Considering how wordy you were in your texts yesterday, I thought maybe I was too forward."

"You can never be too forward with me," Anson said, smiling. "Not when it comes to sex. Consider tonight my full response. You know, my scrub tech had to read it to me."

He walked away into the kitchen and began unpacking the food.

"Holy shit! Are you kidding me?" she exclaimed, following behind him.

"No. I'm dead serious," he answered, cocky as ever, uncorking a bottle of wine. "I was already scrubbed for a procedure when I got the message. Hadn't heard from you yet, so I assumed it would be benign. I told her to read it. She's the one who wrote back. Well, I told her what to write."

"Oh my goodness! Anson: You're terrible! How humiliating! What did I write again?"

"Something about the brain not being the only pink, moist flesh that required my *sexpertise*. You ended it with '*Wet and ready when you are*.' I loved it."

Kendall remained frozen, mortified on behalf of the scrub tech. She scrolled through her phone.

"You wrote back, '*Top of my to do list,*'" Kendall read. "Or rather, *she* did. I can't believe you made her do that."

"It's her job. I can't touch my phone when I'm scrubbed in."

Kendall shook her head in disbelief, finally joining him at the counter with two wine glasses.

"*I* would have refused to read it out loud, telling you to do it on your own time."

"Oh, she tried," Anson said, smiling as he chewed through a heaping bite of pad Thai. "But I can be a bit insistent in the OR. Personally, I think everyone enjoyed it."

He bit his fork seductively, taunting her with his eyebrows. Kendall remained speechless, his audacious behavior deplorable – yet charming, nonetheless.

They ate together as if at the counter of a small diner, looking straight ahead into the kitchen. Kendall enjoyed the arrangement. Removing the pressure of a face-to-face set up opened them up to more personal conversations.

"So, has your scrub tech had to do that before?" Kendall asked.

"Read one of my texts? Sure," he answered.

"No, read a *sext*?"

Anson choked slightly.

"I've never received a text suggestive of anything close to that," Anson said. "So my hat's off to you. Not too many people text me outside of work. On occasion I'll get some from family and friends, but mainly they're all work related. So, your text will have them talking for a while. I'm sure they'll be eager to read more."

"Oh, well, you can guarantee, any sexting from me will be well beyond OR hours now."

Anson laughed and leaned over to kiss her, his mouth full of food, but her bashful nature irresistible.

"So, wait a minute," Kendall said, facing him. "When you've wanted a booty call – you've already admitted to plenty of those so no sense in denying it – there's no sexting involved? I assumed you'd be a pro at it."

Amused, Anson sat back, hiding his irritation. He knew there'd be some sort of recourse from Sunday, regarding his sex life. He took a sip of wine to wash down his food – and soothe out his thoughts.

"I don't give out my number to women. It's more of an arranged hook up. I'm not a dater, just out for the occasional fuck."

Kendall stared at him, astounded, and then closed her eyes, trying to clear her mind. "Wait. So, like online? Tinder?" she asked. "Please tell me you're not one of those creepers that places personal ads on the Internet."

"God, no! Kendall, I'm interested in you. Only you. I'm here with you. Yes, I've had many partners, resulting in a lifestyle I'm not particularly proud of. But I'm trying to put it in the past. Can we please focus on what's happening here, right now, between us?"

She acquiesced, trying to trust his words, and looked back at her food. But he knew: She'd stew in it, if he didn't say more.

"Kendall, look at me," Anson said firmly. "There is only you. I'm not looking for anyone else. I just want to be with you."

He pulled her face close to his and pressed his lips against hers. But his kiss was unanswered, forcing him to search her eyes for assurance.

"I have one more question," she said.

With her face still held in his hands, Anson agreed with a reluctant nod.

"Are you addicted to sex?" she asked sincerely.

He lowered his hands and took in an audible breath, reaching for his glass of wine.

"Maybe I will be with you," he replied, knocking back the rest of the glass. "But no, I'm not. I think I'm one criterion short of a nymphomaniac."

They continued to eat silently through a few bites. But Kendall couldn't let it go just yet.

"You can't blame me for trying to gauge what I'm getting into," she said. "I don't want you starving for sex because our schedules conflict. Then after trolling Dixie Highway for a good time, you force us to double wrap it when we get together."

Anson dropped his fork on his plate and faced her head on. Slowly, drawing in a long breath through his nostrils, he looked her up and down, his eyes lingering over the plunging neckline of her silk robe.

"Last I checked, sweetheart," he said, licking his lips and looking directly at her, "women solicit from me. Not the other way around."

Fuck!

***

"Oh shit. Oh... yes! Oh god. Anson! Anson, please!" Kendall cried out with ecstasy, her arm covering her eyes as she pushed her head back into her pillows. The intensity of another spectacular orgasm was difficult for her body to process, so soon after the other one she'd just shared with him in her bed.

Her thigh muscles relaxed, releasing their spastic grip around his ears and splaying her legs helplessly open. Her body melted into a puddle of euphoric exhaustion. Anson crawled up next to her and flicked his tongue over her firm nipple, teasing her senses.

"No, no. No touching just yet," she whimpered. "Everything's too sensitive right now. I'm like Jell-O. On fire. Fiery Jell-O. Melting. I can't feel my lips. I'm numb. Fiery, frozen Jell-O."

Anson's face beamed with pride as he studied her features. He propped his head up on his hand, waiting for her to return from her higher orbit. Gradually, she met his delectable stare, a sultry smile on her face.

"God, I love that look," he said, kissing the smile off her tingling lips. "Did I wear you out?"

"Just about."

"I like you like this," he confessed. "Like a rag doll."

"I can tell," she said, shaking her head.

"It's fuckin' hot."

Anson kissed her again, then rolled to his back, pulling Kendall into the nook of his arm.

"Is there anything you want me doing that I haven't tried yet?" he asked.

"In bed? Anson, look at me. I'm a pile of putty in your hands. I'm pretty sure you've covered all the bases," Kendall said, laughing. "But thank you for asking. I don't think I've ever been asked that before. How 'bout yourself?"

"Fairly certain you hold the keys to the best sex ever. Just trying to even the playing field."

"How many women have you slept with?" Kendall's thought rolled right off her tongue, missing her filter altogether.

Anson removed his arm from around her and laced his fingers behind his head. "You don't really want to know the answer to that."

"I kind of do," Kendall responded, pushing up so she could see his face. "I mean, if anything, to gloat about how many women I've beat out."

"I'm sure that's it," he said doubtfully. "How many men have you slept with?"

"Dan was lucky number seven. And I wasn't even 21 when we met, so see?"

"Well, good for you. In that case – Grace was my first and I had just turned 20. And that's where this conversation will end."

Kendall groaned, accepting his answer. He curled his arm back around her, bringing her head to rest on his chest. He stroked her hair, brushing it down between her shoulder blades, relaxing her even further. Instinctively, she wrapped her body around him like ivy on a pole. They laid there, quietly, until her body twitched, alerting him to her slumber.

"Babe? You asleep?" Anson asked.

"What? Oh sorry! I was so relaxed," Kendall answered, immediately springing up. "I'm awake. I'm awake."

She shook her head and wiggled her arms, the jiggling of her breasts highlighted by the soft glow of her bathroom lights but the rest of her room serenely dark.

"You're unbelievably cute when you're sleepy," Anson said, smiling. "You don't have to get all riled up on my behalf. We can go to bed."

"But I have to work in the morning. What time is it anyway?" she asked, leaning over him to see her digital clock. "After ten. You have to work, too, right? You should probably get going."

"We're both heading to the same place in the morning. I could give you a ride and bring you back after work. It'd be no problem. Or we could just caravan, if you prefer."

Kendall looked down at her hands. But before she could utter a response, having already picked up on her hesitation, Anson rolled over on top of her.

"Third times a charm? Fair enough?" he asked.

Some fifteen minutes later, he'd sufficiently awakened her entire body once more, sailing them through another orgasmic high, then, finally, surrendering to his own sheer exhaustion.

After saying goodnight, Kendall heaved herself onto her bed, her body weary and irrefutably Zen. His nurturing nature and passionate approach was far more therapeutic to her soul than any drug, counseling session, or work distraction.

She brought the pillow where he'd rested his head close to her nose, swooning in his lingering scent before it faded away. As she fell asleep, a subtle smile settled upon her lips.

Finally, she knew how to shut out the unrelenting chaos within her brain: with unrelenting orgasms.

Chapter 35

Cramming over 50 hours of back-breaking, life-saving, emotional-overspending, and soul-gratifying work into a four-day stretch in a surgical intensive care unit of a trauma hospital could render anyone practically useless by the last day. Kendall was no exception to this rule. Her physical exhaustion, however, was now compounded by the continued advances of a fully charged Double A, who swung by her place Thursday, Friday, and Saturday night, leaving closer to midnight each time. Kendall's haggard look on Sunday morning did not go unnoticed by her coworkers.

"It's like we've been on opposite schedules! How are you?" Courtney asked cheerfully, bounding into the unit just before their shift began. "I haven't seen you since Old Key Lime."

"Day four," Kendall responded, usually enough to get any fellow nurse to pipe down. But this was Courtney.

"Oof," Courtney attempted to sympathize. "Well, I'll keep you fueled. Did you work late last night? You do look tired."

"Again, day four. I'm just happy I have tomorrow off."

Kendall had no intention of making her Allaway affair hospital knowledge. The rumors surrounding their first night had only just let up. And although no one had outright said it, Kendall knew she'd been granted a widow pass from many, including Patricia. So far, Anson had been respecting this as well, remaining Dr. Allaway at GC General.

But Courtney's eyes had a superior level of scrutiny for this kind of extracurricular activity.

By early afternoon, Kendall had already exchanged several texts with Anson, as he wanted her to head over to his place after work. She was leaning toward just going home, to her own house and bed, thinking a night apart would be beneficial to both of them. But he wasn't going down without a fight.

As Kendall bustled around inside an isolation room – stifling in a blue plastic garment and smothered by an itchy, yellow mask – she didn't notice Anson lingering near the doorway, his watchful eye following her every move. She tried, and failed, to brush back some loose hair with her plastic-wrapped arm.

Anson entered momentarily, smoothing the strand back away from her face and around her ear.

"Shit, you scared me. What are you doing here?" Kendall asked.

"Thought maybe you wanted to grab some lunch. It doesn't sound like you'll be coming over tonight," he answered, stepping back into the doorframe.

If only he wasn't so delicious looking every minute of every fucking day.

"I'm smiling right now, you just can't see it," she said. "But I already ate. And just so you know: There aren't any neuro patients in here right now. I'd call this crossing our professional line."

Anson looked down at the threshold of the doorway and stepped back further, technically out of the room. He returned his eyes to hers, a suggestive smile working its way forward.

"Wanna meet in the stairwell?" he asked, jokingly.

"Anson!" Kendall hissed – but the glint in her eyes gave her away. She stepped up next to him and peered out of the room. The unit was fairly quiet. "Go do some doctor things or something. Or better yet, go get a psych consult. I think you just met that last nympho criterion."

He raised his eyebrows, failing to restrain his wryly smile. "God, I want to fuck you right here in your blue gown."

"Go!" she whispered harshly.

"You coming over tonight?" he asked.

"I. Don't. Know," she answered truthfully, her voice now strained – irritation mixed with pleasure.

"I'd like to make you come," he teased, winking.

"Anson!" Kendall shrieked, his comment catching her off guard.

But he simply laughed and confidently strutted away.

She immediately ducked back into the patient's room – aggravated she'd played into his game so willingly. *Damn his swagger.*

"Uh, Allaway just left the unit and your cheeks are pink," Courtney announced, popping out of nowhere as Kendall finally finished in the patient room.

"First of all, he's a doctor in the hospital," Kendall said matter-of-factly. "He's allowed to be in the unit. Second of all" –she ripped off the mask and took a restorative breath– "they probably are pink because I'm hotter than a whore on nickel night. He wasn't checking on my patient, so I don't know what you're talking about."

"Are you still seeing him?" Courtney asked, undeterred.

"I was never *seeing* him to begin with, so if I were *seeing* him, it wouldn't be *still*."

Kendall finished washing up and walked over to her computer to chart.

"To hell with the syntax," Courtney announced, following behind. "Are you and Allaway seeing each other outside of work in a nonprofessional manner – perhaps dating, or maybe something else?"

Kendall filled her lungs, holding the air in for a few seconds, and then exhaled as she spoke.

"We're enjoying one another's company from time to time," Kendall said. "It's not a *relationship* relationship. It's more of a common connection."

"Common connection – like *sex*?" Courtney pried.

"Courtney! It's nobody's business but mine and his. And actually, it relates to grief. He lost his fiancée years ago, and well, he's helping me out in my own loss. We're comparing notes."

Kendall shrugged, wondering if she could really explain it away that simply.

"Oh. Wow... wow. How *are* you doing with all that?" Courtney asked. "The celebration of life was really quite beautiful."

Kendall reflected on her grief status for a moment, then answered honestly.

"Thank you. Actually, I'm doing pretty well. I mean, I think moving forward is possible now, whereas just last month, I thought there was no point to living."

"Oh," Courtney said quietly. "Uh... I hadn't really thought about the day-to-day struggle that continues on. I'm sorry about that. I'm happy to hear things are better. Especially if Dr. Allaway is helping you with it all. That's really great of him. I guess I kind of pigeon-holed him into something, well... a lot less considerate. If you need anything, though, let me know. We can get together outside of work any time."

"Thanks for the offer," Kendall said. "I'm fine, though. Really."

***

Even though she now fully grasped the significant role Anson played in her return to a more normal state of mind, once she reached her Jeep after work, she decided against seeing him that night. She sent him a text.

KM: **Rain check. I'm simply too tired.**

She had just started driving out of the parking garage when she heard her phone whistle.

AA: **What's your schedule for this week?**

She called him to answer – and to keep herself going on the drive home.

"Hey beautiful," Anson answered, immediately triggering a twinge of guilt for driving off in the opposite direction of his house.

"Hey," she replied. "Sorry about tonight. I'm honestly beat. Maybe I'm coming down with something."

"I hope not. Don't apologize. You know, I am capable of restraining myself if you ever want to just come over to chill. It is possible."

"Well, I have yet to experience a *chill* night with you, and I'm not willing to risk it tonight," she said with a smile.

"Fair enough. So, this week. Do you have a few days off?" he asked.

"As of right now, four. I work the weekend again."

"What's *as of right now*? Are you picking up another shift?" he asked, his disappointment poorly disguised.

"There's always that possibility. I need the overtime."

"You short on cash?"

"Anson," Kendall said sharply, her warning unmistakably deliberate.

"What? I was just asking. You're beginning to burn the wick at both ends. That's what will make you sick. But I digress. So," he continued with a playful tone, "I've got a full week ahead again, as well. But I'd like to have my secretary pencil you in for–"

"Pencil me in? Are you freakin' kidding me?" Kendall barked.

He laughed. "I'm messing with you. Ooh, you're feisty tonight. Maybe I should come over there and help you get out a little aggression."

"I'm sorry," she sighed. "I'm just so... there's nothing left of me. You sucked it all out."

"Well, that wasn't very thoughtful of me, now was it? I could try to put it back in you. Like fueling up at the gas station: my pump, your tank."

"Are you buzzed? Why do you sound so chipper?" Kendall questioned, half teasing.

A female voice called out in the background before Anson had a chance to answer; he responded to the mysterious woman's voice first. "Yup, hold on. I'll be right in... Hey, Kendall? I'm going to have to let you go."

"Who was that?" Kendall asked, now contemplating turning around and heading straight to his place.

"My niece, Madison," he clarified and then snickered, clearly a bit tipsy. "I'm hiding out on the balcony right now. She and her friend have been staying here since Thursday. Vacationing at Uncle Anson's. Yay." His sardonic tone humored Kendall immensely, and he took offense. "Oh, I'm glad you find that funny."

"That's so sweet. What – are they on spring break?" she asked, her tone completely changed.

"Something like that. I don't know. They've been doing this for years. They live in Boston."

"And Uncle Anson lives in Florida. How perfect. So, I guess if I had come over tonight, it really wouldn't have been to wear me out further. Hmm?"

"Oh, well. I'm sure I'd have tried a little," he said, smiling. "But yeah, it was actually to save me. But I wasn't sure about springing family on you, so I figured I'd see what you wanted to do first. Then I'd mention the niece and her BFF." He took a swig of a drink, the distinct sound of ice in a cocktail glass clinking the edges. "So I've had bikinis and sundresses and every fuckin' strappy sandal that's ever been made strewed about the house all weekend."

"Aww, you poor thing. Sounds rough."

"It is!" he exclaimed. "My boards have been lying out on the deck in the sun all day, and my bar has been raided every night. Just half a bottle of scotch left to make it through until tomorrow."

"Wait a minute. How old are they?" Kendall asked.

"Madison's got to be 23, 24 now. She's in grad school. When do you graduate college?"

"You did graduate, right?" She shook her head, laughing. "Around that age, maybe younger."

"Well, I was always the young one in class – July birthday. And I skipped third grade, making it that much worse come high school. Late bloomer. So, I'm never sure what the norm is."

Kendall couldn't even picture him as anything but cocky and confident. Picturing a prepubescent Anson, struggling to find his way through high school and college, was nothing short of adorable.

"Aww. So you became an uncle at a young age," Kendall responded in a sing-song voice.

"Yeah, she's my oldest brother's daughter. She's good. As annoying as it can be when they're here, I enjoy it. They head out tomorrow."

Anson stretched out, yawning into the phone.

"But, I'd better get going," he said, wrapping up the conversation. "They want me to fix the surround-sound. So, I'll let you go and we'll talk during the week... and hopefully do more than just talk."

Kendall smiled. "Okay Uncle Anson. Thanks for talking me home."

"Get your rest, Kendall. Lov-" he stopped himself, going silent. After an uncomfortably long pause, he began to laugh. "Okay then. Time for me to say goodnight to Johnny, too. Later, Kendall."

Chapter 36

The following Tuesday evening, feeling playful and ready for a distraction from the hellish work week ahead, Kendall drove over to Anson's house after work. Aside from dropping him off – and getting off – last week, it'd been three weeks since really spending any time at his place. Kendall packed an overnight bag, just in case. Tonight, she felt she just might give in.

She pulled into his open gate with giddy anticipation. Maybe it was his near slip-up from their last conversation – and curiosity over whether he was really ready to say those words. Although she knew it was far too premature in her book, the idea of it all definitely had made her feel a bit bubbly these few days apart. She enjoyed feeling so wanted by a man.

She entered through his unlocked door and looked around. There wasn't any sign of him on the first floor. But she could hear a soulful, somewhat foreboding tune coming from upstairs.

"Anson?" Kendall called out, ascending the stairs.

The music stopped and he emerged from his self-described man cave on the second floor.

"Hey there," he answered, looking sharp in his charcoal gray wool pants and a purple pinstriped dress shirt. "I didn't even hear you come in. I'm pouring a drink. Want one?"

Kendall greeted him with a kiss, his response strangely cool. But she dismissed it.

"I like this color on you," she said, patting the purple shirt over his abs. "And I'll have whatever in a bit. What I really need is a shower. I've been elbow deep in *C. diff* most of today."

Anson stepped back. "Hop to it, then. Unless, of course, you were looking for my help?"

"No thanks. I still smell it – it's stuck in my nose." Kendall stuck out her tongue and laughed. "Not exactly ready for *Double A* action yet."

"Maybe you deserved that," he replied, his voice bizarrely bitter. "Should have spent the afternoon with me instead of picking up a shift. And enough with that nickname already."

"Whoa. Okay. You don't have to be mean about it," she said, taken aback.

"Fine. So, anyway," he began dismissively, "I got this today. Figured you'd be interested."

He pulled a folded paper out of his pocket and handed it to her. She skimmed over the data.

"Lab work?" she asked.

"My clean bill of health. Got tested again yesterday. No more condoms, I guess."

"Oh," she said, smiling again, inviting him to lighten the mood with her. "Well that's good. I bet you're happy to be done with those, hey?"

He shrugged. "Just something I wanted to do for you, since we're doing the whole monogamy thing, right?"

"Anson: What's up with you?" she asked, now offended. "Why are you angry? So I picked up a shift. I'm here now, aren't I?"

Anson audibly exhaled. He didn't want to ruin their entire evening together with snide comments he didn't mean.

"I ran into Leo last night at the hospital," he answered.

"Okay – so?"

"So you've gone out with him a few times?" he asked accusingly.

"Twice. And one of those was while you were in Miami sexing it up. I'm fairly certain I don't deserve your tone," she answered, hurt.

"Yeah, and the other was last Tuesday when I couldn't take you out," he countered. "You had a replacement pretty quick there, didn't you?"

"Okay. Just stop. This is coming out of left field," Kendall said firmly, not wanting to lose her cool and spiral out of control. "That was completely unplanned with Leo. He called, coming out of work, because he had some books for me. *Books*. As in textbooks. I was planning on being out that night anyway, so we met up for drinks. Leo's helping me prepare for school."

She crossed her arms.

"Don't be like this, Anson. I've been friends with Leo for years, long before you were even at GC General. He and I had one lapse in judgment. There's nothing going on between us like that. How did this even come up?" she asked.

Exasperated, Anson ran his hand through his hair. "He threw it out there. I don't know why. To see where you and I were at, I guess. He mentioned your pursuit of school, like it's been your biggest focus. And I looked like an ass, because you didn't bother telling me anything about it."

"About what? *School*?" she asked, the volume in her voice rising several decibels.

"You didn't think the possibility of your moving to Miami was something worth mentioning?" he asked scornfully.

"In. The. Fall," she answered angrily. "Anson, I'm not trying to hide anything from you. I know I mentioned getting into CRNA school. They gave me until May to decide. I haven't made any concrete plans yet. But I also can't make them all last minute. You and I don't exactly talk about the future with one another. That's not what this has been about, and you know it."

"Maybe it should be," he said sullenly. "Is that why you've been picking up so much overtime? Are you saving up?"

"Yes. And I know the overtime won't be available when we head into April and census drops. Right now, I can get the seasonal differential. So, I'm just taking advantage."

"You know I would help pay for–" he began to offer, but Kendall silenced him.

"Stop. I know you would. And I appreciate that. Truly," she said, taking a deep breath. "This is something I need to do on my own right now. I have some savings. And yes, selling my house is one of my options."

They looked at each other with defeat – a new spotlight shining down on their relationship. They were already on two very different roads. She had simply taken a detour. He was driving in a whole new direction. But neither one was ready for the journey to end.

"On that note, as an FYI," Kendall said apologetically, "I did pick up a shift tomorrow night. So I'll probably be sleeping most of Thursday away. Then I work Friday through Sunday." She reached for him again, gently resting her palm against the center of his chest. "So, we can either make the most of the time we have together tonight. Or, we can sit and argue over things that aren't going to change right now anyway."

"There are conversations to be had here, Kendall," Anson said. "Ones that involve more than just sex."

"I agree. But can I at least take a shower first, before we get any deeper? I'll join you in a bit, okay? We can talk more if you'd like," she offered.

But then, she snaked her index finger around the buttons of his shirt, down to his crotch, and cupped him. Slowly, she massaged the hardening pulse beneath his pants. "Or maybe. We'll find. Something else. To do."

"You play dirty," Anson moaned, wetting his lips.

"I've learned from the best."

Kendall bit down on her lip, increasing the pressure, making Anson grow hungrier, his eyes rolling back into his lids.

"You better go now," he said unconvincingly. His eyes remained closed and neither made a move to leave.

"Okay, I'm going," she said softly, not budging. Instead she unzipped him, continuing her massage beneath his pants.

"Kendall," he sighed, gritting his teeth.

"Anson."

Finally, she released her grip, Anson stumbling forward slightly.

"I'll be back in a bit. Hold that thought for me, okay?" Kendall requested, batting her lashes.

He stood motionless as she took the stairs to his loft. He was definitely not ready to give her up.

Chapter 37

Feeling randy and rejuvenated after her shower, Kendall entered Anson's man cave on the second floor wearing a pair of pajama shorts and an off-the-shoulder scoop neck shirt. She wore her hair down, the way he liked it – albeit damp – and skipped her bra, figuring Anson would remove it soon enough anyway.

The sophisticated and sleek design of this room created a dramatic escape to a swank, high-class lounge in the privacy of his home. In one corner, a zebra print chaise lounge sat in front of a gas fireplace filled with turquoise glass beads. Along the interior wall, a recessed backlit bar with a granite counter and five barstools showcased a variety of liquors on thick glass shelves. Her favorite feature was the stunning, 180-gallon saltwater reef tank built into the exterior wall, which boasted all the tropical life of an exotic dive. Of course, no man-cave would be complete without an oversized flat-screen television, and Anson's could be watched comfortably from the long, contemporary black leather sofa arranged in front of it.

The surround-sound system played the soothing sounds of Harry Connick, Jr. All the bar and overhead ceiling lights were on, the room bright and alive – a stark contrast to the dark skies, and the world beyond the glass wall.

And that was where Anson stood.

Out on the balcony, Anson swirled a golden drink and looked out over the black ocean toward an isolated light bobbing along the horizon. He was on the phone, immersed in a heated conversation. Moments of silence, accompanied by his vacant stare, were punctuated with sudden harsh outbursts, his voice carrying through the glass walls.

Kendall recalled the music that'd been playing when she first entered his home that night. That same haunting essence surrounded Anson now. His uncharacteristically jealous nature from earlier now seemed trivial in comparison – the tip of the proverbial iceberg.

She opened the sliding glass door and Anson immediately ended the call.

Without saying a word, he abandoned his drink on the railing and embraced her passionately. There was now a true hunger in his kiss, a yearning he hadn't divulged with his earlier greeting. The heavy scotch on his tongue added a provocative twist to his typical taste.

"God, I've missed this mouth," he whispered, their lips still touching, still wet with one another.

"Is everything alright? Who was that on the phone?" Kendall asked.

Anson walked back to his drink, finishing it like a shot, and ushered her back into the house as he spoke.

"I'm dissolving my business relationship with Xavier," Anson explained. "But we still have some kinks to work out. And you and I will discuss it all sometime. I think it'd only be fair for you to know, even if it's all coming to an end."

Anson walked behind the bar, grabbing the opened bottle of Johnny Walker, and refilled his glass.

"What would you like?" he asked. "I've got a fully stocked bar."

Kendall studied him as he took a swig of the rich, caramel liquid, curious as to how many he'd had.

"Um, I'll just have some water. Haven't had any dinner yet," she said, pulling out a barstool and taking a seat. "Well, what sort of business was it?"

"Entertainment stuff. I don't want to talk about it now. Later. When it's all resolved," he answered.

"Okay. So, are you sure tonight's a good night to be over? I can come over another day, if you need to get things squared away with him," she offered.

"I want you here with me," he said, handing over a glass of water and directing her to the couch. "Here, pick out some music. I've got some food for you downstairs."

Anson grabbed the television remote and pulled up a music library menu on the screen. He then hustled down the stairs.

She browsed through the extensive music list, each song categorized into playlists to fit a particular situation, mood, or season. Then she found a file too irresistible to pass up: *Panty Droppers*.

"Hel-loo, Doctor! What do we have here?!" she shouted out, her voice traveling down the hall.

Kendall selected the playlist and scrolled through the long list of songs, spotting Color Me Badd's *I Wanna Sex You Up*.

"Oh my goodness!" she squealed, choosing it and jumping up from her seat to sing along.

Anson returned halfway through the song, her contagious energy spreading to his face and erasing his more serious vibe from earlier. He stood in the doorway, watching Kendall seductively sway her hips, and croon out the words of the song to him.

"*Making love until we drown*... What does that even mean?" she asked, laughing.

Anson set a plate of fresh fruit, vegetables, cheese, and almonds down on the bar, knowing Kendall generally grazed on rabbit food after work. She danced her way over to him, still humming along to the tune.

"I don't have any grapes. Sorry about that," Anson commented, pulling her waist toward him as she rocked back and forth to the fading beat.

"This is way better," she said, smiling appreciatively, then kissing him. She picked up a carrot and twirled her tongue around it suggestively before biting off the end, making Anson wince.

Whispered words from the R&B group LSG interrupted her game as the song *My Body* pumped through the speakers. Kendall threw her head back with laughter. She picked up the platter and took it back to the couch.

"This is perfect. Perfect, Anson. How much success have you had with this playlist?" she teased.

Anson moved a leather arm-chair close to Kendall's spot on the couch. He then snatched the remote out of her hands and settled into the seat, propping his feet on the coffee table in front of them.

"Hey!" she complained. "You have to stay in the *Panty Droppers* playlist. I think it's high time you introduce me to Double A's secret stash of sweet lovin' from the nineties."

"Kendall. That nickname?"

"Okay. I'm sorry. The all-too-dreamy Dr. Anson Allaway: neurosurgeon-extraordinaire, sex god rocking his god-bod, and keeper of Kendall's fantasies. Play me some of your favorites. Woo me with your musical sexpertise. Drop. My. Panties."

Anson couldn't help but laugh, yet still eyed her dubiously.

"It's not all from the nineties," he said. "And don't think I'm not seeing right through your little plan here." He held up the remote and scrolled through the list of songs. "Okay. So, how 'bout this one? This is a favorite."

The smooth, sultry beat of LSG's *Door #1* filled the room. Anson got up to soften the overhead lighting, ignoring Kendall's muffled snorts. He sank back into his seat and closed his eyes, the sweet harmony slowly dissipating his stress.

"Wow," Kendall commented. "You really get into this, don't you?"

"This brings me back," he answered honestly. He bobbed his head, lost in the beat, and then opened his eyes, only to see Kendall suppressing a giggle. "What?" he asked. "Tell me you at least like some LSG?"

"Um, I know I've heard this song, but I couldn't name another song by them."

"Keith Sweat? You know him, right?" Anson sat up, now on a mission, and selected another song.

The synthesized, viola-like sounds of *Nobody* glided all around them. Again, Anson slid down into his chair, fully swept up in the song. Although the music seemed foreign to her, Kendall did love watching him relax, his mouth whispering the words and his head grooving to the beat again.

After a few moments, he checked her response. And he was not impressed.

"No? This doesn't do it for you?" Anson asked.

She shrugged apologetically.

"You never just get lost in music?" he asked incredulously.

"Sure I do. I have my mood music. It's just not this. Dan was an alternative rock kind of guy, and I've always been an eclectic pop or singer/songwriter fan. So, I just don't have a long-standing relationship with these songs, like you obviously do. Do you listen to this in the OR?"

"Not usually. I love a good bass beat, though," he answered. "I like to feel the thump in my chest. Even if it's slow. I tend to gravitate to jazz, R&B, hip-hop, reggae, calypso, blues. They all have a deeper soul. It just puts me somewhere else. But *these* songs, they have some great memories attached to them as well."

Kendall smiled, enjoying her educational session: The Musical Musings of Anson Allaway.

Anson raised his eyebrows flirtatiously, deciding to play something he knew she wouldn't know. *Freek'N You,* by Jodeci, rippled through the air as he mouthed the repetitive line, *I wanna freak you*, until finally belting out, "*Every time I close my eyes, I wake up feeling so horny.*"

Kendall just about fell off the couch, laughing so hard that a few blueberries rolled off her plate and onto the floor.

And just like that, Anson set the stage for discussing his mysterious, and deliciously dark, past.

Chapter 38

Singer R. Kelly performed, *Down Low, Bump 'N' Grind,* and naturally, *You Remind Me of Something* in Anson's after-hours concert, a playlist exclusively designed for his audience of one. Kendall relaxed into the seduction of it all, little by little, stretching her legs out along the couch as she ate, occasionally singing along to some of the popular lines. It really was an effective way to unwind after her long 13-hour shift.

They hadn't said much to each other all evening, the brooding topic of Anson's business relationship with Xavier put onto the backburner along with the direction of their relationship. Tonight, they were simply enjoying each other's company.

Anson got up to head back to the bar, and as he passed by the couch, he planted a kiss on the top of Kendall's head, simultaneously reaching through the neck of her shirt and giving her breast a quick squeeze. The odd, yet somehow thoughtful gesture, immediately made Kendall think of Dan – he'd often done that very same thing. Except his friendly squeeze had always been accompanied by, *Love you, babe.*

"Okay, so maybe these are too slow for you. I've got something more your style," Anson said, retaking his seat.

The room suddenly transformed into a nightclub as the deep bass of *Pony* by Ginuwine resonated in their chests, spurring Kendall to jump excitedly off the couch.

"Yes!" she shouted. "Perfect. That's what I'm talking about!"

She bounced over to his chair, playfully staging an unrehearsed lap dance: gyrating around and licking her lips with wild-eyed seduction. She spun eccentrically, nearly falling into his lap, but then transitioned the move, dropping low to the floor and shaking her ass around in front of him. Then she grinded against his groin, her hands firmly balanced on his knees.

Anson enjoyed every second of the amateur performance, his hands caressing her hips and pulling her completely onto him. He grabbed her breasts beneath her shirt as Kendall leaned back, resting her head on his shoulder, moaning into his ear. Turning her entire body around, she kissed him with salacious desire. But the restrictive space created by the chair's solid wooden arms prevented her from straddling him comfortably. Anson helped her up, effectively ending her solo show.

"So, *now* I know what gets you going," he said. "Are you a *Magic Mike* fan?"

"I was dancing to this song in the clubs long before *Magic Mike*, thank you very much. But yes, that whole dance routine was hella hot," she said, sashaying back to her spot on the couch.

"Oh, you thought so?" he asked, probing further. "Ever been to a male strip club?"

"Nope. What else you got?" she asked, distracted.

"Would you like to go to one?"

"I don't know. Never thought about it," she answered. "I've seen the Chippendales-type dancers perform at a bachelorette party before. But really, it was just laughable."

"That's because you're cynical. You're the kind of girl who needs a private show, so no one else will see how much you like it."

Next, Anson played Montell Jordan's *This is How We Do It*, his blazing blue eyes tempting her as his observation tickled her thoughts.

The energized atmosphere continued with Blackstreet's *No Diggity*, 112's *Anywhere*; then, Anson slowed the tempo way down with Silk's *Freak Me*. Kendall fixed her eyes on Anson's mouth as it showcased another talent: lip syncing.

Anson got up and slid the coffee table out of the way. He raised Kendall up to her feet, swaying her body back and forth, his hips rotating around with hers as he demonstrated the mastery of his trained dance moves. He whispered the overtly sexualized words of *Freak Me* into her ear, never breaking character. Their pelvises moved seamlessly with one another, his hands holding her firmly against him.

Kendall wasn't sure what to make of the performance, her giggles hushed just below the surface. He directed her back onto the couch. There, he continued his seduction, in spite of her mild ridicule.

Anson bent down between her legs, spreading her knees apart, his whole body waving up with liquid effect as his nose grazed the crotch of her shorts, her belly, and then between her breasts, before he backed away. He hovered over her, locking his arms on either side of her thighs and pressing deep into the cushions. His eyes burned into hers.

"Whoa," Kendall gasped, her giggles still notably absent. "This isn't your first rodeo, is it?"

"You want the real thing?" Anson asked, his voice like spider silk, wrapping her up in his tangled web.

Kendall nodded, needing to know more about this secret side of Dr. Allaway. TLC's *Red Light Special* randomly played next, lining up all her thoughts perfectly as the lyrics sizzled around her. Anson moved about the room like a stagehand, setting up the space.

The fireplace came alive with the touch of a remote, the turquoise glass beads sparkling in the flickering flames. Next, the overhead lights went out, the only remaining light coming from the dim bar behind her. The chaise lounge, positioned at an angle, gave Anson ample room to perform.

The TLC song abruptly stopped and out of the stillness, a few somber acoustic notes played over what sounded like a static ocean wave, the evocative falsetto notes of The Weeknd emerging. After a poignant pause, the beat dropped and Anson reappeared in front of her. He'd unbuttoned his shirt, which framed his sculpted chest and abs beautifully. The intensity in his eyes caused a hitch in Kendall's breathing. But the vulgar words of the song suddenly snapped her out of her trance.

"What song is this?" she asked.

"*Wicked Games* by The Weeknd."

He tossed his belt onto the couch and undid the top button of his pants, folding back the flaps so they hung on the perfect V of his hips. His boxers were nowhere to be found. He moved toward her and touched her face with the back of his hand.

"Get up," he commanded.

Kendall obliged, following his moves closely. He brought her over to the chaise lounge. She sat down, her legs hanging over the side in front of him. Her eyes never left his heady stare, her subtle smile eager for what he had planned.

He stepped back in front of the fire, rhythmically circulating his hips and removing his shirt in synch with the beat. Then he mouthed the potent lyrics, *Just let me ma'fucking love you*, leaving Kendall wide-eyed with wonder. The organic and sensual motion of his undulating abdominal muscles mesmerized her – and she was officially caught in his spell.

He dropped to his knees, onto the wood floor, the words of the song poetically calling the shots between them. He stretched his torso, bending back, as he thrust his pelvis upward, the definition of each muscle exaggerated by the dramatic lighting. His abdomen rolled again in a rippling wave as his hand slid down his entire body to his groin. He grabbed himself, his own excitement growing.

Kendall fought back a shocked laugh, the whole scene unbelievable – a neurosurgeon with mad stripper skills. But it was intoxicating as well, turning her on in a way she'd never imagined. Anson owned this character.

He sprung forward, crawling toward her like a stalking tiger, showing off the sinewy muscles along his shoulders. He parted her legs and moved further in, forcing Kendall into a stunted breath. He placed her hands against his chest. As she felt the heat of his muscles and the pounding of his heart, he again, mouthed the aching words:

So tell me you love me,
(Only for tonight, only for tonight).
Even though you don't love me.

He braced his hands against the edge of the chaise, straddling her legs, then buried his face into the apex of her thighs and dragged his nose up her belly, lifting her shirt slightly before backing away. The distressing cry in the song repeated, and Anson's body called out to Kendall.

He stood her up and guided her hands deep inside the back of his pants. They swayed with titillating angst, the flames of the fire creating long shadows across the floor as the light weaved its way around their tangled legs. Kendall felt the pressure of his erection, tempting her own fantasies.

Anson crouched down in front of her, his hands gripping the flesh beneath her loose shorts as his fingers reached beneath her underwear. He kissed her pubic bone, the words of the song inveigling her senses – *take you down another level, get you dancing with the devil.* Every touch was heightened by the salacious lyrics.

He helped her out of her clothes and cast them out of reach. Kendall stood naked in front of him, the warm glow of the fire enveloping her body as he arched her back, his nose inhaling her sweet skin from navel to neck. He laid her down on the chaise lounge and positioned his body above hers, his arms and legs stiff in a plank position. Then, like a rolling wave, he grinded over her, barely skimming the surface of her highly sensitized skin.

As the chorus returned, he increased the speed of his impassioned move, Kendall no longer fighting back her desire to touch him. She ran her hands down his sides to his happy trail, her fingers following the path and dipping into his pants. She stroked his throbbing erection.

Anson sucked her lips, plumping them up as he gently bit down. Kendall moaned – and that was enough for him. He shimmied out of his pants and hovered above her naked, the heat billowing between them hotter than the scorching flames behind them.

Then the singer cried out again – *So tell me you love me* – and Anson sank below the surface of her ocean, free diving without any barriers.

Kendall cried out, her nails clawing at his back as he thrust deep into her, almost too deep for comfort. But her legs wrapped tightly around his waist, imploring him to continue.

"Oh Anson, love me," she begged, letting go, the power of the moment too overwhelming not to succumb.

The song's lingering instrumental continued for a few moments. Then it all came to a screeching halt as a ring tone erupted through the speakers, the shrill sound destroying their impassioned drive to climactic heights.

"What the fuck?!" Anson shouted as he sprang up, realizing the system's Bluetooth had connected to his phone.

The designated ring belonged to Xavier, and Anson was furious. He rapidly declined the call and returned to Kendall, flipping her over onto her belly. As he grabbed one of her ankles, bending her knee up toward her chest, her ass rose into the air. The position was racy and ribald, exactly what he wanted.

With the music notably absent, the quiet hum of the saltwater tank now the only sound in the hushed silence, the drive behind Anson's performance became more unrefined. He buried his face right below her ass, his carnal tastes unleashed as he licked her pussy from behind, then nipped at the flesh of her bottom. He positioned himself behind her, Kendall dripping in the savory ambrosia he craved, and slammed into her.

Her arms were tucked in next to her breasts, her cheek pressed into the chaise cushion as Anson fingered her hair, eventually wrapping it around his fist and pulling tight like on the reigns of a mare. He laid down on top of her back, pressing his lips to her ear, and whispered deliciously raw and bawdy words, stimulating every erogenous zone. His pace was unrelenting and forceful.

Kendall began to unravel rapidly, her leg muscles stiffening as every fiber tightened in anticipation of a mind-blowing orgasm. But she couldn't take in a deep breath, her chest held in the vice between the chaise lounge and the weight of Anson's body. He felt her struggle and saw the strain in her face. Startled, he jumped back – just as the phone rang out again, further throwing him.

"Fuck, Anson!" she hollered. "Just fucking give it to me!"

"Whoa! Babe. Sorry... I thought..." Anson looked torn, as he'd already stepped away toward the phone. "I thought you needed a minute. Let me just turn off my phone."

"Yeah, I needed a minute to come! What the fuck? Why are you so distracted?"

"Shit. I wasn't sure if it was too much for you. You looked... Shit. I honestly thought I was getting carried away. It looked like I was hurting you."

"I'll let you know if I can't handle it. Handle you," she huffed. "Fighting through the pain can make the orgasm that much more intense, sometimes."

He stared at her, dumbstruck.

"In that case, let me grab something," he said, racing out of the room – and now leaving Kendall stunned.

When he returned not even two minutes later, he found her sitting on a barstool: naked, her legs crossed, impatiently drumming her fingers on the granite. He quietly placed a bottle of personal lubricant on the counter.

"Seriously?" she asked. "How can you let yourself get this far off course, when you were that far inside me?" Kendall asked, exasperated.

"Babe, I'm sorry. It felt like you were struggling and then he was calling again, so–"

"Who was calling?" she demanded.

"Xavier. And he pisses me off so much. I just thought I was getting too rough. I didn't want to hurt you," Anson explained.

"Denying me an orgasm hurts more," Kendall said.

"I doubt that."

"Well, I'm just saying," she continued. "You missed giving me the most intense orgasm of my life because you couldn't keep your head in the game." She then glanced at the bottle of lube. "You'll need a lot more than that to get me wet again."

Anson smiled and sauntered confidently over to her in all his naked glory, still fully erect, his Caribbean blues rapidly assuaging her frustration and liquefying her insides.

"Seriously, Anson," she said, trying to maintain her icy composure. "You were on fire. That whole strip tease? Fucking hot. And then you just up and leave. As a professional, I'd expect you to finish, no matter what. The show must go on, right?"

She rolled her lips inward, reluctant to smile as Anson worked her over with his eyes.

"You're right," he said. "Let me make it up to you."

He stepped behind her and kissed her hair, the warmth of his chest against her back sinking into her skin. He settled his hands around her waist and slid them to the front of her belly, down onto her thighs. She squeezed her legs tighter as he sucked on her neck. Then, he rested his chin on her shoulder and looked down her chest at her crossed legs.

"I've got to get in there to rectify this situation," he uttered softly.

"Actually, you've got to get me wet in order to get in," she replied haughtily.

He swiveled the chair around so that she now faced him, Kendall's mouth contorting as she fought to hide her smile during their staring contest.

"Baby," Anson cooed, brushing his erection up against her, his hand now effortlessly easing one leg off the other, separating her knees so they straddled his muscular thighs. "You couldn't stay dry around me if you tried."

Kendall's mouth popped open in protest. Taking advantage, Anson slipped his tongue inside, overpowering her. He forced her back against the edge of the counter and caressed the slippery surface between her legs.

"See?" he teased. "Now let me *fucking give it to you*, like you asked."

Chapter 39

Kendall and Anson panted, tangled up in one another on the lush white area rug of his bedroom floor. Neither said a word for several minutes, the intensity of the sex they'd just had – in addition to what they'd finished downstairs – surpassing the impassioned second round from their very first night together. With heightened emotions enveloping them, Anson's climactic commentary had danced dangerously close to professions of love.

"I never…" Anson began, but his words failed him. He lifted his head, needing to see the source of his greatest pleasure.

Kendall looked up and smiled. "Glad you liked it."

"Yeah. I *liked* it," he said, shaking his head at her. "Fucking blew my mind. I don't even know how you did what you did. Switching it up like that? While riding me? Shit, Kendall. You realize you've ruined me for life, right? No one else will ever compare."

She graciously sighed, his flattery always excessive after a powerful orgasm.

"Are you sore?" he asked, his curiosity fully fueled. "It seemed like a couple of times, there, you had that *look* again. Pleasurable pain?"

Kendall pushed up and got off of him.

"Aren't you the chatty Cathy right now," she said. "I came, didn't I? Don't worry about my pain/pleasure threshold. You know, considering the unknown number, yet perceived *thousands* of women you've slept with–"

"*Thousands*?" he asked incredulously.

"Yes. I have no choice but to come up with a number – and it's *thousands*. For all that experience you're packing, you sure react like it's all new to you. If I'm into it and all the surfaces are slick, it ain't nothing but a G-thang, baby."

Kendall skipped over to the bathroom, leaving Anson laughing.

"Well you're the *sexpert* here, if you hadn't noticed," he called out, slowly raising himself to a seated position.

"And on that topic of experts," Kendall said, segueing the conversation. "Is it time yet for your *flawless stripper skills* conversation? There's no way you've never done something like that before."

"Yes, there might be a story behind it," he said vaguely, pulling on a pair of boxers.

But then his expression sank, seeing Kendall exit the bathroom.

She walked into the bedroom fully dressed: shorts, tank top, and even her bra. Her overnight bag hung on her shoulder as she walked to his bed and dropped it there. She glanced about the room, surveying it for her belongings.

"Oh right," she said. "We started on the second floor. So what's your stripper story?" She smiled cheerfully, blatantly ignoring her one-sided decision to call it a night.

"You're leaving?" he asked. "It's after midnight."

"I don't want to get into this, Anson. I thought about it, but I've decided to head home. It's no different than any other time, so let's not make it into a big deal."

"It is a big deal! You're completely unwilling to spend more than a few hours with me at a time. Call me crazy, but I just don't get it. We've got something pretty powerful going on here, and you act like it means nothing."

Kendall snatched her bag off the bed and marched down the stairs, Anson following suit.

"Anson," she snapped. "We. Have. Sex! That's all! You, more than anyone, should get that.

"How many relationships have you been in since Grace? How many? Zero! By your own admission! Yet you've fucked all of South Florida! But for some reason, *I* should be ready to just commit again? Well, newsflash! I'm not!"

"That. Is. NOT. Just. Sex!" he shouted at her, pointing back up the stairs. "When will you admit that?"

She disappeared into his man-cave, then abruptly spun around to glare at him.

"You want to know why you *love* sex with me?!" she yelled. "Because I'm fresh out of a goddamn perfect ten-year relationship! Dan and I shared a perfect love. I know exactly what I like and what I want and how to bring the passion and heat to the bedroom. Because. Of. *Him*."

She gritted her teeth, biting back her tears. She stormed away from Anson to find her pajamas.

"But, *you*," she continued, picking up her shorts and shirt strewn near the fireplace. "*You* just know how to *fuck*: no strings attached, no meaning. And I'm sorry that I'm the first person to bring you something other than a robotic release.

"But guess what? That's all I want now. I just want to fuck and be done with it. So, don't put your emotional baggage shit on me. That's *your* shit to deal with. That's not how this started. That's not what *this* has been about, this... this... this fucked-up relationship!"

Anson stood, near the bar, listening to her and absorbing her bullets. She scowled at him from across the room, breathing hard, and waited for his response. She moved to leave.

"You're right," he finally said indifferently, stopping Kendall in her tracks. "I've been this robotic machine for years. Then you come into my life, disrupting everything I've known. Believe me: Everything would have been easier if I'd said no to you that night – my business with Xavier, how I function at the hospital, even my minute-to-minute thoughts.

"You're a passionate woman, Kendall. Christ, the way I feel inside you – there's no comparison. And I want to give it back to you: that feeling. All that emotion that surrounds us when we have sex? It comes from you. But I can't give it back, if you're never willing to experience the cool down of just being next to me."

Anson took a few steps forward, just within her reach, but kept his arms at his sides.

"I want to experience your everyday nuances," he said. "I want to see how you spend the other twenty hours of your day. I want to know about your school plans. I want to know about the birthday party for Gabe. Actually, I'd really like to meet Gabe."

Kendall's hardened expression immediately softened.

Elena and Kendall had been planning Gabriel's 30th birthday party over the phone for weeks, the conversations sometimes happening in front of Anson. Kendall would shush Anson, not wanting her mom to hear him, and then move to another room to finish the party talk, never saying a word about it once they'd hung up.

"I'll be more open with you, too," Anson offered. "I'll tell you what it was like to be an exotic dancer – something I can honestly say I enjoyed. We'll talk about my business with Xavier and why it's ending. I'll even tell you the number of women I've slept with – since you're so hell-bent on knowing. But I can't do this–"

"Wait, what?" she asked, clearing her head with a shake. "You were an actual stripper?"

"Did you hear anything I said besides that?" he asked.

"Well, yes," she answered. "But responding to that's a no-brainer. Everything else is a bit heavier."

"You said so yourself: There was no way I hadn't done that before."

"You're right. I could tell there was actual learned skill behind it. But wow. I thought maybe a few classes at a dance studio." Kendall stood still, pausing to picture it all. "The whole stripping-to-pay-for-med-school persona didn't actually cross my mind. I'm a little shocked."

"It was during my residency. After Grace died. And oddly enough, it wasn't for the money. Well, at first it wasn't. But the money was nice," he said reflectively. "So, what are you? A good shocked? Or a bad one?"

"Just – shocked," Kendall answered with a shrug. "I... I've never known a stripper. At least, not that I know of. But, no judgment from me."

"You're judging me right now."

"Well, I don't mean to," she apologized. "I'm just trying to picture it all."

"What about the other stuff I said?" Anson asked, the tension clearly cut.

"Coupled with what I shouted?" she asked, defeated. "I don't know. I mean... I don't know, Anson. It comes in crazy waves with me. You tell me what you want, and I like that. But I'm not sure it's an option for you to have. At least not yet. Things do get intense when we're going at it, don't they?"

Anson smiled, nodding his head.

"You're right, though. I'm not ready for the cool down," she sighed. "Up there? What we just did? And what we did right here, in this room? It's all-consuming. I don't know how to transition from all that to playing house – and still keep my heart and head about me. It's all or nothing right now. No middle ground. Hot or cold. A take-it-or-leave-it offer. I'm not sure we can even function outside the bedroom. Maybe it's not in our relationship DNA."

"Do you say that because you don't want it to be? Like, why bother when you already have what you want in this relationship?" he asked.

"No. More like, I wouldn't be able to deny that we're dating to my mom and brother any longer," she answered honestly. "They know about you, but don't *know* about you. So, if you're a real presence in my everyday life – well, then they'd have to know about you."

"Ouch. I hadn't realized you were hiding me that much."

"I'm not saying this to be mean," she said. "I tell them we hang out. I mean, it's true."

"I think you want to have your cake and eat it too," he said.

"What does that mean? Anson, we're not dating. Would you call this dating? We've never actually been on a date together, like out and about, among other people. I can't let my family get invested in something that's not real. That's not fair to them. Do your brothers know about us? Your parents?"

"Yes," he replied.

"Oh," Kendall said in surprise. "Really? What do you tell them?"

"That I've actually been seeing a nurse from the hospital and not some affluent socialite over a few nights in Miami."

"But it's only been – what? Just over a week? Really? You talk about me?" she asked, even more surprised by this than by his stripper confession.

"It's been a week – and then some. This all started just over a month ago," he said defensively. "Kendall, it might not be long, but we've managed to pack quite a bit in."

"So, the socialite is your typical type?" she asked, stepping back through their conversation.

"Not really. Those just tend to be the people who call on me from time to time."

"Call on you?" she asked.

"Kendall, are you spending the night?"

She took in a cleansing breath and thought for a moment.

"No, I'm still going to go home," she said. "It's what I have to do right now. I don't know why I'm afraid of the middle ground. But I'll admit: You're getting close to wearing me down, Allaway."

"I don't want to wear you down. There was a moment, tonight – in this room, in fact – when you got lost in us completely," Anson said, reaching for her hand. "Not a thought – just emotion. I think we could have that outside of sex. If you would just give us a chance."

Kendall sighed and looked around the room. "How did we get to this conversation?"

"We got lukewarm," Anson answered. "I'll walk you out."

At her Jeep door they finally kissed, extinguishing any remaining bitterness from inside.

"So we'll play this week by ear, okay?" Anson offered.

"Sounds good," she said, smiling. "And hey: Despite how things ended – tonight's been pretty amazing, Anson. Thank you."

"My pleasure," he said, returning her smile.

They kissed goodbye.

"And don't be thinking that secret world of stripping just up and left my mind," she called out through her open window. "I've got a hankering to know more."

"Maybe if we were dating," he said with a wink.

Touché.

Once home, Kendall immediately dove into the Internet, stretching her evening out until two in the morning since she aimed to sleep away the day in preparation for her night shift. She Googled "Dr. Anson Allaway," typing in all forms of his name along with keywords like *male stripper, exotic dancer*, and even *porn* and *porn star*, stumbling down the rabbit hole of YouTube videos with unsavory links to escort services.

But after hours of looking, she'd turned up nothing – aside from several pictures of Anson in a Miami social life magazine, each shot with a stunning, model of a woman hanging on his arm at a red carpet event.

The photos of the perfectly poised couple didn't settle well with her. She knew they were only *out for the occasional fuck.* And even though tonight that was what Kendall had said she'd wanted – and nothing more – she really hoped that Anson didn't believe her.

Chapter 40

For the next week, Kendall and Anson's relationship developed and transformed, bulking up its internal structure to support them beyond their fervent foundation. Both made the effort to spend time with one another outside of the bedroom. They even went out to dinner twice; one night, after they'd attended a jazz performance at the Kravis Center for the Performing Arts.

These sexless exchanges had been flirty and fun, their chemistry nearly as strong as it was in the bedroom. But the minute Anson had that look in his eyes – one of pure joy – Kendall would panic, seeking out some form of comic relief to lighten the mood.

It was while strolling through City Place in West Palm Beach after the jazz concert, their arms holding each other close, that they'd run into Anson's colleague, Dr. Rodin, and his wife. Anson was completely comfortable with discussing their evolving relationship. Kendall, on the other hand, felt like she'd been caught in a sleazy affair. Her awkwardness considerably shortened the impromptu meeting – and embarrassed Anson. Her constant resistance was really starting to wear on his last nerve.

Another weekend of Kendall working three shifts in a row came and went, with the couple only managing to exchange platonic greetings in the halls at work. Kendall didn't have the energy to keep up her maddening pace and still make time for Anson afterward. So, when they bumped into each other in the cafeteria the following Tuesday afternoon (yet another picked up shift for overtime), Anson decided not to play his Dr. Allaway role. Instead, he kept things familiar.

Very familiar.

"Hey babe. I don't think we've ever actually sat down to have lunch together while at work," Anson broadcasted, cozying right up to Kendall in the cashier line. He was fresh out of surgery, still wearing the black Star Trek surgical cap she'd bought him on a whim the week before.

Kendall laughed awkwardly. "Yeah, well, I'm just grabbing this to go, so... maybe another time."

"Really?" he asked, his eyes echoing his aggravated tone.

"What?" she asked, stepping up to the register to pay.

Anson immediately pulled out his badge for the cashier to swipe.

"I can pay for my own lunch, Dr. Allaway," she said.

"I'm aware, Nurse Matthews. All that overtime you keep signing up for – conveniently keeping us apart outside of work – well, hopefully, it's enough to pay for a meal. But for now, this one's on me."

Anson nodded at the cashier, then accepted his badge back. Kendall was speechless, looking around for a sympathetic eye yet only met with hushed whispers. Embarrassed, she quickly followed Anson as he strutted through the crowded cafeteria, passing by the doctor's lounge and picking up a chair along the way. He set the chair down at a table next to another empty one.

"What was that?" Kendall asked, sitting down where he'd directed her but unwilling to put her lunch on the table. "It's not the same for doctors as it is for nurses. There's a glaring double standard. Don't embarrass me like that again."

"Seriously Kendall? Settle down," he said harshly. "How you manage to beg for it one night and then turn me away the next, I'll never understand." He took a large bite of his steak fajita, the greasy juice running down his hands and dripping onto his lap. "Shit."

Still taken aback by his uncompromising attitude about how they should behave while at work, Kendall got up from the table – but graciously, to grab him some napkins. She walked back, planning to head straight out after handing them over.

However, upon accepting her napkins, Anson caught her wrist as well, pulling her in close and kissing her on the lips.

"Thanks, babe," he said cooly, his cocky smile smoldering, even with a mouthful of grilled steak.

Kendall jumped back, wide-eyed and angry... for about two seconds.

"Okay. I'm sorry," Anson said, his beautiful eyes melting her heart. "I just missed you. Please sit down and eat with me."

"I have to go back upstairs," she said regretfully. "Two other nurses are at lunch. I just wanted to buy something before the cafeteria closed. We'll talk about this later."

But as she turned to leave, she saw the questions written across all the faces around them: Who was she? And why was the most eligible bachelor-darling interested in her?

The gossip train fueled up for departure.

"Are you two dating?" The question shot out like a bullet.

Kendall's neck and ears burned up instantly, panic taking over. "Uh, well, we're–"

"Yes. Yes we are," Anson interjected. "Have been for some time now; we just never made it gossip official until this moment. I'll make sure to update my social media accounts for you all." He shook his head with disgust. "Is it really any of your damn business?"

Kendall looked back at him with surprise. She left the cafeteria, retreating to her patients and her facade of control.

Anson grabbed the remainder of his food and followed her out.

"Are you mad at me?" he asked as she walked briskly down the basement hall to the back stairwell.

"No, I'm not mad. Not really. I just didn't expect that," she answered, not slowing her pace. "I thought we were keeping it private, that's all. Now I feel like I have to answer all these questions."

"What questions?" he asked. "People date all the time around this place. It's like its own dating website. And now it's out there, but they know it's none of their business."

Kendall stopped in front of the stairwell door and faced him. "You think that whole act in there – that just because you said so, there won't be any recourse? Maybe for you there won't be. But for me, it may as well be on the six o'clock news." Kendall swiped her badge at the stairwell door and opened it a crack. "You are *not* following me in here."

Anson laughed. "That happened *one* time."

"Twice, actually. The second time was just a bit more memorable." She slowly smiled. "Really, though. I do have to go."

"Okay, but I want to talk to you about something," Anson said.

"Something good, or something bad?" she asked.

"About us, about this coming weekend. Something pretty neutral, depending on how you view it, I guess."

"Can you give me a little more than that?" she asked.

"Well, the standard DTR talk – and I want you to come with me to Miami this weekend," Anson said. Then he shook his head in amusement, thinking about what he said. "I'm really starting to sound like the chick in this relationship."

"Well, I'll already be in Miami this weekend. Gabe's birthday is tomorrow, and we're having his party on Saturday," she replied, realizing too late that she'd never extended an invitation to Anson. Her brain still compartmentalized him outside of her everyday life.

"Right," Anson said, clenching his jaw.

"Maybe I'll swing by tonight so we can talk. Good?" she suggested quickly.

"Whatever you want, Kendall."

Whereas his callous tone bothered her, his aqua blue eyes positively thrashed her. He was hurt. She pecked him on the lips and raced up the stairs, knowing she couldn't do anything to fix things now. He'd have to wait.

Unfortunately, the rest of her shift careened out of control. First, the rumors from the cafeteria spread over to the unit a couple hours later, via her colleague, Carlos. All her attempts to diminish them just further fueled the fire. She finally caved, accepting the fact that her private life had now become an open book at GC General. Then, an hour before shift change, she received a train wreck of an admission from the trauma ED, tacking two more hours onto her shift.

By the time she called Anson on her way out of the hospital – first to gripe about his PDA, then to dive straight into his *define the relationship* talk – her empathy was gone.

"Well, maybe it wouldn't be so awkward if you didn't fight it so hard," he countered, still standing by his decision to *out* them at work.

"Whatever. So, DTR. What?" Kendall barked.

"Let's just wait until you get here," he said.

"Anson, I'm not in the mood for ambience. I just need you to lay it all out there."

"You're impossible. Fine. Would you consider me your boyfriend?" he asked.

Kendall scoffed.

"I don't know," she answered flippantly. "Is that what you want – will that make this all better for you? We're boyfriend-girlfriend?"

"Yes," he answered confidently.

"Fine. I'm your girlfriend. You're my boyfriend. I'll sit by you at lunch time, only if you chase me at recess."

"I don't even know why I try."

"Oh come on," Kendall said. "That's such a juvenile question to ask. I'm turning onto A1A right now. I'll see you in a minute."

"Honestly, what's the fucking point?" Anson snapped.

"What? Why are you getting angry all of a sudden?" she asked.

"We need the juvenile titles so you understand that you have an obligation to me as well," Anson answered, no longer willing to take every cutting comment she shot back at him. "I'm getting so sick of this bullshit with you: How you dictate what *I* should feel and orchestrate how *we* can act based on what *you* think is appropriate for a widow. You can't live in the shadow of a dead guy forever, Kendall. I'm trying to fucking live here, and you're alive as well. Quit ignoring that monumental fact."

The silence stretched out uncomfortably long, and Anson immediately regretted his eruption – despite the truth in every word he said.

"Fuck... I'm sorry, Kendall. Babe? That didn't come out right. Are you almost here?" Anson asked, apologetically.

Chapter 41

"Hi Gabe! This is Anson, your sister's friend. I hear today is the big three O. Happy Birthday, man. I hope I get a chance to talk to you in person one of these days. Maybe you could teach me a thing or two about fishing. I always manage to hook 'em, just never seem to reel 'em in. I've gotta learn your secret. Have a great day. Tell Kendall I said hi."

Anson's third unanswered voicemail of the day finally struck a chord with Kendall. But she still didn't return his call. She went ahead and played the message for Gabriel and Elena while having dessert in Miami Wednesday night.

"Will he be at my party?" Gabriel asked.

"Sorry, bud. He's got work to do," Kendall said, finishing up her slice of chocolate banana cream pie, Gabriel's traditional birthday dessert. "You'll meet him another day."

"Will we?" Elena asked, a little too eagerly.

"Mom: Please. Don't make this into something it's not."

"It sure sounds like something," Elena commented.

"Well, he'd like it to be," Kendall said, sitting back in her chair. "But I know it's temporary, so there's no point. I've decided to put the house on the market. I'm going to CRNA school in the fall. I won't have time for a romantic relationship. Even if it does sound like it could be something."

"Does he know this?" Elena asked.

"Mom, don't do that – worry about his feelings. You don't even know him. He knows this doesn't have long-term potential. Even if he doesn't want to admit it – he knows. It's just the way things are for me right now."

"Okay. If you say so... But there's something to be said about those people who come into our lives at the exact moment we need them. Even if it's just for a short amount of time. Don't undervalue this relationship just because it won't last. Moments aren't meant to last. But memories are. And I'm guessing, you'll remember him forever."

***

Kendall's shift on Thursday dragged, along with her energy level. Her emotional forecast called for threatening clouds of doom and gloom, with Eeyore sauntering back to her side. She repeated the words her mom said to her, over and over, hoping they'd sink in so she could just let go and live in the moment.

While on her lunch break in the SICU lounge, Kendall finally softened just enough to reach out to Anson.

KM: **We got your message. Gabe really liked it. I had to play it several times. Thank you for that.**

Anson replied close to the end of her shift.

AA: **Will I be seeing you tonight?**

Kendall glanced down at her phone while charting.

KM: **At work right now. I work tomorrow. Doubt it.**

AA: **So are we done?**

She wanted to write something meaningful. Maybe even an apology. She wanted him to find her in the SICU and take her to the stairwell, forgetting all the angry words they'd thrown, knowing it'd been rooted in heartache. She wanted to tell him what her mom said, that even if this didn't end in a fairytale sunset, he meant more to her in the short time they'd been together than anyone else ever could. That he wasn't excessive. That she didn't need to justify him. That she wanted him to stay.

But her body ached, her thoughts were cluttered, and fear got in the way.

KM: **Some things are just temporary.**

AA: **Some things last forever.**

Neither of them responded again.

Kendall pulled into her driveway around eight o'clock that evening and wasn't exactly surprised to find Anson's Porsche parked in it. Anson was leaning up against his door, waiting for her.

She got out of the Jeep and locked the door, barely reacting to his presence. They made eye contact momentarily, but then she walked up the path to her front door.

"So, is this the silent treatment?" he asked. "Will this be temporary?"

She entered her home, leaving the door open for him.

"Kendall? We have to talk about this," he said, closing the door behind him.

Kendall tossed her bag onto the couch, and then her phone and keys on the kitchen counter. She went straight into her bedroom and undressed, Anson watching just outside the door. She brushed past him in her pajamas before entering the kitchen.

Kendall removed a bag of grapes from the refrigerator, then made a crude peanut butter sandwich. She filled a glass with water, grabbed the bag of grapes and her cell phone, and walked past him, carrying the sandwich in her mouth. She sat down on her living room couch and turned on the TV.

Anson looked about the room, as if seeking support from an invisible audience. After a beat, he sat down on the opposite end of the couch. Kendall maintained her glacial stance.

"So, at what point do you clue me in, since you're the one calling all the shots?" Anson asked.

"Don't you ever just want to be left alone? I mean, especially after being told you live in the shadow of a dead guy?"

"Yes," Anson agreed. "But considering I live in the shadow of a dead girl – and that I've apologized umpteen times – you'd think there'd be a little bit of forgiveness by now."

Kendall let out an exasperated sigh.

"Is there something I'm missing? Aside from the obvious. Maybe–" he continued.

"Anson, stop," Kendall said, interrupting him. "Right now I'd rather you just try and *not* figure it out. Sometimes I go into bitch mode. No real reason. It's just how I feel right now. I'm tired, cranky, not in any mood for sex, and I've got you criticizing me on how I'm navigating my emotions. You are welcome to hang out with me, but we both know that's not our strong suit."

Anson sat quietly for a minute, watching her finish her sandwich. She pulled the bag of grapes onto her lap, continuing with her routine. So, he settled further back onto the couch.

"Just curious – and not meaning any offense by it, because I know it's all good and normal – but is this PMS?" he asked boldly.

If looks could kill, Anson's heart would have flat-lined right then and there, his body entering full rigor mortis a mere three hours after Kendall had turned her head to answer his question.

"No, Anson. I'm not PMSing. But thank you for attempting to be tuned in to my cycle. This is just one of Kendall's nuances, that you've mentioned wanting to know."

"I don't think I mentioned wanting to get familiar with *bitch mode*, but if you say so..." Anson muttered under his breath.

"Listen," Kendall said, angling her body toward him on the couch, ready to lay it all out there. "My brother's party is Saturday night, and I've been trying to make a variety of arrangements with my mom from a distance because there's this guilt if I'm not spending my time off with you. I didn't invite you, because I didn't think it'd be your thing.

"My best friend's wedding is May 9th – only three weeks away. I'm maid of honor, and this wedding is extravagant. So, tons of preparation. Then right afterward, she'll be moving to Georgia. Honestly, I don't know how I'm going to deal with that.

"I'm going to be leaving GC General at the end of the summer to attend CRNA school in Miami. My mind is made up. It's going to be full-time, stressful, and three years long. Everything will be changing in just a few months.

"So, on top of all this, I have my – what? My *boyfriend* upset with me because I can't carve out more hours in a day to satisfy his definition of intimacy? This is what I was worried about. You knew that. Anson, there are only so many days I can go without sleep. Eventually, something's got to give. And it will never be my family. Or even my work."

Anson remained quiet, riddling her with guilt. She'd assumed he would jump at the chance to fight back, to fight for her. To defend his place in her heart.

But he didn't.

"And well," Kendall continued, "I'm scared of where this is headed."

"Scared? About what?" he asked.

"About us."

"*Us* – what?"

"I'm not sure I want this anymore," Kendall answered softly, staring at the grapes in her lap. "Knowing where it could lead."

"With me – or any relationship?"

"The relationship," she said. "Well, not exactly. I do want it at times. I want it with you. It's just... I need the distance every now and then."

"I get that," he agreed, his voice quiet, almost pensive.

"Why aren't you saying more? Why do I feel like I'm the only one talking here?" she asked.

"Because I need to hear it from you," Anson answered. "You already know how I feel about you: how I want you in my life, how I want this relationship to work. Kendall, I've laid it all out there for you plenty of times, to either pick up or kick to the curb. And for some fucking reason, I've become a glutton for punishment when it comes to you. So, if you're telling me you just need some time, I'll ride *this bitch mode* out until that more favorable version of you returns. But I'm not going to sit by and take this rejection, time and time again. I can't. I've got some pride as well."

Anson shook his head, his expression crinkling with frustration. Then he looked back at her, sharply.

"You know, if you included me in your family and work, you wouldn't feel so divided in your time," he said. "But I'm guessing that's where the problem lies: not cataloguing me in your brain as one of your important people."

"Anson, you are important – important to me. And in many ways, the most important per–"

"Goddammit, Kendall!" Anson cut her off. "Don't say shit like that if you don't mean it."

He wanted to say more, but resisted. They both knew the truth.

"I know you're ready for more," Kendall said softly. "But I... I just don't think it can happen with me. Not now. Not the way you need it to be. It wouldn't be fair to you."

Anson rested his head on the back of the couch, now looking vacantly at the TV. The TV Guide Channel had been running the entire time, announcing upcoming shows and movies, unsympathetic to their plight. He methodically nodded his head, her words sinking in slowly, the spoken truth now impossible to deny.

"So where does this leave us?" he asked, his voice lacking any hope.

"I'm not sure. I'm not looking for anyone else," Kendall answered honestly.

"Well, that makes two of us."

Anson met her eyes, then moved closer to her.

"I'll leave it up to you then," he said, placing his hand affectionately on her leg, his energy singeing her immediately. Then he stood up from the couch and got ready to leave.

"Are you going then?" she asked, confused.

"You just finished telling me you want to be alone – and your preemptive strike on the drive up from Miami comes to mind. If you're not making time in your schedule, I shouldn't take offense. The whole *it's not you, it's me* speech. In all fairness to you, you warned me and I accepted those terms. I'm trying to hold up to my end of the bargain. So, I won't push you. I won't act hurt."

He then walked to the front door.

"Wait, *are* you hurt?" Kendall asked him, standing up from the couch with mild panic.

"I'm definitely not feeling great about this," he said. "But we all need to know when to cut our losses."

Anson grabbed a hold of the doorknob to exit.

"Well, wait just a minute!" Kendall demanded, setting down her grapes and swiftly meeting him at the door. "You're here now. Suppose I don't want you to go quite yet?"

Anson grasped Kendall's upper arms with his hands; the restrained touch cooled her skin. "You'll need to make up your mind. You can't have it both ways. I've tried."

"What both ways?" she asked.

"The thrill of someone chasing you and the security of not falling in love."

Kendall's expression sank, his words towering over her. *Of course*. He was so right. She had wanted flirty fun, to feel alive and in control, but only if she could manage it devoid of all emotion.

Rather than wait around for his heart to break further, Anson opened the door and left.

Kendall stood paralyzed in fear, the static sound of her stunned nerves crackling in her ears. There was no goodbye, no plan for talking later or meeting up, no real closure to whatever they'd had. And in that moment of willingly letting him go – because of her fear of vulnerability, her fear of getting hurt, her fear of falling in love again – she felt the crushing weight of standing alone once more.

And it broke her.

"Wait!" Kendall shouted, racing out her door onto the driveway.

Anson had already backed up onto her street, shifting the Porsche into drive, when he spotted her running toward him.

He rolled down his window and waited.

"Wait," she repeated feebly, her voice choked as that suffocating sadness threatened to move back in. "I don't want you to go."

Anson pulled his Porsche back into her driveway, throwing the road behind him into a ghostly darkness as his headlights turned away from it. Kendall followed him back up the cracked concrete drive until he came to a stop.

As soon as he stepped out of his car, Kendall threw her arms around his neck. Anson embraced her tightly – raising her to the tips of her toes – and drew in a long breath over her hair.

"How's that for chasing?" she asked, burying her face into his neck.

She sniffed, a few isolated tears breaking free, and leaned back to look at his eyes. But the sober expression from when he'd left remained unchanged.

"I'm not one for dramatics, Kendall. If you need the time, take the time."

"I'm not saying I know what I want from this. But I do know: I don't want you to go," she whispered.

"I can't make this work only when it's convenient for you," he replied. "I'm working full time as well."

"I know. And you're so good about checking in and planning nights together. I'm trying, Anson. Just be patient with me. I need time."

"That's what I'm doing. So, we'll touch base again in… I don't know. A couple of days. After we're back from Miami," Anson suggested.

"I want you to give me time, not space," Kendall argued.

"Actually, you did ask for space earlier."

"Fuck what I said earlier! Gaah!" Kendall jumped back, pacing around like a trapped animal. She stopped, squeezing her eyes shut, and pinched the bridge of her nose as she fought through the pain of letting him in.

"I like you, Anson. I *really* like you. And maybe it's more. But there's this uncomfortable dichotomy going on internally, since I'm still very much in love with my husband. And on top of that, there's this mortifyingly daft side of me waiting for Dan to come home – and it would end me if he found you here. And I know he's dead and I know this sounds like I'm having a complete psychotic breakdown – but that's the truth. That's what's buried so deep down, that… when I'm with you" –Kendall looked back up at him, opening her eyes, her vision clear, her voice steady– "and you make me laugh. You make me feel… happiness. I feel… cherished. And then, you take me into your arms – and it's like the never-ending orgasm, for fuck's sake."

Anson blushed, his face softening with a smile. But Kendall carried right on, her cathartic momentum fueling her words.

"When that happens with you," she continued, her voice quiet yet strong as she closed the gap between them, "it breaks me. It absolutely breaks me.

"Anson, in the middle of it all, I look at you. Into your eyes. And I see how you look at me. Like he did. I never expected to see that again. To see it so soon.

"And I feel it. The way you make love to me. It's beautiful. You're far from robotic. You've got such depth behind those eyes. Such passion.

"It's just too much right now. I can't look at you that way. Not when I see him. I can't be open to love like that again – to pain like that again. And because I don't know what to do with those feelings – I'm sorry, Anson, but I have to shut you out."

With his thumb, Anson brushed away a tear as it rolled down her cheek. She leaned into his large palm, his loving touch supporting her so tenderly.

"I really don't want to shut you out. If anything, please fight to bring me in," she whimpered.

Anson took in a few slow breaths. Finally, he closed the car door behind him, opening up his hand to hers and walking her back up to the house. Her heart raced along at a blinding speed.

"Anson?" she asked, unsure whether he was coming or going.

"I'll give you the time you need. But first, I need something from you," he answered.

"Will you stay for a while then?" she asked.

They reached the front door, still wide open from Kendall's theatrical exit. Anson stepped into the house, pulling Kendall in behind him. Slowly, he backed her up against the inside of the closed door, his hips meeting hers. With those Caribbean blues confirming every word she'd said, Anson looked directly at her, holding her head in his hands.

"If you asked me to," he said, "I'd stay forever. Do yourself a favor tonight – keep your eyes closed."

Anson kissed her, inhaling her fragile state deep into his lungs, guiding her further in than ever before. Their chests rose with one another in synchrony, the borders of their physical bodies washing away like footprints on the beach as their souls danced in the flames of the other.

Kendall's entire being dove in, safely swimming in Anson's unapologetic love.

Chapter 42

Anson didn't sleep over that Thursday, the night of their unequivocal lovemaking. In fact, he had quietly left Kendall's home an hour after they'd made love. And although neither of them said those three game-changing words, they'd both felt them and welcomed them, thriving in the hope they carried.

She and Anson had left things up in the air once again, agreeing to take the weekend to think about things. Although they both worked Friday, they never reached out to one another, wanting to respect their open-ended decision – or at least continue to ride on the good vibes of Thursday night.

Kendall woke up on Saturday morning feeling refreshed, rejuvenated, and in a word, reborn. It was just after seven o'clock, the perfect time to get things ready for a morning out on the great Atlantic Ocean before heading to Miami for Gabriel's birthday party.

She smiled as she stretched, the idea of experiencing love once again frolicking about in her thoughts. Dan seemed more present when she was at peace – even if brought on by another man.

Gabriel and William rifling through drawers and cabinets in the kitchen interrupted Kendall's relationship analysis.

Ariel and William had driven down to Miami the previous afternoon to pick up Gabriel, as his biggest birthday request had been a day out on the boat. Considering the party kicked off at Elena's gallery later that night, Kendall had decided a morning trip would start the day off beautifully, giving Gabriel the best of both worlds: the ocean and his family. It'd been a while since all three of them crashed at Kendall's house, especially for reasons other than supporting her emotionally.

The aroma of a freshly-brewed dark roast coffee woke Kendall further, enticing her to leave her master bedroom. William stood behind the kitchen counter, shirtless in his sweatpants, arguing over omelet ingredients with Gabriel. He looked up at Kendall as she entered the room.

"Good morning!" William said, greeting her exuberantly. "So the hot debate in the kitchen is whether this omelet should have a little kick or not. We've got scallions, tomatoes, mushrooms, a bit of parsley, and a whole lot of nothing else." William danced around like the host of a cooking show. He shook the crushed red pepper jar like a maraca, showcasing his zesty culinary skills and making Gabriel laugh.

"Good morning, sleepyhead," Gabriel said, smiling at Kendall.

"You two are super bright eyed and bushy tailed. Can I get a cup, please?" Kendall asked, pulling up a barstool next to Gabriel. "And sorry, Will. But trying to get Gabe to add a little spice to his life is like trying to brush your teeth while eating Oreos. This boy likes it bland, always has."

"I had blueberries in my cereal," Gabriel countered. Of course, he'd already had his morning orange juice and bowl of cereal.

Kendall reached out and rubbed his back. "I love you, Gabe."

William skipped the extra spice, settling on salt and pepper, and poured his omelet mix into a heated skillet. A few moments later, they heard a boisterous squeal from Ariel, stretching awake on the hide-a-bed couch in the living room. Together, they ate their omelet breakfasts around the peninsula counter as they mapped out their leisurely cruise down Florida's Gold Coast.

Once they'd finished, Kendall turned on the satellite radio and pumped up the volume, switching everyone into high gear. Ariel and Kendall headed into the master bath to get ready for the day – giving Kendall a chance to update Ariel on certain highlights from Thursday night. Gabriel got ready in his guest room, while William put the kitchen and living room back in order.

While folding the hide-a-bed back up, William heard a knock at the front door. He grabbed his T-shirt off the couch and looked through the peep hole. A fairly familiar, well-dressed man waited casually on the front step. Unconcerned, and still shirtless, William opened the door, his deeply defined abdominal and pectoral muscles on full display. Standing in the doorway, William pulled a crisp white undershirt over his head, only further enhancing the chiseled cut of his torso against his dark chestnut skin. He looked up – and directly into the raging eyes of his forgotten past.

"Oh shit. Anson-fucking-Allaway. Of course. I didn't even..." William sputtered off, dumbstruck.

"You'd better start talking before I fucking lose it," Anson growled, stepping right up to William and ready to brawl.

"Aw, hell! This isn't what you think," William said, pushing Anson back and onto the porch. "I'm a friend of Kendall's. In fact, I'm getting married to her best friend next month. Maybe she's mentioned her – Ariel? I've been out of the business for years." He paused, shaking his head. "Damn. I can't believe you're the one she's dating."

Anson's eyes went wide, taking it all in as he stepped back from William. Running his hands through his hair, he suddenly felt weak, almost dizzy. Anson bent over, supporting himself on his knees, and took in a deep breath. He looked back up at William.

"Does she know?" Anson asked in a panic. "I haven't told her yet. Oh, fuck! Johnson, did you tell her? You've told her, haven't you? I was going to tell her. I'm in the process of ending everything with Xavier."

Anson's uncharacteristic pleading was so desperate, so unexpected, and so uncomfortable to witness that for a moment, William felt bad for him.

"Relax. I didn't tell her anything," William said. "She doesn't even know about me. Until seeing you now, in the flesh, I had no clue she was dating *the* Dr. Anson Allaway. I only hear bits and pieces of what's going on through Ariel."

William's reassurance relaxed Anson considerably, his confidence partially restored. He straightened out and approached the door again.

"Thanks, man," Anson said, shaking his head as if he'd dodged a bullet. "I'm definitely taking care of it. It's just a bit crazy right now... And it's really strange seeing you here. So... um, is she home?"

William looked at him like he had two heads.

"You think your secret is safe now? I have no loyalties to you, *man*," William said incredulously, his stance broadening, blocking the entryway completely. "Just knowing you've strung Kendall and her broken heart along for the past month – I'm ready to dropkick your motherfucking ass right here on her doorstep! But before I knock you senseless, let this sink in: You will never be anywhere close to the man that Dan was. You're the shit he scraped from his boots. And Kendall will see that, the minute you tell her the truth."

The stinging words were like a vacuum to Anson's lungs, snuffing out his next breath. He'd thought those very thoughts, but never imagined hearing them come from someone else's mouth. He stared, wild-eyed, searching for a retaliating response, but came up empty.

Then Gabriel swung the door open, curious as to what was going on outside. He studied Anson and looked back at William inquisitively.

"Gabe, I've got this. Go ahead and get Kendall," William instructed, his expression instantly easing up. Gabriel obliged.

"Was that her brother? He's here, too?" Anson asked. "Fuck."

William shook his head in disgust.

"Anson," Kendall said in surprise, glancing at William and amused by his bodyguard presence. "What are you doing here?"

"Um, just wanted to stop by," Anson answered, his eyes darting over to William.

"We're good, Will. Give us a minute," she said. They walked out into the driveway.

"Hey, I'm sorry I just showed up," Anson said, stealing a quick peck from Kendall. "I didn't realize you'd have such early company."

"Oh, well, they slept over. We're taking Gabe out on the boat today before heading down to his party at my mom's gallery." Kendall looked over at the black Lincoln Town Car parked behind William's Audi. "Is that your ride?"

"Yeah, I'm heading down to Miami now," he said. "I thought maybe you'd want a ride, so I had him stop by. Clearly, not well thought out. This isn't exactly giving you the space and time you needed, now is it?"

Kendall shrugged, giving Anson the benefit of the doubt. The pulse of his touch along her hips glided effortlessly into her heart. She kissed his neck and then his mouth, a suppler kiss this time.

Anson broke away.

"I can't. Unless you're getting in the back of that car with me–" he said. He then wiped his face with his hands. "Sorry about this. I shouldn't have stopped by. I'll just see you next week sometime, okay?"

"You're fine. Don't worry about it, Anson. You're here now. At least come in and meet my friends? My brother, too! Might as well, right?" Kendall suggested, smiling sweetly.

"I'd love to, but I really need to get going."

"Oh come on. It'll only be a minute. Besides, you already met Will, so only two more," Kendall said persuasively, nuzzling him just below his chin.

"Honestly, Johnson doesn't think much of me. Or Will rather. Let's just say, I made an ass of myself. So, I'm not exactly starting off on the right foot here," Anson said. "We'll do it some other time."

"*Johnson*? He introduced himself as *Johnson*?" Kendall asked, snickering.

"Uh, well. Dr. Johnson, right?" Anson said, trying to cover his tracks.

"*Dr. Johnson*? Oh my goodness! That's even worse!" Kendall laughed at William's cockiness but loved his presumably protective antics.

"Oh, well... I may have formally introduced myself first," Anson offered, grimacing as he dug himself deeper into his hole of lies.

"Did you two get out a ruler and measure your dicks as well?" she asked crudely. "I must have missed some showdown. Okay, so whatever. Bad first impression. Want to correct it? I mean,

Ariel would be seething if she knew she'd missed out on judging you as well."

Begrudgingly, he directed her back to the front door, hoping to make the introductions quick and painless. Kendall opened the door to her crew, all hanging out in the living room and eagerly awaiting their return. Except for William.

"Okay everyone, this is Anson, aka Dr. Allaway," Kendall announced, looking right at Ariel, smiling broadly. "He's a brain surgeon over at Gold Coast General, and well, the guy I've been dating." She looked closely at Gabriel, trying to gauge his reaction.

Anson nodded, feeling unusually reticent. Typically he walked into a room as *the* guy everyone looked to for direction. Families hung on his every word, confident he had everything under control. Women wanted him to complete their picture of perfection and to fulfill their sexual fantasies. But now he was the new guy, with a not-so-secret alternative lifestyle, brusquely trying to fill some unparalleled fireman's boots. Or just covering them with dog shit.

"Anson, this is everyone," Kendall said, continuing her introductions. "That's my amazing brother, Gabriel, aka Gabe – whom you've sort of heard over the phone. He's a fisherman extraordinaire and star employee of Gold Coast Reefs."

Gabriel immediately got up from the recliner and shook Anson's hand, always mindful of his manners.

"Here's Ariel, aka Dr. Duval. She's a professor of linguistics over at Gulfstream University. Not to mention my best friend and voice of reason. And you've already met Dr. Johnson, aka William or Will, aka Ariel's fiancé. He's a forensics expert and entomologist in hot demand with the FBI. They're a power couple extraordinaire, harboring more degrees than a thermometer."

"What's with the formal titles?" Ariel asked after shaking Anson's hand.

"Well, apparently these two boys were having a pissing contest outside. So, I thought I'd just throw it all out there. You know, to clear the air," Kendall answered with a smirk.

After being warmly greeted by Gabriel and Ariel, William played along, extending a firm handshake to Anson but retaining his level of contempt. William's past had been right where it belonged: in the past. But with Anson there, that past was very much present.

"Well, he has to go down to Miami now," Kendall said, wrapping up the meet-n-greet. "There's a car waiting for him outside. I just wanted everyone to meet, so maybe down the road we can all get together."

Kendall squeezed Anson's arm tighter. She then slid her hand into his, not shying away from the attachment they'd developed, letting him know it wasn't the space or time she needed – it was him. Anson visibly relaxed with her support, and Ariel noticed.

"Why don't you come to the wedding next month? It's in Miami as well," Ariel blurted out, William's scowl immediately showing his disapproval.

"Oh. Well, he might be on-call, right?" Kendall suggested, not wanting to put Anson on the spot – and just now sensing the boiling tension between the two men.

"Probably. But I'll look into it. And I appreciate the invite," Anson said.

"Well, the rehearsal dinner then," Ariel suggested persistently. "You eat, right? Come to the rehearsal dinner. It'll be Friday night, the eighth. It's outdoors and relaxed, like a huge barbeque. More time with Kendall. Can't go wrong with that, right? William and I would love to have you there."

"Uh…" Anson stalled.

"Sure. But only if he has time," Kendall interjected. "We can talk about that later. He's got to get going now." She pulled Anson back to the door.

"Sounds good. It was nice meeting you. And congratulations to you both," Anson said, waving goodbye.

"Bye Dr. A. Come on over when you want to go fishing. My mom wants to meet you, too!" Gabriel called out.

Although genuinely pleased by this, Anson forced a smile as the knife already piercing his heart plunged in deeper.

Right after closing the door behind her, Kendall whispered to Anson, unable to suppress her giggle. "What did you do to Will?"

"I don't know," he lied. "I was hit by the music when he opened the door and well, he's a guy answering your door on a Saturday morning. What can I say? I acted like a jerk. He said I'm not worth your time. I can't say I disagree."

"Oh please. Spare me. Dejection doesn't look good on you," Kendall said, pulling him in tighter as they walked arm-in-arm to the Town Car. "It was just a misunderstanding."

But then she winced in pain, holding her side.

"What's up? You okay?" he asked, looking her over carefully.

"Yeah, I'm fine. Just a little belly pain. Cramps, maybe. I might be getting my period," Kendall answered dismissively.

"You don't know when you get it?" Anson asked.

"Well, it's irregular. I have an IUD with hormones. It doesn't come every month."

Anson continued questioning Kendall with his eyes.

"I'll be fine. Anyway – so if you do come to the rehearsal dinner, you'd better bring your A-game. Ariel seemed quite taken with you, though, so that's always good." Kendall pushed up against him, planting a kiss on his doleful lips. Then she looked at him with a great big smile. "Hey, what do you know. We're actually planning into the future!"

Anson smiled and kissed her again. Despite the perfect South Florida morning weather and the beautiful moment he was sharing with Kendall, there was still a marked sadness in his kiss. Kendall looked up at him, the sheen of his clear blue eyes reflecting only regret.

"Anson, what's wrong?" she asked.

Anson took a deep breath and leaned up against the car door, pressing her into him, wanting to keep her close.

"I have to talk to you about something," Anson said, stroking her hair, then weaving and looping the long strands between his fingers. "I wanted to last week, but then the shit hit the fan and well..." He sighed heavily. "I need to explain my business in Miami to you. Who Xavier is and what we do."

"What do you mean *explain*? It's something in the entertainment business, right?" Kendall asked, now thrown by his tone.

"Well, once again, we don't have the time right now. It's just that, if you feel comfortable heading into a relationship with me, committing to the idea of us a bit more – it's only fair that I give you the full picture." Anson casually met her eyes, studying them for clues. "Fuck. I can't lose you over this."

Kendall, taken aback, instinctively placed her palm alongside his cheek. "Anson, what is it? Just tell me."

Kendall then recalled his drunken desperation over the phone the last time he'd been in Miami, followed by the unknown number of women revelation. The entertainment business. As in male strippers!

"Oh my goodness! Do you still strip?" she asked, the question out before she really planned to say it.

"What? No! No... not exactly–"

"*Not exactly*?!" she asked in shock.

"No, Kendall. Fuck! I'm not explaining myself very well. I don't dance at all anymore. There's a connection, though... This was such a shit-brained idea, stopping by. I'm such an ass. I'll just call you tomorrow to see how the party went, okay?" He kissed her goodbye, then abruptly climbed into the Town Car.

Dumbfounded, but without any hope for actual answers, Kendall walked slowly up the drive and watched the car back away – until it came to a stop.

"Kendall, hold up," Anson called out, climbing out of the Town Car and opening up his stride.

Before Kendall could say a word, his hands clasped around her head with such fierce conviction, she couldn't imagine standing on her own once his support was gone. He claimed her mouth, their tongues intertwining as he rapaciously fed on the sweetness of her love.

Anson broke away, their foreheads still pressed against one another. He panted, his breath heating up Kendall's face. He kept his eyes closed, finally using his words to speak from the heart.

"Kendall, I'm in love with you. And I know you told me not to get attached, but I couldn't help it. I am so in love with you. I started to fall for you the minute we kissed outside my house that first night. I don't know what will happen between us after this weekend, but I just need you to know: I love you."

More to Come

I hope you enjoyed the first book in my Gold Coast Romance series. There is so much more on the horizon for Anson and Kendall. The second book, *Heal My Broken Heart*, will be here before you know it. And you won't want to miss it! Thank you for reading.

Love, Elle G. Mraz

About the Author

Elle G. Mraz has several not-so-secret love affairs: peanut butter *M&Ms*, sweet champagne, and writing run-on sentences. She merged all three one day in 2014, continuing off and on until completing her first romance novel, *Love Me Back to Life*.

Elle met her Canadian husband in Guatemala and got hitched in Las Vegas. Together they laugh, dream big, and ponder life's great mysteries ("When did our junk drawer become a junk room?") while raising their two children, a couple odd rescue cats, and two even-odder rescue greyhounds. While she's done her fair share of traveling and has lived abroad, Elle was raised along the briny Atlantic coast of South Florida, which she'll always call home.

Writing spicy dramas for others to enjoy is a welcome distraction from Elle's on-the-job drama as a full-time registered nurse. When she's not working, spending time with her kids, or paying a bit of attention to her main man, she tries to squeeze in some writing and reading time – preferably on the beach with a mimosa. One can dream.

Contact the Author

Thank you for reading my book – it makes my heart so very happy. Please let me know what you think. THANK YOU!

ellegmraz@gmail.com
www.facebook.com/ellegmraz
@ellegmraz on Instagram
Elle G. Mraz on Goodreads.com

A portion of this book's proceeds will go directly to the Gold Coast Down Syndrome Organization. To learn more about this wonderful nonprofit that supports families who have children with Down syndrome in Palm Beach County, Florida, please visit: www.goldcoastdownsyndrome.org